HUSH, THE WOODS ARE DARKER STILL

THE WICKED WOODS CHRONICLES BOOK TWO

L.V. RUSSELL

Cover designed by Jorge Wiles

@JorgeWiles

www.facebook.com/JorgeWilesillustrator

This book is a work of fiction. Names, characters, places, and incidents either are products of the author's imagination or are used fictitiously. Any resemblance to actual persons, living or dead, events, or locales is entirely coincidental.

CONTENTS

This one is for my girls. To the moon and back, my darlings. To the moon and back.

CHAPTER ONE

*G*et up, Teya, we need to go."

I blinked as Laphaniel shook me awake, then stretched out my aching limbs until they cracked, willing warmth back into them. The skin over my hands split; the chill bit into the wounds, making them sting.

For a moment, I lay on the cold ground, staring up at the stalactites dripping from the cave roof. The early morning sun peeked into the cave enough to illuminate them, casting an eerie glow, so they looked like giant teeth.

Wincing, I shoved myself to my feet and bit into the strip of dried meat Laphaniel handed me, the last piece we had. We had been fortunate enough to stumble across a travelling merchant, purchasing some warm clothing and scraps of food. The food was mostly stale and the clothing old and threadbare, nothing more than a small bundle of roughly woven shirts, trousers, and cloaks with holes in them. We would have likely perished without them though, and the merchant had taken in our desperate state and had charged us extra for it.

Winter had stopped nibbling at the edges of Faerie and now crept further in until everything was blanketed in unforgiving snow and ice. It was too cold for us to sleep outside, forcing us to seek shelter in caves, if we were lucky enough to find one, or shallow hollows if we weren't.

It was too barren for Laphaniel to hunt for food. He would lay traps deep in the snow, and we would wait. Days crept by, but they remained empty.

The wolves were quicker than us, hunting, unburdened by the snow and cold, to pick off the last straggling animals. Everything else had hunkered down for the winter. The howling would keep me from sleep, always sounding too close to us, despite Laphaniel assuring me we were downwind.

But we had more to worry about than the wolves. Luthien had sent her fey to hunt us down.

Three weeks had passed since Laphaniel and I had broken the curse, binding all the Seelie Court to a mortal queen, broken it when we fell in love, just like a human fairy-tale.

My sister Niven had been chosen to be the next mortal queen, bound to the ruined Seelie castle for fifty years where she would wither and die, and then another girl would be chosen. Again, and again and again, for all eternity. Until, on the evening of my father's funeral, I had walked into the woods and demanded my sister back.

But found Laphaniel,

And fell in love.

I gave up the chance to spend forever with him, safe and loved beneath the branches that stretched throughout his home. Instead, I traded my life for my sister's, bargaining with Luthien, the rightful Queen of Seelie, to spend the rest of my life in a dark, abandoned castle alone. I thought it would fix the ruins of my family.

It didn't.

Years spent alone in the castle had ignited a darkness within Niven, a darkness that had lingered in her. She had always been cruel, cold... wrong. The girl I had found in the mouldering tower of the Seelie Castle was a nightmare in ruined silk. I would never forget the look of ecstasy on her face as she plunged a knife through Laphaniel's chest.

Laphaniel had not let me come alone.

He had died in my arms. He died for me, a mortal girl, which broke the curse on the Seelie Court—doesn't love always conquer all?

"Did you sleep at all?" I asked Laphaniel, noting the bruise-like shadows beneath his eyes. His face, like mine, was streaked with dirt, his hair matted with it. Stubble darkened his chin, a stark contrast to the pale skin beneath the filth and blood.

"A little."

I narrowed my eyes as I helped to roll up the thin blankets we had, tying them tight as we readied ourselves to move on from the damp cave we had stumbled upon. I knew he barely slept. Every night he tossed and turned ever since we had ended the curse. Something had dragged him back from the dead, a colossal shadow of fury and rage that had descended upon the castle and brought everything inside back to life…husks of flowers in long dry vases…desiccated spiders in the rafters…trapped birds, and Laphaniel.

I no longer woke screaming from my nightmares, but every night Laphaniel was dragged from sleep by his.

I woke with him each time, reaching out while he clamped a hand to his mouth to force the scream back down his throat. He would wake, shaking, drenched in sweat until the chill caught hold, and he would tremble. He wouldn't tell me what he was dreaming, but I could guess, as sometimes the shadowy fingers that had hauled him from death still plagued my dreams.

With the curse on the Seelie broken, it made me the last mortal queen, with my reign ending upon my death. Luthien had no plans to allow me a long and happy life.

"You can't stay awake forever," I said, taking his hand.

Laphaniel curled his fingers around mine before shrugging. "I can try."

Staring out of the cave mouth, I noted the fresh snowfall and the heavy skies, thankful at least that our footprints had been erased.

"You can talk to me," I said as he shoved a hand through his filthy hair, making it stand on end. I doubted mine looked much better. "I just wanted you to know that."

He nodded, his voice cracking as he spoke, "Every time I close my eyes, I feel like I'm dying all over again."

The words came out in a quick rush as if they had been pressing against his lips for too long. He wouldn't look at me, staring instead at the hostile landscape before us. I reached for him again and hesitated, terrified he would pull away, but he wrapped his arms around me and held me close.

"I wish I could take your nightmares away like you once did for me," I said against him, not letting go until he pulled away.

"This helps," he answered. "Thank you."

"The talking or the hug?"

He gave me a small, wonderful smile. "Both."

"Can I ask you something?" Laphaniel nodded, so I continued, "If you had the choice and you found me again in the woods, would you force me to turn back, knowing where it would end up if you helped me? Or would you still take Niven, knowing this is where it would all end?"

Laphaniel said nothing for a few agonising moments, but then he leant forwards, his lips moving close to my ear so I could feel each word he whispered back at me. "I would choose you, Teya—for every day of forever, it will always be you."

I closed my eyes against the words, knowing how much choosing me had already cost him. In the days following our flight from the castle, we had circled back to Laphaniel's house for supplies...only to find it engulfed in flames, fire licking the dark clouds like they were trying to set the sky alight.

I could smell it burning before I saw it, could hear the dying trees as they were forced away from the walls, turning to kindling as the fire consumed them. Glass shattered...nothing was left but the stone, a cold and brittle shell that offered only helplessness.

It hurt more than I thought it would, to know we would never make a home there together.

"Are you ready to go?" Laphaniel asked. "We need to keep moving."

I took his hand and followed him out of the cave, wincing as the wind hit me. The snow crept over my boots, soaking the hem of my cloak. The surrounding trees offered no shelter, all the branches stripped back, so they resembled spindly naked limbs. The lakes were frozen too, some of the ice so deep in places, we could walk across it.

Laphaniel kept trying to summon a flame in his hands, flicking his fingers until they were raw. Nothing came, nothing had come for the past week.

He was too tired,

too hungry,

too cold.

"We're not going to last the winter," I said.

"We just need to keep going."

"Until we can't go on anymore?" I asked, eyeing the heavy white clouds overhead. "We are either going to freeze or starve, Laphaniel."

"Then what do you want me to do?" he snapped, turning to me. Against the blinding white of the snow, his eyes were as black as coal. They were always black. "Luthien has hunters everywhere. If we stop, she will find us. And you're right. If we go on, we'll likely starve, so what do you want me to do, Teya?"

"I didn't mean…"

"No," Laphaniel interrupted. "I'm really asking you, what do we do?"

I shook my head. "I don't know."

Laphaniel sucked in a breath. "There is somewhere we can find food, somewhere warm we could stay until we think of something."

I knew he would never suggest such a place if we had any other choice if death wasn't chasing us down.

"No."

"Then we are going to die."

"No, Laphaniel. I am not going back there."

"I haven't found food for days," he said, exhaustion hissing through his voice. "Luthien won't need to catch us soon; she'll just need to wait until winter finishes us off."

I stepped away from him, wrapping my arms around myself as the bitter wind tugged at my ragged clothes, biting the raw skin beneath. I wanted to scream at the unfairness of it, at knowing he was right and that we had no other choice. I had to go home.

The thought of it would have once been a relief to leave the chaotic world of Faerie behind and return to my quiet village. Now it only filled me with dread.

"Niven killed you."

"Luthien wants to kill us," Laphaniel answered, bringing his cloak up over his face to ward off the wind. "I have been thinking about it for the past few days, trying to come up with another plan, but there's nothing. We need food, Teya. We need warm clothes, a night spent away from the frozen ground so we can *think*. If there was any other choice..."

"There isn't," I said, knowing he was right. "I'm sorry."

"What for? This isn't your fault."

I shrugged. "I should have chosen to stay with you."

Laphaniel caught my arm, his hands coming up to rest against my face, his touch icy cold. I could feel the calluses as he stroked my cheek, his fingers as raw as mine. "That wouldn't have made you happy, I made sure of that. But I'm right here now, I'm not going anywhere."

He pulled me closer, his mouth pressing against mine in a moment of warmth that made me remember how wonderful it felt to be alive. I moved my hand beneath his ruined shirt, searching out the miraculous thump of his heartbeat. My fingers stilled over the smooth scar tissue, and he tensed at my touch, his hand coming up to pull mine away.

"I just want to feel your heart beating," I said, and his hand stilled. He moved mine back over his chest so I could feel his heart thump against his ribs, beating the same wonderful song I had fallen in love with. I swallowed a sob, leaning my head against our entwined hands.

"Don't cry," Laphaniel breathed, pressing a kiss to the top of my head. "Your tears will freeze."

I smiled, not moving away. "What's the going rate for frozen tears?"

"In winter? I think they're pretty worthless." He kissed me again. "So, stop."

Even now, I could barely believe he was mine, that I belonged to someone who would follow me through death and darkness and still be eager to hold me...to know he was mine as much as I was his.

We walked and walked, on and on. Even when the skies above darkened and let loose a storm made of snow and despair, we carried on. We walked even when the blisters on my feet popped and my boots squelched. When Laphaniel fell, his feet slipping from beneath him on black ice, I dragged him up, and we kept on moving.

"Where's the edge of the wood?" I called out over the relentless storm. "How far until we leave Faerie?"

"There's a path this way that is rarely used," Laphaniel called back, the wind snatching away his voice. "It should take us near your home town...if we're lucky."

"And if we're not?"

"Then I don't know where we'll end up, or when."

I skidded to a stop. "When?"

"If I misjudge the path, Teya, we may end up in China a hundred years from now."

"You didn't think to mention this to me until now?"

Laphaniel shook his head, grabbing my hand to help me through the snow that was piling up around our feet. "If we don't find shelter from this storm, then it won't matter."

I understood why he hadn't said anything. Our future was measured in hours...days if we were fortunate. There was no use in finding something to worry about too far ahead; it was a bleak outlook, but an honest one.

"Teya, look," Laphaniel said, quickening his pace as he hauled me uphill. "There's a house up there."

"Who on earth would live all the way out here?" I asked, squinting past the storm to see the dark outline of a crooked hut shrouded by twisted trees.

"I think that was the home of the Harp Witch," Laphaniel answered, wiping the snow from his face to get a better look.

I stilled, remembering all too clearly the last time I ended up in the house of a witch. "Please tell me she was a nice old lady who just loved her music."

Laphaniel gave me a grim smile. "She strung her harps with heart-strings, so when she played them, they would reveal the secrets of those she had butchered. Don't look so worried—she's long dead."

I followed Laphaniel up the narrow, winding path to the witch's house, torn between the desperate need to find shelter, and the terror of what might still linger in the Harp Witch's home. Even though Laphaniel said it was empty, I could still sense the horror that had taken place within its walls, the terrible deeds so dark they left an echo that had bled into the eaves and timbers and begged to be left alone.

We reached the gate, and I placed my hand beside Laphaniel's on the railing, noticing too late it wasn't made from wood, but bone. Bones surrounded the cottage in a grotesque parody of a fence, all yellow with age, all picked clean. I couldn't fathom how many lives had been snuffed out to create it. Atop each post sat a skull, the tops cracked open to allow a candle stub to be wedged within.

"Those aren't adult bones," I said, recoiling as Laphaniel swung open the gate and walked into the courtyard.

"No, they are not."

I hurried after him, ducking under the low doorway as we entered the cottage, my heart hammering against my chest at the darkness within it. Laphaniel grabbed hold of my hand, pulling me close.

"There is nothing here but bad memories," he said softly. "It's a horrible place, but I won't let anything happen to you, I promise."

I nodded, taking a breath to calm the fear that threatened to overwhelm me. I had faced worse than a dark room and had come out fighting.

"I need to light a fire," Laphaniel said, rubbing his hands together and blowing into them. I took them in my own, trying to warm them up. "Grab one of the candles."

I did as I was told, plucking a candle stub from a nearby table. Slimy, yellow wax squelched over my fingers, but I held the wick under Laphaniel's hand and hoped. He clicked his fingers over it, furiously blowing into his hands to get some warmth behind them. A flame flickered and faltered. He clicked again as I cupped my free hand around the candle to ward off any breeze.

Flame finally danced over Laphaniel's fingers, weak and stuttering.

"Go light the rest, don't let it go out."

I ignited the rest of the half-melted candles around the cottage, collecting a small handful to take back to the table. After lighting them, I took Laphaniel's hands and held them over the flames.

"Do you think you'll be able to get a small fire going after you warm up?"

He nodded, "I think so."

Brittle light cast shadows against the stone walls, glittering against the cobwebs that hung so thickly overhead I couldn't see the beams. Spiders scurried back into the eaves, huge and bloated, disturbing the carcasses of long dead birds so they dropped to the floor with a dry thud.

"I think I preferred the dark," I half joked, not daring to look up again. I glanced around the room, noting the macabre harps that lined the walls. "On second thought-"

"Don't touch them," Laphaniel said, filling the fireplace with old, dusty logs. "Unless you're curious as to what they have to say."

"I'm really not."

I took a step closer anyway, to look at the delicate etchings that had been painstakingly carved into the wood. I didn't dare touch the strings which were knotted and red and still impossibly wet looking. Even though I hadn't touched them, I could hear a faint hum that quivered through their strings, as if they were singing to themselves. I moved away, swallowing my disgust.

Against the far wall stood an ancient bed, the wooden headboard so rotten, chunks of it lay crumbled around the base. I pulled off the mouldering covers and blackened pillows, replacing them with our blankets. There was nothing I could do about the mattress.

Laphaniel managed to get a meagre fire crackling, and for the first time in ages, I began to remember what it felt like to be warm.

I sat on the edge of the bed, its creak echoing around the room, and watched as Laphaniel pulled his knife from his belt and disappeared outside. He was gone only moments, and my heart sank at what he brought back in to roast over the fire.

"Is there no bacon running around out there?" I asked, eyeing the long tails that dangled from his fingers.

Laphaniel smiled, a quick quirk of his lips that did nothing to lighten the shadows in his eyes. "The place is infested with them."

He readied himself to clean them, but I stopped him, holding my hand out for the knife. "Can I help?"

"You don't have to, Teya," he replied but handed me the knife when I didn't back down.

We prepared the rats together, some of the tension lifting ever so slightly as we worked. Laphaniel's skilled fingers showed me how to skin them whole, how to take out the bits we didn't want, and then how to skewer them over the fire.

"They didn't teach this in the Girl Guides," I said, as the fat bubbled and dripped from the tiny carcasses making the flames hiss.

"It is a privilege to teach you, Teya," Laphaniel replied, turning the meat, so it blackened and cooked. "Despite the circumstances."

"It seems a shame to waste these." I held up the skins, each of them looking like empty glove puppets. "Maybe we could sew them together and make a really small blanket?"

His laugh was wonderful and too brief. Any fragments of joy we managed to scavenge between us were always too fleeting and too few.

"I never thought I would be so hungry I would look forward to eating rodents," I said, as Laphaniel passed me one. "But, these look like the most delicious things in the world right now."

"Try not to get too excited. They're mostly skin and bone," Laphaniel answered, watching as I sunk my teeth into my food before starting his.

The feeling of having hot food was almost overwhelming, and before I knew it, I had a pile of little bones in front of me. Laphaniel picked his clean also, snapping the bones to suck out the marrow inside. He did it with such practised skill, one only someone who had known true hunger could possess.

"How was your first rat?" he asked, a smile dancing against his lips.

"Better than roast chicken," I said, reaching for another. "Which is something I thought I'd never say about eating rodents."

We finished eating and crawled under the covers of the bed, trying to ignore the reek of mould and damp that rose from the ancient mattress. Laphaniel had covered the fire, so only the embers glowed, barely giving any warmth but not sending smoke up the chimney like a beacon.

It was still cold inside the cottage, and my breath fogged in front of me as I wrapped the blankets tight around myself, but it was still a much more forgiving chill than what we faced outside.

"Close your eyes, I'll keep watch," Laphaniel said beside me, his head resting against mine as he ran his fingers along my arm.

"You need to get some sleep," I answered, turning to face him. "We both do."

He looked set to argue, but he said nothing as he ran a hand over his face, breathing out a heavy sigh I recognised as defeat. He closed his eyes, exhaustion dragging him under as if someone had flipped a switch.

I stayed awake a while longer, listening to the faint murmurs of the harps as they whispered in the shadows, the cold breeze teasing their strings as it crept through the cracks in the walls. I was just drifting off when Laphaniel kicked out, his hands tense on the mattress as he struggled with whatever dark dream had hold of him. He gasped, a frightened and broken sound that rasped through his lips, he took another breath, and it caught and another...the sound scraping against his throat as his nightmare choked him.

"I'm right here," I whispered to him, catching his hand as he made to lash out. "You're not alone, I'm right beside you."

The blankets twisted around him as he struggled, his breaths almost barking up past his lips. I pulled him closer, my lips at his ear.

"I love you," I breathed. "I love you, and I'm here, and I'm not going anywhere."

With a shuddering sigh, he opened his eyes, blinking at me in confusion before swiping a hand over his face.

"Teya?" My name slipped strangely from his mouth, his black eyes not quite looking at me. "Can you close the window, it's cold."

I had missed him rambling in his sleep, the feel of him mumbling incoherently in my ear as I slept. He seldom did it anymore. Stroking the dark hair back from his face, I watched as his breathing settled, the nightmare retreating elsewhere for a while.

I wished I had Glamour like a true Queen of Faerie should. I would have loved nothing more than to weave threads of dreams from starlight just for him, to have the wind sing a lullaby. To hold the nightmares at bay simply because I willed them away. Like he had once done for me.

But I didn't have Glamour because I was a human girl. The mortal Queens held no true power but were merely figureheads…something to hold the Seelie crown and to be hated from a distance. I would have gladly given it up to Luthien if I could.

If the price for losing the crown wasn't my life.

Burying myself closer to Laphaniel, I closed my eyes, keeping my arms wrapped tight around his body, my forehead to his. Sometimes… just sometimes, it was enough to keep his nightmares away, a tiny fragment of magic only I possessed.

I fell asleep to the sound of his breathing, accompanied by the almost gentle plucking of strings.

CHAPTER TWO

*T*he stench of mould filled my nostrils as I woke, making me recoil from the damp mattress. Laphaniel stood by the cold fireplace, his back to me.

"Here," I got up and passed him the cloak he had tucked over me. "You need to keep warm too."

"You were shivering."

"Have you been up long?" I hadn't felt him get up, but his side of the bed had been cold.

"A while." He gave the crumbling logs a kick to ensure they were all out. "The storm is clearing."

Early morning sun filtered through the grimy windows, catching the dust motes swirling down from the webs above us. Light bounced off the ancient table, revealing bloodstains that had seeped deep into the wood. The floor bore marks too, splatters of red, which went unnoticed in the darkness. We had eaten at that table.

Away from the harps, stood a cabinet, shelves filled with bottles. Yellowing labels curled around the glass, the ink faded and barely legible. Many were empty, with whatever they once contained, long shrivelled up. Bottles of baby teeth remained beside broken fingernails and a couple of eyeballs all milky with age.

I had seen worse. It was the jar almost hidden at the back, which caught my attention. Thick webbing crackled around my hand as I reached into the cabinet, causing little black spiders to scurry indignantly into the corners as I tugged it free.

Light danced from within the glass, radiating through the filth covering it. But there was a manic feel to it, a desperation against the brightness. Peeling back the label, I read the scrawl and cried out.

I had seen so many awful things in Faerie. Too many.

"Laphaniel?"

He was instantly at my side, moving with fluid grace, and took the bottle from my hands. "Why do you always have to touch everything?" There was no anger in his voice, only mild exasperation.

"All those little skulls outside, do you think she bottled up their souls in here?"

"Most likely," Laphaniel said, holding the bottle up to the sunlight, causing the souls inside to spin and swirl. "Looks as if the witch died before she could use them."

He took a step away from me, lifting the bottle higher before dropping it to the floor. Glass shattered on stone, spilling chaotic light around the room. At first, they screamed, and the harps screamed too.

Then they laughed, even as the harps carried on screaming.

Bright orbs of light circled us, flickering through the dusty sunbeams to tease at our hair, squealing with the kind of laughter only children truly possess.

The lights vanished before the sound of joy did, each little orb seemingly soaked up by the light until nothing was left. The harps continued shrieking, their strings plucked by ghostly fingers that drowned out any remaining echoes except horror and pain.

"Where will they go?" I called out over the wails.

"I don't know," Laphaniel answered. "Perhaps wherever I went."

He wouldn't talk about it, saying he didn't remember much about dying and what happened after. But far beneath the nightmares and fear, I could sense an odd longing in him.

He had been dragged back from wherever, kicking and screaming... as if he didn't want to come back at all.

"Let's get out of here," I said.

The miserable song of the harps followed us as we left the witch's cottage far behind, the cries drifting over the wind-torn trees until they, too, began to moan.

My footsteps grew leaden as we walked on, the fulness in my belly long gone, leaving nothing but an aching hollowness. I felt sick with it, my head throbbing. I stumbled. My hands reacted too slowly as I fell forwards, but Laphaniel's didn't. My legs gave way as the world tilted; shadows formed around the corners of my vision.

"Teya?" Laphaniel's voice sounded too far away, even though his arms were around me. "Look at me, can you hear me?" He tapped my cheek before gently guiding my head to my knees.

"I'm fine. I just got a little dizzy…" I forced myself to my feet.

"Wait, don't stand up—"

I barely heard him over the ringing in my ears, then everything went black, and I didn't hear anything at all.

Darkness swam around me, warm and comforting. How long it kept me, I didn't know. Hours…days, it didn't seem to matter.

The world righted itself slowly, leaving a thickness in my head and mouth and a strange heaviness everywhere else. Laphaniel's arms were still around me, my head cradled against his chest as he walked. He saw my eyes flicker open, and a sigh hissed through his lips.

"You fainted," he said, concern stark across his face. "You've been out for hours."

He set me gently to my feet, keeping one arm around me until I found my footing.

"You carried me all this time?"

"I didn't want to stop and risk getting caught up in another storm," Laphaniel said, tightening the cloak around my shoulders. "How are you feeling?"

"My head hurts," I answered honestly. "Is it much further?"

"No, the path is just through those trees. It looks like we've been granted a little bit of good fortune."

I smiled. "I think we're owed some." He made to scoop me up again, but I placed a hand on his arm. "I'll be okay to walk from here."

The trees thinned out around us, creaking in the wind. They had started to unwind from each other, bare branches pulling apart as we moved from Faerie back to the place that had once been my home.

I could sense the magic fading as we walked away; the world around us hushed its whisperings, and the wind stopped singing. The strange brightness of the world we were leaving, dwindled while my world closed in around us. The echo of the sun vanished, the ordinary sky no longer having room for the magic of a double sunrise.

There was a fence at the edge of the trees, the wood glistening with a thin layer of frost while the beginnings of dawn peeked over the distant houses. I looked to the looming hills and at the soft glow of the streetlights casting shadows on the ground. The shadows remained still —no matter how hard I stared, they didn't dance.

I closed my eyes against the little village, realising I had outgrown it. The home I longed for, had gone up in flames.

"It's still winter here," I said as Laphaniel helped me over the fence. "I left when it was winter and walked into spring. It is freezing in Faerie, and it's freezing here. I can't even work out how long I've been away."

Laphaniel glanced over at the rows of houses, and I wondered if he remembered which one was mine. Where once he had promised to bring my body back if I died on him.

"You're trying to find logic in the rules of faeries when there is none."

"Time really means nothing to you, does it?" I said, taking his hand to lead him down the road. He squeezed my hand.

"It does now."

Beneath the streetlights, he looked pale and filthy, and I knew I looked no better. If anyone happened to pass us, we would look like a couple of homeless youths.

I took the lead, walking past the row of cottages that led to my house, pausing at the gate. My hand slipped from Laphaniel's to slide along the perfect paintwork, my eyes darting from the clear, neat path to the perfectly trimmed rose bushes each side of the door. Their naked branches glinted with frost, giving nothing away about how magnificent they must have looked when spring woke them.

"Your mother watered them," Laphaniel said, turning to me as I reached for one of the vines curling up over the doorframe.

I didn't look at him. The roses I knew had been dead and brittle. "You remembered."

"Six Mulberry Close," he replied, pointing to the gleaming number on the door. "I would have kept my word."

The curtains were open, the well-maintained driveway empty.

"Can you get us inside?" I asked, peering under the doormat in a futile attempt to find a spare key.

"Of course."

I made a sweeping gesture with my hand, and with a smile on his lips, he moved past me, running his hand over the bottom left panel of glass.

"Don't you dare..." I started, closing my eyes as he used his elbow to smash out the panel, reaching inside to flick the catch on the door, so it swung open.

"And we're in," he said, sounding too pleased with himself.

"Yes." I shook my head as I moved past him. "Well done you."

The smell hit me first, a flood of memories pouring over me as the scent of fabric conditioner and stale smoke filled my head. I recoiled instantly, feeling Laphaniel's hand on me as I fought the urge to turn and run.

"I don't want to be here," I began. "I'm not ready for this."

I hadn't thought of what I would say to Mum if I saw her. How I could even begin to explain where I had been and why I looked so ragged and bruised...and lost. But she wasn't there, and suddenly all I wanted was to fall into her arms.

I couldn't bear the thought of seeing Niven.

Laphaniel followed me as I wandered into the living room, flicking on the light switch to banish the shadows the early morning sun could not. The wallpaper had changed, and it no longer curled up from the wall where my mother hadn't used enough paste.

Stepping closer to the fireplace, my heart twisted at the familiar faces staring back at me. I ran my fingers over the frames, hardly noticing that they shook as I brushed against photos of my mum and dad, smiling and posing for the camera.

They looked much older than I had ever remembered them being; more wrinkles around Mum's eyes, and my dad had silver in his hair.

With a jolt, I realised they were recent pictures.

There were six photographs along the fireplace, many more scattered over the bookcases and windowsills in the cosy room. There were only a few with four people in them. My own face beamed at me, held up in the arms of my dad or smiling at a birthday party I couldn't remember.

I appeared in only a handful, some as a baby then as a toddler. There was one of my first day at school, holding hands with a scowling Niven...then nothing.

"No..." Dread curdled in my stomach as the unfamiliarity of everything began to sink in.

"Teya?"

I brushed off Laphaniel's hand as I rushed upstairs. Pausing at Niven's door, I sucked in a quick breath before pushing the door open.

The room had been painted a deep blue, the mirrored surfaces of the furniture were flawless, reflecting the black bed that dominated the area. The covers were rumpled, pillows strewn across the floor to lie amongst the dirty laundry that was gathering in a heap at the end of the bed. Mingling with the scent of perfume was the sickly-sweet smell of smoke, one that didn't come from smoking regular roll-ups.

I backed out of her room, slipping past Laphaniel who silently watched me, and reached out my hand to what had been my bedroom door. The wood was discoloured where countless stickers had once been.

With a sob, I opened the door.

I remembered back when it had just been Mum and me. I remembered the phantom dinners and all the gifts that would never be opened. I remembered Niven's shrine. Her untouched bedroom that would always belong to a young girl. And wondered why I was so... so different.

My pink room had been painted a soft yellow, cream curtains flowing to the floor, held back by a string of golden beads. A double bed replaced my old one, overflowing with scatter cushions in every shade of cream and dusky pink. A different desk stood at the far wall, pristine and unmarked by my attempts at makeup.

The only essence of me in the room was a single shelf. Carefully-placed trinkets stood polished and shining, and I wondered if mum ever allowed them to gather dust.

I picked up a small teddy bear that sat between a sparkly unicorn and a music box, and held it close, breathing in its scent that should have meant more to me.

"It's as if I was taken," I breathed, still clutching the frayed bear. "As if you stole me away and not Niven."

Laphaniel visibly flinched at the thought.

"Niven came back," I continued. "She came back, and my family stayed together."

Laphaniel moved closer, taking the bear from my hands and tossed it onto the bed. I stared at it, and its beady eyes stared back as if wondering where it knew me from.

"Why is she enough for them?" I asked, my voice hollow. "Where is my empty place setting? Do they keep presents in the loft for me, knowing I'll never open them?"

"I didn't know it would be like this," Laphaniel said, "We can just grab a few things and leave."

"Why didn't they miss me like they missed her?"

Unable to give me the answers I needed, Laphaniel pulled me close and pressed a gentle kiss to my forehead. "Do you want to go? We'll find somewhere else."

I shook my head. "And go where?"

I didn't know the house I stood in, nothing about it was familiar apart from its scent, and even that had been tainted. My memories didn't belong anywhere within the newly painted walls and plush carpet. I didn't belong.

"This reality is a better place without me," I began, breaking away from Laphaniel. "My dad is alive here, I don't think my mum is crazy." I swallowed, wiping at my eyes. "The wallpaper isn't hanging off."

Laphaniel touched his forehead to mine, his breath soft against the bridge of my nose. He opened his mouth to say something, then paused, his head snapping towards the sound of the front door creaking open.

"Stay here," he said, and cold panic seized my body at the thought of him confronting Niven again.

"No!" I caught his arm before he took a step onto the landing, tugging him back so frantically he almost lost his footing. "No, the last time you met Niven, you bled out in my arms. You can stay here."

I walked down the stairs gripping the banister with a shaking hand, knowing I was not ready to see my sister again.

At our last meeting, I had been terrified. I had gone to her out of guilt and a sense of duty, to try to dull the shame that ate away at me, blaming myself over and over again for something that had never been my fault.

"I'll pay for the window," I said, taking the last step, watching as my sister knelt on the floor to study the shards of broken glass that were scattered across the hallway floor.

Niven stood to face me, an eyebrow arching. "With what? You look like a war orphan."

If she was surprised to see me, she hid it well. Her blue eyes skipped over my tattered state, lips curling into a smile that revealed the loosely hidden cruelty beneath. She exuded a strange radiance standing there, watching me.

A simple clip held her black hair up, a few curls let loose to tease her face. The black dress she wore barely skimmed her thigh, showing inches and inches of pale bare leg despite the cold.

Sweat and stale alcohol mingled with her sickly perfume, the strange smoke I had noticed from her room, clung to her clothes. Despite her obvious hung-over state, nothing about Niven hinted at vulnerability. It only made her appear more dangerous.

"I just want to grab some clean clothes and some food. Then we'll leave."

Her head bobbed forward once, lazily. With a bored gesture, she motioned for me to continue what I was doing.

"I doubt you'll fit in anything left in your room," Niven smirked, bending down to unlace her boots so she could fling them off. Her smile widened as one of them struck my leg.

"Then, could I have something of yours?"

She shrugged. "Whatever, if it is lying on the floor, take it."

I stared at her, unable to believe she could act like nothing had happened. Niven glared back, her too-bright eyes fixed on me as her smile slipped into a scowl.

"I don't want to know why you're not decaying in that castle with the corpse of your lover," she hissed. "Take what you want and leave."

"I gave everything up for you, Niven," I said, the words pointless. They meant nothing to her. They never did.

"I don't care."

I nodded, turning to walk back upstairs. The sudden hand on my arm stopped me going further.

"Wait," she said, her nails digging into my skin. "Who are you with?"

She didn't know, and the thought sparked a new rush of fear through me. "Who do you think?"

She moved surprisingly quickly, slipping past me to bolt up the stairs before I could stop her.

"Niven, wait!" I slipped on the stairs as I ran after her. "Stop!"

I grabbed her arm as she stepped onto the landing, and she spun to face me. I let go at the look she threw me. There was no fear in Laphaniel's eyes as she turned back to him.

"You should be dead."

"I was," he said, the words deathly calm. "Shall we call it even?"

Nothing human lingered in the way he spoke, the timbre of his voice sounding all wrong. His subtle accent had deepened into something strange and terrifying.

Pushing past Niven, I stood in front of Laphaniel, pressing my hand against his chest. His eyes flickered to mine, and I gave a tiny shake of my head, silently ordering him to calm down.

"I think we need to talk," I said, facing Niven again. Her eyes dropped to my hand, covering the erratic thump of Laphaniel's heart. I would never forget she had been the one to still it.

"I have nothing to say to either of you," she said coldly.

"We wouldn't have come here if we weren't desperate, Niven," I said. "We need somewhere we can sleep for the night, food, and clothing. I want to know why everything is different. You owe me that at least."

"I owe you fuck all," she spat, her head snapping to Laphaniel as a deep snarl rose from his throat. "Control him."

I kept my hand against his chest. "He doesn't need controlling; he wasn't the one lashing out with a knife."

Niven's grin showed teeth. "I was in control when I stabbed him."

I closed my eyes at the memory.

"You weren't, though, were you?" Laphaniel said, pushing closer. The haunting edge to his tone slipped away into something softer... colder. "You aimed for Teya, I just got in your way."

I withdrew my hand slightly, so only the tips of my fingers brushed against Laphaniel. "Please, Niven."

I didn't have the strength to fight on the landing.

"You can have ten minutes, then I'm done."

She pushed herself off the wall and walked downstairs, leaving behind the odd lingering scent that surrounded her.

CHAPTER THREE

he circle of steam snaked up from my mug, and I breathed in the comforting smell of coffee, not realising how much I missed it.

We sat at the dining table, Niven opposite us using her own coffee to chase down a couple of painkillers.

"So," Niven began, after I finished explaining. "You made a bargain with Luthien to take my place?"

I nodded, taking a sip of my coffee before adding another sugar to it.

"You promised to spend the rest of your life alone in that miserable castle; instead, you ended up breaking a centuries-old curse binding mortals to the Seelie throne." Niven tapped her fingernails against her mug. "All because you two fell in love. How tragically romantic."

"Yes," I said. "I am the last mortal Queen of Seelie. If Luthien kills me, the natural line will be restored, and she will inherit the throne. It's been a tough few weeks."

Niven looked up from her mug, "You've been gone just over a year, Teya."

"What?"

"Well," she continued. "I know you have been gone only a year, everyone else believes differently. I was thrown from that cursed place like a rag doll and dumped back here. I thought I was finally home, but everything was different... everyone remembered everything differently." She paused to take a breath, eyes flashing with sudden anger. "The timelines changed, and it was you that had been taken all along, not me. Dad is alive, and he remembers things about me that have never happened, do you know what that feels like? There are photos of me in places I have never been, and I have just had to deal with it and watch as they mourn for you."

"They stayed together," I said. "I couldn't keep them together."

The scowl on Niven's face slipped into something far crueller. "Jealous?"

I took in the room around me, the neat stack of cookbooks above the range, the little matching spice jars. All the plates rested in the rack. "How could I be, Niven? My dad is alive."

Laphaniel reached for me beneath the table. "What have you been doing for the past year, Niven?"

She shrugged. "Whatever I damn well please."

"I can smell them on you."

Niven leant forwards, steepling her fingers to rest her chin on them. "I bet you can."

"What's going on?" I demanded, "Niven?"

Laphaniel didn't look at me as he answered for her. "Your sister is playing with the Unseelie."

"And what business is that of yours?"

"You are a child dancing with shadows," Laphaniel began, his hand resting against his untouched drink. "You know nothing of the madness of the Dark Court."

"I know more than you can comprehend," Niven hissed. "I have seen their shadows, and they welcomed me without flinching. I have found my place within the Unseelie and I will not sit here and be judged by you."

"The Unseelie Queen will tear your head off."

"The Unseelie Queen is dead!" Niven snapped. "The Barren Queen is gone..."

"Leaving behind no heir," Laphaniel cut in. "You're going to end up in the middle of a civil war, Niven."

Niven leant back on her chair, a smile on her face. "There was a boy the Queen loved, a human infant she simply couldn't resist snatching up for herself. You should see how the Court loves him, it's like he belongs there. The Seelie have been too wrapped up in their own affairs for too long to notice the Unseelie were raising a King."

"He's human?"

Niven shook her head, lighting a cigarette and blowing a perfect circle of smoke at us. "Not anymore."

"How?" Laphaniel asked, visibly unnerved.

"I wasn't there to see it," Niven answered, flicking ash into her empty mug. "But Phabian told me it was like being reborn. Just before the Queen's last breath, everything that made her fey flooded into him. He found me shortly after I came back, surrounded by dancing shadows that listened only to him. He offered me a place within the darkness, and it felt like finally going home."

Niven stood, her eyes focused upon Laphaniel. "You are looking at the Queen of the Unseelie. I may dance with shadows, you pathetic creature, but at least I know how to waltz with them."

"They're going to kill you, you stupid girl." Laphaniel hissed back. "The Unseelie will sniff out any weakness…"

"They love him!"

"Do you?" I demanded.

Niven tilted her head, thinking for a moment. "Yes."

"Enough to die for?"

"Enough to kill for."

I looked at my sister, really looked at her. With a jolt, I realised I felt nothing for her but a crushing understanding that I had tried to save someone I no longer deemed worth saving.

"Maybe, Niven," I said. "One day, you will learn to love someone more than you love yourself. Until then you have no idea what love feels like. You couldn't possibly imagine the gaping hole left behind when it's gone. I don't ever expect an apology for what you did, because you don't comprehend the pain you've caused. One day you'll love someone enough, and you'll finally get it."

I stood, scraping the chair back against the wood flooring so it screeched. Moving to the kitchen, I rinsed the cups in the sink. It gave my hands something to do, so I didn't throttle Niven.

"What do you want from me?" she asked from the doorway.

"I don't know. Nothing." I placed the cups on the draining board and dried my hands. "I didn't come here to seek you out. Luthien is going to kill me, Niven."

She rolled her eyes. "Phabian is still getting used to controlling the Unseelie…"

"You don't control the Dark Court," Laphaniel cut in, having moved silently to join us.

Niven ignored him. "We don't want the Seelie to start sniffing around us."

"So, what are you saying?" I asked.

Niven sighed, "We probably want Luthien on the throne as much as you do. It may well be beneficial for us if she didn't kill you."

"I do like being helpful."

"It may be worth helping you keep your crown, little sister," Niven said, smiling to herself. "I'll have a talk with Phabian and see if we can work something out."

"At what price?" Laphaniel asked, stepping into the kitchen beside me.

"I'm sure we can come to an agreement," Niven answered.

"I am not bargaining with the Unseelie Court."

"Then you will both die," Niven countered, a shrug lifting her shoulder. "Without Phabian's help, it is only a matter of time before Luthien finds you and rips you apart."

"And you think he'll help us?" I asked, "This wonderful new king of yours?"

"As I said, we don't want Luthien on the throne, the Unseelie are too unstable at the moment to handle an outside threat."

"The Unseelie are always unstable; it is a court of madness, and they would sooner slit our throats than help us," Laphaniel snapped, stepping closer to Niven so he towered over her. Niven didn't flinch as she tilted her neck to stare up at him.

"Do they frighten you?" she mocked. "Because they should. You should see what Phabian can do with his shadows, it's wondrous. There is madness there, but can you really say that your own court is not controlled by it? The Seelie hide behind a veil of civility, but it is only a disguise. You are as feral as the rest of them. You are all monsters."

"Niven..." I began, but she cut me off.

"Do you deny it?" she asked Laphaniel. "You are the monster that steals away children from their beds, are you not?

Laphaniel smiled, black eyes flashing, "You skipped beside me Niven. You took my hand without a thought. What kind of child follows a monster into the shadows with a smile on their face?"

Laphaniel caught her wrist as she made to slap him, holding it a breath away from his face.

"Are you going to break me?" Niven said, her words hissing through her teeth.

Laphaniel dropped her hand, shaking his head. "I'll leave that to the Unseelie."

"I wouldn't stay long if I were you," Niven said, stepping back. "Luthien may think to search for you here."

"I don't know where to go."

Niven curled her lip, our barely disguised desperation likely disgusting her. "Mum and dad have this awful holiday cottage down in Cornwall, one they were going to fix up but never have. Stay there. I'll send word after I've spoken to Phabian."

"Where are Mum and Dad?"

Niven's smile bloomed on her mouth, but there was something else mingling with the cold twist of her lips, darkening her beautiful face. Only Niven could make scorn look lovely.

"They're on a cruise with another couple they met from Mum's Bingo club. I don't blame you for forgetting about them."

"I haven't forgotten them."

"Ever since you got here, you've barely taken your eyes off him." She nodded in Laphaniel's direction, her eyes filled with disdain. "You keep protecting him, unconsciously shielding him. Though you know, he is capable of killing both of us before we could blink."

"You killed him before I could blink, Niven," I said softly.

"I did, didn't I?" she smirked, absently chewing on her fingernail. "The keys are hanging on the hook by the microwave, drive safely."

"You want me to drive to Cornwall now?"

She looked down at my filthy clothes, and I hoped something stirred the humanity hidden within her.

"Stay one night," she said finally. "Then go. There is a pile of clothes in the cupboard destined for the charity shop, help yourselves. You both stink."

She gave one last hateful look at Laphaniel and pushed past, only turning to face me when I called to her.

"Where are you going?" I asked, though I was sure I knew the answer.

"I needed a change of clothes, then I'm going home."

I blinked at her word choice, and for just a moment, her eyes softened.

"This is not our home, Teya. We belong to our monsters now. You seek happiness in the shadows as much as I do. Take what you want from this place, it means nothing to me."

Niven disappeared upstairs without another word to either of us, and after a few minutes, I heard the front door click shut, leaving us alone in a house that should have meant more to me.

Back in the kitchen, I found a bag of dried pasta and dumped handfuls into a saucepan and waited for the water to boil.

"How does dinner and a shower sound?"

"There is nothing I want more right now," Laphaniel answered, filling two glasses with fresh water and handing me one.

I found a jar of sauce in another cupboard, stirred it into the cooked pasta, and heaped it onto plates. We ate until there was nothing left, and I had to force myself not to make another batch so I could eat that too.

"You'll make yourself sick," Laphaniel warned. "Have more later."

"Oh, I will," I said, taking Laphaniel's hand and leading him back upstairs. "After we shower."

We stopped on the landing and found the bags of clothes Niven had mentioned. I handed him a small pile of clothes before finding something for myself to wear.

"Come with me."

He smiled, the first real smile I had seen from him in too long. He followed me into the bathroom, as eager as I was to feel clean again.

I switched on the shower and watched as the water cascaded into the bathtub, quickly filling the room with steam. The fabric of my clothes crunched as I peeled them from my body. I moved to Laphaniel, my hands taking over from his as I undid the buttons of his shirt, lingering over the scar on his chest. He leant forwards, his mouth against mine as he shrugged his arms out of his sleeves. He kissed me like he needed me to breathe, hungry and desperate, his hands coming up to tangle in my hair.

Laphaniel broke the kiss first, his eyes bright as he lifted me under the wonderful heat of the water. He stepped in after me, sweeping the wet hair from my shoulder so he could kiss the skin just beneath my neck. I turned to face him, leaning my head against his chest as he wrapped his arms around me.

I lathered up a sponge with minty shower gel and scrubbed my body before washing the dirt from Laphaniel. He closed his eyes as I ran bubbles over his face and down his neck. Dirt ran in rivers down his lean yet muscular body.

Taking the sponge from me, he pressed a soapy kiss to my lips, and without a word, he lowered himself down in the tub, bringing me with him.

The water lapped around our bodies, washing away blood and dirt and some of the bad memories. My head rested against Laphaniel, soap still clung to his chest, trailing bubbles down over the flat planes of his stomach. With a wet hand, he wiped away the tears that slipped down my cheeks, pulling me close when they refused to stop, and rocked me gently in his arms. We didn't talk, we didn't need to.

There was nothing to be said out loud that would have meant more than having him hold onto me, his bare skin against mine as the steaming water rained over us.

Reluctantly untangling myself from Laphaniel's water slicked body, I turned the shower off before rummaging through the bathroom closet to find two towels. Laphaniel watched me, perching on the edge of the bathtub, his eyes following the droplets of water sliding over my skin. It had been a while since either of us hungered for anything but food.

"I found these in the medicine cupboard, I thought they might help." I passed the bottle of pills to him. "Mum took them when Niven disappeared too."

He rattled the bottle. "What are they?"

"Prescription sleeping tablets…"

"No." He tossed the bottle back to me.

"When was the last time you had more than a couple hours' sleep?"

"Probably before I met you," he said dryly.

"Very funny."

"I want to be able to wake up if I need to, Teya."

I sighed. "You can't carry on like this, snatching moments of sleep when you can't stay awake any longer."

I passed the bottle back to him. "We have a proper roof over our heads for the first time in weeks. There's a warm bed."

"Just for tonight?"

Nodding, I watched him tip a small handful of pills out, swallowing them with a gulp of water from the tap. He followed me into my old bedroom, resting back against the pillows. I lay with my head on his chest, the heavy duvet pulled right up to my chin.

The clock on the wall announced it was just after ten-thirty in the morning. I hadn't looked at a clock in ages. Time had lost all meaning to me, days, weeks, even years meant nothing in Faerie. When time didn't leave a mark upon you, it was all too easy to ignore.

"Do you think the Unseelie will help us?" I asked, threading my fingers through Laphaniel's.

"If it means they get what they want in the end," he said, closing his eyes. "I wouldn't trust them."

"It's Niven I don't trust."

"The Unseelie will either destroy your sister, or she'll live long enough to rule it," he said. "There is a spark that drew us to her...a darkness we hungered for. We just tried to force her into the wrong court."

"Is there darkness in me?"

Laphaniel turned to face me and ran a hand over my cheek. "Not yet," he replied.

I closed my eyes and nestled against him, listening as Laphaniel's breathing slowed down and deepened. I couldn't help but wonder what lay ahead for us, what demons would be coming to shadow over my soul, what nightmares I would have to embrace just to be free to live. I wondered the price of it all.

Sleep came fitfully at first, restless and filled with too many thoughts, but then my exhaustion took over and dragged me down into a merciful and dreamless black.

CHAPTER FOUR

$\mathscr{I}$ woke with no idea where I was, the feeling of being under warm covers so disorientating that for a moment, I thought I was back at Laphaniel's house. Never again would I wake there, beneath the twisting branches of his bedroom where it rained blossom, a place where, despite everything, I had begun to fall in love with him.

Laphaniel still slept beside me, sprawled out on his front with one leg hanging off the bed. His arms draped over the pillows, hugging them tight, and with every couple of breaths, he let out a soft snore. The fingers of his left hand twitched as he dreamed.

Not wanting to wake him, I carefully slid out of bed and fumbled in the darkness to the landing, where I flicked on the light and wandered downstairs. Outside it was still black, the stars twinkling in the indigo sky, barely hinting at dawn.

It was cold in the kitchen with a frost lingering at the windows, slowly dripping down the glass like melting tears. I filled the kettle and waited for it to boil, grabbing two mugs and heaping coffee and sugar into both. I popped some slightly dry bread into the toaster and rummaged in the fridge for a pot of raspberry jam.

My head felt strangely heavy. Glancing up at the kitchen clock I discovered why, it had just gone half five in the morning and we had been sleeping for nearly nineteen hours.

As I made the coffee and toast, I spotted an old map on the kitchen counter, folded back with a hastily drawn circle around a village in Cornwall. Niven had scribbled an arrow in black Sharpie and written "HERE" in capitals. She left no note, nothing else except the keys to Mum's ancient Micra. It would take hours to drive down, and I just hoped the car was up to it.

I took breakfast upstairs, resting the tray on the bedside table before I curled back against Laphaniel, still not having the heart to wake him. I watched while he slept, lost within some dream that caused him to mumble something against the pillows. Smiling, I ran my fingers over his back, stopping at the edge of the covers. I trailed my fingers up his spine, and he stirred, his body tensing. He moaned softly when I kissed his neck, his eyes flickering open.

"Good morning." I smiled.

"Yes, it is," he replied, voice still thick with sleep.

"I have coffee and toast."

Laphaniel stretched and rolled onto his back, taking his time before propping himself up against the pillows. I passed him a steaming mug, then nestled in his arms with my coffee warming my hands.

"Wouldn't it be wonderful, just to stay like this?" I tilted my head back, catching the look that flickered in his eyes, before realising that it was exactly what he had once offered me: warmth, happiness, and eternal love.

"One day," he began, "you will lie on a bed of silks wearing nothing but that devilish smile of yours. The world will be ours, and nothing and no one will ever be able to take it away."

"Am I always naked in your imagination?" I said, my face warming. The black of his eyes had begun to lift away, replaced by a sleepy violet. "Because if by some miracle, we get through this and we defeat Luthien, I will be ruling with my clothes on."

"Disappointing."

I elbowed him with a chuckle, "Just eat your breakfast."

"You're blushing," he said, brushing his long fingers against my face. "Your cheeks have gone all pink."

I tried to look away, but Laphaniel refused to drop his hand.

"What is it?"

The doubts and niggles prickled at me as a little voice resurfaced and whispered that I wasn't good enough. Not special enough, too broken, too weak…too human.

"Why me?"

"Why you, what?" he asked, genuine confusion sweeping across his face.

"What made you fall in love with me?"

"I don't know," he said, his fingers softly brushing down my cheek to the edge of my lips. "Does it matter? I wanted to keep you because I was bored and lonely, I didn't want you because I fell instantly in love with you, and you know that. I love you because my soul sings out for yours, and because I need you. More than I have needed anyone. I don't know which part of you I fell in love with first, but I do know I love you, wholly, completely and desperately."

"You think I'm your soulmate?" I asked, the word falling from my mouth both wonderful and strange.

"If that's what you want to call it."

I blinked, unable to find words to question him…but he spoke so plainly, so honestly, how could I? His words settled over me, solid and comforting, sounding like home.

Laphaniel reached for a piece of toast, as I drank the last of my coffee, swirling the dregs around in the mug. We lay in comfortable silence as we finished breakfast, quietly enjoying each other's company within the chaos we had been swept up in.

It was still dark outside when we left, the chill of the early morning biting through my gloves as I scraped the thin layer of frost from the car window. It crept through the cheap coat I had found in the cupboard, the smooth black fabric crinkling with every move I made. There had been no coat for Laphaniel, only an oversized grey hoodie with holes in the sleeves.

I tossed a bag of supplies into the back seat while Laphaniel stood back, eyeing the car as if it would turn around and bite him.

"Are you going to be okay?" I asked, noting the rust around the car door, worried that I was making him climb into an iron box with wheels.

"How long until we reach the cottage?" he asked, still looking wary.

"A few hours, longer if I get lost."

He forced a smile, hiding his hands in the pockets of his borrowed black jeans so I couldn't see him fidget. "Try not to get lost."

Laphaniel took a breath and climbed in beside me. I gave him what I hoped was a reassuring smile before starting the car, stalling it instantly. "I'm sure it's like riding a bike…"

I never knew someone could put their seat belt on so quickly.

The car jolted and shuddered as I struggled with the gears, the petrol gauge tilting very close to empty.

"Do you know how to drive?"

"It's been a while," I admitted, easing out of the driveway.

I pulled up to the nearest garage, paying for the petrol, bottled water and snacks with the fifty pounds I had found whilst snooping around Niven's room. I also purchased a road map after leaving the old one on the kitchen top.

"Turn left at the end of this road," Laphaniel said as we got going again, the map perched on his lap. "Your other left, Teya."

He had the window down, blasting the car with freezing air. I was thankful for the hat and coat I had found in the bag of unwanted clothes. Laphaniel caught my eye and smiled before pointing back to the road.

"Look ahead, you're making me nervous."

"I'm just checking you're okay."

"Don't worry about me," he said. "Just look where you are going."

"My driving is not that bad."

The roads were fairly clear, as few people were out so early in the morning, and for that, I was incredibly grateful. We wound around country lanes, glimpsing the sea over the cliff edge as the first rays of wintry sun broke through the miserable clouds.

My hands on the steering wheel were freezing, and I had to search for the road signs as an hour into our journey, Laphaniel had dropped the map and slumped in his seat.

"We're over halfway there," I said. He only nodded, sitting up and fumbling for the water I had brought and took a small sip before wincing. "Do you need a break? We can stop somewhere if you want."

He shook his head, a low moan escaping his lips. "I won't get back in again."

"You don't look good," I said, worried.

"Thanks," Laphaniel muttered and closed his eyes.

I hummed along to a song on the radio, earning a tired smile from Laphaniel. "Join in if you want to."

"You're doing a fine job on your own," he replied quietly.

I laughed, shaking my head as the song changed to something I didn't know. "At least our lives never depended on my singing skills."

Laphaniel shifted in his seat. "To which I am eternally grateful."

"Do you want me to shut up?"

"No," he breathed, keeping his eyes closed. "It's oddly endearing."

I continued to hum as I drove, tapping my fingers on the steering wheel, glancing at the road signs to ensure we were headed in the right direction.

The roads remained empty, the passing landscape stark and bleak. The radio played on, song after song, passing the time and filling the quiet. Laphaniel didn't speak again, his head rested on his chest, his skin grey.

Lights flickered on the dashboard, a flash of colour that was gone in a blink. It happened again just as quick, everything lighting up like Christmas before going dark. The overhead light clicked on, buzzing incessantly until the bulb blew.

"Laphaniel?"

He didn't answer.

My headlights brightened, flooding the still dark roads with white light. I pressed my foot to the brake. Nothing happened.

"Laphaniel, wake up!"

Hectic Glamour sparked around the car uncontrolled. My hands tightened on the steering wheel, the car jolting as I caught the edge of the road.

Glass shattered over the tarmac as the headlights blew. I hit ice and skidded, spinning the car.

Again, I tried the brakes, stomping down hard. We left the road.

The car tore through bushes and dirt, breaking through winter brittle trees, and I couldn't stop it.

But the ditch did.

I slammed against the seatbelt, instinctively reaching for Laphaniel, but he was already clambering out of the car.

With shaking hands, I unbuckled myself and forced the door open, rushing to his side as he retched.

He wiped at his mouth, his words little more than gasps. "Are you okay?"

"I'm fine—" I began, moving my hand to his back when he bent double and was violently sick. "You're not. What happened?"

I didn't expect him to answer, and he didn't... couldn't.

"I'm going to grab you some water," I said, "I'll be right back."

I ran to the wrecked Micra, knowing we were both lucky to walk away from it. The bonnet was a mess, smoke curling up from within, and I quickly turned off the ignition. One of the wheels had popped too.

Careful of the pieces of glass littered over the back seats, I grabbed the bag of supplies and made my way back to Laphaniel. He sat on the frosty grass, head bent forwards, taking in deep breaths of fresh air.

"Here, take this." I passed him a bottle of water, and he rinsed his mouth out. "Is that better?"

He shook his head.

I winced for him. "Are you going to throw up again?"

A nod.

"Why didn't you tell me to stop the car?" I asked gently, my hand making little circles over his back while he continued to lose his breakfast over the grass. "I would have stopped."

Laphaniel sat back with a groan, draining half the water. "I was going to...I...I left it too late..."

"Did you know you would react like that?"

"No."

I had seen first-hand how iron affected him, how quickly it poisoned his body. We were both foolish to believe a car would be any different.

I swept the damp hair away from his face, one hand still trailing over his back. "We're going to have to walk the rest of the way, you blew all the electrics in the car. And it's currently stuck in a ditch."

Laphaniel finished the bottle of water, taking another deep breath. Colour began to seep back into his face. His voice sounded much steadier as he asked, "Are you sure you're not hurt?"

"I'm going to have some colourful bruises, but I'm fine." He didn't look convinced. "I'm okay, Laphaniel, I promise. I'm worried about you though."

He rested his head on his knees, his voice muffled. "How far did we get?"

"We made it to Cornwall," I said, "It's a few miles walk to the cottage— we got pretty close. Do you want to stop a bit longer?"

"No," he answered, pushing himself to his feet. "I'm feeling a lot better already."

We found a coastal path not far from where we had crashed. It wound down over wild hills, its steps slick with the drizzle misting above us. It led us through a little copse of trees not far from the beach, then onto a gravel path with a rundown cottage at its end.

Laphaniel tugged at my hand as I made to step inside, leading me instead over the front lawn to the fence at the side of the house. He rested his arms on the wood, and I followed his gaze out over the endless dark sea. The waves churned as they crashed against the rocks, sending white spray high into the air. Dappled sunlight crept through cracks in the grey sky, catching the rain drops as they fell, setting them alight.

"I've always loved Cornwall," I said, leaning my head against his shoulder. "We used to stay at this old caravan park when we were little, which Niven hated of course. I fell in love with the utter wildness of it." I smiled wistfully. "It reminds me of Faerie."

"Do you miss it, then?" he asked, not turning from the furious waves.

"Parts of it, the parts you showed me at least. Will you miss it?"

"I've never spent long outside Faerie. There's always a pull to go back, and I've always listened to it. Fey get banished to your world as a punishment, so it's harder for us to live here, there's too much iron and not enough magic." He paused, catching the look I couldn't quite keep from my face. "I don't see this as a punishment, Teya, that's not what I meant...I just don't understand how your world works."

I remembered all the warnings he had given to me on our first meeting, how I would be torn apart by monsters in the woods, my soul cleaved from my body. Oh, how he had enjoyed tormenting me. I gave him a wicked smile.

"Just imagine everything here wants to kill you and you'll be fine."

"Ha ha," he replied, "I warned you, and you still didn't listen."

Reaching up, I pressed my lips to his cheek. "Because you were just being a bastard, and you know it."

His eyes lit up as he laughed. "You ignored me anyway."

"And nearly got myself killed," I said, shaking my head. "Come on, let's go take a look at our seaside cottage."

Old paint peeled away from the door, the lock stiff. Inside, dated wallpaper covered the walls, the embossed patterns stained a nicotine yellow. Greying net curtains hung limply from the windows, spots of mould creeping up the tattered lace.

Upon one wall, blocks of bright colours had been painted in neat squares, little tins of paint stacked up upon one counter. The whole place looked barely touched.

"It could be a lot worse," I began, placing our bags onto the table before wandering into the living room. An inglenook stood at one end, a pile of old logs waiting in a tattered basket beside it. "Care to light a fire?"

"If we can get something to eat after," Laphaniel replied, stuffing logs into the fireplace.

"You're hungry already?" I asked, wondering how he could possibly want food so soon after spilling his guts up.

"Starving,"

Fire danced at his fingertips, sure and strong before catching the logs and setting them alight.

"I have some money left over from what I took from Niven," I said, fumbling in my pocket. "and since we're at the seaside, how about I treat you to fish and chips?"

"Let me clean up first," Laphaniel answered, pulling his shirt off. "I won't be long."

I didn't blame him for wanting to freshen up. Settling on the old sofa, I snuggled beneath a faded knitted throw and closed my eyes for a moment, drained from the car journey and the shock of crashing the car.

The sudden cold stirred me. Darkness settled in shrouds of shadow, and I knew I was no longer at the cottage. Standing up, I disturbed the dust that clung to everything. Candlelight flickered weakly in tainted holders, dripping wax onto the stone floor in puddles. The weak flame barely cast any light in the dark room.

Laphaniel lay asleep on the bed, and I moved over to join him, reaching out to brush the hair away from his face. I jerked back at the chill of his skin, my hand barely touching his cheek. His lips moved, and I bent low to hear what he was saying, flinching at the coldness swamping him. Something tickled against my cheek, and I recoiled back as the fat body of a spider pushed its way past his lips. The skin around his mouth cracked, peeling away to reveal white bone that crumbled as more and more spiders crawled from his lips.

They poured over the covers, scurrying over each other in a frantic dance, leaving nothing beneath the mouldering blankets but bone and the echo of death.

"Teya." Laphaniel's voice swept over me, sending the darkness and shadows back into hiding.

I forced my eyes open, fighting against the desperate sob clawing its way up my throat. I fell against him, his hand coming up to the back of my head, drawing me close.

"I closed my eyes for just a minute," I began, breathless. "Only a minute."

"I know," he answered, smelling of soap and mint. "One day we will bargain away our nightmares and make a fortune."

The nightmare slipped back into my subconscious, lying dormant, waiting. "Go finish getting dressed," I said, trailing a hand over his still bare chest. "You're very distracting looking like that."

Laphaniel's eyes lit up, the wickedness within him flaring to life as he moved closer. "How distracting?"

Leaning forwards, I kissed him, tasting his little moan that caressed my lips. "You completely muddle my thoughts until I can't think straight."

"Is that a bad thing?" he breathed back, deepening the kiss.

"No, it's wonderful."

He pushed against me, a hand sliding up against my waist as he kissed my neck, his teeth nipping the skin just below my collar bone.

"Laphaniel..."

"Hmmm?" His hand skimmed over my thigh, barely touching as I reluctantly pulled it away.

"Wait..."

"Why?" he murmured, clasping his fingers through mine. His mouth found my lips again, chasing away all reason.

"Because..." His tongue brushed against mine, and I dragged him closer, needing him...wanting him. "We don't..."

"Don't what?" The huskiness of his voice nearly undid me, rumbling over the hollow of my throat.

One hand slipped from my fingers, moving lower, brushing beneath my clothes, against my breast. It skimmed my side, soft and gentle, moving lower and lower.

"We don't have..." I tried not to arch into him, drawing back before meeting his dark gaze. "If I end up pregnant..."

He let out a groan, head buried against my neck. "Oh."

"Put a shirt on, and we'll get some food," I said, catching my breath "then we can nip to the shop. It'll be like a date...something humans do."

"I had you dancing to the trees and drinking wine made from moonlight. Did I not court you well?"

"You held me against my will." I remembered all too well the strange coldness of that glowing wine, the crispness, the way I could almost taste the stars themselves.

"You didn't want to leave."

I closed my eyes at the memory. "No, but is there anything wrong with wanting something more..."

"Human?" Laphaniel finished for me, and I sensed the barest hint of uncertainty in his voice, a thread of vulnerability that rarely surfaced.

"Maybe, I don't know," I said quickly. "I long to dance under the trees until my feet can no longer hold me up, to fall asleep in your arms under the moonlight and carry on dancing when the sun rises again. I want that more than anything, but a part of me misses chips on the beach in the drizzle."

"I sometimes forget how human you are," he said, brushing a strand of hair from my face.

"Sometimes it's easy to forget that you're not."

Laphaniel's hand lingered against my cheek before he pulled away with a small smile. "Come on then, let's go and get your soggy dinner."

"Thank you."

He smiled as he took my hand, and even though we had run away and were in hiding and the ever present threat of death hung above us, it was nice to laugh, and to walk in the rain, and eat chips on the beach in January.

CHAPTER FIVE

The wind had more than a little bite to it, with the winter sun unable to do anything but brighten the otherwise grey sky. The small collection of quaint shops and boutiques stood either side of a winding cobbled lane, leading away from our cottage down to a rustic harbour, where half beaten boats bobbed happily on the water.

The village was serene, a place where the pubs had real log fires and candle stubs on the cosy tables. Beside the charming pub stood a gift shop selling new-age type jewellery, all silver stars and crystals beneath a soft fog of incense smoke. I peered in, distracted by the twinkling fairy lights hanging from the shelves.

"See anything you like?" Laphaniel said beside me.

"Why, are you planning on buying me something?"

"No."

I elbowed him before I walked off.

"I believe I bought you once," he called after me, humour rich in his voice.

"So romantic," I replied, not caring to dwell on the memory of him, bargaining with the witch who had captured me. Slimy Soo had demanded a high price for me…a small fortune for a dying girl.

Laphaniel leaned against the shop front, his eyes flicking to a pair of girls that were staring at him as they walked past. I could see their cheeks redden as they caught his eye, and their steps quickened.

"Not really," he said with a smile. "I was looking for a goat to fatten up."

I gave a snort, shaking my head, "Well, I will always be grateful you chose me and not the livestock."

"So am I." The fairy lights caught the violet in his eyes, making them glimmer like star shine. "Though the goat smelled better."

"Do you want anything from the shop?" I asked, laughing. "I'm just going to grab some tampons if you want to wait here?"

"Could you get some more bottled water? The water from the tap tastes wrong."

I knew it was stupid to feel uncomfortable buying tampons around Laphaniel, but it just felt too human. I didn't know how female fey bodies really worked, I had no one to ask. It had been mortifying enough to ask Laphaniel for supplies in Faerie.

I didn't know if fey menstruated at all, if they bore children like a human woman would. They could lay eggs for all I knew, though I hoped to god they didn't.

Inside the shop, I grabbed what I needed, along with a few chocolate bars simply because I missed them. Handing over what was nearly all my stolen money, I caught the date on the local newspaper.

January Twenty-sixth.

"What's the matter?" Laphaniel asked after I joined him on the cobblestones, noting the look on my face.

"It's my birthday today," I replied, unsure how I felt about it.

Laphaniel gave me a quick kiss on the mouth, and as birthday presents went, it was by far the best. "I've got you a gift."

I looked up at him, my eyes narrowing as he passed me a small black box. "You only found out it was my birthday ten seconds ago."

"I didn't intend it to be a birthday gift."

"When did you get it?" I asked. "Did you just steal this when I was in the shop?"

There was a sudden, wonderful wickedness in his eyes as he shook his head. "I was given it."

"In the five minutes I was gone, you managed to Glamour a poor shop assistant into giving you this?"

"She seemed happy to help."

"She?"

Laphaniel cocked his head, a slow smile itching at his lips. "Jealous?"

"No," I lied, not liking the thought of him bewitching anyone else, knowing how easy he was to fall in love with, how it started with the touch of Glamour, and the knowing smiles. I just wasn't going to tell him that.

"Do you want me to go back and pay for it?" he asked, his tone sharpening.

"I don't think they accept blood and nightmares."

Laphaniel's eyes narrowed as I snapped at him. "Shall I go find out for you? See if I can make her scream instead of smile?"

"I have money, you don't have to use that here." The word came out before I could stop it, and I regretted it instantly. "I didn't mean…"

"That?" he repeated, mimicking the way I had said it, like it was a dirty word. "Glamour? Do you have endless riches in your bag I don't know of then? Let me see."

He snatched my purse from me before I could react, emptying the pitiful amount of money we had left into his hand.

"Give it back," I hissed.

"How much is here?" Laphaniel demanded, shoving his hand towards me so a few coins fell to the ground. "Enough to buy food? What about wood for the fire? Did you buy matches or is my Glamour only okay when it's for something you want?"

"That's not what I meant, and you know it."

"I don't know what you meant, Teya," he said, suddenly cold and distant. "Would you rather I was human? Is that it?"

"I've never once wished that." I shook my head, grasping at words. "You enchanted me…literally, from the moment I first met you. Everything about you was wonderful and extraordinary and frightening, and I found it so easy to fall in love with you…too easy." Stupid tears pricked at my eyes, and I bent to pick up the few coppers that had fallen, before snatching the crumpled note from Laphaniel's hand. "I didn't fall in love with a human boy."

An awkward silence settled over us, neither of us willing to break the tension, both too stubborn to reach out. I didn't mention the gift again, and Laphaniel had placed it into his pocket without a word.

"Let's just go back," I began, tightening my coat against the chill.

"I thought you wanted to get something to eat?"

A bitter laugh slipped past my lips. "I wanted to buy you dinner and sit on the beach. I wanted to show you a little of my world, even though it's grey and damp and not magical in the slightest. Because you showed me yours."

Laphaniel held out a hand. "Then show me."

I glanced at his hand. "It is a grievous offence to yell at someone on their birthday over here. In some countries it is still punishable by death, did you know that?"

He cocked his head slightly as he tried to work out if I was lying or not. I would have fooled him if I was able to keep the smirk from my face. Grinning, I took his hand and pulled him close, knocking the shopping bag slightly, making it clink.

Laphaniel lifted the two bottles of spiced rum from the bag. "Teya Jenkins, did you steal these?"

I winced.

"You little hypocrite," he said, though he seemed more impressed than anything.

"I stole those the old-fashioned way."

"You have a skewed sense of morality, Teya," Laphaniel said, rolling his eyes as we started to walk down to the seafront.

I bought us a bag of chips to share and a bottle of coke, which Laphaniel turned his nose up at. I drank half the bottle in one go, the taste both familiar and comforting.

The beach was deserted, the sea choppy and grey with waves crashing up the sand to leave a trail of seaweed behind. We wandered along the shoreline, allowing the icy spray to wash over our feet, meandering down to the tiny cove just beyond our cottage.

I sat between Laphaniel's legs on the damp sand, the chips

balancing on my lap as the sun finally broke through the grim sky, tearing the grey to reveal the bright blue beneath.

"Here." I passed a bottle of rum to Laphaniel before opening my own. "I chose these because of the pirate on the front."

Laphaniel's laughter rumbled against my back. "Are you planning on getting wretchedly drunk on your birthday?"

"Would you stop me?"

"No," he replied, clinking his bottle against mine. "It would be nice to forget about everything for a little while."

I took a mouthful of rum, closing my eyes at the warmth sliding down my throat. I took another and another and another until the world began to dance around me, and everything became much softer...more bearable.

Laphaniel kept one arm around me, his fingers stroking back my hair as he quietened his demons with alcohol. He stayed there for a moment, just holding me, his head resting on my shoulder.

We lit a bonfire with pieces of driftwood, Laphaniel sparking it to life with a flick of his fingertips. I watched the flames lick at the broken wood, spitting and hissing as it crawled across the edges and turned them black. His fingers were still warm as I reached for them.

"How do you do it?" I asked, and he flicked his fingers again slowly, so little flames danced in his hand.

"Like that."

"I wish I could do it."

He took my hand carefully, pushing my third finger and thumb together, twisting my hands ever so slightly, so he made me click my fingers. "Try that."

I did as instructed, the lazy tone of his voice sending a shiver down my back that had nothing to do with the frigid wind.

Nothing happened, my fingers didn't even make a decent clicking noise. Laphaniel held my hand tighter, leaning in to whisper in my ear.

"Again."

I moved my fingers, his hand beneath mine, mimicking the exact gesture he had taught me only moments before. Flames instantly brushed against my skin, nestled between both our hands, burning but at the same time, not.

Warmth flowed over my skin, and I knew that if Laphaniel slipped, even a fraction, I would burn.

"Don't set me on fire." I laughed, amazed at the feel of his Glamour in my hands.

"I could always toss you in the sea if I did," he replied.

"You wouldn't dare."

I was up over his shoulder before I could make another sound, his eyes flashing with pure impishness as I struggled against him, squealing at the sudden icy spray of the sea as he ran towards the water.

"Laphaniel! Put me down." I clawed at his back, while the water crashed against him. "No! Don't put me down."

I slipped closer to the water, his hands tightening when he staggered slightly.

"I thought you wanted to get down."

"Not here." I tried to clamber back up him, but he was as unsteady as I was. I managed to overbalance him further, and we both plunged beneath the frigid water.

Laphaniel dragged me back up coughing and spluttering, the saltwater burning in my throat. I shivered instantly; the weight of my sodden jeans dragged down my legs. I yanked them up, but the waves crashed against me, and they slipped down again.

"It's freezing!" I yelled at him, noticing he was trembling too, but only because he was laughing at me with deep breathless gasps.

Seeing him laugh like that awoke something deep within me, I couldn't remember a time when we had both laughed so freely. I never wanted it to end.

With a manic glee, I shoved him hard, watching as he stumbled back, unable to catch himself, so he crashed back under the water.

I ran for the shore, not having the courage to look back. A wild scream fell from my lips as his arms came up around me, lifting me up out of the water to spin me around. With my arms around his neck, I closed my eyes as he spun, relishing a moment of pure unhindered freedom, our laughter mingling together with complete abandon.

Burying my head into his shoulder, I kissed the soft dip of his neck and tasted salt. His head lowered, mouth finding mine with clumsy kisses that stole my breath away.

I slipped from his arms, not breaking away from him as I half dragged him back to shore. We slipped and stumbled over each other, before landing in a heap beside the fire.

Reaching up, I tugged Laphaniel's shirt over his head, wincing when I accidently threw it into the flames. I fumbled at the button on his jeans, the soaked denim refusing to push past his hips as I descended into giggles again.

"Lift your bum up," I said, my chuckle morphing into a sharp snort. The sound startled us, with Laphaniel collapsing against me, his entire body shaking with his laughter. He gasped against my neck, struggling to take a breath.

Tears streamed down my face, my ribs hurting from laughing…my body so unused to such joy it was literally hurting me to be so happy.

"You really are wonderful," Laphaniel murmured, lifting himself over me so I could see his face. He took a breath, leaning in to kiss me again. His fingers trailed over my face, tracing over my cheeks and down my neck, his gaze never leaving mine until I blushed and turned away, unable to hold his eye any longer.

Teasing kisses followed where his fingers had been, and I arched my body towards his, tasting the sea against his lips as I found his mouth, enticing a gasp from him as I bit down.

Glamour sparked and swirled around us, exciting the flames nearby, so they danced and spat. My head swam with the wonder of it, the magic and the rum swirling my world until nothing else mattered. I barely noticed the chill of the wind against my bare skin, the rough sand against my back, or the spit of flames. I barely noticed Laphaniel reach over me, his breathing hard and frantic while he fumbled around in the shopping bag.

We made love like the world was ending. Like we didn't know when or if there would be a time to be happy again. We snatched the moment and devoured it until the waves began to creep up the sand and wash against our bare legs, reminding us that we no longer had forever.

"You're shivering," Laphaniel murmured in my ear as I lay against him.

"I want to stay here for a little bit longer," I replied, my words slipping thick and heavy from my mouth. "Just lie here with me?"

I reached out for the rum, both bottles near empty and took a large swallow before Laphaniel prised it from my hands.

"I think that's enough," he said as I laid my head against him. "Come on, get up…Teya?"

He tapped my cheek and I prised my eyes open. My hand was strangely heavy as I brushed it against his cheek. "You are really pretty."

"Okay." He smiled. "Up you get, come here."

He lifted me into his arms, and I snuggled against his chest, feeling safe and warm and very, very loved. "Can I go to sleep?"

"Yes, close your eyes, you drunken wretch."

Laphaniel rolled me against his chest, and I nuzzled closer. He staggered once, snickering into my hair. Then everything just faded away as I fell asleep in his arms.

CHAPTER SIX

A strangled gasp stirred me from a deep sleep, the bed shifting from beneath me. At first, I thought Laphaniel was having another nightmare, and I grabbed for the lamp. I knocked it over with fumbling hands, filling the room with a trembling light.

We were not alone.

"You stupid boy," Oonagh hissed. The silver-haired faerie straddled Laphaniel, her white gown sprawling around her like mist. She pressed a knife to his throat, a thin dribble of red slipped from beneath the blade. "How fortunate for you that it was me who found you."

The last time I had seen the lithe, beautiful faerie, she had been dressing me for Luthien's ball. There had been a strange warmth to her, not quite a kindness, but she had been the only faerie who hadn't been cruel to me.

In the dim light of the bedroom, however, she was terrifying.

"I'm not feeling very fortunate at this moment," Laphaniel replied with frustrating calmness. "Get off me before I throw you off."

Oonagh bared her teeth. "I dare you to try."

I sat up, ready to pull Oonagh off Laphaniel, not caring in the slightest that I was naked beneath the covers. "Did Luthien send you?"

Oonagh's ghostly eyes shot to me, dark and livid. "Yes."

In an instant, Laphaniel had grabbed at Oonagh's pale hands and flipped her over onto the mattress, the knife at her own throat. The beautiful faerie laughed without humour, spreading her arms wide against the bed, tilting her chin up to meet the blade.

"What are you doing here?" Laphaniel asked, warning darkening his voice.

"I was sent to take Teya back," Oonagh replied, reaching over to trail her fingers down my arm, and I flinched. "But that is not what I am going to do."

She kicked her legs upward, catching Laphaniel and in one swift motion, had deftly rolled off the bed. I had felt the softest touch of her lips against mine when she moved.

Laphaniel's snarl rumbled in his throat. He took one step towards Oonagh before he paused, whipping his head around to the doorway.

"What are you doing here too?" Laphaniel hissed as he noticed a second presence. He snatched a shirt from the floor, still wearing the jeans from the night before.

I turned to the doorway, catching the glare on Laphaniel's sister's face. Nefina curled her lip while I tried to cover myself, but beneath the scorn in her blue eyes there was a new vulnerability surfacing which almost softened the hatred in her expression. She was dirtier too, her green silks unwashed and ripped, her white-blonde hair knotted.

I didn't know the reasons behind the fraught tension between Laphaniel and Nefina—Laphaniel wouldn't talk about it. I just knew his sister disliked me because I made her brother happy.

"You should have just stayed away," Nefina said, turning to Laphaniel.

"Believe me, I wish we had. What's the matter, Nefina? Has Luthien finally tired of having you as her lap dog?"

"I was never her lap dog!" Nefina snapped. Bruises marred her slender arms, the gauzy fabric of her dress not quire hiding them. "You were her little obedient puppy, yapping at her heels. You have no idea what she did to me after you left. Who she took her anger out upon."

"You cannot blame me for all the bad things in your life."

"Oh, I can. You took me away, remember? Because that's what you do. You take things and promise things that you cannot give, and then you leave."

Laphaniel stood, taking a single step closer to his sister. "Would you have preferred to stay with your father?"

Nefina took a breath, looking up to meet Laphaniel's furious gaze. She didn't waver. "Better a rich man's whore than the life you gave me."

"You are a thankless, ungrateful bitch," Laphaniel snarled. The light began to flicker from its displaced position on the bedroom floor.

"Oh!" Nefina gasped, clutching her elegant hands to her chest in mock adoration. "Should I be thankful to you, then? For the nightmare that was my childhood? Thankful to leave one hell only to be thrust into another and another after that? Do you even remember any of it, or were you too lost in an Ember fog to even know where you were?"

Nefina caught the shock on my face and sneered at it. "You never told Teya that delightful part of your life, I take it?"

"What he tells me is no concern of yours, Nefina," I said, gaining an unreadable look from Laphaniel. However, I made a mental note to ask what Ember was.

"I kept you safe," Laphaniel said to his sister, some of the anger ebbing from him.

"You need to rethink your meaning of that word," Nefina spat. "You didn't keep me safe, you are not keeping that dumb creature over there safe. She is going to die because of you."

"Is that why you came here? To list all my shortcomings and tell me that I'm going to fail?" Frustration replaced what was left of Laphaniel's simmering anger. "You are not telling me anything I don't already know. I have no plan on what to do next. We have reached out to the Unseelie for help, I am that desperate…I have nothing in mind but to throw ourselves at their mercy, hoping they will listen before they slaughter us."

"That's a fool's hope," Nefina said.

"It's all I have."

"How did you get here, Laphaniel?" Oonagh asked, the edge to her voice revealing she already knew the answer.

"I drove down," I said, reaching under the cover for my top, which was crunchy from my dip in the freezing sea. I yanked it on and fumbled for my jeans. The air was almost crackling from the tension in the room; the hateful words left unsaid.

"You drove down," Oonagh repeated, nodding slightly, so her soft hair tumbled over her shoulder like cobwebs. "How was the iron sickness?"

"It was unpleasant," Laphaniel answered.

"Oh, I bet it was." Oonagh reached for something concealed in a pocket of her long silver cloak, the edges ragged. She tossed the map onto the bed. I winced, and Laphaniel closed his eyes. "I had a feeling you would return to Teya's house."

"Because Luthien had mine scorched to the ground," Laphaniel cut in.

"You left this behind!" Oonagh rounded on him. "Have you any idea what would have happened if one of Luthien's fey had found it? Are you really that stupid, Laphaniel?"

Laphaniel made a low sound in the back of his throat, a warning that caused the hairs on my neck to prick up. Glamour swirled thickly around the room, restless and angry. My head swam with it.

"I'm in no mood for this," Laphaniel said, pushing past Oonagh as he made to leave. She grabbed his arm with a snarl of her own.

"Perhaps drowning yourself in drink wasn't the smartest idea then. I can smell it on you both. I can still scent the iron on you."

"It probably wasn't the best idea, Oonagh," Laphaniel snapped, yanking his arm back, "But it felt fucking good at the time."

"Laphaniel! Wait," I called after him, but he didn't listen, he just left. Oonagh and Nefina turned to me as I ran my hands through my hair, swallowing the lump in my throat while I fought the urge to scream.

"That car journey could have killed him," Oonagh said, the accusation sharp. "Where is the car now?"

"In a ditch."

Oonagh took a step closer, long fingers reaching to touch just below my collarbone. I wondered what colour the bruising was. "You could have been killed."

I swiped the knotted strands of my hair away, feeling a headache starting to pound behind my eyes. "I need coffee if we are going to continue this, lots of it. You two go and make coffee, I'm going to find Laphaniel."

"I don't know how…"

"No, Nefina. Figure it out please, stop talking to me."

I found Laphaniel in the garden, beneath a wooden gazebo that had seen better days. Pulling up a chair, I sat beside him, the peeling paint coming off in my hands. He didn't look up.

"Nefina's right," he said.

"No, she isn't."

He scrubbed a hand over his face. "Did you know Luthien once flayed a girl alive because she spilled a drink on her dress?"

"Luthien has to catch me first."

"It took three days for her to die."

I took his hand, forcing him to look at me. "Stop."

"I don't know what I'm doing," he admitted.

"It's not on you to figure it all out. Are you going to tell me what happened between you and Nefina?"

He shook his head, "Just leave it alone."

"What's Ember?"

He looked away, "Nothing but a bad memory."

"Are you going to add that to the list of things you won't talk about?"

"I think I will."

I sighed. "Bottling everything up won't make it all go away."

"Here." Laphaniel placed a little black box onto the table. "Now seems as good a time as any to give this to you."

He watched me pick it up, turning it over in my hands before lifting the lid and peering inside. It was a star. Small and silver, simple and perfect. Each one of its six points was different lengths, curving inwards ever so slightly.

I carefully lifted it from its box and fastened it around my neck, my fingers lingering on the delicate points.

"Thank you."

"It is about as useful as a real star to wish upon, but I thought you might like it."

"I love it," I said, reaching across the table to take his hand. "You are my star, Laphaniel. Never forget that. My light in this darkness."

"I think sometimes you put too much faith in me," he answered, his dark mood not seeming to shift.

"I wish you would talk to me."

"I am talking to you."

"Laphaniel…"

"It won't stop the nightmares, will it?" he interrupted softly. "Or mend the rift between Nefina and me, or change the fact I was dragged back when all I wanted was to stay—"

He stopped, closing his eyes. Having him say it out loud was like a kick to the stomach. "You told me you didn't remember."

"I don't remember much, but it hurt." He stood, creating a distance between us.

The memory of him dying in my arms was too clear. "I know. I saw."

He shook his head, the violet of his eyes slowly swallowed up by black. "No…no, not that. I was never meant to come back. It was like being ripped from somewhere and tossed aside, and now I feel like I am drowning."

Laphaniel paced against the damp grass, agitated and withdrawn. His fists curled and uncurled at his side. Glamour swirled around him, unchecked.

"Did you forget about me?" The words were the barest of whispers, I hadn't really meant to speak them, but his head snapped towards me.

"I don't know."

"Why wouldn't you want to come back to me?" I asked, the words holding no comfort at all, just a bitter accusation that rose unprompted, hungry for answers I wasn't ready for, and he wasn't ready to give.

Laphaniel took a breath, and it hissed through his teeth. Tendrils of feral Glamour whipped at my hair, sparking the pounding in my head. I could barely hear anything over the sudden ringing in my ears. Wet slipped from my nose, red upon my fingertips.

"Wait," I called out as he took another step back, panic flashing over his face when he noticed the blood. His breath caught again. "Laphaniel—"

"Don't." There was a lull to the word, heavy and strange. I had no idea if he meant to thread his Glamour into his voice, or if it were completely out of his control. "Leave me be."

For a moment, my mind went blank, and my body soft as the lilting melody of his voice settled over me. My feet moved, but I barely felt them.

It felt good to walk away, better than good. Wonderful.

I forced myself to stop, remembering well the pull of Glamour, the need to listen and obey. It was getting easier to fight it.

With leaden feet, I closed the gap between us, pulling him close enough, so his heart thumped wildly against me. His Glamour dropped like a dying wind.

Laphaniel tilted his head to rest against my shoulder, his breathing calming, but he tensed when Oonagh called out to us.

"We better go back and talk to them," I began. "Do you need a moment?"

I knew he would hate for the others to witness his vulnerability, the sudden lack of control over his Glamour...his emotions. He pulled away from me and nodded.

"Okay," I said.

"I don't...I can't talk about what happened, Teya. Not yet. I don't know what just happened...I don't—"

"I'm sorry," I cut in, sensing his rising panic. Noting the sparks of Glamour stirring up again.

Oonagh called out again and I gritted my teeth, wishing she would stop. "Do you want me to stay for a bit?"

"Oonagh won't stop yelling for us," Laphaniel replied quietly. "I'll follow in a minute."

I walked back to the cottage on my own, finding Oonagh and

Nefina in the living room. A tray of weak looking coffee sat upon a little table.

"What happened?" Oonagh asked, her ghostly eyes following me as I sat down.

The coffee barely warmed my hands. "I tried to force him into opening up to me, and I shouldn't have."

Tears pricked at my eyes, and it was an effort to keep them in check. Oonagh offered me no comfort, no kind words, she just waited, and for that, I was thankful to her.

"He said he didn't remember...I didn't think. I didn't realise..." I rambled, my words fast and useless. "I pushed him, not even noticing how he was hurting."

"You're noticing now," she said, taking a sip from a dainty china cup.

"I may have left it too late."

"This is forgivable, Teya. Selfishness is forgivable, after all we faeries are selfish creatures." Oonagh said, waving a hand over the branches of a dying houseplant. Tiny buds appeared beneath her fingers, only to die again when she pulled her hand away. "Do you quarrel often?"

"We've started to."

"Good." Her eyes lit up. "You're both hungry, frightened and lost, so of course you will bite at each other. It is when indifference sets in, then you can worry."

My hand reached for the star around my neck. "I can't lose him again."

"What do you mean?" Nefina asked, leaning against the far wall, away from us. I turned to face her, noting the dark circled beneath her bright eyes. She didn't know how we had broken the curse.

"We went into the Seelie castle so I could take Niven's place, and she stabbed Laphaniel. He died in my arms. It's what broke the curse." I swallowed, unable to explain how his soul was dragged back to his body. Unable to think how it had been dragged kicking and screaming from a place where apparently, it had found some sort of peace.

Oonagh held a hand to her mouth, exchanging a quick glance with Nefina, whose lovely face had turned ashen.

"What are you two actually doing here?" I asked, wary.

"Would you believe we are here to help you?" Oonagh answered.

"By attempting to slit Laphaniel's throat?"

Oonagh dismissed my words with a wave of her hand. "I was merely demonstrating how easy it would have been."

She reclined in an overstuffed leather armchair beside the fire, which she had lit with a delicate twist of her hand. Nefina settled by the window, looking out fearfully when she wasn't glaring at me. She jumped when the front door opened, as did I, sloshing warm coffee over my legs.

"Sit down if you are joining us," Oonagh said as Laphaniel walked in, curling her long legs up beneath her like a cat. "We have much to discuss."

Laphaniel sat beside me, his leg touching mine. "Have you caught up on our situation?"

Oonagh narrowed her eyes. "Must you be so flippant? And yes, Teya just explained how the curse was broken. True love really does conquer all, doesn't it?"

"I don't believe we've conquered anything yet," Laphaniel replied.

A sly grin spread over Oonagh's lips. "We are beginning to gather a rebel group."

"How many?" Laphaniel asked sitting straighter, the faintest thread of hope warming his voice.

"Not enough," Oonagh said. "But it's a start. Luthien does not know that I have betrayed her, not yet anyway."

"And you?" Laphaniel turned to his sister, who visibly recoiled. "Why are you here?"

"Luthien found out that I helped you," Nefina said, her voice wavering. "I made the antidote the night Teya drugged you with Goodnight Kisses, and she found out. I am no longer welcome at Court."

Oonagh shifted in her chair, leaning forwards. "The consequences Nefina faced for helping you were horrific, Laphaniel, there are scars she..."

"That's enough, Oonagh," Nefina cut her off with a hiss. "I need no one's pity."

"There are fey loyal to you," Oonagh said, turning her pale, pale eyes onto Laphaniel. "Those who will follow you in a rebellion against Luthien."

"Loyal to me?" I asked, confused.

"Of course, not you," Nefina scoffed, then nodded towards her brother. "Him."

How could I have forgotten that Laphaniel would have been king, ruling alongside Luthien, on elegant thrones in a castle that bore no signs of ruin? If Sorcha, Luthien's sister, had not cursed the Court of Seelie in her last breaths, we would never have met.

Niven would never have been taken. Luthien would hold the Seelie crown with Laphaniel at her side.

It was not impossible to imagine Laphaniel as a faerie king, wicked and beautiful, watching over fey that fell to his feet as he commanded.

Though it was much harder to picture Luthien beside him, a heart-wrenching siren sparking with Glamour and power. A faery queen so merciless she would make you plead for death, just so you could see her smile when she did. Luthien, the Queen of Seelie, only equalled in the consort beside her.

It was only hard to picture her beside Laphaniel, her slender hand holding his, because I couldn't bear it.

"The last rebel army that followed me didn't fare too well," Laphaniel said, speaking of the war that had raged between Luthien and her sister, resulting in Sorcha conjuring the curse that doomed the Seelie to a mortal queen.

"And yet they still come," Oonagh replied. "What hope could you possibly have for the Unseelie?"

"They have a new king, untested," Laphaniel said. "With Luthien on the Seelie throne, they are at great risk. She could quite easily slaughter them all."

"Soren had no heir…"

"Soren found herself an heir, Nefina. The Unseelie Queen plotted a way for her court to survive after her death, while we were all too busy snatching away children. Stop talking and listen," Laphaniel snapped. "The Unseelie may back Teya's claim to the throne."

"Who is he?" Oonagh asked, pouring more tea. "This new Unseelie king?"

"Human, or used to be," I answered. "We don't really know what he is yet."

Oonagh stared at me over her teacup before placing it untouched back onto the table. "Two human rulers? I do not think Faerie will like that."

"You talk as if Faerie is a living thing…"

"Is it not, then?" The silver-haired fey crossed her long legs, an unease settling over her. "What if this king will not help?"

"Then Luthien will gain the throne, and we will lose," Laphaniel said, tilting his head back to rest against the sofa. "It won't matter how many rebels you have. Teya won't win against Luthien without The Unseelie."

"You are waiting for word from them?"

"Niven said she would speak to Phabian, she sounded genuine… but who knows, it may just be one of her cruel games," I said, hoping I was wrong.

Laphaniel rubbed his eyes. "I don't know what we are bargaining with, and I don't know what it will cost for them to help us."

Nefina leaned forwards, her eyes fixed on mine. "What are you willing to pay?"

"I don't know…"

She smiled at me, cold and cruel. "If you truly wish to rule over us, you must know what you are willing to sacrifice for us, how much blood you will shed. Fey can sense fear, we can taste it. If you fear us, we will destroy you."

I glanced at Laphaniel, foolishly thinking he would contradict his sister, but he said nothing, and a heavy, awkward silence settled over us. I had no idea how to become a queen, how to rule over a court. I wasn't fey, I didn't have the wickedness that they possessed…the fondness for cruel games and sheer spite. I wasn't like Niven.

"Will you teach me?" I asked Laphaniel, wondering how much of my humanity I would lose to become the queen they needed. How much of my soul.

"Yes," he said, drawing me close, so his words ghosted over my neck.

I pictured him then, sitting beside me on a throne made new, made of twisting branches that bloomed in spring and burned gold as winter whispered to them.

"What happens when I die?" I asked, understanding that I was the last mortal Queen, and my reign couldn't last forever.

"Your heir would take the throne," Oonagh said as if it were the most obvious answer in the world.

"My heir?" I echoed stupidly.

"Your daughter, to be exact. The Seelie crown always passes down the female line."

"What if we don't have a daughter?"

"Then keep trying until you do," Nefina said. "Queen Aria of the third age had fifteen sons before she finally produced a girl."

"Oh."

"Can we focus on one problem at a time, please?" Laphaniel sighed. "Nefina will likely have a claim for the throne as my sister."

"I have no desire to become Queen."

Oonagh smiled. "No one wants that, dear."

Laphaniel rose, hand slipping from mine. "Are we done here?"

"For now," Oonagh replied, stretching her arms above her head. "Stay here until you either hear word from the Unseelie or from us. Luthien's fey are everywhere. Stay indoors, stay hidden, stay safe."

I stood beside Laphaniel, and Oonagh stepped toward me, embracing me quickly. Her hands lingered on my shoulders, close enough that I could smell the sweetness of her skin, like morning rain.

"You are not alone in this," she whispered to me, touching her forehead to mine. "Whatever happens, you brave girl, you were never alone."

She pulled away to embrace Laphaniel, and he held her back in a hug that lingered as mine had done. She whispered something, and he shook his head. Oonagh's eyes darkened, then with a sigh, she kissed his cheek and broke away from his arms.

Nefina watched from the doorway, her face a blank mask while we said our goodbyes, and she said nothing. She didn't wait for Oonagh before she left, slipping away with only the briefest glance at Laphaniel.

"If this all goes wrong, you may never see her again," Oonagh said softly. "She's your sister."

"Do you expect me to heal a void carved out over decades in one afternoon?"

"No," she sighed, disappointment weighing her words. "Goodbye, Laphaniel."

We both watched them go, and the cottage suddenly felt small and cold without the other faeries in it.

CHAPTER SEVEN

The nightmare struck without warning. Horrific and violent, nothing I did would reach him.

Laphaniel kicked out at me, twisting in the bed. Hands scratched against my arms when I tried to wake him, his eyes utterly black and focused on something I couldn't see. Waves of Glamour shrieked around the room, a frantic rush of power I had never witnessed before. It sent everything crashing to the floor, ripping books from the shelves to scatter in heaps of torn pages. The lightbulbs exploded, showering the bed in glass. I rolled away, shielding my head, but the shards cut into Laphaniel's bare skin as he tossed and turned, splattering the sheets in red.

He didn't wake when I screamed his name.

Over and over again.

Until my voice was hoarse, and I could only wait in the trembling darkness for the nightmare to let him go.

To be done with him.

Laphaniel woke, gasping, fighting against me. He shoved me away, still struggling to get a decent breath in. He made it two steps before crumpling to the floor, head smacking against the doorframe.

I was at his side in an instant. "I can't help you with this if you won't speak to me," I implored him.

"You can't help, Teya." He shoved himself to his feet. "There is something waiting for me every time I close my eyes. Something black and angry and never ending."

"Your nightmare?" I pressed, not wanting him to shut off again. Laphaniel shook his head before tugging on a shirt. The little cuts on his body were already healing.

"I think it's something else."

"Like what?"

Laphaniel leant back against the wall, closing his eyes. He let me take his hand, looking utterly lost. "I don't know."

Slow and lingering days passed us by, though neither of us could enjoy the much-needed rest from running. The cottage grew claustrophobic, with Laphaniel pacing the rooms like a caged animal.

He had barely slept, choosing instead to prowl the cottage and gardens, coiled up like a spring. He would come to bed each night, and we would lie together until I fell asleep in his arms. Then he would leave, just as he had once done while I was Glamoured at his house.

Rain fell in lazy sheets against the window, the long hours slipping by in a wash of grey cloud and constant drizzle.

On a particularly grey morning, I lounged on the old sofa, stretching my legs out, careful not to nudge Laphaniel, who sat beside me with his head back and eyes closed. It was only in those few moments he would allow himself to doze off, stealing the briefest of respites when he couldn't keep his eyes open any longer.

"We watched this yesterday," he said thickly, as I flicked onto a documentary on meerkats.

I sighed. "That was prairie dogs. They're completely different animals."

He scrubbed a hand over his face, reaching for his lukewarm coffee. "I don't think they are."

I smiled. "I know you hate waiting. I do too. I know you don't like being cooped up in here."

"I'm not eager to go to war either, Teya," he replied, stretching his arms above his head until they clicked.

It wasn't too much of a stretch of the imagination to picture him sat astride a massive warhorse, plunging deep into battle, though the thought of it clawed at my heart. There wasn't a part of me ready to bear watching him disappear into a mass of clashing swords, to be wounded in a fight, to come home bloodied and broken. Or not at all.

"I don't want you going to war for me."

"I would go to hell for you," he said. "And it seems others are willing to as well."

"They are following you."

He shrugged, a soft lift of his shoulders that hinted at an indifference I knew he didn't feel. "Become their queen, and they will think differently."

"I'm just a girl," I stated, not seeking pity, knowing Laphaniel wasn't one to give it. "Human."

"I thought that once, you proved me wrong."

Thunder roared with such fervour it shook the house, the unexpected noise making me leap up. The lights in the living room flickered, dimming quickly before sparking back to life. Laphaniel stood to move closer to the window, and I followed, marvelling at how dark the sky had become. I could almost taste the storm as it rolled across the indigo clouds.

"Come with me." Laphaniel snatched my hand to drag me into the garden. I stumbled after him, shivering as the heavens opened, crashing rain down on us. He stopped at the fence, pulling me into his arms as the storm began to scream over the sea, enraging the waves until angry foam dashed at the nearby cliffs.

The skies erupted with bright light. The storm ripping through the black in a sudden violent flash, the thunder followed instantly, booming across the beach with an intensity that made my heart roar with it.

It was a cacophony of fury and chaos, a song of beauty and destruction, and I understood why Laphaniel was so entranced with it.

It was the closest he could get to home.

I turned my face up against the rain to watch Laphaniel while he watched the storm, his eyes the same colour as the livid sky. Rain plastered his hair to his face, inky strands whipping back in the wind. His entire body was tense against mine, and it was in that moment I truly realised how homesick he was, how much he longed for his world of frenzied bedlam and strange creatures.

My t-shirt squelched as I wrapped my arms around him, thankful he had found this tiny piece of release. I could smell the storm on him, a new wildness that had faded while we waited at the cottage.

Laphaniel blinked and looked down, gazing at me as if he had forgotten I was there until that moment. I smiled up at him through the sodden nest of my hair, but he frowned.

"You're soaked," he said, drawing me closer.

"Yes," I grinned back. "That's usually what happens when you stand outside in the pouring rain."

"I just…" He trailed off, turning to face the sea again. "It doesn't matter. Let's go back."

"No, I miss it too," I said, climbing the slick fence, so I sat on the top post. "I don't belong here any more than you do. I miss Faerie, Laphaniel. More than I ever thought I could."

He pushed his dripping hair away from his face. "You do?"

"I miss the singing trees," I answered. "I miss the hidden glens where you first kissed me, and the hollow by the brook where you showed me the unicorns." My cheeks heated. "And more…I miss the smell of your bed, the way autumn scattered those tiny pink flowers over the covers. I miss dancing with you until the twin suns rose, then lying in your arms when they set again." I swallowed and tilted my head back, allowing the rain to mingle with the sudden tears. "I miss our forever."

He kissed me then, soft and slow, tasting of the storm. "No one really gets forever, Teya."

"Then I just want to stop running," I said, leaning into him as the rain thrashed against us. "I want to remember a time when I wasn't terrified of being torn to pieces, of being part of something I don't really understand."

Laphaniel looked helpless. "I hate not knowing what to do. This is so far from what I hoped for us. I truly thought you would share my bed for a while until I convinced you to go home."

I punched his arm, and he laughed. "Is that all you wanted from me?"

"In the beginning, yes. You were wearing that little black dress, and your hair was up." He tugged my hair into a ponytail, looping it up, so tendrils of red fell across my face. "Just like this. You had mud on your face, and your tears were black."

"I had just come from my father's funeral," I said.

He tilted his head slightly, wickedness creeping into his eyes. "I know. I could smell the vulnerability on you a mile away."

"What did I smell like?"

"Like despair and fury."

I looked up, shaking my hair from his grip. "And you wanted that?"

"Yes. Does that bother you?"

"What if I had told you no?"

He looked at me like I was stupid. "You did say no."

I hopped off the fence, stretching and shivering at the same time. "What do I smell like now?"

"Wet," Laphaniel replied, and I shoved him. He grabbed me before I could move, sliding a leg around me so I tumbled to the ground, his arms catching me just before I hit the grass. "You smell of the storm, of feral things and nightmares. I can smell the dreams on you, the love and raindrops, and the tang of fear. I could pick you out blindfolded in a sea of people."

"Less despair?" I asked, my breath catching at the wild grin on his face.

"Oh yes, but much more fury."

He pulled me to my feet, awakening something within me, the thrill of when we first met, of running through the woods and knowing he would chase me. I grinned, and his eyes lit up.

My feet slipped on the sodden grass as I darted past him, not hearing him give chase, but then I never did. He caught me. Of course, he caught me, and though I was winded from my sudden sprint, Laphaniel's breaths were even.

He flung me over his shoulder and began to walk back to the cottage, his hands cold and wet on my skin. The rain had started to slow, clouds parting enough to allow thin rays of sunlight to trickle down. We were both drenched to the bone, and I wanted nothing more than to share a hot bath.

Laphaniel slowed before we reached the back door, setting me down on my feet without a word. His hand moved to my mouth, soft against my lips, yet the meaning was clear. His head tilted, listening, his eyes sharp. I could hear nothing.

"How many?" I mouthed, as Laphaniel held up two fingers. "Have they seen us?"

He gave a slight shake of his head.

I suddenly felt too hot, even the raindrops from my dripping hair were uncomfortably warm against my skin.

"They're coming for us?" My voice was a hoarse whisper, panic pushing the words from my mouth in a rush. "It's too soon…."

"Hush." Laphaniel breathed, sensing my panic. "Look at me. I need you to trust me."

"What?" He grabbed at my wrists. "Why?"

"Because I need to keep you safe," he said, hands tightening as I continued to struggle.

"You're hurting me," I hissed "What are you doing? Laphaniel?"

"Stay quiet."

"Why?" His hand clamped over my mouth, and I realised with sudden horror that he was dragging me towards the coal store. "No…"

"Don't scream." His words were a hiss against my cheek as he opened the store, shoving me in even though I fought hopelessly against him. I turned just as he shut the hatch down, plunging me into complete and utter darkness.

CHAPTER EIGHT

The dark was absolute. A smothering, suffocating shadow of air that clawed at every part of me, dragging my nightmares back to the surface.

With frantic hands I fumbled over the walls, desperate to find any source of light...a vent...a crack in the stone, anything. My fingers broke through thick webbing, sending their hosts scurrying over my hands and down my arms. I bit down on a scream, sucking up air through gritted teeth as I fought to stay quiet.

The echo of the hatch slamming shut was all I could hear, the desperate look in Laphaniel's eyes as he tossed me into the darkness, all I could see. It was torment.

I couldn't hear anything from the cottage, no screams or shouts or sounds of fighting, just silence. Unbearable, unforgiving silence. I couldn't think of what I would do if it wasn't him that opened the hatch. I wasn't sure if I would fight...I didn't know.

Light flooded in with the creaking of the hatch finally opening, and I recoiled. Wood grated against stone as slick hands reached in and grabbed me. The coppery tang of blood filled my senses, and I choked on a scream.

"It's not mine. It's not my blood," Laphaniel stammered, dragging me close. "Most of it isn't mine."

Blood was splattered over his face, his shirt dark with it.

"Are you okay?" I ran my hands over him, "Are you hurt?"

"No, I…"

"Don't you ever lock me away again!" I hissed, shoving him away. The blind panic began to ebb away. Anger quickly took hold in its place. "Don't you dare."

"I was keeping you safe."

"I had no idea what was happening," I snapped, "I don't know what has happened, Laphaniel, because you shoved me in the dark."

"There were two scouts," he said through gritted teeth. "Either one of them could have killed you. I did what I thought best, and you can be damn sure I would do it again."

"Are they dead?"

"Yes."

"Don't you walk away from me!" I grabbed his hand, and a snarl rumbled up his throat. The flesh on his palm was blackened and raw. I stared down at it. "This looks like a burn."

"The knives in the kitchen are steel," he answered, holding his hand to his chest.

"That needs cleaning."

He followed me into the cottage without protest and I gaped at the destruction. The table lay shattered in pieces, the chairs broken, shards of glass glinted from the tiles. Blood smeared the walls, red handprints on the tiles, the cabinets and the floor. The fight had been swift and brutal. Violent.

Picking my way over the floor, I turned my gaze to one of the bodies sprawled across the mess. He looked as broken as the furniture around him, with blood seeping into the threadbare rug. His mouth hung open, gaping. The angle of his neck all wrong.

"Teya."

I heard Laphaniel's voice behind me but didn't turn around. I couldn't tear my eyes away from the second faerie lying dead in the kitchen, or from the knife used to slit his throat with such vehemence that it had nearly decapitated him.

"Teya, we need to go," Laphaniel urged, his good hand tugging at me. "Stop looking at them."

"I need to fix your hand," I replied, still focused on the bodies lying on my mum's kitchen floor.

"It can wait."

"Sit down!" I almost screamed at him, hysteria bubbling up from somewhere deep inside me.

He looked like he was going to bite back but moved instead to sit on the sofa, while I rummaged in the cupboards until I found a battered first aid box. I perched next to him, dropping coal dust over the faded yellow throw, blood had already seeped into the fabric from where Laphaniel sat.

"Hold your hand out." I inspected the weeping mess on his palm, wondering how long he had held onto the knife. "This is going to sting."

He hissed while I rinsed his hand with the ancient bottle of antiseptic, the strong smell drowning out the tang of blood. I applied a burn dressing and bound it tight to keep it clean.

"My mum always loved a well-stocked first aid kit," I said, running a hand gently over his. "She'd keep a mini one in her handbag too. Sometimes she even bought princess plasters."

"Are there none in there?"

"I'm afraid not." My lips lifted into a tight smile, my anger gone, leaving nothing behind but a shaking relief he was okay. With my head resting against the sofa, I blew out a shuddering breath, my nerves frayed. I had no idea if I was shivering because I was cold or in shock. It was likely both.

"We can't stay here," Laphaniel said. "Go and grab what you can, then we need to go."

"To the Unseelie?" I asked, and he nodded. "What if they won't help us?"

"I don't know, Teya."

Laphaniel stood, peeling off his sodden, bloodied shirt. I noted the bruises down his side and the blood that had soaked through to his skin.

"Wait here a minute," I said, not looking at the bodies as I dashed to the kitchen to run a cloth under some hot water. "Hold still."

I washed as much blood off him as I could before passing him a clean shirt, my hands lingering for only a moment on his chest.

Laphaniel tugged on the black t-shirt while I changed out of my still damp clothing, quickly rifling through the clothes to find another pair of jeans and a stripy top three sizes too big.

"Black or purple?" I asked, holding up two faded hoodies.

Laphaniel held out a hand. "Black."

"But the purple matches your eyes."

He gave me a tired smile before he plucked the black hoodie from my hands.

"What about the bodies?"

"Leave them," he said, then held a hand up before I could say anything. "Did you hear that?"

"I didn't hear anything."

Laphaniel's body tensed as he walked towards the window. "Hounds."

"Dogs?" Panic rose up like a tide when I saw his eyes widen. "What is it?"

"A Huntsman," Laphaniel said, backing away and ushering me out of the kitchen. "A mercenary. Luthien paid someone a very high price to get to you."

"What do we do?"

"Run," he said, shoving me out of the cottage. "Now! Go."

Laphaniel grabbed my hand as we fled the cottage, the sounds of braying hounds finally reaching my ears. We tore down the garden, skidding on the rain-drenched grass. I clung to his hand as he sprinted down the winding coastal path, our feet crunching the stones.

His strides were longer, and my legs practically skipped to keep up with him. My breath gasped from my lips in freezing clouds. From behind us, I heard the echo of the dogs, the sound of heavy hoofbeats. We could never outrun a man on horseback.

"Where are we going?" I shouted, my voice ragged.

"The harbour," he yelled back, pulling me on as I fought to keep up with him. "I'm hoping there's a warehouse or something we can hide in. I need to think."

"And if there isn't?"

"I'm not really thinking that far ahead, Teya."

I stopped dead, grasping his arm as he spun around to face me. "We'll be just like cornered rats!"

"Have you ever cornered a rat?" he snapped, face wild. "We need to get up high and away from the hounds. Keep moving."

He didn't give me time to argue before he dragged me on, his grip around my hand unforgiving as we pounded the damp Cornish streets. Cries of outrage followed us as we shoved past people, all seemingly deaf to the howls of dogs and the stomp of hooves. Their ignorance was unbelievable and infuriating, making it much easier to elbow them out of the way.

We tore around corners, down narrow alleyways and over fencing. Laphaniel bent low to shove me up and over the high chain-link before he vaulted over with the nimbleness of a wild cat. My hands stung from the cold, sharp metal, my feet smarting from landing on the hard ground.

Laphaniel landed beside me, using his hoodie as a barrier between the top of the fence and his hands so he didn't touch the steel.

"Okay?"

"Yes," I replied. "Don't fuss, keep going."

The tang of saltwater and fish intensified as we neared the harbourside, the neat, well-kept buildings that had dotted the seafront replaced with crumbling industrial units, many falling beyond repair as the little town lost its fishing heritage and made way for tourists.

Graffiti stained most sides of the concrete maze we had entered, a flash of bright paint amongst the grey. Homeless people squatted in the doorways, huddled beneath damp blankets, sharing bottles of clear liquid and watching us with vacant, uncaring eyes.

"Up here," Laphaniel urged, leading me to a building that looked like a stiff breeze would blow it down.

I followed him in, coughing at the smell of dank and mould that hit my face. Glass lay scattered across the floor, every window smashed to pieces, so the cold wind blew through, disturbing the thick dust that coated everything,

Blankets lay abandoned in the corner, covered in mould and stagnant rainwater. Broken bottles caught the meagre light, discarded needles nestled between the glass shards. The place reeked of hopelessness and pain.

The staircase was rotten, the wood splintered and peeling, the banister long since gone, likely pulled off to be used for firewood. Laphaniel tested a foot on the lowest step; it creaked and bowed, and the entire building seemed to shake with his weight.

"I think it'll hold," he said, climbing up, outstretching a hand to me.

"You think? It's a long way to fall if you're wrong."

"Fine. I am pretty sure it will hold, now hurry up."

I clambered up behind him, the staircase swaying beneath the both of us, pieces of damp decaying wood crumbling off under my feet. The brackets holding it to the wall were rusted and useless, straining against the walls and threatening to give way with each hesitant step I made.

Laphaniel grabbed me on the last step, hauling me up as the doors below us smashed open, sending a pack of hounds tearing around the ground floor. My shout rebounded off the walls, mingling with the howls of the dogs below as they started towards the stairs. Laphaniel dragged me out of the way, ignoring my hiss of pain when he caught my foot and jumped down on the middle step, shattering the wood on impact. He sprang backward just as the staircase crumbled and collapsed, sending debris smashing to the floor below. Laphaniel caught the overhang by his fingertips, dangling while I crouched with my mouth open in frozen terror.

He scrabbled on the ledge, the dogs below us jumping and snarling as he dangled over them. I dragged him up by his shirt, hauling him over the ledge by his belt, where he fell against me with a breathless gasp.

"You cannot escape me," a deep voice boomed. "I am coming for you."

"Perhaps," Laphaniel called back. "But, your dogs are not."

The laugh that followed was chilling. "My hounds will chew your insides, boy. I will have you begging for death, and you will die, that I promise you, though not before you watch while I ruin that pretty whore of yours."

"Laphaniel…" His name was a desperate plea against my lips, my fingers a frantic pull at his shirt. He turned, his eyes so black that I startled.

"Go!" he said. "To the top…trust me."

I did as I was told, numbly, running beside him as we climbed four more sets of stairs that had aged better and were clinging to the walls with determination. There was no way we would be able to stop the huntsman from following us up. We ended up in an old loft room, filled with abandoned pieces of ancient machinery that had been left to rust, the coppery smell mingled with the lingering stench of must and urine, making my eyes sting.

A thick length of rope trailed across the floor, a heavy and rusted old hook tied to one end, the remnants of an old winch used to haul heavy sacks up to the storeroom. Empty sacks lay deflated, chew marks splitting the greying fabric. Ancient piping lay broken and rusted, orange flakes seeping into the decaying floorboards.

"There's nothing up here," I said, spinning around to face Laphaniel. He staggered, bracing himself against the wall before slipping to his knees. I scanned the dank corners in a pointless search for an exit. I was hoping for a fire escape…a window…anything that would lead us back outside.

I was hoping for anything more than nothing.

CHAPTER NINE

*L*aphaniel shoved himself up from the floor, swaying slightly. I caught his elbow whilst frantically looking around for something to pick up.

"Don't touch anything," I said, grabbing a piece of piping from the floor. One end glimmered a metallic orange, the rust crumbling off in my hands. Laphaniel backed away, his sleeve covering his nose and mouth.

The door splintered open with a howl of rage, and I spun quickly, crashing the pipe down upon the Huntsman.

He screamed, the flesh on his cheek sizzling. I swung again, but his armoured hand shot out, viper quick to clout me across the face. I sprawled hard onto the floor.

Darkness flickered at the edge of my vision, but I could just make out his face, scarred and hideous, greasy black hair clung to his face, one eye nothing but a drooping grey orb. Rank breath hit me, warm and wet.

"Scream for me." A heavy boot pressed against my stomach.

My hand fumbled for the pipe, fear making my fingers numb. I braced myself as the Huntsman raised his fist again. Laphaniel slammed against him, sending them sprawling to the floor and away from me.

Wielding the pipe, I brought it down hard, aiming for the Huntsman's head. Metal smacked against the wooden floor when he rolled, sending up sparks of rust. Both faeries cringed, Laphaniel hissed, the sound feral.

The Huntsman snarled, backing away with unsteady feet. Blood dribbled from his cheek in an angry smear.

"Think you're clever, girl?" He spat a mouthful of blood and spittle at my feet, grinning while he drew his sword.

I didn't move fast enough as he slashed out, and the edge of his blade struck the pipe in my hands. It crashed to the floor and skidded away. He lifted the sword again, twisting to Laphaniel.

The floorboards splintered when I launched myself at him, throwing him forwards. The rotting wood crumbled beneath us, swallowing up the sword, so it crashed to the floor far below us.

Laphaniel grabbed me before I slipped down, dragging me away. My cry of warning came too late, lost as the Huntsman came up behind him, kicking him with so much force across the head that he skidded to the edge of the room.

His name tore frantic from my lungs, but Laphaniel lay motionless a few feet away from me. I slipped further, flinching as heavy boots hovered close to my hands. The Huntsman crouched over me, enjoying my struggle. His grin was a filthy slash on his face. Thick hands caught mine, holding me over the gaping hole.

"Do you know how many pieces I could carve you into and still keep you alive?" he said, words slurring. "I could let you count if you want?"

I was frozen in his grip; the stench of blood and bile on his breath made my stomach lurch. The creamy white of his scarred eye rolled in its socket, the other fixed on me. He grinned, tongue lashing over his teeth, and forced one of my fingers back until it cracked.

"Ten fingers," he began, while I flinched. "Two eyes. I'm going to peel the skin from your bones. I'm going to feed it to your lover, then I'm going to feed him to my dogs."

"Luthien wants me alive," I bit back with much more bravado than I felt.

"I never said I was going to kill you," the Huntsman began, lowering me back onto the floor. "Just break you…"

A choking gasp cut off the rest of his words. Laphaniel sprang from the shadows, twisting the huge rope around the Huntsman's neck before yanking it tight. His grip on the rope was relentless. They scrabbled with each other, the rope knotting around them. The massive hook at the end scraped along the wooden planks, catching and cracking the wood before lodging onto the ancient framework.

"Laphaniel, move!" I hurled myself at him, skidding as I reached for his hand. The floor beneath them shattered. Laphaniel's hand was torn from mine as he fell, the rope racing after them in a flurry of broken wood and dust. The hook held with a screech of metal. There was a soft grunt when the rope went taut, then nothing.

My feet skidded from under me as I raced down the stairs to the floor below. The rope had stopped about twenty feet above the floor, swaying with the weight of the bodies wrapped up in it.

The Huntsman's eyes were open and bulging, his head lolling against his shoulder as he swung back and forth, back and forth like the pendulum on a macabre cuckoo clock.

"Cut the rope!"

My breath whooshed from my mouth so fast my head spun, the sound of his voice flooding me with a relief that nearly floored me. The rope hadn't caught around Laphaniel's neck, instead, looped around his chest to pin one arm behind him at a crippling angle.

"Teya, go back upstairs and cut the rope," he repeated, pain straining his voice.

"You'll fall!"

"I'm aware how gravity works. Unless you have a very long ladder, please cut the rope."

"But…"

"Please," he said through gritted teeth, squeezing his eyes shut while he rocked back and forwards, the rope tightening, pulling his arm up further.

I snatched the Huntsman's sword from where it had fallen, surprised at its weight. I heaved it back upstairs, keeping back from the massive hole in the floor. The wood creaked under my feet as I held the blade aloft over the rope. Giving a tentative swing, the sharp edge sliced through the rope with ease, and uttering a small, pointless prayer, I swung again, severing the rope completely.

The sickening thud echoed cruelly, sending rats and pigeons scurrying under my feet as I bolted back down the stairs. My feet pounded over the steps, my heart in my throat at the sight of the still bodies lying in a heap on the floor.

"Laphaniel?" I rushed to him, dropping to my knees and untangling the rope from his body. "Open your eyes, look at me."

He groaned when he tried to sit, shifting away from the corpse of the Huntsman. I spared him only a fleeting glance, quickly looking away from the purple bruising around his neck and the way his thick tongue drooped over his lips. A foul dampness had spread over his trousers.

Laphaniel leant against me, one arm hanging limp at his side, the other wrapped tightly around his stomach as if holding himself together. Blood trickled from his nose, his head, and his mouth.

"I've dislocated my shoulder," he said, taking a small breath. "And I think I've broken a few ribs."

I gently placed a hand to his side, and though I barely touched him, he flinched.

"Yeah," he concluded. "They're broken."

"Can you move?" I didn't touch him again. "Is there anything I can do?"

"I need you to put my shoulder back."

"I don't know how," I answered, terrified of causing him more pain.

"I'll talk you through it," he said, words coming out faint and soft. "It's easy."

I swallowed. "Tell me what I need to do."

"I need you to help me lie back. Then hold my arm out and slowly pull it until you hear the bones slide in place. Brace your legs against me if you need to."

"Your ribs are broken."

"I know, we'll deal with them after."

I took his hand. "What if I get it wrong?"

"You won't."

I steeled myself, wiping my damp palms over my jeans before I helped him lie back, slowly easing him to the floor. He hissed in pain, blood gleaming on his teeth. I caught his wrist, feeling the bones in his arm grind together as I pulled.

"Harder."

I did as instructed, but struggled to get enough force behind my grip without pushing against Laphaniel's side. The audible clunk of bone echoed with his yelp, leaving him breathless on the dusty floor.

"Did it work?" I asked, pushing the damp hair away from his eyes. He gave me the barest of nods.

"Can you rip up some of those cloths?" He gestured to the dusty material heaped in the corner. "And bind my ribs?"

"How long will they take to heal?" I asked, shaking as much dust as I could from the old sheeting, before tearing it into filthy bandages. "Laphaniel?"

He stared at me, unfocused. His next words sounded drunk. "I'll… I'll sleep it off…I'll be fine."

I lifted his shirt and winced for him, unable to look away from the mottled red marks forming over his ribcage. Taking a strip of fabric, I wound it tight around his middle. Laphaniel sucked in a breath, his hand clawing at the floor beside me.

"Do you think you can stand?" I asked. "It's cold and filthy in here, we can find somewhere warmer for you to rest. Away from all the iron upstairs, away from the dead body."

"Here's good," he mumbled, lowering himself down. Small grunts of pains slipped from his mouth as he moved. "Here's fine."

I moved, so I was behind him, taking his head into my lap. His eyes closed, his body forcing him into sleep so it could mend itself.

"If anyone else comes," he began thickly, "I won't be able to stop them."

I gave his hand a gentle squeeze. "But I will."

Laphaniel stretched his legs out, holding his breath until he made himself more comfortable, letting it blow past his lips in a shuddering rush. He coughed and flinched, but I felt him fall asleep while I stroked the edge of his cheek, his breathing laboured before calming as he slept deeper.

He didn't stir again until the sun began to filter through the broken windows, the light catching on the shards of glass dusting the floor.

CHAPTER TEN

y sleep was plagued with nightmares, of shadow men chasing me in the darkness, bodiless monsters that had no voice or substance, just a menacing aura…a memory of something terrible.

I dreamt of Laphaniel, of course I did, his arms around me, alive and warm. But every time I turned to kiss him, he would turn away, and my mouth brushed over nothing.

No

I kissed him again, and he shoved me away.

No

A cold, wet hand slid over my shoulder, prising me away from Laphaniel, and I shuddered as Lily curled her sopping naked body onto his lap. The Unseelie faerie grinned, lips bloodless, dull eyes bulging and lifeless. Her lithe, graceful body was bloated and drowned.

Mine

Her rasp ended in a soft purr, her sodden body flickering and changing until it melted away completely, replaced with the soul-breaking form of Luthien. Her fingers raked up through Laphaniel's hair, forcing his head back as she bit deep into the curve of his neck. The moan she enticed from his lips dripped with ecstasy.

I lay awake on the cold floor, waiting for Laphaniel to stir. The dream left behind a pang of jealousy I shouldn't have felt, a lingering sense that I was simply not enough, not for him or his court.

"Hey," I said as he woke up. "How are the broken bones?"

He stretched and rolled his shoulder, moving much more smoothly. "Still a little sore, but no longer broken at least."

"Let me take a look." I lifted the bandages, running a hand over the blackening bruises that wrapped around his ribs. Dried blood caked on his skin, a scab crusting over where bone had broken through. "I think you should rest for a bit longer."

"We can't afford to linger here, Teya," he said, standing up. "The hounds would have scattered back to Luthien, and she will find out her Huntsman failed. More will come. We need to keep moving."

"Where do we go from here?"

Laphaniel eyed the Huntsman's body with disgust. It had already become a feast for the nearby rats. "We need to find a witch."

I blinked, pushing myself off the filthy floor, hoping I had misheard him. "What?"

"Witches are neither tethered to the Seelie nor Unseelie," Laphaniel said. "They are part of both, able to roam through the lands unhindered. They like the mortal lands too, easy picking with gullible people all too eager to offer up their souls."

He walked beneath the massive hole in the ceiling and stared up, head turning to the splatter of blood on the floor near his feet.

"It shouldn't be too difficult to track one down around here," he continued. "Amongst all the charlatans, I'm sure we'll find one."

"Then what?" I asked. "We bargain our way into the Unseelie lands? With what? We don't have anything."

"There's always something to bargain with."

"Like blood and nightmares, teeth, bone, and heartstrings? What are you willing to pay?"

"Whatever it takes to get you where you need to go," Laphaniel snapped, whirling around to face me. "Stop second-guessing everything I do. What did you expect? That we just wander into the Dark Court? We will have to walk through miles and miles of woodland if we just enter through the trails I know. We would have to go through Seelie first because I don't know the trails directly into Unseelie. We would wander labyrinthine paths for days, that's if we weren't slaughtered first. I am hoping to bargain for safe passage close to the Unseelie castle, which itself is deadly enough."

"I'm not second-guessing you…"

"Yes, you are," Laphaniel said, his words weary, heavy. "I'm getting sick of it."

I held my hands up and took a step away. "I'm not just going to follow you around like an obedient pup. You should have realised that by now."

"I'm not asking you to blindly follow me…"

"But you won't let me question you?"

Laphaniel gave an impatient snort, raking a quick hand through his hair. "We are going to find a witch, Teya. We are going to the back end of Unseelie. We will pay whatever price is demanded unless you have some wonderful new plan you've been hiding up your shirt?"

I gritted my teeth against the retort I wanted to throw at him; a night spent in a cold warehouse taking its toll on my temper. "I think rushing off anywhere now isn't a wise decision. You just fell twenty feet."

"I don't need reminding," he snapped, pacing the floor, not quite hiding the flinch of pain as he moved. "Fine, we'll find a Solitary house. There must be one around here somewhere, they're scattered all over your world."

"What's a Solitary house?" I asked.

"A place for faeries without the protection of their Court," Laphaniel explained. "They're usually abandoned old houses, away from humans, away from too much iron. They stand as havens for banished fey, places for fey that no one else wants. Faeries are not meant for solitude."

"How will we find one?"

"They are marked, so it shouldn't be too difficult, but we can't linger. We'll just stop for food, maybe a night's sleep, then we go, okay? There is an honour between Solitary fey, but they are still faeries after all."

"Why couldn't we have gone to one before, rather than face Niven?"

Laphaniel was quiet for a moment, and he wouldn't look at me. "I wanted to take you home."

What he had always set out to do.

"I didn't know it would be like that," he continued. "I thought...I thought perhaps you would get to see your mother."

An ache pressed against my chest, deep and unwanted. "If we hadn't gone back, we wouldn't have seen Niven, and we wouldn't have this scrap of hope. We'll go back another day; when this is over. I think my mum would like you."

I outstretched my hand, and together we walked back down the creaking staircases and vaulted down the huge gap left behind from the shattered stairs. We passed by the broken bodies of the few hounds unlucky enough to get caught in the collapse, the others had fled in the night.

Laphaniel led us down narrow lanes away from the warehouse, keeping his head low against the onslaught of winter rain. I held onto his hand, my fingers entwined with his.

Now and then, he would run a hand over a stone wall, or the side of a house, changing direction as he followed some unseen map.

After what seemed like hours of walking down cobbled lanes, Laphaniel finally stopped in front of a beaten-down building, standing alone and crooked. Three storeys of moss-covered stone stood before us, ivy growing up over the roof and forcing itself between the cracks in the paint, splitting it down to the ground. The windows were surprisingly unbroken, but so covered in grime that it was impossible to see inside. The whole place had a faint acidic smell about it, like urine or old sick.

Laphaniel trailed a finger over a symbol carved deep in the stone, jagged edges loosely resembling a crooked S. It glowed blue beneath his fingertips, subtle and flickering, touch of magic and nothing else.

"Here we are," Laphaniel said beside me, noting my look of despair. "It'll be warm and dry at least."

"It will beat a dilapidated warehouse with a dead body in it," I answered, catching his smile as he held the door open for me, and I was instantly hit with the heat of a roaring fire.

It was cosier inside than I had expected, looking much more like a quaint inn than the exterior suggested. Nearly every table was occupied, but apart from the few fey sitting by the doorway, nobody glanced up. There was a buzz of conversation in the air, mingling with laughter and the soft, lamenting melody of the piper in the corner.

Laphaniel ushered me to a table in the corner, and I shrugged my soggy hoodie off over the back of a chair before sliding into the worn bench beside him. Little candles wavered on the tables, pooling dribbles of wax onto the stained tops of the wood. Above us, more candles burned on rustic chandeliers, the light catching the cobwebs draped over them.

"Can I get you anything to eat, lovelies?" said a young girl who skipped across the floor to our table, placing two full mugs of mulled cider down in front of us. "We have the house stew, or the pot-luck roast," she added with a wink.

"What's in the stew?" I asked, warming my hands on the mug.

"Whatever's left of the roast."

"Which is?"

The girl laughed, revealing sharp canines. "I have no idea."

"We'll have two bowls of the stew," Laphaniel said. "Do you have any rooms left?"

The girl thought for a moment, glancing around the full room with her hands on her hips. She stood up on her tiptoes, peering over the crowd, and it was then I noticed the sleek fur coating her legs and the fact she didn't have feet, but hooves.

"Briar!" she bellowed, and a dark-haired man turned her way. "Are you all staying tonight?"

"Just Grace and me!" he shouted back. "The others are going to wreak merry hell somewhere else!"

"The loft will be free if you want it, nothing fancy, but it's comfortable." The waitress turned back to us with a pretty smile, then skipped off towards the bustling kitchens.

I took a sip of my drink, the thick foam coating my nose and mouth. It slid down my throat with a heartening embrace, leaving behind the heat of cinnamon and the crisp sharpness of apples.

I leant closer to Laphaniel, resting my head against his shoulder while I listened to the sound of the pipes a woman was playing, sitting on a stool at the far end of the room. Her long, golden hair was plaited down one shoulder, her tan skin decorated with tattoos. Vines and vivid flowers were inked down her arms, over her bare legs, winding up over her neck. She played beautifully, and by the rapt attention she was getting from the surrounding fey, I wasn't the only one to think so.

"She's not a faerie," I whispered to Laphaniel, noticing how she swung her legs while she played. "She's human."

Laphaniel nodded. "That would be Grace, then. She's with the dark-haired fey."

"How do you know that? Grace could be any of the other three women over there."

"Look at how he is watching her."

I looked and understood what he meant, even though everyone was watching Grace play her pipes, there was something far more primal in the eyes of the dark-haired faerie. He stood back, not touching her, he didn't need to. The claim was there.

"Possessive bunch, aren't you?" I joked as our food was placed down in front of us, two steaming bowls of stew that were nearly over-flowing. I tore off a chunk of bread and dipped into the thick gravy, not caring in the slightest what the brownish meat was. "I'm surprised you don't mark your lovers."

Laphaniel chuckled into his drink. "We do."

I nearly choked. "What?"

"They can scent me on you. They know you have been claimed, and you are mine."

"I don't belong to you," I said, the words coming out wrong and sounding harsher than I intended.

"Yes, you do."

Having spent so much time alone with him, I had almost forgotten how intensely possessive he could get. He had revealed that side of him when I had danced with Gabriel at Luthien's ball, and he had nearly killed him.

"Do you feel that way because you bought me?"

The look he gave me was all the answer I needed, and I regretted the words instantly.

"You are not my whore, Teya."

"I know…"

"Do I make you feel like that?"

"No. Never."

"You have claimed me, as much as I have claimed you."

I finished my drink, then used the last of my bread to mop up the remains of my stew, noting how Laphaniel had only eaten half of his. "Humans don't tend to go around scenting people, that's all. I never realised I was walking around smelling like you."

Laphaniel gave me a feral smile. "Why do you think no one else has made a move on you?"

"You could have told me," I said, rolling my eyes. "So, can you scent Grace on that other fey?"

"Yes."

"I had no idea how keen your sense of smell was," I began, picking at my dirty clothes. "I've been pretty damn stinky lately."

Laphaniel pulled me close, laughing softly into my hair. "You smell of the earth and the woods…of you. I like it more than the strange soaps you use."

I brushed a quick kiss on his lips. "I like being yours, Laphaniel."

"Good."

Our bowls were promptly taken away, and two more mugs of cider were brought over, along with a large pitcher of ice water. I drank and watched while Grace played a faster tune, her heels clicking against the wood as she was hoisted onto the tabletop. Everyone sprang to their feet, a rowdy folk song filling the room as they sang along to the notes of Grace's pipes. I laughed at the lyrics, tapping my foot along to the tune, grinning at the filthy story it was telling. From the tabletop, Grace shouted the verses between notes, and the inebriated fey shouted back, drunk on music and good drink. She didn't miss a beat, dancing on the top of the tiny space above her audience, her face a beaming beauty.

Someone picked up a fiddle, another, a flute, and before long, the place was alive with music, real faerie music that sang to my soul and finally made me feel I was home. I turned to Laphaniel, and we laughed together, a feeling of absolute freedom within a tiny inn, surrounded by faeries who didn't care who we were. Laphaniel pulled me closer, his breath close to my cheek was sweet with the tang of apples.

Grace finished her song with a graceful curtsy and a breathless shout of thanks. From where we sat, I could see the flush against her cheeks, the glimmer of sweat on her skin. She curtsied again, and without warning, jumped from the table into the arms of the dark-haired fey, who caught her as if she weighed nothing.

"Another drink?" the waitress asked, appearing back at our table, waving to Grace as she and her lover escaped upstairs.

"I think I would really like a bath first," I said, already feeling my head swim from the two large mugs of cider I had drank.

"Of course, anything else I can get for you?"

"We are looking to find a witch; I don't suppose you know of any local to here?" Laphaniel asked, and the waitress's smile faltered.

"Is it a charm you're after?" Her voice was hopeful. "A wish? Because Old Anna Crow lives not far from here, she's wonderful at herbs and trinkets." She paused, closing her lovely brown eyes. "You don't want herbs and trinkets, do you?"

"No," Laphaniel answered, and the girl began to wring her hands. "I need a Hag Witch."

The waitress sighed, pity spreading over her face. "Arabelle lives close to the moor. Be careful how you offer payment because she'll take more than you can give. Unless you truly have no other options, don't go to her."

"We don't have another option," I told her as she plucked a key from her apron and handed it to me.

"You shouldn't get any bother here, whatever it is you are running from. Allow yourself a brief respite. Rest up, gather your strength, and good luck to you both."

"Thank you," I said, almost weeping at the kindness she was showing us.

"If you need anything while you're here, shout for Darby."

Darby's hooves clicked on the scruffy wooden floor as she walked away, handing out more drinks and clearing tables as more faeries came and went.

I climbed the narrow staircase with Laphaniel following me, stopping on the landing as Grace dashed past me, carrying a change of clothes and a slightly grubby looking towel.

"Shared bathroom I'm afraid," she said, darting into the bathroom. "Hop in after me, lovely Briar can wait. You look like you could do with some hot water." She looked at Laphaniel and gave him a sweet smile. "It'll be a cold shower for you, handsome, sorry."

She closed the door, and I heard the latch slide in place. Briar was standing outside his room, leaning against the doorframe, watching Grace disappear into the bathroom. He nodded at me when I walked past, and I smiled back, but then his entire demeanour changed when he glanced at Laphaniel.

He bared his teeth, a soft growl rumbling from somewhere deep within his chest. His eyes narrowed, the deep green darkening to black as he backed away. Laphaniel's fingers curled tight around my waist as he pushed me forwards. A snarl slipped from his lips when he passed Briar.

"You're not solitary," Briar hissed, and Laphaniel whirled around to face him.

"What business is that of yours?"

Briar straightened, matching Laphaniel's height. "Why would a Seelie brat be lingering around here?"

"For my own purposes," Laphaniel answered. "Back off."

Briar didn't move, his lips twisting into a sneer. "Finally tired of being ruled over by little girls?"

I thought Laphaniel was going to lunge at him, but to my surprise, he caught himself. A wicked grin crept onto his face. "Oh, it's still better than the fate befallen you. Don't the Unseelie burn their traitors? What did you do to deserve your exile?"

Briar's fist collided with Laphaniel's face. He made to retaliate, but I grabbed his arm to stop him. With a furious snarl, he shoved me off, swinging a punch at Briar.

The space was far too small to brawl in, but it did nothing to deter them from trying to tear each other apart. It was a sudden, ancient rush of hatred, both feral and unstoppable as if they were both hardwired to do as much harm to the other as possible. I yelled for Grace, who came running from the bathroom, utterly naked and dripping in bubbles. She launched herself at Briar, giving me a chance to grab Laphaniel, hauling him back.

"Are you both children?" Grace berated. "This is a place where it doesn't matter where you've come from, why you're here or what you've done. Briar, you should know that better than anyone here. Both of you should be utterly ashamed of yourselves. Shake hands and make peace now. Hurry up because I'm bloody cold."

Grace was smaller than I was, a slim waif-like girl with her dripping blonde hair trailing over her naked breasts, but she had an authority I could never mimic. She stood there, in the cold, dark corridor, stark naked without an ounce of shame. Tattoos covered most of her body, more vines snaking over her hips and down her legs. No vines decorated her back, however, but a pair of beautiful blue and purple butterfly wings.

"When these two have kissed and made up," she said to me. "Come and meet me up on the rooftop. Do you smoke?"

"Um…no."

"That's okay, I'll teach you how." She waved me off and turned back to Briar and Laphaniel. "Shake hands before I rip your arms off and beat you with them."

Briar was broader than Laphaniel, but with one glare from Grace, he held his hand out. Laphaniel hesitated until I kicked him, reluctantly taking Briar's waiting hand.

"Grace was a quiet little thing when I first met her," Briar said, as they broke away. "I had no idea what a spitfire she was going to turn into."

Laphaniel nodded, taking a step back. Both had blood on their faces and knuckles. "Well, I've had no end of trouble since the day I met Teya."

"See, and now you're bonding over your lovers!" Grace cried, clapping her hands with manic glee.

Briar rolled his eyes. "For the love of the gods, woman, put some clothes on!"

Grace disappeared into the bathroom, and after giving Laphaniel a wary look, Briar retreated into his room, leaving us to walk up to the loft together.

"You deserve your cold shower," I said, examining his bloodied fist as I sat on the bed. "What the hell came over you?"

"I just really needed to hit him."

I was relieved when Grace called my name to say she had finished with her shower. "We are going into the Unseelie lands, so are you planning on fighting everything that moves there?"

"No."

"I'm taking a shower," I said, plucking a towel from the stack in the cupboard. "Why don't you try and get some rest? You didn't eat much earlier, are you sure you're okay?"

He nodded, lying back against the pillows, though I knew he wouldn't sleep. I closed the door and made my way to the bathroom, feeling I needed more than hot water to wash my troubles away.

CHAPTER ELEVEN

The bathroom was cramped and grubby, with cheap plastic tiles peeling away from the floor. Black mould crept up the far side. The tub stood avocado green against the wall, a grimy rim around the edge, suggesting it hadn't been scrubbed since its installation.

I ran the water, waiting for it to warm up, and stood beneath the weak spray. Despite what Laphaniel had said about my natural scent, I poured a generous glug of shower gel onto a sponge and scrubbed the dirt away. It still felt good to be clean.

Tipping my head back, I drowned out everything except the rush of my blood in my ears. I needed that moment, that quiet stillness away from the chaos, the barbed words, the tension, and the fights. I needed time to comprehend I would never live a normal life, that Laphaniel... no matter how much I loved him, would always be volatile, a wild being that made no claims on being human.

I had to accept there would always be a part of him that enthralled me, overwhelmed me, and pushed me to be someone I never thought I could be. I knew I pushed him too. Most likely, more than anyone had ever done before, and he had yielded for me. There was a gentleness to him that had not been there when I had first met him in the woods, but he made it too easy to forget how dangerous he truly was. I doubted I would ever get used to how quickly his eyes blackened.

With the water growing cold, I got out and dressed, passing Briar in the corridor as he made his way to shower. I peeped around the door into our room, seeing Laphaniel shift and sit up on the bed, the speed he had moved telling me he hadn't slept.

"I'm going to meet Grace up on the roof. Will you be okay on your own for a bit?"

"I'll be fine," he answered, swinging his legs over the bed. "How was the shower?"

I shrugged. "The bathroom is pretty nasty, though it's nice to be clean. I just needed some space and time to think."

Laphaniel cocked his head, waving a hand absently over the candle on the nightstand, igniting it with his fingertips. "You don't need an excuse to want some space to breathe, Teya. What were you thinking about?"

I smiled, but it felt forced. "How I keep forgetting you're not human, then being surprised when you don't act like it."

"Do you want me to act human?"

I thought for a moment, and Laphaniel waited. His violet eyes caught the candlelight, the ring of silver shining against the deep black of his pupils. He waited patiently, and tears pressed against my eyes, falling quickly onto my cheeks before I had a chance to scrub them away.

"No."

"What do you want?" he asked gently, as I picked paint off the peeling doorframe.

"Just you."

"Are you sure?" he asked with such uncertainty that it broke my heart. I took a step into the room, then another and another until I was in his arms, and he was holding me tight against him.

"I want to stop being frightened," I said, my voice breaking on a sob.

"Of me?"

I shook my head. "Of something taking you away from me...of all this constant bickering driving a wedge between us."

Laphaniel pulled away. "I'm not going to leave you, Teya."

I looked down, away from the intensity of his gaze. "You left Luthien."

"I'm not going anywhere," he said, his hands coming up to frame my face. "When it got too hard when everything was so hopeless, I left Luthien. She didn't want to come with me, and it hurt, but I was able to walk away from her. I never could walk away from you, Teya, not from the moment I met you. I will be by your side when you are crowned Queen of the Seelie Court, or I will die by your side if after everything, we fail."

"We always seem to argue..."

Laphaniel smiled, leaning forwards to kiss my forehead. "Well, that's nothing new, is it? You have challenged everything I say, and I don't like being told no. Pair that with the tension of running for weeks, then being cooped up, I think we're doing pretty well."

"Thank you," I breathed, needing the reassurance more than I realised. "I just want this to be over."

"I know, so do I," Laphaniel said. "Go and meet Grace on the roof and spend a few hours talking to someone that isn't me."

"I think I need that," I said, feeling more weightless than I had in a while. "Will you get some sleep after you shower?"

"Possibly."

I gave him a look telling him I didn't believe him but headed up to the roof garden where even though it had stopped raining, the air was still damp and cold. Someone had attempted to make it look appealing with a few plant pots scattered over the small space, but they had been left to wither, so it just made everything look even more sad and depressing.

Grace sat on the edge, her legs dangling over the stone, a thick cloud of smoke drifting around her head like a halo. She didn't turn but patted the space beside her, and I sat, accepting the worn blanket she passed me and wrapped it around my shoulders.

"I'm sorry for what Laphaniel did," I said in way of greeting, but

Grace just barked a laugh that was so at odds to her elfin frame that I jumped.

"I have no doubts Briar threw the first punch," she said, taking a slow drag on her cigarette, blowing out a stream of greenish-blue smoke. "I think, no, I know, he was just jealous that you belong to a court. It's pretty shit being solitary."

"I'm not sure where we belong yet," I replied, shaking my head as she offered me the cigarette. The sweetness of it filled my nose, tickling my senses, smelling of wonderful things, and forgetfulness.

"Do you want to talk about it?"

"I would rather talk about anything else."

Grace smiled, her hazel eyes almost black. "Faerie is intoxicating, isn't it? How it draws you in, promising the world for the small cost of your soul. It is not for everybody, though, only for those who can see the light beyond the shadows."

My hand moved to the star around my neck, my fingers running over the curled points. "It makes coming home a lot harder, doesn't it? I feel like I don't really belong here anymore."

"I miss it more than I thought I ever could," Grace said, drawing her knees up to her chest. "We've been back here for a few years now, but before that, the last time I saw England was in 1942."

"You've aged beautifully," I said, earning a wonderful grin from Grace.

"Why, thank you." She laughed, before seriousness spread over her face, her eyes seemingly gazing at something far away. "The years won't touch you in Faerie, I'm guessing you know that, and I spent decades there. I went looking for adventure, and I sure as hell found it."

"What happened?"

"Come here." Grace beckoned me closer before sucking on the end of her roll-up, puffing her cheeks as she held onto the smoke. I hesitated before leaning forwards, tensing as she covered my mouth with hers and blew.

I coughed and staggered back, tasting the strange spiciness against my tongue, a cloying heat that coated the back of my throat and made my eyes water. The warmth melted through my body, taking every-thing away until there was nothing left but wonderful softness.

I took the joint when she offered it again, less hesitant, more curi-ous. The smoke fizzed against my lips, and I breathed it in until I slouched against Grace, barely remembering my name.

"It won't hurt you," she said, her voice a lulling whisper. "You won't even wake with a hangover. We call it Fizz, from what it feels like against your mouth. Like popping candy. You looked like you really needed it."

The taste lingered on my tongue, little sparks of life. "Is it anything like Ember?"

"How do you know about Ember? Don't you ever touch that," Grace said sharply, eyes narrowing. "It's for whores and gutter rats and will burn through you until nothing is left but ashes."

Oh, Laphaniel…

"Tell me about your adventure," I said, my words slow and soft.

Grace pulled me close, dragging the blanket I had shaken off back around my shoulders. "You'll still get cold, even if you can't feel it. You want to hear my story?"

I nodded, the world around me slowly nodding too.

"Everything started when I went looking for trouble and found Briar," Grace began. She smelled like apples and woodsmoke. "I was evacuated from London when the war broke out. A group of us were sent to this sprawling mansion in the middle of Yorkshire, you could explore the rooms for days and still not see it all. It could have been a wonderful experience…a haven away from the horrors back home. It should have been wonderful."

Grace smiled, a forced twitch of her lips before continuing. "We all learned quickly to stay out of the way, to stay hidden. I favoured the woods at the edge of the estate because they were dark and creepy, and no one liked to go down there. In the middle of this copse of trees stood a beautiful old labyrinth which had crumbled so badly you could see into the middle. In the centre was a well, fed by a spring that ran through the woods, but the water was always tinged orange and growing darker each day."

"Rust?" I asked, and Grace nodded.

"You can see where I'm going with this. I didn't know Briar was a faerie, didn't really believe they existed, but I knew something was different about him— you just know they're not like us, don't you? I found him by the well, and he looked like he was trying to vomit up his spleen. He was a mess, covered in bile, and heaven knows what else, convulsing on the ground. Briar is completely colour-blind, so didn't notice anything was off with the water until, exhausted from a hunt, he filled his canteen and drained it dry."

"He didn't smell the iron in the water?"

"He later told me he could scent iron but had no idea it was from the well. He had drunk from it many times before. The railings up further had been damaged by a storm, breaking off into the water supply. Have you ever witnessed iron poisoning?"

Something punched through my foggy haze, a nightmare I would relive for every moment of every day. "Yes. How on earth did you save him?"

Grace grinned, looking utterly pleased with herself. "Charcoal, and lots of it. A friend of a friend once drank too much of her papa's home-brew and nearly killed herself, charcoal worked for her."

"You didn't get help?"

Her lovely eyes darkened. "And risk a beating simply for existing? No, thank you. I found lumps of charcoal in the bonfire, and had no idea if it would work or not...but I wasn't willing to get the shit beaten out of me for a dying stranger. I found fresh water and a bowl, mixed it all up and force-fed it to him, unsure if I was just going to kill him off quicker."

I turned to watch as the sun began to sink below the rooftops, the last rays reaching out to set the sky on fire. "You saved his life."

"I did," Grace answered, blowing more smoke against my lips as I turned to face her. I brushed my hand over hers, and she squeezed it back, keeping hold of my fingers. "It's hard being surrounded by them, isn't it? We delight in the world that they show us, the magic and the wonders, but there will always be a part of us that seeks this, a human friendship, and that's okay, Teya. Never forget that it's okay to be human."

"Were the Unseelie good to you?"

"Were the Seelie good to you?" Grace said, tilting her head, not needing me to answer. "Briar was. I didn't go into Faerie often to begin with, so he watched me grow up, and our friendship evolved into something new. Something wonderful. He offered me the choice to live in Faerie with him, or I could stay at the boarding house and receive my daily beatings."

"You couldn't go home?" I asked.

"Orphaned," Grace said; the years of mourning had long turned to acceptance. "I chose Briar."

"Why was he exiled?"

"We were stupid." A bitterness darkened her voice. "So goddamned stupid. So filled with young love, we thought we were invincible, that we lived far enough away from the Barren Queen to believe we could be truly happy...to have everything, unburdened, unpunished."

"You were pregnant," I guessed, watching her eyes fill with tears as she nodded.

"We ran away, we ran and ran, and I lost the baby." She quickly swiped a hand over her eyes.

"You don't have to continue," I said, but she did.

"Soren still wanted us for being within reach of something she could never hope to grasp. She caught us...of course, she caught us! They always do. Briar was to be executed, I was to watch." Grace gave a shuddering breath, her hand going to the place just above her heart. "I bargained my soul for him. Soren took it with glee, and I have no idea what she did with it. Nothing waits for me after death except eternal damnation. I cannot follow Briar into whatever life exists after this one. I am mortal, I will age and die where Briar will not. Where once we had forever spanning out in front of us, we now have a fragment of that."

The sky bled away into blackness, the clouds drifting away to reveal a blanket of stars. They were brighter, more alive than I had seen them in a while, and I guessed I had the Fizz to thank for that.

"No one gets forever," I said, and Grace chuckled darkly beside me.

"As good a toast as any, I guess. No one gets forever."

We shared the last of the Fizz as the night chilled around us, both trying to make shapes as we blew out the greenish fog. Grace managed rings, blowing out smaller and smaller ones, so they passed through one another. I managed to spit down myself.

"I didn't mean to fill the night with my sad little story," Grace said, laughing as she clapped me on the back.

"Actually, it's quite nice to hear someone else is having a terrible time too," I said, my words slurring so much I had to repeat myself three times.

"I hope it works out for you, Teya, I truly do. Whatever it is that you're running from, what you're fighting for, I hope you make it."

"If we make it out of this, I'll come back for you," I said as I heard footsteps behind us. I didn't need to turn to know it was Laphaniel.

"I'll hold you to that," Grace answered, embracing me tightly before she stood. She gave Laphaniel a dazzling grin. "She may need a little help getting to her room."

I giggled, feeling the last of the fizziness dance on my tongue. "Did you want some?"

Laphaniel bent to scoop me into his arms. "I think it best if one of us stays sober tonight."

"Are you cross?" I asked, clinging to him when he spun around, making the whole world spin in a riot of colour. "Do that again."

Laphaniel obliged, allowing my head to drop back as he spun, and I marvelled at the sudden explosion of colours I had no name for.

"Again."

He danced on the rooftop with me in his arms, painting the sky with a palette of indigos, blues, and blacks, struck with slashes of silver that tore the night as they chased through the sky.

"Again."

I was gasping for breath when he stopped, grinning as I waited for my world to calm. Laphaniel grinned back, his bright eyes finding mine, and I kissed him until everything erupted once more. I knew he could taste the Fizz against my lips, but he didn't draw back.

"Take me back downstairs."

"The bed's filthy."

"I don't care."

Laphaniel carried me to our bedroom without further protest, sprawling me onto the dingy mattress while I yanked his shirt over his head. He let out a low groan when I kissed him, brushing my lips against the hollow of his neck until I felt him crumple. His hands tangled in my hair, tilting my head back, exposing my throat to him as he bit down. My gasp was muffled by his lips crushing against mine.

I ran my hands over the mottled bruising on his ribs, my eyes locked on his, grinning up at him as his pupils swallowed up the purple. He closed his eyes, while my hands wandered down the contours of his chest, his lashes leaving spiky shadows against his skin. His breathing hitched when I trailed my finger down to the dark hair circling his bellybutton. My mouth followed where my fingers had been, moving lower and lower until his hands were tangling in my hair, and his body was arching off the bed. I undid him with every kiss, every touch, until my name was a curse on his lips, an oath…a promise.

With a low hiss, he dragged me up and kissed me hard, pushing me back onto the bed. There was something hungry and wanting burning in his eyes, I felt it too…a desire to be as close as we could physically get, to seek solace in each other's arms without having to talk.

I lay awake after, tangled in Laphaniel's arms, while he slept deeply beside me, too exhausted to keep his eyes open any longer. I didn't dare move, knowing if I shifted just a fraction, he would stir, and he needed to sleep.

As the moonlight trickled through the window, I rested my head against Laphaniel's chest, and listened to the song of his heartbeat, beating in time with my own.

CHAPTER TWELVE

*A*re you sure you don't have any other choice?" Grace asked the following morning, perching on the edge of our bed, handing us a steaming mug of coffee from the breakfast tray she brought. Briar stood in the doorway, chewing on a piece of bacon.

Grace had knocked on our door just as the sun began to rise, sensing we didn't intend to linger, and wanting to say goodbye before we left. She hadn't pried into what we were doing but found out through Darby what it was we were looking for.

"Can you get us into the Unseelie lands?" I asked Briar.

"Not since the banishment," he answered. "The paths I know are closed off to me, and even if I could get through, I would be killed on sight."

I had expected his answer, but it didn't stop the flash of disappointment I felt. If only it could have been that easy.

"Arabelle is a vicious piece of work," Briar added, leaning on the doorframe a respectable distance away from Laphaniel. "Even Soren was wary of her. That witch is ancient and cunning. I truly hope you know what you are doing."

"We don't," Laphaniel said, looking a bit more rested than he had for a while.

"I've heard rumours of the new Unseelie King. He is fighting to prove himself to a court already unstable. Now is not a good time to seek his help."

"Luthien poses more of an immediate threat," Laphaniel countered, placing his untouched coffee onto the nightstand.

"Are you certain they will help you?" Grace asked, dipping toast crusts into a pot of jam and nibbling on them, spreading crumbs all over the covers. "Why would they even entertain the idea? Surely they would love nothing more than to tear a Seelie faerie to pieces?"

I winced at the thought. "My sister is their Queen."

Grace and Briar shared a look.

"I know," I said at the shock on their faces. "I imagine she's fitting in quite nicely."

"Two mortal Queens?" Briar mused, echoing Oonagh's unease. "The new King is human too, so I have heard?"

"Was."

Briar pushed off the doorframe, green eyes bright against the dim room. "This will end in madness."

Grace reached for my hand, her fingers sticky with jam. "Please be careful."

"I'm trying to be," I replied, squeezing her hand back. "If this all goes well, and there is anything we can do to help you and Briar, we will. I promise."

Grace smiled, a sad quirk of her lips told me that she had lost any hope she may have once held onto, too used to listening to empty promises to find any comfort within them. "You're very kind, Teya. Don't let them take that away from you."

Leaning forwards, she kissed my cheek before bouncing off the bed with a spirit that had not yet been broken. Worn down and beaten maybe, but not broken.

I stared after her as she leapt into Briar's arms, marvelling at the adoring gaze he gave her. He looked at her like there was no one else in the world.

Laphaniel gave me that look. Every time he thought I wasn't looking or paying attention, I would catch him staring. He would turn away with a grin, embarrassed I had caught him. I was his world, as much as he was mine.

"Are you ready to go?" Laphaniel asked after Briar and Grace had left. He rose from the bed and stretched, looking better for having a few hours' sleep.

"Yes. I'm completely ready to haggle our lives away." I caught his look and held my hands up. "I'm joking, Laphaniel. Hey, what's wrong?"

He stumbled slightly when he stepped forward, reaching out for the bedpost to steady himself. All colour drained from his face as he clamped a hand to his side.

"I think I pulled something last night," he joked, the words more than a little breathless. "I blame you."

"You look like you're going to pass out," I said, not buying his flippant attitude. "And you didn't touch your breakfast."

He rolled his eyes, grabbing a slice of cold toast and finishing it in three bites, chasing it down with a gulp of orange juice. "Happy?"

"Depends, are you going to throw up now?"

"I'm fine, Teya. You try mending broken bones overnight and see how you feel."

"Don't snap at me."

He held a hand up. "I'm sorry. I'm okay, Teya. Just tired and grumpy. I'm sorry."

"You weren't grumpy last night," I said, shouldering a small bag of supplies Grace had given us. "I seem to remember you being very, very happy."

"And that's probably why my ribs are sore this morning, you insatiable woman."

I laughed as we left the room, the sound echoing cheerfully around the gloom. Downstairs, a few fey sat around tables with plates of bacon and eggs in front of them, mismatched cups of tea steaming up from the tables. Some were even reading the local newspaper.

It looked odd. Something off about it all, that wasn't glaringly obvious, but it niggled at me. Everyone just seemed less bright, less wild. Less alive.

"We draw strength from our Courts," Laphaniel said, giving the room a quick glance. "These fey no longer belong to any, and there is not enough magic in your world left for them to thrive."

"What happens to them?" I asked, keeping my voice low as we left the inn.

"Some of the weaker fey probably waste away, the others keep on existing without ever belonging anywhere."

I thought of Grace and Briar, of him having to watch as she aged, and he lay untouched by the passing years. I missed Faerie—the idea of never seeing it again was unimaginable.

I wanted to dance beneath the blossom with Laphaniel again, watch a double sunset seep down over the too-green hills. I longed to hear the trees whisper to me as night swept up around us, and the stars came out. I missed the way the wind sang.

Faerie had left a hollow deep within me, I feared not going back would only lead to madness.

I could only imagine what it was like for the Solitary fey, being away from Faerie for so long with no hope of returning. My heart yearned for it, and I'd been away only days.

Outside, the early morning sky was free from clouds, allowing a light frost to settle on the ground, crunching with each step we took. We wound around lanes into tamed woodland. I couldn't even begin to admire the countryside opening around us.

My last encounter with a witch very nearly cost me my life. Laphaniel had paid over the odds and saved me. I never liked to dwell on what would have happened if he had simply passed me by.

I hated the thought of what we would be forced to bargain, of what would happen if the price was just too high.

ARABELLE LIVED AWAY from the village, bordering the moorland with its sweeping lilac heathers. Her house was ordinary, a white stone cottage that looked just like all the other quaint little cottages, complete with a wisteria bush growing over the porch. There were no railings of children's bones, no animal carcasses offered up to ancient gods, no sound of music played on human heartstrings, but still it felt…wrong.

There was an otherworldliness to it that crept into my bones, fraying my nerves as it stood pretty in a mirage of belonging.

We followed the tidy path to the front door, and I steeled myself as Laphaniel reached for the knocker and banged three times. We waited, and just as I was going to knock again, the door opened. Humid warmth struck my face in a fog of choking smells.

"Yes?" A girl peered around the doorway, skinny and dirty, her eyes wide and blinking against the sunlight. "What business do you have here?"

"To see Arabelle," Laphaniel answered, as the girl glared up at him.

"She is busy at the moment."

"It is very important," Laphaniel insisted, shoving his foot against the doorway as the girl made to close it. Chains clanked around her ankles, locked tight enough that the flesh beneath bled raw.

"Please," the girl whispered, her eyes pleading. "Please go away."

She was strong for a girl her size and made a good attempt to slam the door in Laphaniel's face, but he pushed back until she stumbled.

"Go get your mistress before I shout for her," he hissed, making her flinch.

"Laphaniel!"

The girl shoved against the door, her knuckles white. "She says she's not to be disturbed…if I get her…"

"Bethany Wilkins!" screeched a voice from within the darkness. "Do your little ears not listen? Do you not heed what I have to say, what did I tell you, my filthy worm?"

Bethany Wilkins shrank back, hate-filled eyes flicking from Laphaniel to me before she turned away. "They wouldn't go, mistress, I was worried the knocking would disturb you…"

"Oh, do shut up, you withering slime," Arabelle sneered, pushing past the girl as she stood before us. "Get back to your work before I find another use for you."

Arabelle watched the girl leave, reaching out to yank a handful of dirty hair as Bethany ran past, visibly delighted in the yelp she tore from her.

"Little Bethany is the great-great-granddaughter of a woman who came to me in need of a bargain," Arabelle said in way of greeting, beckoning us into her home with a sweep of an elegant and unlined hand. "I own the first-born girl of each generation until the end of days. I own them all. Some I keep and some I sell, the smaller ones I have devoured whole."

The door creaked shut behind us, and I kept close to Laphaniel as Arabelle led us deeper into her home. Black beams stretched across the ceiling, with pots and pans and drying herbs hanging over us. She gestured for us to sit at a table cluttered with glass bottles, a few were corked, most not and oozing a strange smog that gave off a sickly scent. My head swam with it.

Arabelle sat in a worn velvet chair and crossed her long legs. Her fingers drummed against the armrest, painted red nails tapping out a rhythm that made my teeth ache.

"What have you two lovelies come to buy from me?"

She fixed me with eyes the colour of smoke, a whirl of grey and silver that were fathomless against the deep black of her skin. She grinned, canines pointed beneath painted lips, and there was nothing behind that smile that held even a thread of kindness…of mercy. I had no doubts that her soul, if she possessed one, lay withered and ruined, an ugly thing betraying the beautiful skin she wore.

"We need safe passage into the Unseelie Court, as close to the castle as possible," Laphaniel said, and Arabelle turned to him, her nostrils flaring as she scented him.

"Indeed?" Her glee was obvious. I feared what she would ask of us. "That is some request."

"I'm guessing a pint of blood would not be sufficient payment?" Laphaniel offered, and I balked at his nerve.

Arabelle reached forwards, almost caressing him, her fingertips stopping just shy of Laphaniel's face. She licked her lips, masses of dark hair falling over her bare shoulders as she leaned in.

"Oh, my lovely one," she breathed, her voice a caress. "I would bleed you dry, and yet it still would not quench my thirst. Tell me why you require passage, and then perhaps I can set a fair price."

I met her stare, fear rising like a tide. "I believe we have different ideas on what is fair payment."

"That may be so," Arabelle said, ghostly eyes unblinking. "But I want to know how much it means to you both, how much you are willing to give up."

Laphaniel leaned back in his chair. "Perhaps we are visiting relatives."

Not quite a lie, but Arabelle's lip curled as she withdrew her hand from Laphaniel. Quicker than I could see, she snared my wrist, her long fingernails slicing deep. The smoke in her eyes lifted, leaving behind a filmy white.

"Ah," she breathed, her grip on me vice-like. "Teya Jenkins, the Queen of Seelie, fleeing from Luthien herself. You dare throw hope upon the newly crowned King of the Unseelie. I see rebels, an uprising of discontentment." She paused to lick the blood trickling over my wrist. "And a beautiful war, all resting on me helping you."

My hand dropped hard against the table when she released me. I felt violated, knowing she had clawed into my mind and picked out the parts she wanted. Her voice still filled my head, a crooning echo left behind as she sifted through my thoughts.

"There was no need to do that," I said, recoiling from her.

"I don't ask twice."

"Demand your payment then," Laphaniel hissed, pulling me tight against him. "What do you want from us?"

Arabelle clicked her long fingers, and Bethany came stumbling over, her chains dragging behind her. "What would you give for your freedom, little worm?"

"Anything, mistress," Bethany said, her eyes firmly on the ground. "I'd give you anything."

"Would you gut these two if I asked it?" Arabelle sneered, twisting Bethany's head around, so she was forced to look at us. "Would you skin and tan their hides if I demanded it from you? Would you do it for your freedom, Bethany Wilkins?"

Bethany looked up, hope flaring behind her miserable eyes. "Oh, I would, mistress. Yes, if you willed it. Anything."

My heart twisted for the girl, even as she contemplated murdering us. I knew how quickly that spark of life...that fragment of hope long thought lost, could diminish forever. Arabelle's next words ensured it did.

"Your freedom is not up for sale, my little worm," Arabelle said, her hand going to Bethany's cheek. The girl let out a long howl of grief. "Never will you know anything but this life. As will your children, and your children after that and all who follow, until this world is no more."

"Mistress...please..." Bethany begged, tears making filthy tracks over her face. Arabelle wiped one away and brought it to her lips.

"Away with you," Arabelle said, turning away from the girl to face me. "Do you understand what price my little worm would be all too willing to pay? Just to save her pitiful self? What would be sufficient payment for the two of you to get what you wish? Bearing in mind what a big wish it truly is."

"What do you want?" I demanded, my voice echoing around the cottage. I silently vowed never again to deal with another witch for as long as I lived.

"I want your spark," Arabelle hissed, spittle flying from her mouth. "That vain hope you both cling to, thinking one day it will bring you joy. I want the misery that seeps from your marrow, the fear you reek of. I want to watch the love you share decay and rejoice as it buries you."

I cringed back when Arabelle lunged for me again, sharp nails dragging across my skin before Laphaniel caught her.

"Leave her!"

Arabelle swung around, a snarl ripping from her lips as she whirled on Laphaniel. "I can sense the horrors on you, boy! The shadows and the monsters. I can hear your heart shrieking!"

Arabelle slapped Laphaniel's hand away, and as quick as an asp, she grabbed him, dragging him close to her. "What blackness is there for you, lovely one?"

The candles all spluttered out, the room suddenly only illuminated by grimy sunlight struggling through the blackened windows. A gasp slipped from Arabelle's lips before the witch began to scream.

"What have you done?" Bethany demanded, running to her mistress. Arabelle's screeches tore through the small cottage, her neck straining back, mouth agape.

Laphaniel was desperately trying to prise his hand from the witch. Blood seeped over his skin as Arabelle's nails dug in, her grip relentless.

I grabbed at the witch. "Get her off of him!"

Arabelle's screams grew hoarse, milky white eyes seeing something none of us could fathom. Foam dribbled from her lips. Red snaked down her nose to mingle with the spittle on her chin.

"Don't you touch her," Bethany snarled, sending me sprawling across the floor as she backhanded me across the face. "Let her finish what she is seeing."

"Laphaniel?" I called his name, but he didn't answer. His eyes were closed, squeezed tight. The slices in his hand opened further as he continued to pull away. Blood began to pool upon the table. "Laphaniel!"

At last, the witch drew away, her words a scratch against the darkness. "Impossible."

She sat up slowly, smearing blood, and spit across her face with the back of her sleeve. Her breathing rattled. Arabelle eyed Laphaniel with her teeth bared, eyes once again pits of shadows. She stood, bracing herself against the table.

"What did you see?" Laphaniel asked, enticing a hollow chuckle from the witch.

"Here." Arabelle twisted her hand in mid-air, conjuring a sphere of gleaming glass that floated inches from her fingertips. "Take your boon and leave this place."

"What did you see?" Laphaniel repeated, kicking his chair over as he stood. "Tell me."

Arabelle shrunk back, not even glancing my way as I snatched up the glass ball. "I cannot speak of what I saw, lest it changes things. I am bound by my oaths."

"Like hell, you are, witch."

Arabelle sneered. "You will tear this world apart."

Dread coiled in my stomach, heavy and unyielding. "In this war?"

Arabelle spared me a fleeting glance. "Not in this war, little lovely. Perhaps not the one after that or the one that follows the one before. Know this though, all you hold dear will go down screaming."

"You give us prophecies and half-truths?" Laphaniel asked, a growl slipping into his tone. "An open destiny you cannot reveal, for fear it will force me on a different path?"

"I gave you what you came for and took no payment."

"You will allow us to leave here without an exchange?" I said, looking down at the ball in my hand, its smooth sides cool to the touch.

"I ask for mercy," Arabelle said, looking back at Laphaniel. "When the time comes, I ask for mercy."

"You're just planting nightmares," I said. Arabelle gave me a chilling smile. "You revel in chaos."

"I will tell you something." The smoke in her eyes twinkled. "I will tell you of a hunger both desperate and consuming, an air heavy with lust and the tang of flesh. I can still taste the sorrow, the pain, and the rich scent of filthy bodies entwining together." Arabelle pointed an elegant finger at Laphaniel. "I can see him, but not you, my little lovely. In your place, I see a vision of midnight hair and cold eyes."

The dread in my stomach curdled. Niven.

"You're lying," I said, the words a breathless plea.

"You know well that I cannot," Arabelle replied, raising a finger and pointing it at us. "Nothing good will come of the love you two share."

"We're leaving, Teya. Come on." Laphaniel grabbed my arm, his hands rough. "You can go to hell, witch."

Arabelle grinned from the shadows she was steadily retreating into. "We may all end up there yet."

Laphaniel said nothing while he pulled me away, his fingers tight around my wrist as he took three long strides towards the door, his other hand curled around the handle.

"You shouldn't be here," Arabelle whispered from the darkness. Laphaniel paused, tensing. "But you already know that, don't you?"

"What of it?" Laphaniel hissed through gritted teeth, keeping his back to the witch.

"You wear death like a cloak."

Laphaniel shook his head, yanking my arm as he flung the door open and stormed out. Arabelle's last words followed us as if she had spat them in our ears.

"But you wear it well."

Laphaniel didn't stop until we reached a stream, tall willows banking each side like long-limbed guardians. Only then did he release my hand, not noticing the way I rubbed my throbbing wrist.

"What the hell was that all about?" Arabelle's ominous prophecy echoed around my head, planting fear and doubt deep into my mind.

Laphaniel held a bloodied hand out for the sphere in my pocket. "You know better than to trust the words of witches, Teya. Arabelle picked pieces of a vision and used it to frighten you."

"It worked," I said, passing him the sphere. "She saw you with Niven."

His eyes flashed. "You believe that?"

The thought of it was unbearable. "Arabelle can't lie."

"She has had centuries to hone the skills of manipulating truths, Teya," Laphaniel began. The anger ebbed from his eyes, leaving them cold. "Fey learn how to distort the truth from a very early age. Don't dwell on the nightmares of witches, they trade them as currency."

"And the rest?" I asked, rubbing my hands over my arms.

Laphaniel barked a hollow laugh. "I highly doubt I will cause the end of the world, Teya."

I bristled. "Don't mock me."

"We do not matter to this world," Laphaniel hissed. "It cares not if we live or die or fall in love or hate each other. It is huge and unwavering and constant. Witches speak in metaphors and riddles because it brings misery." He took a breath. "Creatures a lot wiser than you have driven themselves mad attempting to decipher the prophecies the witches spit out. The world is still spinning."

I nodded, wanting to glean some comfort from his words, but Arabelle's warnings bore hooks and were not so easily dislodged. "She knew you're not meant to be here."

"But I want to be."

With those words, he twirled the sphere in his hands, balancing it for a moment on his fingertips. He threw it against the trees where it shattered.

The trees bent and bowed, branches growing and twisting until they knotted together. Flowers bloomed and burst, spitting their petals down upon the ground where they curled and died. The trees creaked as they moved, groaning as they worked to form the shape of a doorway.

Laphaniel held out a hand, face unreadable. "To the Unseelie."

"To the Unseelie," I echoed, and stepped through the doorway.

CHAPTER THIRTEEN

The doorway decayed and crumbled the moment we stepped through, leaving us standing upon a cliff edge with the light of twin suns beating down upon us. Stark, silvery trees swayed around us, though there was no wind. Branches stretched up into points, trying to pierce the sky.

A light frost covered the bleak landscape, no snow to be seen as if winter had yet to seep into the Unseelie. I wondered if it too was wary of slipping in uninvited.

Grass crunched underfoot as I took a step forwards to peer over the edge, down to the swirling waters below. Foam crashed against the rock, the swirling black waters cascading over boulders to tear down the riverbed. The waves screamed against the stillness of the clifftop.

"So, this is Unseelie?"

Laphaniel nodded, joining me to look across the water. "On the boundary line by the looks of it—not as far as I had hoped."

"How do we get down?"

"We jump."

My stomach dropped. "Of course, we do."

"Watch," Laphaniel said, picking up a rock to launch into the furious waters. It didn't even ripple. "The River of Tears runs from the furthest reaches of the Seelie lands, all the way up into the Black Mountains to the north and to the Wyld Woods to the south, ending up somewhere at the end of the world. As far as we know, it travels the entire breadth of Faerie. It is endless."

"Does Faerie really have no end to it?"

"None that anyone has ever found," Laphaniel replied, shoving the hair from his eyes and eyeing the waters like they would rise and take him. "I don't know what you will see in the waters, Teya. It will try to keep you, you need to remember that whatever it is you see, it isn't real."

"What do you mean? What's in the water?"

"Just keep fighting for the surface, okay?"

It wasn't okay, but standing at the edge, I curled my fingers around his and swallowed back the fear rising inside me. I couldn't break my gaze away from the churning waves. "We jump together."

Laphaniel squeezed my hand, locking our fingers as we stood on the precipice. The roar of the waters bellowed at us, daring us to jump.

"Ready?" he asked.

"Nope."

Laphaniel braced himself beside me, but I tugged him back. There was every chance we would plunge into the swirling void and never surface again. "Wait."

"There is no other way down."

I closed the small gap between us, keeping my hand tight in his. "I know. I was just thinking about what Arabelle said about you and Niven..."

"Teya." My name was a warning on his lips.

"I don't expect you to spend eternity alone, if after everything, I don't make it through this. I just need you to promise me it will never be Niven."

"Never Niven," he snarled her name like a curse. "If I lost you, know that I would never give my heart to another. All that I am would be lost with you. Without you, I would burn this world to the ground and turn everything to ash and dust."

"Perhaps that's what the prophecy foretold?" I said, leaning into him in a brief embrace.

"I would tear this world apart for you."

I smiled. "I believe you."

We stepped off the edge together, plunging so fast my breath was stolen away. Laphaniel's hand wrenched away from mine when we hit the water. There was no splash.

An invisible current swept me along in thick smog that sounded like crashing waves but was no more substantial than cool mist. I was weightless, drifting along on some riptide that dragged me further and further under.

I couldn't breathe. I opened my mouth to call out for Laphaniel and choked on nothing. My lungs screamed for air. Kicking upwards, my hands fumbled against the fog as it dragged me down. I kicked and struggled and gasped, desperately fighting against the blackness that began to creep in. A wordless exhale of mist bubbled up from my mouth and drifted away. Blackness seeped in, and I carried on sinking.

"Teya?" My name punctured through the black, sounding too far away. "Teya, wake up."

I opened my eyes to Laphaniel shaking me gently. Bright light stung my eyes as he moved from over me, and I squinted at the deep blue sky overhead.

"Oh, that wasn't so bad," I said, pushing myself up. A dull burning lingered in my chest, an echo of nearly drowning. "Are you okay?"

Laphaniel smiled, sprawling out beside me, and stretched his arms high over his head. "You've been asleep for ages."

"Sorry."

"Don't be, you look lovely when you're dreaming." He moved closer and rested his head against my shoulder, his hand seeking mine. "What do you want to do now you're awake?"

"What should we do?" I asked, sitting up. The warmth of the sun settled upon my face, the trees around us sang in the breeze. The scent of wildflowers, moss, and pine overloaded my senses with a familiarity that brought tears to my eyes.

"Where are we?" I dared ask.

Softly, so softly, Laphaniel cupped my face in his hands and kissed me. It was a kiss I had almost forgotten, one without fear or hunger. A kiss heavy with the promises of so many more. It didn't feel like the last one, as many of our kisses had.

"Where are we, Laphaniel?" I asked again, pulling back enough to see the wonderful violet of his eyes, void of darkness and shadows.

He pointed to a gap in the trees, and I turned my head, my heart breaking. "Home."

Standing tall and proud and untouched by flames was Laphaniel's house. The stone gleamed white against the sunlight, the wild blossom around the doorway bursting open at the warmth.

"Do you want to go in?" Laphaniel asked. "We don't have to stay long if you don't want to."

I hesitated, staring at his outstretched hand. "I don't think I should."

"Wouldn't it be wonderful if you did?" he said. "If only to refresh your memory."

I swallowed. "Just a quick look?"

"Stay as long as you like," Laphaniel replied. My blood froze at his choice of words, words he had uttered to me once before, and I had danced the seasons away.

I wanted to leave, a nagging voice at the back of my mind urged me forwards...but I would never get to see his house again. I stood before a ghost of a life I still longed for with every fibre of my being, a life free of fear and pain and bloodshed.

"I just want to say goodbye."

"Do you want me to come with you?"

I stood, brushing the grass from my clothes. "Yes."

The house stood perfect. Soft candlelight bathed the rooms, all ignited with a wave of Laphaniel's hand. The branches winding around the walls stirred, blossom stretching open into pink flowers that rained down from the boughs overhead.

I climbed the stairs, blinking petals from my eyes as they fell around my feet into a gloriously scented carpet. My feet knew the way to Laphaniel's bedroom, the one I had shared with him when he enchanted me. Throws and furs and threadbare blankets covered the large bed, all smelling of spice and liquorice...of Laphaniel. Of home.

Streams of light flooded through the open window, catching the dust motes dancing on the air. Thick, twisted branches covered the ceiling, coiling out from the walls to drip more blossom onto the bed. Slowly, I walked to the window and gazed out over the forest and to the lake beyond.

I didn't hear Laphaniel come up behind me, and I jumped slightly at his arms wrapping around me. "Stay."

"Don't."

Gently he turned me, so I faced him, hands soft against my face, kisses soft against my cheek. "Stay with me."

"I can't," I choked, feeling the bitter words on my lips again, the same argument we'd had all that time ago. I couldn't believe I was giving the same answer, one I had regretted ever since.

"Why?"

The torment on his face almost broke me. "Because this isn't real."

I tore my arm free of his grip and fled the room and the memories it brought with it. Laphaniel called after me, his voice raw and broken.

I stopped running in front of what had once been Lily's room. Soft yellow paint shone from the door; a garland of wildflowers hung in the centre all tied up with a ribbon that blew in the wind. It looked nothing like the dank dwelling of the faerie who had once tried to kill me.

With my curiosity getting the better of me, I pushed open the door. Inside stood a smaller bed, the posts carved with little creatures that leapt from the wood. A patchwork quilt pooled over the mattress, a worn stuffed bear sat propped against the plump pillow, gazing up at me with black eyes.

"She'll miss you too."

"Who?"

My hand lingered on the doorframe, my fingers brushing against little notches in the wood. Height markers.

"Our daughter."

I snatched my hand away from the door, backing away, shaking my head at the impossibility of it. The unfairness of it.

"How old is she?" I asked, my heart stuttering against my chest at the thought of a real family...unbroken. Where there were no ghostly place settings at the table, no empty chairs, no missing children, and dead fathers.

Laphaniel shrugged. "Four."

So young.

"Where is she?" I dared to ask, a sudden need to see her taking over everything else within me.

"Playing in the woods."

"You let a four-year-old play in the woods alone?"

I darted down the stairs and back outside, running to the back of the house and through the rose garden to the woodland beyond. I came to a staggering stop at the sight of a mud-stained little girl doing handstands to the delight of a swarm of tiny sprites.

"Mama! Look!"

"I'm looking," I said, unable to move any closer. She beamed at me from upside down, her dark hair falling in her eyes, almost obscuring the bright violet of her irises. Her bare feet were caked to the ankle in mud, her dress torn.

"She's as feral as you are," I said to Laphaniel, who had followed behind. The little girl did a daring flip in the air, slipped and tumbled to the floor.

"And with all of your grace," Laphaniel replied with a wince, as screams broke through the tranquillity.

"Mama!" The girl cried, lifting her hands out for me, and I instantly made to go to her...and paused. "Mama?"

Laphaniel stepped forwards, scooping the girl into his arms as she continued to reach out for me, her eyes wide and tear-stained.

"Teya?"

"No," I blinked, shaking my head, even as my body urged me to reach for the little girl, my own heart hurting with her. "This isn't real."

"Does it matter?"

"I think it does," I replied, stepping back. "I can't stay here."

"Please?" Laphaniel begged, closing the gap between us, shifting the girl, so she rested against his hip. "Don't leave us here. Stay. Be happy."

"I am happy," I said, tears sliding down my face. "I am happy."

"No, you're not."

It took all my strength to shake my head, squeezing my eyes shut to drown out the promises he was feeding me. I held my hand over my aching chest, feeling something spike my hand.

Looking down, I clutched at the star on my necklace and imagined Laphaniel...my Laphaniel... alone on the riverbank. If I never went back, he would know I left him for a dream, and that I would rather die for an illusion than face reality with him.

"Stay," Laphaniel urged.

I backed away. "No."

"Why?"

"Because whatever dream this is, died a long time ago," I said, allowing the grief of it all to wash over me. "This dream is out of my reach now, and that hurts more than you will ever know, but I will not give up what I have to get it back. I will be happy again, but not here, not with you. My Laphaniel is hurting, and he needs me. Whatever part of him you represent is long gone, and he's a better person for it."

Laphaniel screamed at me, reaching out as water began to spill from his mouth. The girl in his arms turned to white foam and crashed to the floor in a wave. I staggered back as Laphaniel collapsed into a torrent of furious water that rushed up against my legs.

Around me, the trees, the rocks, and grassy mounds exploded into murky waters. The gleaming stone from the house crumbled into the swirl, the waves swallowing it up until there was nothing left.

The waters rose to my waist, up and up until it dragged me under. The strong current snatched at my body like hungry arms, all fixed on keeping me from the surface.

I could see nothing in the darkness. With every bit of my flagging strength, I fought for the surface and finally broke free. I sucked in air, only to be thrown back under as wave after wave crashed against me.

"Laphaniel!" I shouted his name over the thundering waters. "Laphaniel!"

Strong arms wrapped around my middle as I was sucked under again, hauling me up so I could breathe.

"Stop thrashing about!" Laphaniel gasped, struggling against the current. "We need to get out of the water, now."

He looped an arm around my waist and dragged me towards the riverbank. I kicked through the current with him, straining to keep my head above the water. My legs cramped, the wild waters growing cold.

The river refused to release us without a fight, launching us up over the rapids and down into the foam, forcing us closer and closer to the rocks at the edge.

Laphaniel was thrown backwards, his head striking the rock. I yelled his name when he slipped beneath the waters and didn't surface. Clinging to the rocks, I grabbed his hand again, hauling him up to me. He sucked in a breath, coughing up a mouthful of gritty water. Blood seeped from the back of his head, running over his neck into the water.

Shadows moved beneath the waters, monstrous black shapes the size of buses, swept through the swirling tide, long tails sweeping through the current with ease.

"Get up onto the rocks." Laphaniel hissed, shoving me up. "Move."

I turned to help him up, grabbing him by his sodden shirt, as an enormous head reared up through the water, its mouth a gaping maw of teeth. The eel-like creature lunged forward, striking the spot where Laphaniel had been just moments before.

It roared its fury, flicking out a forked black tongue to suckle at the stone, lapping up the blood that had dripped down into the water.

"Go, go, go!" Laphaniel urged.

Another head sprang from the water, biting down on a chunk of stone, narrowly missing my leg. I cried out, and it turned, whipping its tongue at me.

Pain exploded along my arm, sharp suckers biting into my skin. My shoulder wrenched back as Laphaniel grabbed for me, the skin on my arm, tearing away from the barbed tongue.

The creature pulled back its slick head, my blood dripping from its mouth and lunged again.

Laphaniel slammed into me, shoving me over the rocks and down the riverbank. Rocks tumbled after us as teeth collided with stone. Black heads lifted from the river, coiling bodies thrashing against the current. They opened their mouths, rows, and rows of jagged teeth glinting in the sunlight, and screeched at us.

With barely a ripple, they slipped back under the inky waters.

"My arm," I panted, cradling it to my body

"Let me see it," Laphaniel said, kneeling beside me. "I need to remove the barbs. Stay still."

He turned my arm over, running a finger down the ruined flesh. Pain spiked up over my shoulder, and I swore.

"The barbs are poisonous," Laphaniel said, his careful fingers prising them from my skin. "If you feel faint, lie back."

I watched as he slid one free, the jagged edges catching my skin. Blood swelled from the tiny hole, along with a blob of white pus.

"I'm not going to faint," I answered, even as the world began to spin.

"Just lie back before you hit your head."

Everything tilted, and I braced myself against him until the dizziness passed. "I'm fine…"

He caught me as I pitched forwards, the pain in my arm fading with everything else around me.

CHAPTER FOURTEEN

The worried look on Laphaniel's face melted away into relief when I opened my eyes and blinked up at him. He helped me sit up on the damp grass, his fingers tightening the makeshift bandage around my arm. The pain had gone, leaving behind an odd tingling ending at my fingertips.

"How are you feeling?" he asked, stroking the hair from my face. He had moved me away from the riverbank, but I could still hear the roar of the water. Above us, the sky was tinged with a strange indigo, pale sunlight beamed down and bathed everything in an eerie twilight.

"I'm okay," I answered, noting the dried blood on Laphaniel's neck. "How's your head?"

"I'll live."

"What did you see in the water?" I breathed in the familiar scent of him. Under the smell of murky river water lingered the scent of spice and warmth, of dirt and shadows and everything that made him mine.

Laphaniel buried his head into my shoulder, one hand tangling in my hair. "I saw you," he breathed, "and you were drowning over and over again. I couldn't get to you fast enough. I kept finding you face down, and it didn't matter that I knew it wasn't real, because it almost was."

I pulled back, meeting his eyes. I could never forget how he had pulled me from the mermaids, what it had felt like to drown beneath the cold water. How could I forget the feel of his mouth on mine, warm breath over frozen lips. My name echoing as he called for me. I just hadn't realised how much it still haunted him.

"You did get to me in time," I began, resting my head against his. "You seem to have a knack for saving me."

He huffed a small laugh. "What did you see?"

"A memory," I said. "Nothing but an echo."

"Of what?"

I smiled, pushing myself to my feet. "Of everything you once offered me."

Laphaniel rose beside me with fluid grace. "Did you want to stay?"

"I wanted to say goodbye," I answered. "And I did."

I stepped away from the sounds of the river, staring up at the twisting woodland stretching out before us. Towering trees stood so close together they knotted around each other. The branches still clung to the fragments of leaves, some were still tinged with gold, winter not yet having found them.

The Unseelie trees did not sing, but I could sense them listening.

"What monsters live beyond those trees?" I asked, peering into the thicket. Brambles and vines had swallowed up the path, and the shadows themselves seem to devour everything.

"Ones I hope to avoid," Laphaniel answered, his entire body tense. "There are creatures in the Unseelie I have only heard about in stories. It would be unwise to venture in there after dark. I think we should make camp here tonight."

He looked like he would rather walk straight into Hell itself than the shadows of the Unseelie.

I peered up at the strange sky, the light of the suns' sinking low. "I'll gather some wood."

"Don't go far." Laphaniel shot out a hand, startling me.

"I won't," I promised him, pointing to the sticks dotted over the ground around us. "I've learnt not to go wandering the woods on my own."

Laphaniel dropped his hand, still looking uneasy. "I sincerely doubt that. You're too curious for your own good."

I smirked as I gathered firewood, piling it up for Laphaniel to ignite. The air was cold, and our clothes were wet. The warmth of the fire was a welcome relief, a little light against the surrounding darkness. A beacon, too—we both knew that.

Everything Grace had packed for us was lost to the River of Tears, leaving us once again with nothing. Laphaniel slipped into the shadows, silent, coming back shortly after with the body of a thin rabbit dangling from his hand.

He skinned it with a piece of sharp flint, the firelight catching the red on his hands, making it shine against his pale skin. I made a wobbly spit using sticks and strands of thick vine, and together we sat and waited for the meat to cook…or flop into the fire.

"Who taught you to hunt?" I asked over the crackling and spitting of the fire.

Carefully, Laphaniel turned the rabbit and browned the other side. He could have easily made a better spit, though kept mine in a gesture I found oddly endearing, "My mother."

"With Nefina too?"

"No. Nefina doesn't know how to hunt."

"I've never heard you talk about your mother before," I said, drawing my knees up to keep warm. "What was she like?"

Laphaniel shuffled closer to me, his leg touching mine. "I don't really remember her," he said, poking the fire, so the flames danced. "I remember this game she used to play, though. She would blindfold me when I was very young and lead me into the woods after nightfall. For three days, she would leave me to see if I could survive on my own."

"That's awful, Laphaniel," I said, failing to keep the shock from my tone. "How old were you?"

He shrugged. "I think I had seen my fourth midwinter, maybe."

I swallowed, for a moment utterly lost for words. I couldn't begin to understand how anyone could leave their child alone, to abandon them in a sick game to see whether they were gobbled up.

"I burned my hands to begin with," Laphaniel continued, lifting the rabbit from the flames and passing me a strip of meat. "I wasn't good at lighting fires, but I didn't want to be alone in the dark, so I kept practising until I could summon a flame without thinking. I could use a small knife, but the bow I was given was too big. After the three days had passed, my mother would find me, and we went home."

My heart twisted at the thought of him as a frightened child, but he spoke as if it wasn't cruel. Perhaps all fey children were raised in fear and darkness.

"Did you ever get lost? Or hurt?" I asked, and he smiled.

"Not until the dragon came along."

"Dragon?" I echoed, and his smile turned into something wicked and wonderful.

"It was young," he continued, picking off flakes of rabbit meat. "And sickly, hardly bigger than a bear. You could see its ribs, it was so scrawny and had these tattered wings that dragged along the ground, a pathetic thing really. Oh, but its teeth were still sharp, and it was faster than me. Stupidly, I ran, regretting my decision the moment my feet began to pound the floor. It lunged, and I felt its teeth and claws scrape along my back. Then it stopped, dropping down dead with one of my mother's arrows through its skull."

A laugh trembled past my lips. "She never left you."

Laphaniel nodded. "I was so angry with her. I refused to go hunting with her again; she continued to ask, but I wouldn't go. I thought I had done it on my own, scared off the beasts in the shadows with my ridiculous little knife, when all along she had been there, keeping me safe. I hated her for it."

"I can imagine you as a stubborn child," I said, grinning as I stripped juicy meat from the bone. "You really never went out with her again?"

"Not long after, she found out she was carrying Nefina."

"Couldn't you have gone out after she was born?"

Laphaniel set aside his half-eaten food. "No."

I watched as he closed his eyes and pinched the bridge of his nose as if warding off a headache. He didn't touch his food again.

"What's wrong?"

"I think I hit my head harder than I thought," he answered, rubbing a hand over his eyes. I moved my hand to the back of his head, my fingers finding a small bump.

"You sure that's all it is?"

Laphaniel sighed and lay back against the cold grass, tugging me down too, so I fitted snugly against him. "I just need a good night's sleep."

"At least we can both agree on that," I said, noting the odd warmth coming from him. He closed his eyes and didn't move. Something he hadn't done in months.

I wondered if he was still feeling the effects of the iron, first from the car journey, and then from the warehouse. I had seen how lethal iron was to faeries, so it made sense for it to take time, leaving his system entirely.

Sleep didn't find me so easily. The surrounding woods were alive with the baying of creatures I had no name for, the whispers I couldn't understand, the echoes of distant screaming.

The strange sunlight bled over the horizon, the moody sky darkening like an oil spill. Shadows stretched along the ground, wavering with the wind, thick fingers of black that jutted out from the spindly armed branches.

I moved closer to the flames, tugging Laphaniel with me and prayed it didn't go out.

Dawn came slowly, lazily. It brought with it a thin layer of frost, a hint of winter, and nothing more. The dusting of white gave a softness to the surrounding land, concealing the darkness lingering below the surface. It may have fooled someone else with its veiled wonderland. It would have fooled me once.

Laphaniel stirred as the sun crept higher and melted the frost away, shattering the illusion. Beads of sweat slipped down his temple.

"You're like a fussing nursemaid," he said, knocking my hand away. He sat up and glanced around, eyes blank for a moment.

I rolled my eyes, "How's your head?"

He picked at the dried blood on his neck. "It's fine, how's your arm?"

"It's itchy," I replied, noting the change of subject.

"Well, don't scratch it."

I stood and stretched hard enough for my bones to click, my clothes crunching as I moved. I gave them a quick sniff and winced.

Laphaniel kicked dirt over the remains of the fire, looking just as filthy and bruised as I did. It was becoming harder to remember how he looked when clean and rested and unbloodied. I wished to see him less haunted, missing the quick smiles and wicked glances that were already becoming less frequent.

Slipping my hand in his, we entered the twisting woodland of the Unseelie. Strange light dappled down over the thick roots, striking the ivy creeping over the ground. Violet tinged everything, the few clouds overhead the colours of bruises. Endless twilight surrounded us, casting everything with long winding shadows.

The bones in my hand creaked as Laphaniel tightened his grip. His footsteps over the ground were silent.

"I may need this hand in the future, Laphaniel."

"What? Oh, sorry." He dropped my hand, and I flexed my fingers. "Stay close."

"I'm not going to wander off," I said, straining my head to take in the trees towering above us. Some stood so wide and tall they blocked out all light. Branches wound up and around the trunks, looping from tree to tree like moss-covered bridges. I caught sight of movement above us, lightning-quick and utterly silent.

Laphaniel huffed, unconvinced. "I would rather you stay where I can see you, Teya, judging by past experiences."

I opened my mouth to reply, the teasing words on the tip of my tongue, but I swallowed them back. Laphaniel stood tense, head tilted to listen, eyes following the movements above us. It wasn't the time for jokes.

"What's following us?"

"Nothing worth worrying about yet," he answered, glancing at me with black eyes. "Cait Siths are trailing the shadows above us. Likely hoping something bigger will come along and kill us, leaving them to devour our souls. Lazy creatures."

One sleek black creature leapt down from the branches, landing without a sound at my feet. It sat in front of me, the size of a beagle, its wide green eyes unblinking. I stepped back, and it rose, slinking around my legs.

Flame licked at Laphaniel's fingertips, and the Cait Sith turned, hissing. With a flick of his wrist, Laphaniel sent sparks at the creature, and it darted back into the treetops.

"They have sharp claws and a nasty bite," Laphaniel explained, as I scanned above us. "But Cait Siths will rarely take on larger prey. They prefer to wait."

"Will they keep following us?"

"They deem us most likely to provide them with a meal, so yes."

I caught sight of the lean bodies slipping through the trees, soundless, and graceful. The knowledge they wouldn't harm us didn't reassure me, given they were waiting for something else to bring us down.

Sweeping blossom trailed down from one of the thinner trees as we walked on, seemingly untouched by the passing season. Birdsong filled the air, high and quick. Vivid red flowers bloomed over the black branches, petals so downy soft they left glittering scarlet dust on my fingertips.

"Don't do that," Laphaniel snapped, knocking my hand away.

I jerked back. "Is it poisonous?"

"Lucky for you, it's not," he replied, exasperated. "It's blood."

I frantically wiped my hand over my jeans, glancing up at the tree with a shudder. The blossom at the top gleamed black, curved petals wet with droplets that gathered like dew. Blood dripped onto the flowers beneath. Like a rose bush, thorns covered the stalks, needle-sharp. The noises I had mistaken for birdsong were not birds at all, but flittering creatures impaled upon the thorns. Iridescent wings beat helplessly while the flowers drank them dry.

"It's a vampire tree," I gasped, my eyes darting to the hollow husks of long-dead faeries, mouths all agape in a final helpless cry. Webbing covered their mouths, left behind by scavengers that had come after death.

Laphaniel gave a humourless laugh. "I have never heard it called that before. Perhaps you will finally learn to stop poking everything."

I grimaced. "I really do try; I have curious fingers." I waggled them in front of him, earning a real laugh. He grabbed my hands and yanked me into a quick embrace.

"I don't want you to change, Teya," he said, his mouth at my ear.

"I think I am, slowly." I pulled back, touching my forehead to his. "And so are you. I'm not afraid like I used to be. I know what it is I want, and I will fight for it. This world is making me grow up, and I think I needed to."

"Have I changed?" Laphaniel asked, black eyes narrowing. "How?"

He sounded so outraged I snorted, but all humour slipped away as I said, "You no longer find amusement in my pain."

Laphaniel said nothing for a moment, even the Cait Siths above us stilled, listening. "Tormenting you, entertained me in a way I had almost forgotten. I enjoyed the way you jerked away from me, how your eyes filled with anger, then with tears. Then I made you smile, really smile, and I heard you laugh."

The further we walked, the darker it became until the sky above glowed a sullen violet. The little sunlight filtered down in silvery pools, striking the edges of stone jutting up from the ground.

Fragments of buildings stood amongst the stone. They were not in ruins, but all perfectly built, just not finished. Like they had been forgotten. We passed a complete fireplace with nothing surrounding it; smoke curled up from the chimney, but the grate remained cold and unlit. A blue painted door stood perfectly on its own, brass letterbox polished to a high shine. Hundreds of black tulips surrounded the door, unmoved by the chilly breeze passing through. A carved stained-glass window cast rainbows over the ivy-strewn floor. A gravestone stood beside it, bearing no name. A wishing well brimming with ancient coin, sat next to a child's playhouse, complete with gingham curtains and dolls with no faces.

"Dreams and nightmares," Laphaniel whispered beside me. "Wishes and forgotten things."

I stepped over a lost-looking teddy bear, a chill creeping down my spine. "Can we move on?"

Laphaniel took my hand, quickening his step as the dolls turned their heads to watch us pass. "Gladly."

A sudden, piercing cry shattered the quiet. We ducked as the noise disturbed a nest of inky birds above us. The birds screeched, swooping low in a swarm of black. Wings beat against the back of my head, claws tangling in my hair. Another echoing cry sent the birds to the skies, cawing their fury.

"What was that?" I shook feathers from my hair and plucked them from Laphaniel's.

"I have no idea." He turned one feather around in his fingers. "Nor do I care. Just keep walking."

Another scream ripped through the woods, then another. Terrified. Helpless. I paused, glancing back. Laphaniel tugged me on, but the sound roused something very human deep within me...an instinct I couldn't ignore.

"It's likely a banshee," Laphaniel hissed, sensing my struggle. "Or a wisp or a phooka wanting to lure gullible prey like you to their death. Ignore it."

"What if you're wrong?" I asked, cringing at the screams.

Laphaniel spun, furious. "Then it is their misfortune and not ours. They get to die beneath these forsaken trees and not us. Move."

"What if you had ignored me?"

A snarl slipped past his lips. "Move. Now."

He clicked his fingers for me to follow, and I gave him a withering look, taking three steps before I heard a cry that stopped me dead.

"Mummy!" it cried, sounding heartbreakingly young. "Please, Mummy!"

Laphaniel grabbed my wrist, and I made to protest, to fight him. He swore through gritted teeth, dragging me towards the terrified cries. "Damn it, Teya!"

CHAPTER FIFTEEN

*W*e raced through the trees, following the cries that had subdued into helpless sobs. Laphaniel cursed under his breath, his grip on my wrist relentless. He let me go as we came to a stop by a gnarled, blackened tree. It stood away from the others, the ground beneath dry and dead. Its branches were bare as if winter had already stripped it back. Spindly limbs curled upwards, broken and weeping boughs that swayed in the wind.

From where I stood, I could just see the makings of an enormous nest, a crude thing of black twigs and dripping moss. It reeked of rot.

"Harpies," Laphaniel said, sighing. He pressed a foot against one of the lower branches; it creaked but didn't snap.

Something crunched under my foot, and I looked down to the ground, littered with bones, all picked clean and forgotten in the yellowing grass. "Where are they?"

"I don't know," Laphaniel answered, placing a finger to his lips. "But I doubt they've gone far."

We looked up at the sound of a muffled sob, the nest suddenly tilting as someone scrambled to the edge. A little girl peered over, wide eyes meeting mine, and for one terrible moment, I thought she was going to topple over. I held my hands out, silently signalling for her to stay still.

The nest jostled again, this time under Laphaniel's weight as he climbed up with the quick grace of a mountain cat. The little girl cried out, pitching against the edge, dislodging clumps of wood and dead things, so they plummeted to the ground.

"Keep still." I heard Laphaniel hiss, making the girl jump and cry out again. She looked no older than six. I remembered my first meeting with Laphaniel and how afraid I had been; he had looked significantly less feral back then too.

"You're scaring her," I hissed back, hoping he could reach her before the nest crashed to the ground.

"My brother…" she whimpered, and I could see her point to a corner of the nest.

"Your brother is dead," Laphaniel said, impatient. "Come here."

"I don't want to leave him," she sobbed, and I winced as her cries echoed.

"Then stay here. I'm not risking my neck for a corpse."

More twigs fell to the earth as Laphaniel backed away, one hand tight on the branch above him. The girl scrambled forwards, foot breaking through the bottom of the nest.

"Don't move," Laphaniel ordered, reaching forwards. The nest creaked when he touched it. The branches holding it up creaked too. "Keep still, or we're both going to fall."

The girl let out a choked, petrified sob.

"Maybe less honesty, Laphaniel!" I called from the ground, desperately wanting them down.

Laphaniel swung away from the nest, balancing upon a branch that groaned from beneath him. "I'm going to count to three, and you're going to jump to me."

"I can't."

"One."

The girl didn't move, Laphaniel took a step down.

"Two."

She shifted, her little body shaking with her sobs. Laphaniel climbed further down, he peered up and shrugged his shoulders. She lunged to the edge as he disappeared from her view, and more of the nest disintegrated from beneath her.

I choked on my cry when she fell forwards, toppling over the ruined pieces of the nest, straight into Laphaniel's waiting arms.

He pulled her close, arms tight around her. "Three."

Laphaniel balanced on the branch, finding his footing. He climbed down slowly, the boughs he stood on groaning with the extra weight. I didn't take a breath until they were both firmly on the ground.

"Thank you," I breathed.

He shifted the girl in his arms, keeping her against him as she clung tight to his neck. She looked up at me, brown eyes wide and terrified, standing out against her too-pale skin. Matted hair stuck to her face, so coated in dirt and blood, it was impossible to tell what colour it should have been.

I made to take her hand, recoiling when she lifted the mess of her own. Something had chewed her fingers right to the bone.

"We're going to help you," I began, forcing my eyes away from her ruined fingers. "Can you tell me your name?"

"Alice." The word fell past chapped lips in barely a whisper.

"We need to get out of here," Laphaniel said, glancing at the remnants of the nest. "Before the harpies come back and realise something is missing…"

High shrieks cut him off, and we both snapped our heads up to search the skies. Alice squirmed in Laphaniel's arms; a low keening sound slipped from her mouth.

We swore, and Laphaniel backed away, motioning me to follow. We ducked into a dense path of low trees, the ground tilting ever so slightly to form a small hollow. Shadows cascaded over us.

"We're too close," I whispered, pressing my back against the slope.

"I know," Laphaniel answered helplessly. "but if we run with the girl, they will catch us."

I helped lower Alice to the ground, my heart somewhere in my throat. With trembling hands, I sought out hers, the one left whole, and squeezed. Alice squeezed back with surprising strength.

We crouched in the hollow, peering through gaps in the branches as the thrashing of wings drew nearer. I pressed close to Laphaniel, wrapping an arm around Alice to hold her against me.

Together we stayed huddled, watching three winged creatures alight upon the blackened tree. They screeched and cawed at finding their nest empty and ruined.

"Thieves!" one called out, the word hissing through a long, dark beak. "Which one of you greedy maggots thieved my meat?"

It stood larger than the others, and they cowered as it loomed over them. Its beak clicked close to their faces, curved and wicked. Another screech erupted as it threw back its black, avian head.

"It was not me, sister mine," squawked the smallest harpy, keeping its head low so matted hair fell over its drooping breasts. "Why would Nessa steal? Why, sister mine, when she is still so full of the boy child?"

Laphaniel moved his hand over Alice's mouth, silencing her cry.

"So, you blame me, do you?" spat the third, stretching her wings out and snapping them back with a furious cracking sound. "It was not I who stole her, you mouldering hag. She likely fell, horrible thing that she was. Good old Arla only took her fingers. Nibbled them down to nothing, she did. Oh, and so juicy they was, the only thing worth chomping on, they was. Skinny little brat she was!"

The harpies cackled, the sound carrying over to the hollow where we huddled. Alice's head rested upon my shoulder, her breathing hitched and shallow. Hopeless tears travelled in silence down her cheeks.

Laphaniel tore a strip from his shirt and wrapped it around what was left of her hand; he caught my eye and gave me a tiny shake of his head. I held Alice tighter.

"I reckon some creeper creeped along and stole her away." The harpies sniggered in the treetop. We tensed in the hollow, barely daring to breathe. "Took her away as she lay broken on the ground, sisters mine."

"Dirty, thieving creeps," one cackled. "Toss these bones and make room for more."

Branches snapped, and any withered leaves still clinging to them tumbled to the ground. The harpies flung their wings out and took to the skies with a scream of delight.

The smallest circled back, kicking the ruined nest with clawed feet. Twigs and moss and sludge slopped to the ground, along with the thud of something heavier.

Thankfully, Laphaniel had the good sense to force Alice's face away as the picked remains of her brother lay shattered amongst the dead leaves.

"I can see you creeping."

Alice's scream tore through the hollow. The largest harpy alighted just above where we hid, her strangely human neck twisting over us. She hadn't made a sound.

Instantly, Laphaniel was in front of me, shielding us. With Alice in my arms, I scrambled back. The harpy watched, amusement glinting in her black eyes.

The other two creatures landed in absolute silence, their beaks clicking a breath away from my face. Rancid breath blew hot against my cheek, turning my stomach.

"We do love rotting meat, don't we, sisters mine?"

"Tastes all the sweeter for it, it does," the smallest replied, outstretching a wing to run a talon down my face. "You are a little too fresh, little creeper."

Flame flickered at Laphaniel's fingers, wavering and small. He tried again, but nothing appeared.

The harpy lunged, a shriek of laughter bursting from her beak. Claws scraped over Laphaniel's face, forcing him down. Talons shot towards me, splaying out to clutch at the tattered clothing of Alice. I held tight, twisting the girl in my arms. Claws raked along my back, shredding the fabric of my hoodie.

Blindly, I thrust my hand out, grabbing a fistful of feathers. I yanked the smallest harpy from the air, my fingers digging into its damp body. It shrieked at me, beak clamping tight around my arm.

My hand went for its throat, fighting it off. I shoved its head to the side, the bones crunching under my fingers. It went limp, beak sagging open to release my arm.

Blood trickled over my hand, my fingers sticky with gore.

I snapped its neck. Without trying.

Outraged screams drowned everything else out. I fought the urge to throw up, bile rising in my throat.

Fire bloomed within Laphaniel's hand, real and angry. I watched in horror as he threw himself at the largest harpy, pinning her down as whatever greasy substance coated her feathers went up in flames.

"Oh, more for me, sisters mine!" squawked the last harpy, shoving off from the ground with Alice dangling from her claws. "More for Arla, sisters gone!"

"Laphaniel!"

He looked up from the still smouldering remains, wavering slightly when he stood. Alice thrashed in the harpy's grip, unbalancing the creature as it struggled to remain airborne.

It pitched sideways, slamming into a tree with a sickening crunch and a burst of red. We both ran as Alice, and the harpy plummeted to the ground, the little girl's scream swallowed up by the harpy's piercing cries.

Laphaniel snatched Alice from the air, stumbling with the momentum to crash against the ground. They rolled together, neither moving when they slammed to a stop.

The harpy struck the ground with a dry thud, bones cracking on impact. She did not get up again.

I skidded to a stop beside Laphaniel, who lay on his back, breathing heavily. Alice lay sprawled over his chest, her good hand clenched tight around the fabric of Laphaniel's hoodie, her knuckles white.

"Are you hurt?" I dropped to my knees, scanning both. "Laphaniel?"

"I sincerely hope this isn't becoming a habit," he said, panting.

"What?"

He lifted a hand and gestured to me and then Alice, who still clung to him like a limpet. "Risking my neck for human girls."

I allowed myself a small smile, relief making me lightheaded. "Thank you."

"You killed one," he said, sitting up. Pride filled his voice. "I saw you yank it from the air."

I shuddered at the memory. "I think their bones are hollow, just like a bird."

"I want to go home," Alice whimpered. "I want my mummy."

"What are we going to do?" I asked Laphaniel, noting the high spots of red on Alice's cheeks, standing bright against her pallor.

Laphaniel stood with Alice still in his arms. He spoke in a hushed whisper, so quiet I barely heard him. "We can't take her home. We don't know where she lives. Even if we did, we would never find the path back to Unseelie again."

I ran a hand over Alice's cheek, feeling it hot against my fingers. "I know. We can't take her with us. She has a fever—she needs somewhere to rest."

Laphaniel closed his eyes and sighed. "Get some firewood."

"We're camping here?" I asked, hopeful.

"For tonight," he answered, lowering Alice to the ground. He stepped beside me, pulling me close as he whispered, "I can't save her, Teya. You know that, right?"

Tears pricked at my eyes, slipping pointlessly down my face. Laphaniel wiped them away, but they kept coming.

I nodded, swallowing. "I know."

"Because of you, she will not die alone," Laphaniel said softly. "And I will do what I can to make it easier."

A sob hitched in my throat. Words failed me. I just nodded again.

"Find some firewood before it gets too dark. Look to see if you can gather any mistweed."

"What's mistweed?" I asked, swiping a hand over my face.

"A plant that grows in the shadows. Look for thin, trailing stalks bursting with tiny white flowers. It has some healing properties; it may help with her fever"

Set with a task, I took a deep breath and searched the ivy-covered ground for the mistweed, setting aside dry logs for the fire. Beneath a sprawling old tree, I spotted the plant winding its way around the trunk. White flowers adorned the deep green stalks, little buds with peaked petals that were sharp to the touch. I pulled a handful, placing it with care upon the stack of firewood I had gathered.

I built the fire, with Laphaniel igniting it. The flames licked at the wood, hot and hungry. Alice lay beside it, settling down with her head in my lap; quiet sobs shook her body. My heart twisted, aching with something I hadn't felt before. A new longing that had slowly crept over me, unbidden.

A vision of a young girl playing in the woods flashed before my eyes, the squeal of laughter so real, I turned to look. I could see the wild dark hair, the flash of violet eyes brimming with mischief.

Even though it had never been real, I missed my child, our daughter.

Holding Alice tighter, I watched while Laphaniel carefully unbound her fingers. He chewed the little flowers, smearing the white paste over the livid wounds. Alice flinched as he worked but didn't pull her hand away.

Crows settled on the branches above us, a swarm of shining black, all regarding us in silence, eyes gleaming with too much intelligence. They cocked their heads, all watching. I hated to think they were simply waiting for Alice to pass.

Laphaniel glanced up, eyes narrowing. "I never thought I would bring you here," he said, turning his head as more crows settled nearby. "I really didn't think I would take you to Luthien. I never wanted anything like this for you."

"Both our choices brought us here," I said, gently stroking Alice's hair. "It's so far removed from what we both wanted, but we're together. We're still together."

His lips quirked up in a tired smile, though the black of his eyes didn't lift. Alice coughed wetly and groaned, shifting in my arms.

"I don't feel very well," she murmured.

"I know, sweetheart," I said, "Try and get some sleep."

Laphaniel shuffled closer. "Close your eyes."

He whispered something to Alice under his breath. I couldn't make out the words, but I recognised the way they lilted, the softness behind them, the ever so gentle tug that was just too tempting to ignore. Laphaniel threaded Glamour into his voice until little Alice lay limp and heavy in my arms, her mouth parted as she snored softly.

"Will she wake up again?" The words were out of my mouth before I could stop them. I had just as good as asked Laphaniel if he had killed her.

He stared at the girl in my arms. "I don't know."

I gripped his hand. "Thank you for going back for her."

"You would have run off if I hadn't," he answered, running a hand over his eyes. He tilted his head up again to look at the crows.

"That's not why you did it."

"Perhaps not."

"Why do you keep looking at the birds?" I asked, peering into the treetops. Countless black eyes stared back. "What do they want?"

"Maybe nothing," Laphaniel began, running a finger along a piece of flint until a bead of blood bloomed at his skin. "Maybe they are messengers."

"For whom?"

He lifted his hand, not moving when one of the inky birds alighted upon it. With a quick dip of its head, it coated its beak with the droplet of blood and took to the skies. "We may have somewhere to take Alice."

CHAPTER SIXTEEN

*L*aphaniel continued to watch the skies; the crows surrounding us remained stoic in the branches, still as the night.

"What are you waiting for?" I whispered, unease prickling at my body.

"To see if the bird will come back," Laphaniel answered, not looking away from the darkening sky. "These crows belong to a Scara, an Unseelie tree spirit."

"Why would it want to help Alice?"

"It covets children," he replied, and my unease turned to dread. He noticed, and his eyes hardened. "Do you have a better idea?"

I shook my head, holding Alice tighter.

The crow returned as the last rays of silvery light drifted over the treetops. It landed at our feet, opening its beak to drop a round stone onto the ground, rune-like etchings carved into its shining surface.

"What does this mean?" I asked, turning the stone over in my hand.

"It means we follow the crows." Laphaniel scooped the still-slumbering girl into his arms.

The birds flew from the trees in a swirl of cawing black, scattering ahead of us so we had to run to keep up. I kept the stone tight in my hand, unable to think what a tree spirit could want with a child. We had no way of knowing if it were a worse fate than the harpies.

The crows stopped deep in the woods, the night sky blotted out by the thick branches of the massive trees around us. Specks flittered in the shadows, casting dancing bursts of light along the ground. The lazy flittering grew manic as the crows descended upon them, gorging themselves until there was nothing but darkness.

The Scara's dwelling nested beneath a sprawling ancient oak that stood hollow with rot and decay. More crows surrounded the creaking branches, dark beaks clicking against the eerie silence as they watched.

Skeletal leaves fell to the earth, turning to dust the moment they hit the ground. Black sap oozed from cracks in the trunk, seeping down the dying wood to congeal at the base like old blood.

It was a horrible, desolate place, and even Laphaniel gave pause as we stood before it.

"There must be somewhere else." I grabbed Laphaniel's shoulder. "We can't leave her here."

We both jumped as the door swung open, disturbing the crows above us, so they took off, screeching into the twilight sky.

"My darlings told me you were coming," sang a voice from the darkness. "Show me what you have brought me."

"Laphaniel! Don't...please." Laphaniel ignored me, shrugging me off.

"Ah, I see," the Scara said, delight ringing loud in her voice. I could do nothing but follow Laphaniel into her home, my heart sick. "Come, come in."

I blinked in the darkness, my eyes slowly adjusting to the soft candlelight struggling in the corners. The Scara waved a hand to ignite more, flaring up the waxy stubs on the table and shelves and bringing to life the dying embers of the fire.

A sheer gown of black silk hung from her lithe body, her legs bone-white beneath the gauzy fabric. Long delicate fingers reached for Laphaniel, desperate to touch the young girl he held. He stepped back, eyes wary, as she turned her sleek raven head to the side, her long black beak clicking in warning.

"She's near death," the Scara said, one black eye fixed on me. Her voice held the melody of rustling leaves and dying storms. "What will you give me for the burden you carry?"

"You want us to pay you?" I blurted, disgusted. "Maybe we don't even want you to have her."

The Scara laughed, a soft cawing that set the few crows lingering by her doorway to join in. "Better me than anything else out there."

"What is it you want?" Laphaniel demanded, keeping his back to the door.

"Seelie, aren't you, boy?" she asked, smoothing down the inky feathers on top of her head, which were longer than the others on her body, trailing down her back like hair. "I could smell you a mile off. I could use more Seelie blood. Do you think a pint would be fair price?"

Laphaniel glanced at me. "I think blood is the going rate for dying girls."

"What will you do with her?" I asked, taking in where we were to abandon Alice. Roots dangled above us, curling to pool upon the dirt-covered floor. A bed sat in one corner, low and crooked. Threadbare covers dripped over the edge, deep green moss spreading up from the fabric. Everything reeked of damp. The only window let in no light, nothing more than a slit in the rotting wood.

The Scara watched me take in her home, her head tilting, her bird eyes black and unreadable. Without turning from me, she took a long blade from a shelf and placed it beside an empty glass jar.

"If she lives," the Scara answered at last, "I need an apprentice, and I will love her until my soul aches. If she dies, I will feed her to my crows."

"We want your word you won't harm her."

She twisted her head to Laphaniel, bending it around without moving her body. "Dear boy, she will be mine. Nothing on this earth would dare to touch her. She will be beloved of mine, and all that is mine, she will control the flocks and the dying trees. She will bring death upon those who have wronged her, and it will not be swift. It will not be with mercy."

A dank home within a world of nightmares was so far beyond the childhood that anyone could have dreamt for Alice. The ache deep within me turned hollow, leaving a void I wasn't sure I could fill.

I feared what a life raised by shadows would do to a child, how quickly it would suck the innocence out of someone like Alice if any innocence remained after what the harpies had done to her.

"Place the child onto the bed, then hold out your arm," the Scara instructed Laphaniel. "Your blood will go towards paying for the healing herbs I need to save her life."

Alice didn't stir as he lowered her onto the moss-covered bed, but her breathing hitched. I just prayed we were not too late.

"Will she live?" I dared ask.

The Scara kept her attention on Laphaniel, drawing a blade without hesitation over his arm. "She will either live or die—I know no more than that."

Blood dripped into the jar in a steady flow, filling to the top before the Scara drew it away. She pressed a wad of moss to the wound, then licked her fingers clean. Laphaniel swayed when she released him, reaching for the wall to steady himself.

"Keep your hands off me," he hissed as the Scara caught his elbow before I could. Her eyes flashed, not with ire, but with mirth.

"Be mindful, Seelie boy," she sang, placing her jar of blood high upon a shelf. "Do not give more than you can afford."

"Come on, Teya," Laphaniel said, swiping the moss from his arm. The bleeding had stopped. "There's nothing more to be done here."

The Scara gestured for us to leave, her beak slightly open in what appeared to be a chilling smile. We made it to the door before Alice flung herself at Laphaniel.

Her screams were devastating, her grip relentless, suddenly realising she was being left. Tears of utter terror flooded down her face, both hands grappling at Laphaniel. I could only imagine the agony it was causing her.

The Scara waited in silence, watching. Tears of my own slipped down while I helped prise her away, her little body weighing barely anything as I forced her into the Scara's arms.

I shoved Laphaniel through the open door as the Scara dragged Alice back to the bed. I didn't look back. I didn't dare look back.

Alice's cries followed us beyond the rotting tree, the sound shredding through me so thoroughly, I knew I would never unhear them.

Laphaniel staggered ahead of me, doubling over to retch into the bushes. He pushed my hand away. "I'm dizzy from the loss of blood, Teya, that's all."

"You've given three times that amount and barely wobbled," I reminded him, sitting beside him when he sunk to the ground. "Put your head between your knees. You look like you're going to faint."

He did as I told him, which surprised me, leaning forwards to suck in long deep breaths. Then he pitched against me, eyes rolling back.

"Laphaniel?" I tapped his cheek, and his eyes flickered open. "Look at me. No, don't get up yet. Just stay there a moment." I placed a hand on his chest before he could sit up, relieved to see more colour seeping back into his face.

"The other girls used to scream like that when I left them behind," he said, voice soft. "When I left them to rot in the Seelie castle."

"Under Luthien's command," I replied, helping him sit up. His eyes were glazed, lost in some dark memory brought on by Alice.

He shrugged. "I still did it."

"Stop."

"Niven didn't scream, not right away."

I placed a finger to his lips before bringing my head to his. We sat like that for a moment, sharing breath, listening as the echoes of Alice's screams grew silent. I hoped the Scara had found a way to calm her, or that she finally slept. I wouldn't think of the alternative to the sudden quiet.

I would hope.

And keep hoping, until nothing else remained. I had little else.

The sound of snapping twigs had Laphaniel instantly alert and on his feet, the movement so swift I hadn't seen him move.

"What is it?"

He scanned the trees, listening, eyes wide. "Keep walking."

Laphaniel took my hand, leading me through the forest as quickly as we could without running. He kept looking behind him, choosing paths that twisted and turned until we doubled back on ourselves.

Something followed in the shadows, bending branches just out of sight, and as much as Laphaniel tried, we couldn't seem to lose whatever was stalking us.

We quickened our pace, me practically jogging to keep up with him, my hand locked firmly in his. He didn't run, so I knew whatever followed was too close, and that if we fled, we would be hunted down.

"Are you hurt?" he asked, stopping suddenly to run his hands over my body. "Are you bleeding from any wounds you haven't told me about?"

"What? No," I said, startled by the panic in his eyes. "Could it be the blood on your arm?"

Laphaniel ran a hand over me, lifting my sleeves to check for himself. "They're not scenting me; I don't know how they're tracking you if you're not bleeding."

"Oh." Realisation hit. "I am, just not from any injury."

Laphaniel scrubbed a frantic hand through his hair. "They think you're in heat."

"Who?"

"A herd of satyrs." He grabbed me by the shoulders, his eyes blazing. "I need you to run."

"They're going to chase me," I began, panic threatening to swallow me whole.

"I'll stop them."

"You can't, no!" My voice hitched. "I'm not leaving you."

"Yes, you are," he snapped. "As fast as you can, head north."

My eyes darted to the thick woods looming around us. "I don't know which way north is."

"Keep going through those trees, stay on the path…"

"I can't see the path without you!"

He gave a strangled sound, and instinctively I reached for him, shocked when he shoved me away, forcing me to stumble.

"Go!"

Whatever was out there, I wanted to face it together. Leaving him behind was incomprehensible.

Laphaniel drew me close for one quick embrace. "I will find you, I promise."

I ran.

Even though I didn't know what I was running from or running towards. Even though I had run from faeries before and knew it was always futile, that no matter how fast I ran, they were faster.

Always.

My breath became agony in my chest. My gasps fogged before me as I sprinted through the forest, tripping over low branches and jagged rocks that jutted up from the ivy strewn ground. I had no idea what direction I ran in—I simply ran.

Sprawling natural bridges twisted overhead, and I tried to get to them, clambering over the thick tree trunks. The lower branches snapped with my weight, the stronger ones too high for me to reach.

Laphaniel would have leapt up with ease.

So, I ran and ran until I lost all sense of where I was. No light trickled down, the woods lit only by dancing lights skimming over the ground.

It didn't matter how quickly I fled, I could still hear the heavy pounding of feet close behind, hunting me down. With a cry of despair, I sagged to my knees as they finally surrounded me.

A group of massive beasts emerged from the shadows, curved horns stretching out along their heads, cutting through the mist coiling around us. Yellow goat-like eyes fixed on me, wide nostrils flaring out puffs of breath into the cold air. I cringed in the dirt as one stepped closer, hooves gouging out rivets as it stomped.

Pain exploded in my head when it shoved me back with a heavy paw, my skull smacking against rock. The world blurred around me, and for a moment I thought I might black out and it would all be over.

I wanted it to be over.

A paw grappled at my hair, coiling around to drag me back to the others. I kicked and lashed out. I screamed, all for nothing.

I was thrown near Laphaniel's feet, skidding over the hard

ground. Thick hands held him down, a filthy gag shoved into his mouth, tied so tight I feared he couldn't breathe. I fought to get to him, a shout lodging in my throat as they clouted him around the face.

A cloven hoof came down upon his newly healed ribs, and he roared around the gag, curling into himself.

I didn't move again.

The reek of rot surged over me, and I recoiled as a massive paw came out to touch my face. Grease coated its ruddy coat, twigs, and decaying leaves buried deep within the fur. Creatures moved between the coarse hair, fat squirming things that slipped down to burrow beneath my clothes. To tangle in my hair. To writhe on my skin.

Tears ran down my face, my breath catching in my throat. A thick tongue darted from between black lips and licked them away.

I turned my head away from Laphaniel, who still fought against the beasts holding him down. I turned away.

Clumsy paws petted over my jeans, rummaging beneath my hoodie then my top. My bra-strap pinged against my shoulder, snapping. It inched lower, its hot breath puffing over my face.

Then stopped.

A sudden, guttural rasp spilled from its mouth. An arrow jutted from its eye socket, causing it to jerk once before toppling onto me.

I couldn't breathe, couldn't see. Couldn't move.

Someone dragged the weight from me, and Laphaniel was there, on his knees, hands coming around me to haul me close. "Say something, speak to me."

I blinked and met his eyes. "I'm really cold." My voice sounded like it belonged to someone else.

I shifted my gaze to the other bodies surrounding us. Arrows stuck out from all their heads. Their yellow eyes remained open.

"I ran as fast as I could," I said, noticing the armour-clad knights surrounding us.

"I know," Laphaniel answered, his voice unsteady. "I know you did."

A blanket was draped over my shoulders, soft and warm. Laphaniel made to lift me into his arms, but hissed in pain as he bent low, one hand going to his ribs.

Another set of hands lifted me up, quick and rough, shoving me into a waiting carriage before I could draw breath. I cringed at his touch, brief as it was. Laphaniel's low snarl echoed off the brittle trees.

Soft black velvet surrounded us, the seats covered in thick furs. Candles swung from bronze cages above, the glittering light illuminating the moody decadence. The luxury unsettled me. Rattled me.

Anger began to seep through the growing numbness, I clung to it like a life raft.

"I couldn't get to you. I was so close, but I couldn't get to you." Laphaniel lifted a hand to tuck my hair behind my ear, and for the first time, I sensed him hesitate before he touched me.

"Don't," I snapped, "Don't treat me like I'm broken."

"I wasn't—"

"I'm not broken."

"I know, Teya"

Someone rapped on the carriage window, startling both of us. I turned to meet the deep hazel eyes of what I assumed to be an Unseelie knight, the eternal twilight caught the black of his armour, making it gleam like old oil. Laphaniel tightened his hold on me.

"Ready to go?" asked the knight.

"Yes," Laphaniel replied, the word a soft snarl.

"You are fortunate we found you when we did. If we were not expecting your arrival, then I doubt there would have been anything left to save." He flicked his eyes to me again, lingering on my torn clothes. "Nothing much, anyway."

I cringed at his implication before realising what he had just let slip. "My sister knew we were here?"

A slow, cruel smile spread over his lips, his eyes dancing. "We knew the moment you crossed the river."

"She waited until now to send help?" I asked, searching the knight's face for any hint of remorse, mercy, or kindness. I found none.

"Does that surprise you?"

My body and soul hurt. "No."

He turned his dark eyes onto Laphaniel, the coldness within them, turning to something with more malice. "Welcome to the Unseelie court."

He moved away and called to someone up ahead, then there was the sound of snapping reins, and the carriage lurched forwards. Laphaniel remained tense even as he drew me back into him.

"At least Alice wasn't with us," I said, unable to wipe the greasy feeling from my hands. It covered my clothes. Everything. "If they had caught her…"

"But they didn't," Laphaniel cut in.

"Does this feel like a huge mistake to you?" I asked, jolting in the seat. The carriage thundered through the woods, banked either side by knights with cloaks of raven feathers that snapped behind them like wings.

"If it is, then neither of us will leave these lands alive."

CHAPTER SEVENTEEN

ranches rattled against the carriage as we rode on and on, thin boughs dragging along the glass like spindly limbs. I jumped the first time I heard the scraping of wood, and the second and third. By the time we drew to a stop, my nerves were on fire.

The carriage doors opened upon a wide courtyard, the stone walls utterly black and so smooth they reflected everything like dark mirrors. Bonfires smouldered in the centre, the embers barely flickering. Ash swept over the ground, dragged up into the air to eddy around us.

"Traitors," one of the mounted knights pointed out as he passed by. "Scum."

He spat on the ground, giving his horse a sharp kick to move it on. I looked away from the bonfires, away from the stakes I could see through the thick smoke.

"You would look good tied up there, pretty boy," smirked another knight. "Though we have wagers on who will skin you first."

Laphaniel bared his teeth, a snarl rumbling its way up his throat. The knight took a step closer, stopping a breath away from Laphaniel's face.

I grabbed Laphaniel's elbow in warning as his fist curled at his side. "Don't."

The knight turned on his heel, not giving us a backwards glance.

I held a hand to Laphaniel's chest, feeling the anger and fear and hate bubbling just below the surface. "You can't fight them all."

He didn't look at me, his heart a wild thump against my palm. "I know, Teya."

I kept my hand on his arm, the muscles beneath my fingers tense. Together we stepped through the thick smoke smothering the courtyard to behold the towering castle of the Unseelie.

It stood black and sprawling. The stone was the same gleaming ebony that seemed to suck in the eerie twilight, so it glowed from within. Countless towers loomed tall and twisted, each turret piercing the skies far, far above us. Bridges connected them all and swayed in the breeze.

It was so vast I could see nothing of the land beyond it.

"The castle is built within a labyrinth," Laphaniel said, looking like he was facing the gates of the underworld. "Stories say that even the servants get lost at times and are never seen again."

We stopped in front of an enormous door with vines of curling silver, which trailed up over the archway to loop around the handles. "Perhaps they escaped?"

Laphaniel shook his head, giving a glance to the burning pyres. "No one escapes this place."

How could I forget that the Unseelie butchered the Seelie king, tore him up, and sent him back in pieces to his queen?

As damned as the Seelie castle was, it held nothing of the unfettered cruelty practically screaming from the obsidian stone of the Unseelie.

"This way."

I swirled around at the voice, the sound coming from all around us and from nowhere all at the same time. A doorman bowed to me as I turned back, standing where, just a moment before, there had been no one. Its grey hooded cloak pooled to the floor, dissolving into mist where it touched the flagstones.

"Follow me."

It had no face that I could see. No mouth, no eyes, nothing. Only an empty void where its face should have been. It bowed again, sweeping an arm of shadow out to us. The door opened without a sound, revealing a long and dark hallway. The walls dripped in shadow, coiling down from the carved, vaulted ceiling to follow us as we walked.

The doorman waited ahead, the strange mist gathering around it while it floated a few inches above the black marble. There wasn't a sound as the door closed behind us.

Fat candles burned away in sconces along the walls, licking over the burnished silver holdings to cast strange shadows. Black upon inky black, the walls moved with the eerie light, revealing shadows that looked like trees, like bears. Like monsters. They appeared out of the corner of my eye, turning to nothing but ebony stone when I looked directly at them.

Laphaniel held my wrist, keeping me close to him. I could feel his pulse race. My own heart hammered within my chest.

"Through here."

The doorman didn't materialise again, settling instead to linger as mist and whispers, sending chills down my spine as it traced ghostly hands over my shoulders. Laughter sighed over my neck; teeth grazed my skin.

Another set of doors opened, the wood carved to resemble a gaping maw, shards of silver dangled from above like fangs. Red stained the tips, ruddy and old. The hallway opened wider; the ceiling above domed with glass. Light pierced down onto the black marble floor and bounded off the mirrors lining the walls.

Antlers hung from corded ropes; candles balanced on each tip to drip wax upon the floor. A few still had the skulls attached, more candles glowing from the empty eye sockets. The flames did not show within the mirrors.

Our reflections, however, bounced back infinitely. I looked once, twice, noting that my reflection didn't always look back at me. I looked again to see it grinning madly, but I wasn't smiling.

One panel of glass held little glowing orbs that skipped between the mirrors like trapped fireflies.

"What are they?" I asked, but I had seen similar lights before.

There was a cold breath at my neck. "Souls."

I flinched at the sound.

"Beautiful, are they not?"

Beside me, Laphaniel made a conscious effort not to look at the mirrors, keeping his gaze straight ahead. I took his hand as we reached the far end of the room.

Two knights flanked the doors at the end of the mirrored hallway. They stood utterly still, yet their cloaks billowed around them like black wings. They didn't look at us, but their reflections never took their eyes off Laphaniel's.

Twisted smiles opened to reveal pointed teeth. Clawed hands reached out to grab at Laphaniel's mirror image and dragged him down. Snapping jaws tore at his throat, splattering blood across the glass.

The knights still didn't acknowledge us when they pushed open the doors.

I dragged Laphaniel past them as he stood frozen, forcing him into the throne room where a sudden hush descended. All eyes snapped to us.

It was nothing like the lazy cruelty of Luthien's court. A savageness overfilled the cavernous room, rumbles of snarls echoing from the stone walls. Eyes flashed in the shadows— creatures scuttled within the darkness, quick and un-clothed.

The Seelie Court, at least, held onto veiled civility, the cruelty hidden behind lovely smiles and tempting promises. There was a mask of elegance, a gilded wickedness. Everything shone and sparkled and gleamed and sang. Though underneath, it was all rotten.

The Unseelie Court did not obscure their nature, there was no pretence. It burned raw and feral and savage.

The massive room itself had been carved from black stone. Distorted statues stretched to the height of the domed ceiling way above us, clawed hands outstretched to hold the dark glass ceiling.

Two thrones sat at the far end, high upon a stone dais, shining so purely, that for a moment I mistook them for glass and not silver. Long, violent shards protruded from all around them, entwining with each other in a convoluted knot of twisted metal, forging them together for all time.

My sister sat upon the left, dressed in swirls of black mist that clung to her body like a second skin. Her blue eyes stayed on me, cold as always, while a knowing smile played at the corner of her too red lips. Her black hair fell loose over her shoulders, a circlet of twisted silver rested upon her head.

Niven leant to the side, listening while the man beside her whispered in her ear. Her smile bloomed, full and wicked. Mocking laughter echoed around the room as whatever joke they were sharing trickled through the court.

The Unseelie King turned to me; ordinary brown eyes roamed over my body. His crown was larger than Niven's, the points jagged and sharp. With his bright red hair, it looked like the crown sat on top of a pool of blood. His lips lifted in a smirk. "I didn't invite you here."

I took a step forwards, keeping my chin high. "If we had waited any longer, we would be dead."

The Unseelie King leant forwards, his gaze sharp. "And what concern is that of mine?"

I dared a glance at the surrounding fey, listening as wings rustled in the quiet and claws scraped along the marble. "If Luthien takes the throne, then she will send an army here to slaughter you. You are a new king, and you will not be able to save this Court with Luthien as queen."

Every bloodthirsty face snapped to me. Around me, the shadows quivered and stretched out toward where we stood. I wondered if he could command them to tear us down.

"Is that so?" the Unseelie king drawled.

A rebellious smile threatened at my lips, but I held it back. "It's what Niven has told me."

The Unseelie King turned to my sister, and everybody in the room shrank back, waiting with a mix of fear and hunger. Niven turned her head, raising a gloved hand to lightly trace the King's cheek. Her smile had not faltered.

"It's true," she purred, relaxing back against the silver. "In time, we will bring this world to its knees, but you are not yet a match for Luthien. If my sister dies, it will end in our ruin."

The Unseelie King threaded his fingers through Niven's, while shadows coiled around his feet like lazy cats. "I could spare you a few of my knights; I am sure they would delight in tearing your rival's head from her body. I could ensure you sit upon the Seelie throne."

"At what price?" I asked, unsure what he would ask for. Unsure what I would be willing to give up.

"You're smarter than you look."

I inclined my head slightly. "This is not my first time in Faerie."

"Indeed." The Unseelie King steepled his fingers, and the shadows surrounding him trickled back to their original resting places. The stone glimmered with the tentative things, quivering beneath the candlelight, desperate to wreak havoc. "I will think about what you owe me, I am sure we can come to an arrangement that suits both Courts."

I hated not knowing the cost and wanted to push the matter further. A light touch at my arm from Laphaniel kept my silence.

"We have your aid, then?" Laphaniel asked, ignoring the sudden torrent of snarls and flash of teeth. The Unseelie King lifted a hand, and silence fell at once.

"They don't like you, do they?" the Unseelie King smiled. "I don't believe there has ever been a Seelie faerie within these walls that hasn't been ripped to pieces. This is the dawning of a new time, of new allies to a greater threat. It is enough to stir the blood, is it not?"

"You didn't answer my question."

"I will give the help you so desperately need." Shadows trembled across the floor, snaking towards the two thrones. They coiled around the Unseelie King's legs, and over his arms. They tangled in Niven's hair, lifting the ebony strands away from her face. "But first, I wish to play a game."

I dared a glance at Laphaniel. "What kind of game?"

The Unseelie King bared his teeth. "I promise it will be fun."

"For whom?" Dread curdled in my stomach, leaden, and cold. "If we win at this game of yours, do we have your word you will help us?"

"In all its entirety."

I took a step forward. "And if we lose?"

"Oh, you'll see," the Unseelie King replied, leaning back in his throne as cruel laughter seeped up from the surrounding fey. I caught Niven's smirk, the shadows looping around her arm as she lifted a goblet in salute.

"What is this game of yours?" I asked, already knowing it would be awful and bloodthirsty.

"I will choose a knight, Miss Jenkins, to fight your own. Whoever is standing last will be declared the winner."

A fight to the death. I could have begged for anything else, but it wouldn't have made a scrap of difference, I knew that.

I knew that.

"I'll fight."

"No," I breathed. "No, Laphaniel."

The Unseelie King rose to his feet, calling more and more shadows to him. They settled over his shoulders, sweeping to the floor in a constantly roving cloak. Niven stood beside him, tangling her fingers in his. The glee on her face sliced at something deep inside I had thought long healed.

With a click of his fingers, the Unseelie King summoned a scrawny, crooked creature from the masses of eager fey. It stopped and bowed at the foot of the dais, thin wings buzzing behind it like a fly. It held a sword in its hands, a long blade of shining silver that it passed into the waiting hands of its king.

"Look how eager your lover is to fight for you," the Unseelie King began. "How eager he is to die for you." He shared a terrible smile with Niven. "Again."

He sent the sword sailing through the air towards Laphaniel, who caught it with ease and swung it around in a slick and graceful arc. The blade sang, and I swore I saw Laphaniel's eyes light up.

"You're exhausted," I hissed, barely breathing. "What if you lose?

He said nothing to me but gently touched my cheek before brushing past.

Laphaniel stopped in front of the two thrones, his back straight and head up, and he should have looked out of place there…filthy and dishevelled in ripped jeans and a black hoodie, but with the sword in his hand, he looked just like a knight.

My knight.

A spark of pride ignited my body, turning to horror as his opponent walked up and stood before him.

He was immaculate in his shining black armour, cropped hair woven through with raven feathers that matched the ones on his cloak, so it looked like he had wings. His face was a cruel mask with hungry eyes.

"To the death, then!" the Unseelie King called out, his voice bouncing off the mirrored walls, stirring the watching fey into a frenzy.

The screams of the Unseelie Court had barely begun before the Raven Knight lashed out, his movements almost too quick to see, sword slicing down to the exact spot Laphaniel stood a fragment of a second before.

Laphaniel spun, ducking low to avoid decapitation, slashing out in a savage attempt to sever the knight from his ankles. Both swords met screeching, Laphaniel still low to the floor as the Raven knight sent blow upon blow down upon him.

My voice was swallowed in the cacophony of jeers and howls that rattled the walls. The rising bloodthirsty cries grew louder and louder with the crashing of metal. Glamour grew thick and heavy, swirling around the room to send the shadows and candlelight crazy. It was a riot of noise and chaos and madness, and the Unseelie drank it up as if starved for it.

Laphaniel and the Raven Knight danced around each other in a violent waltz, both covered in sweat and blood as they tore at each other. They moved with a terrifying grace, swords meeting screaming, bodies turning, ducking, slashing.

Laphaniel staggered when a blow caught him on his arm, and he spun quickly to avoid the knight's blade, bringing his own sharply down against his opponent's side. The Raven knight howled, spittle flying from his lips while Laphaniel backed away. Laphaniel spat blood, gasping.

Cold laughter seeped through the mayhem, and I looked up from the fight as the Unseelie King raised his hands. Beside him, Niven clapped as dark shapes materialised before them.

"You said, one opponent!" I called out over the chaos, watching in mute horror as massive black dogs took form from the shadows. Their teeth glittered in the manic candlelight.

"No," the King answered, keeping his hand high to keep the hounds at his feet. "I said last man standing."

"Cheating bastard!" I swore, my voice utterly swallowed by the roar of the dogs as he thrust his hand down. "Laphaniel!"

Laphaniel turned, swinging his sword upwards as one of the snarling dogs leapt at him. He impaled it to the hilt, the dog whimpering before it died. More lunged at him, ripping and tearing his clothes, biting at his arms and legs, fighting desperately to get to his neck.

The Raven knight stood back, catching his breath while the dogs did their best to take Laphaniel down.

I ran forwards, narrowly missing Laphaniel's sword when he swung and hauled one of the hounds away. It turned to mist in my hands, swamping over me in cold tendrils that wrapped around my body. They held me tight, looping like shackles until I could hardly move…barely breathe.

Three more hounds fell by Laphaniel's sword, one caught mid-air when it jumped up, splitting in two as Laphaniel dragged his blade through the air. The dog jerked, twitching across the floor, its detached left side still working for a few more seconds.

"Behind you!" I screamed, fighting desperately against my bindings. The Raven knight brought his sword down upon Laphaniel's head, catching his cheek when he moved at the very last moment. Laphaniel lifted his sword, stumbling with its weight. He snarled and slashed out at the Raven knight, using his dwindling strength for one last blow.

And missed.

I screamed with him as the knight jerked forwards, piercing Laphaniel's shoulder with the length of his blade that sent him sprawling to his knees. His sword clattered to the floor, streaked in red.

I tore at the shadows around my body, ripping them quicker than they could materialise. Shoving myself to my feet, I lunged for Laphaniel's sword and, without thought or mercy, flew forwards and struck the blade through the raven knight's chest, impaling the armour with a force I didn't know I had.

He fell to the ground, dead. A triumphant smirk remained upon his face.

I grabbed Laphaniel, hauling him up and taking his weight as he grunted against me. I faced the two thrones, dropping the sword onto the blood-soaked marble, its echo singing around the sudden silence. "Last man standing," I panted. "We win."

The Unseelie King lounged in his throne, surveying the death and blood with an amused eye. He shrugged, the shadows around us all, stilled. "Do you know what I would have done if you had lost?"

Laphaniel's blood trickled over my hands, I fought to look up at the two thrones. "No."

"I still would have helped you. It is in my best interest to do so, but it is good to know what you will do to secure your throne, Miss Jenkins."

"You just wanted someone to die." I wanted a sign that I was wrong, to see a shred of mercy…of something human still left within him.

"I did. It was beautiful."

"You hateful c—"

"Careful," the Unseelie King warned, straightening. "Don't you forget who you are talking to. Go and get him patched up before he bleeds out over my floor."

"Do we have a room, or are we to stay in your dungeons?"

"You are guests of the Unseelie," he answered, gesturing for a rake thin creature to step forwards. The creature curtsied, ragged gown rustling as she moved. The decaying leaves making up her skirts crumbled to the marble. "Ithir will show you to your quarters. Do try not to get eaten during your stay."

With a final look at Niven, I walked away. She glared back, bringing a cigarette to her lips, which the Unseelie King lit it with a wave of his fingers. She said nothing, exhaling a plume of smoke.

Ithir escorted us into another mirrored hallway, her long winding fingers clicking against the glass while we walked. She turned to me, moss slipping from her mouth as she spoke.

"Up and up the stairs," she began, deep brown eyes darting from me to Laphaniel. "The fourth door on the left is for you."

She grinned at us and backed away, licking her lips before leaving us alone.

I kept hold of Laphaniel's elbow while he stared at the space just above my head. "How are you feeling?"

"Where does this hallway lead?" he murmured, still not looking at me. "This isn't the right way. We're going the wrong way."

"We're going to our room to get you cleaned up so we can rest. Let me see your shoulder." I lifted the torn fabric, relieved to see he wasn't bleeding heavily. "This doesn't look too bad. Does it hurt much?"

"No."

"What are you looking at?"

I followed his gaze, frowning as his reflection crumpled to the floor, twitching and jerking while tiny winged creatures with needle-like teeth picked at him.

I placed a hand beneath his chin, forcing him to look at me. "Don't look in the mirrors."

"I don't want to be here." He backed away, bumping against the glass as he shrugged me off, his lovely eyes black and frightened. "I'm going back."

"Back where?"

"Home."

"It's gone, remember? It burnt down."

He shook his head. "What did you do?"

"I didn't do anything," I replied softly. My hand brushed over his cheek. "You're burning up."

"Teya? I..." His knees buckled, and he slammed hard onto the marble. I sunk to my knees beside him, catching him just before his head struck the floor.

I shouted for help.

"No..." The single word was a desperate plea. "I'll get up."

Laphaniel forced himself upright, leaning heavily against me. He sucked in a rasping breath and coughed. Blood trickled down his chin

"Something's wrong..."

"I know," I said, bringing his head down into my lap. I tried to stop my hands shaking as I held onto him. Another cough rasped from his mouth, the sound wet and pained. I shouted for help again, despite him begging me to stop. I shouted again and again and again until someone came at last.

Something came.

"I heard you," the Spider said. "I heard you."

CHAPTER EIGHTEEN

*L*aphaniel groaned beside me, shrinking back while the faerie that filled the nightmares of all other fey loomed over him.

Soft white hair trailed over thin shoulders, spilling down the four arms that protruded from them. Four long, lithe legs came off a swollen abdomen, the skin pale and sleek. Her feet were bare and clawed. A tattered gown covered the top of her body, draping over full breasts, the sleeves long enough to cover her four hands, but not enough to hide the sharp talons at the end of her slender fingers.

"I'm Charlotte," she said, turning her otherworldly face to mine. Two huge black eyes blinked down at me, framed by six smaller ones, all twinkling in the light. She smiled, revealing a row of cruel-looking teeth that were nothing compared to the razor-sharp fangs that lay neatly tucked in the side of her mouth.

"You're the spider fey," I said, sliding in front of Laphaniel.

"You have heard of me?" she asked, the words soft and strange. She stretched closer, her hands hovering just over my face. "Are you afraid?"

"Should I be?"

She thought for a moment, then turned her attention back to Laphaniel. "Perhaps."

"He's really sick, at first I thought it was the iron, but I don't know, I don't know what's wrong…" The words poured out in a rush. I couldn't help but think I had just brought death upon Laphaniel. The thought terrified me.

"You need to come with me."

"Will you hurt him?" I asked, noting the red stains on her finger-tips. Charlotte stared at me, not saying anything, slowly contemplating my question.

"Not if I can help it," she said finally, her voice haunting. "Not with any malice or intent at least."

"She is going to kill me, Teya," Laphaniel breathed, something so beyond terror on his face, I had no word for it.

I helped Laphaniel back on his feet, keeping hold of him. He sucked in a sharp breath, his knees almost buckling again. "I won't let anyone hurt you."

Charlotte dipped her head slightly, mulling over my words. With a strange smile, she ran her claws over the glass wall, so it shimmered and melted away like water. The liquid mirror lapped at our feet, the ripples sounding like shattered glass. A staircase stood within the gap left behind, the steps slippery with the glittering water.

Charlotte fixed all eight of her eyes on Laphaniel, who recoiled away from her. "Best get him downstairs before something else scents his blood."

We circled down the steps, down and down and down, deeper into the bowels of the Unseelie labyrinth. I had to pull Laphaniel down beside me, forcing him to keep walking. With every other step he let out a small moan of pain, his hand in mine, slick.

We followed Charlotte into a nightmare.

Moss spread over the stone walls, the high ceiling above us was so thick with cobweb I could see nothing beyond it. The room was dark and dank and cold.

Crumbling bookshelves lined the walls, filled up with ancient tomes all locked shut with faded clasps. More shelves hung from the walls, straining beneath the weight of countless jars, each brimming with things floating in thick yellow liquid. Fat candles burned in the gaps in the stone, dripping wax onto the stained floor.

An old bed sat in the corner; sheets splattered with dark stains. Attached to the railings were four leather straps. A collection of old surgical tools dangled from hooks, swinging slightly although there was no breeze.

"Teya..." Laphaniel was breathless, his hand trembling in mine. I took a step back with him, turning to face the way we had just come.

"Do you think you can reach the stairs before I catch you?" Charlotte said, not looking at us.

"He doesn't want to be down here."

"No one ever does," the Spider said sadly. "Now, if you would just help him onto the bed over there, I can take a look at him."

Laphaniel shook his head frantically, trying to back away. I had never seen him so helpless, and it frightened me.

I forced him to look at me. His face was ghost white, eyes utterly black. "Let her bandage you up, then we can go, I promise."

In the far corner of the room stood another bed, made with crisp white sheets and soft pillows. Very reluctantly, Laphaniel sat upon it, his arms tight around his middle. He swallowed quickly, his breaths hitching.

Charlotte brushed past me, one hand lingering on my hip, claws digging into my skin. She brought her head close and whispered in my ear. "If you want him to live, hold him down."

She caught my eye before she slipped away, and I nodded, not knowing what else I could do but listen to her and pray she wasn't planning on devouring us.

"Lie back," I said to Laphaniel, squeezing his fingers, feeling his hand hot and damp in mine.

He didn't move, his entire body tense. "Why?"

"Because your shoulder needs stitches, and it's going to hurt," I replied, not quite lying to him. "Just lie back, and it'll all be over."

In the gloom, I watched Charlotte draw up some greenish fluid into a syringe. Laphaniel followed my gaze and instantly tried to tear his hand from mine.

"What are you doing?" he snarled as I clamped my hand back on his. "Teya?"

"Charlotte is going to make you feel better," I said, swallowing a sob as he fought against me, kicking out when Charlotte approached him

"Don't!" he cried. His fingers dug into my hand to try and prise it away. "Let me go! Get off me, Teya!"

It broke me to pin him down like some sick animal, fighting against him while he bucked on the bed. His eyes shone utterly wild as he dragged his arm away, his body giving him one last surge of strength to try and escape.

I grabbed him again, hissing in pain when he sunk his teeth deep into my arm. Using my wrist as a gag, I shoved against him to keep him down. I forced his other arm out, moving my fingers so Charlotte could curl her claws around it to expose the inside of his elbow.

Laphaniel tore his hand away, raking fingers over Charlotte's skin, his face a mask of desperate panic. The Spider was quicker, slipping the needle deep into his arm. She pulled away the empty syringe with a satisfied nod.

"You're going to be okay," I said, guiding Laphaniel's head back onto the pillow as he slumped against me. He attempted to sit and failed. "I won't let anything happen to you; I promise."

"Don't leave me here," he said thickly, words slurring together. His hand slipped from mine.

"I'm not going anywhere." I pressed a kiss to his burning skin. "I'll be right here when you wake up."

"Don't..."

His eyes drifted shut, and he didn't move. If it were not for the slow rise and fall of his chest....

"This boy reeks of blood and death," Charlotte said, passing by in silence. I leapt backwards into a table, sending everything on top crashing to the floor. "Did I startle you?"

"You're very quiet," I replied, sucking in a shaking breath. I knelt on the floor to pick up the things that had scattered, scalpels, needles, and little dishes to keep things in. Charlotte reached over me, picking up an assortment of tools from the floor, holding out her clawed hands for the rest.

"I will need new ones," she sighed, dropping the handful into a bucket on the large worktable. "The needles are in the second drawer over there. They are formed of ice-glass; I made them myself."

"And the scalpel?" I dared to ask, my stomach churning as her eyes lit up.

"Do you want to watch?"

I moved, sliding closer to Laphaniel. "I won't let you hurt him."

The Spider cocked her head. "And what would you do, little one, if I chose to cut him up instead?"

Fear and fury battled inside me; my heart crashed against my ribcage, my pulse a scream in my ears. "I will find a way to burn this place to the ground with you inside it."

Her touch was cold as she ran her fingers over my face, fangs glinting behind her strange smile. "I do not doubt you, little one."

I didn't move from Laphaniel's side, watching while the Spider came closer, her talons clicking upon the floor as she approached the other side of the bed. I tensed, but she didn't lay a hand on Laphaniel.

"Lift his clothing up."

I kept her gaze for a moment, then reached for the tattered hem of Laphaniel's hoodie and lifted it gently. My hands shook as I peeled back his t-shirt, the fabric sticking to the wound oozing over his ribs.

A sob clawed its way up my throat. "You stupid…stubborn…"

Charlotte pulled back more of his shirt, revealing mottled bruising snaking all the way over his chest. Her fingers stroked down his ribs before pressing down. Laphaniel writhed under her touch, a low groan on his lips.

"Stop that!" I slapped her hand away, and she caught it with her own, hissing.

"Can you feel it?" she whispered, bringing my hand down upon Laphaniel's skin. "That fever could well be the end of him, little one. These ribs have been broken and not had the chance to heal properly. There is a wound deep inside, and it is festering. He has a mark on his arm, I am guessing from blood-giving? Yes? It is all too much. His shoulder does need cleaning and stitching before that begins to poison him too."

"I thought...I thought it was from the iron, from the car...the warehouse." I swallowed, unable to look away from the wound on Laphaniel's side. "I didn't know, he didn't tell me...we just kept on running. I didn't know it was this bad. I didn't know."

"Fey heal quickly," Charlotte began, face softening, "when they are not exhausted and hungry. When they have a safe place to rest, with clean bindings for their wounds. I can smell the faint tang of iron on this boy. He is lucky not to be dead already from his stupidity."

"We had nowhere to go." Tears rolled over my cheeks, hot and useless.

"Well, you are here now," Charlotte said, lifting Laphaniel's wrist and pressing her long fingers against his pulse. She frowned, and my heart lurched. "Ah, there it is."

I released a shuddering breath, taking Laphaniel's hand from her. "Why are you helping us?"

Charlotte moved over to her worktable, claws scraping over the stone. "You are guests in the Unseelie Court," she said, sifting through bottles. "In any other circumstances, that Seelie boy would be strapped to my other bed while I carved him up."

"We weren't invited here," I began, suddenly wishing I could swallow the words. "I mean..."

"Hush," Charlotte said, swivelling her head to me. "You think I do not know that?"

"Then why help us?"

Charlotte laughed, the sound both awful and lovely. "I think it would aggrieve your sister, would it not?"

"You don't like Niven?"

The Spider's smile widened. "Do you?"

I brought Laphaniel's hand to my lips, hating how still he was. "Is he going to be okay?"

Charlotte turned back to her potions, crushing something purple into dust with a grinder before setting it over a burner. "Let's get him through tonight, and then we will see."

It wasn't the answer I wanted.

Silently, the Spider tipped the molten purple liquid into a section of jars, corking them all before leaving them high upon a shelf to cool. She lifted another bottle into the candlelight, twisting the bottle, so the contents gleamed a wonderful rainbow of colours. She peered over her shoulder.

"Moonlight and Starshine, little one," she said. "Amongst many other things you couldn't possibly fathom. My healing elixir, it takes an age and a day to create."

"Are you going to get Laphaniel to drink that?"

"Not unless you want him to choke," Charlotte replied. "But first he needs to be cleaned up. Strip his clothing, then fetch that bowl of clean water by the stove."

I did as I was told, eager to help, eager to do anything but stand by and watch. The water was heating gently by the fire, a pile of clean cloths folded nearby. I gathered both, settling the bowl on top of the bedside table. I lifted Laphaniel's clothes, and hesitated.

"I don't want to hurt him."

"You will not cause any more damage, and those clothes need to come off before I can help him."

"Including his jeans?"

"All of it, please," Charlotte replied without looking at me. "I expect you have seen him un-clothed before?"

I eased Laphaniel's hoodie and shirt off, his body remaining unresponsive, lolling against me like a ragdoll. I tugged his boots off, then his socks, running my fingers over the arch of his foot, where I knew he was ticklish. He didn't flinch.

I ran the cloth over his face, down his neck, and over his shoulder, rinsing it out in the water. With another cloth and more clean water, I washed what I could of the wound at his side.

"What is this?" Charlotte asked, slipping in beside me. Her hand lingered over the raised scar above Laphaniel's heart. "This is an iron mark—this should have killed him."

I wrung out the cloth in my hands, turning the water a ruddy brown. "It did."

"Oh?" Her head tilted, teeth clicking as her curiosity piqued.

"It's why we are in this mess. The curse binding the Seelie Court to a mortal queen broke after he gave his life for me." I stopped, the words catching against my throat. "He didn't want to come back."

Charlotte's hand stilled, her fingers stretching out until they curled over mine, her skin soft and cold. "Even fey are not immortal, not really. Death is a certainty even for us, though we may evade it, it will always come. It does not let go easily."

"He's not the same since he came back," I said, unable to stop everything from tumbling out. "It's like he has lost something, but he doesn't know what, and the nightmares...he won't sleep, he barely eats."

"No wonder he is in such a mess," Charlotte said with a shake of her head. "But I may be able to help with the nightmares. Though now, I need to treat the sickness that has taken hold of him."

I held Laphaniel's hand out to Charlotte so she could slip a drip into the back of it, her long claws quick and agile.

Purple liquid dripped slowly from the glass bottle she suspended from above Laphaniel's bed, slipping down a glass tube into his hand. Charlotte wrapped a bandage tight around his hand.

"I do not trust him not to yank that out," she said. "Please make sure he doesn't."

I nodded, settling onto a small stool close to the bed. I tucked the blankets around Laphaniel, not letting go of his hand.

"A witch foretold he would tear this world apart," I said, hating the silence.

"And what witch was that, little one?" Charlotte answered, glancing down at Laphaniel. She stroked the matted hair away from his face with a delicate touch and frowned. "Witches have prophesied the end of days many times."

"What if Arabelle is right this time?"

Charlotte laughed, a quick cold sound that held no humour behind it. "Then there will be nothing you can do to stop it. Kingdoms have fallen by lesser fey."

"You don't know him."

She shrugged, passing me a bowl of cold, clean water. "There are not many faeries that would come this far for a human girl."

I laid a damp cloth over Laphaniel's forehead, and he shifted slightly but didn't wake. Bitter self-pity crept over me, a worthless feeling that nagged and mingled with the regret I carried. The unfairness of it all overshadowed everything until I could barely breathe.

"I should have just stayed with him when I had the chance," I said quietly, not looking up. "What if I lose him now?"

"Would you have been happy if you had stayed?" the Spider asked, claws running along the wound at Laphaniel's side.

I hesitated a fraction too long. "Yes."

"Liar."

I bristled, looking up to catch the Spider's eyes. She watched me unblinking, head tilted to the side, soft white hair trailing over her bare shoulders. Her claws remained outstretched over Laphaniel. She clicked her fangs, waiting.

"I wish it had been enough."

"We all love to wish, little one," Charlotte said softly. "And to hope."

"What do you wish for?"

"So many things," the Spider mused. "Sometimes, I wish for things of beauty, of dreams long forgotten."

Her eyes were black pits when she looked at me again. I jumped back, sloshing water over myself.

"Sometimes," she breathed, lips curling away from her fangs, "I wish I could drag the shadows from the walls and weave them into horrors unseen by this world."

I glanced at Laphaniel, remembering his stories of the Spider-witch who gorged on fey that wandered into her webs. The same Spider that watched over Laphaniel's prone body with her teeth glinting.

"I can smell your fear, little one," she said, reaching over to tuck my hair behind my ear. "Not as strong as your lover's, but you are afraid."

I pointed upwards, to the white sacks hanging in the thick webbing.

Some had bones dangling from iridescent threads. "It would be foolish not to be."

Charlotte brought another pair of hands up to cradle my face. "Why did you bring him down here, if you are so afraid?"

Tears slipped down my cheeks. "Hope."

"Even in a place such as this?"

I nodded. "Especially in a place like this."

Charlotte withdrew her hands from my face, slipping one claw into her mouth to taste the teardrop she had collected. "I mean neither of you any ill intent, little one, if knowing that is any comfort to you."

"Thank you," I said after a moment, having nothing else to say.

"Keep that cloth cold." She nodded to the bowl on the nightstand. "and the water clean."

"What are you going to do?" I asked, watching as she lay out a selection of tools on top of her worktable.

"I am—" She cut off mid-sentence with a sharp hiss. "Hush! Who dares come down here?"

I snapped my head around to face the doorway, unable to see anyone else in the low light. Slow, skittering footsteps dragged along the stone floor. A jittery, hunched creature emerged from the shadows, horned head bent low.

"It is only Nigit, Dark Widow..." spluttered the cowed, twisted thing. "The Queen sent me, mistress...else Nigit would not be down here. No, no, no, Nigit would not be down here."

With arachnid grace, Charlotte sprang against the wall, scurrying up with ease until she perched upside down from the ceiling. Her mouth opened wide, jaw clicking as she drew back her lips to reveal her fangs. She tilted backwards, hair floating around her as she twisted her neck, stopping a breath away from the petrified creature.

I cringed beside Laphaniel, silently thankful he was sleeping and wouldn't see the nightmare crawling overhead.

"I did not invite you here," she said, words lisping around her bared teeth. "I should suck you dry where you stand."

"Wait! Wait, mistress, I beg of you...don't eat Nigit, he is tough and bony, and his blood is weak. Nigit comes only at the request of his Queen."

Nigit wrung his gnarled fingers, eyes darting around the gloom until they settled on the bed. His entire stance changed instantly as he scented blood. His squat nose twitched, jagged teeth slipping down from his gums, his eyes flickered to me briefly before settling on Laphaniel. Drool slopped from his black lips.

"No!" I raised a hand, fingers curling into a fist. "If you take another step, you won't have to worry about Charlotte. I'll tear your head off myself."

Charlotte clicked her teeth. "I do not doubt it," the Spider said to me. "What does the Queen want?"

Nigit hunched lower, his tongue flicking out over his lips, leaving a slobbery mess behind. "She wishes to speak with her sister, immediately."

"No," I said. "Tell her she can wait. I'm not leaving Laphaniel. I promised I wouldn't leave him."

"The Queen demands your company."

I craned my head up to face Charlotte, but her furious eyes were still pinned on Nigit. "I promised him."

"Go, little one," she said, lifting a finger as I began to protest. "Your sister is a malicious creature—it would be best not to keep her waiting. I will keep watch here; he will not notice you are gone. I do need to tend to that wound of his, and it will not be pretty. Perhaps it is for the best you won't be here to see."

She leant down to place an icy kiss against my forehead, the points of her teeth grazing my skin.

"I'm trusting you with his life," I said, breathing in the spider's scent of dew and cobweb.

Charlotte pressed another chilling kiss upon my skin. "Yes, you are."

I turned back to Laphaniel, adjusting the covers though he hadn't moved at all. "I don't know if you can hear me, but I won't be long. I'm not leaving you, I'm not." I watched the slow rise and fall of his chest, my hand resting to feel the thump of his heartbeat. "Don't do anything stupid. I love you."

Stepping away from the bed, I glanced up at Charlotte. "If Laphaniel does stir, could you not be on the ceiling?"

Her answering laugh was strangely musical. "I may just have to keep you, little one."

"Nigit will go now too, Dark Widow." Nigit backed away, keeping his beady eyes upon the spider overhead.

Charlotte lowered herself with a strand of silk. "Oh, I think not."

I brushed past Nigit on my way out, and though my feet thudded against the floor, and I nearly threw myself back up the stairs, the noise didn't quite drown out his strangled cry. The sound followed me up, slowly gurgling into a whimper until it silenced completely.

CHAPTER NINETEEN

My hand lingered upon the wall of the dark stairs leading down to Charlotte's lair, my heart aching to ignore Niven and to just go back down and be beside Laphaniel.

Where I was wanted.

And needed.

I took a breath and held onto it, composing myself before I met with my sister. Then I took another step until I stood once again in the mirrored hallway. Splashes of dried blood flecked the glass, a smear of it over the black marble where Laphaniel had fallen. My reflection was nowhere to be seen.

"This way."

I hadn't noticed the faerie waiting for me. He gestured for me to follow with a wave of his slender fingers. Pale blue eyes observed me from a bone white face, while a little smile played out on his lips.

He bowed his head to me, tumbleweed hair crackling over his shoulders. "Let us not keep the queen waiting."

"No," I answered, following behind. "We wouldn't want to do that."

Down more winding corridors we walked, snaking through labyrinthine passageways that tapered off in countless directions. Tall windows slashed against the black stone giving me the barest glimpse of the sprawling grounds below, all lit by a fat moon and thousands of stars. I kept hold of my star, its weight a comfort in my hand, a light in the dark.

My guide led us up steps that seemed to ascend into the heavens themselves, on and on we climbed, the steps curling around in a tight narrow spiral. It was the second tower I had climbed to face Niven.

I would never forget my first.

"My Queen is waiting for you," the faerie said when at last we reached the top. He knocked upon a solid wooden door, pushing it open for me with a nasty grin. "My lady! I bring to you, your sister."

He bowed so low to the ground his nose touched the floor. I didn't wait to be invited in, pushing past the creeping faerie to step inside.

The room itself was breathtaking, stuffed full of velvet sofas and thick white furs that cascaded over every chair. The walls were carved from the same obsidian stone, all so black it looked like night itself. The black was everywhere, shining, glittering without end. It should have felt suffocating, oppressive, but like the sky, it was endless.

A window had been sculpted from the stone, opening onto a moon-drenched balcony. I could see a lake from where I stood, so perfectly still, it reflected the night like glass.

Niven sprawled over one of the sofas, the dark silken mist of her gown dripping onto the plush rug beside her. She bared her teeth as I came in, the smile feral. Tilting her head back, she puffed out a bluish circle of smoke as she finished her cigarette.

"You wanted to see me?" I said, not returning her smile. "Apparently, it could not wait."

She didn't move from her position, drawing another lungful of sweet smoke into her mouth. "If you want our help, there are a few conditions you need to agree to first."

I sighed, sinking into the sofa opposite her. "Can we make this quick? I really was enjoying Charlotte's company."

Niven sat up then, swinging her long legs forwards and reaching for a crystal jug on the marbled table in front of us. She poured a generous amount of amber liquid into two glasses. Niven took a sip, the blue of her eyes like ice.

"Has she eaten your lover yet?"

I refused to bite. "Charlotte seems lovely. She has promised to take care of Laphaniel, and I believe she won't harm him. Your messenger didn't fare so well, though."

Niven lifted an eyebrow. "How is dear Laphaniel?"

I took a sip of my drink, savouring the warmth it left behind. I didn't want to play Niven's games. "Do you really care?"

"No."

"I thought not," I answered, leaning back into the plush cushions, resenting the comfort that my sister had, the warmth and security. I wondered if she even knew what it was like to be afraid, if she remembered the feeling at all. I wore fear like a second skin.

"Phabian was impressed that he won," Niven said, draining her glass before refilling it. "Especially given the state he was in."

"Laphaniel is lying sedated underground while Charlotte stitches him back together." I took another drink to soothe the ache in my throat.

"The Spider doesn't much care for me," Niven said, running a hand through the air to fill the room with a phantom breeze that lifted the scent of the jasmine winding over the balcony.

"I wonder why?"

Niven just flashed a grin, the candles flickering around her with the wind she had stirred up, the shadows waiting in the corners of the room wavered, waiting like leashed dogs.

"How did you end up here, Niven?" I asked. "Why, after everything, did you still end up in Faerie?"

"You don't approve?" Niven barely moved, barely raised her voice, but the shadows around her shuddered, the light quivered against the wicks. "Phabian found me a few months after you broke that damned curse. Everything had changed, but I was still the same. I remembered everything that happened to me, but the world remembered differently, wrongly. You threw me back into a world without faeries, with grieving parents and photos of things I didn't remember because I

188 | L.V. RUSSELL

wasn't really a part of it. I was abandoned in a house filled with a childhood that didn't belong to me, an entire reality that didn't belong to me, and you ask me why I chose this for myself instead?"

"Why Phabian?"

"Why Laphaniel?" Niven hissed the word as if it were poison. "It's sickening."

"You left him to die in my arms," I reminded her, noting the absence of any regret or remorse on her face. There was not even a trace of guilt. "I didn't know what happened after the curse was broken. I'm sorry."

The shadows around Niven calmed. "I didn't ask for your pity."

"I don't pity you, Niven."

She brought her glass up to her painted mouth, amusements alight in her eyes. "Do you hate me, then?"

"I don't know anymore," I answered, draining the last of my drink, resisting the urge to pour another. "I think you deserve to be hated."

"You've changed."

I played with my glass, running a finger over the rim until it sang for me. "You haven't."

"Faerie seems to suit you."

I blinked, glancing up as a ghost of a smile appeared at her lips, making her look so achingly beautiful. "A compliment?"

"Perhaps."

"I think you were born to rule the Unseelie," I said, and she laughed, the sound like poison and wonder.

"Look at us," Niven said, tipping more liquor into her glass. "Having an almost civilised conversation, next we'll be hugging."

"And if I tried?"

"I'd snap your neck."

I didn't doubt her. Niven truly made the perfect dark queen, with her porcelain skin and midnight hair, and glare as sharp as her tongue.

I placed my empty glass back onto the table, Niven never took her eyes off me, eyes darting across the bruises on my arms and the dirt that caked my ruined clothes.

"If you knew we were here, why didn't you send help?" I asked, folding my arms back on myself, hiding the marks, crushing down the memory of heavy paws on my skin. "Did you make us wander the woods just for the fun of tormenting us?"

"Yes," Niven purred.

"I was nearly raped." I choked on the words.

Cold eyes met mine; a lazy lift of her head sent her long, long hair rippling down over her body. "But you weren't."

"I could have lost Laphaniel again. Niven, I still could."

"I don't care, Teya."

"Why?"

She paused, her shoulder lifting into a slight shrug. "I think that perhaps, I was born wrong."

"No one is born evil."

"Do you think I am evil?"

"I think only time will reveal what you really are."

She said nothing as she reached for a cigarette, holding it over the candlelight until it glowed, though I had no doubts she could ignite it with her fingers if she had wanted to. How she controlled the shadows, I had no idea...why they obeyed her, I couldn't begin to fathom. She offered me one before sucking the tip of hers when I declined.

"Shall we get on so you can run back to your lover?" Niven crossed her legs, the ebony shadows of her dress caressing her skin. "Phabian has set some terms which you must abide by if you want our assistance."

"What is it you want from us?" I asked, trying not to breathe in the cloying smoke that rose around Niven.

"You do not ask for our help again," she said, puffing out a perfect circle. "You are not welcome here."

"You have made that abundantly clear."

"We take the Northern edge of the Broken Woods as our own—that is where the new Unseelie boundaries will begin."

"I've never heard of those woods..."

"They belong to us now," Niven snapped, and I didn't bother to argue, hoping the Seelie wouldn't miss a few trees. "Any Seelie fey found upon our lands will be executed without mercy."

I blinked. "We stay on our lands, and you stay on yours."

Niven nodded, apparently satisfied.

"Is that everything?" I said, wondering why our conversation couldn't have waited until Laphaniel had healed.

"Those are our conditions, Teya. Agree to them, and Phabian will give you enough aid to destroy Luthien."

"I agree to the terms," I said, standing up to leave, eager to get far away from my sister and back to Laphaniel's side where I belonged. "Goodnight, Niven."

Her dark laugh had me stopping before I had taken a step, my heart sinking. "We can't just take your word."

With an elegant flick, she threw a piece of paper onto the table between us, and I grabbed it quickly, sliding off the ribbon, holding it together.

"A contract?"

"Legally binding." Niven smiled, tilting her head up to blow smoke into the air. "Sign it, then you can go."

"I'm not signing this until Laphaniel has read it."

Niven stood, swirls of shadows creeping past the skirts of her gown, shifting into dogs that strained at her feet. "You will, or you both leave this castle tonight, where my monsters will carve you up before Luthien does."

"I have done nothing to you," I implored her. "Nothing. Nothing I have not atoned for a thousand times over."

The dogs snarled at her feet, tails tucked low as they stuck to her side, their legs fading in and out of shadows as they fought to stay corporal. I wouldn't back away, my gaze fixed on Niven and not her hounds, though I may as well have been staring into an abyss.

Unfurling the papers in my hand, I read the neat script, not for a moment doubting Niven would throw us out if I refused to sign.

*By order of the Unseelie King and his Consort, I
hereby swear to the terms and conditions laid out to
me in return for defeating the false queen of Seelie.
In addition to the terms already stated it is noted
that further payment may be demanded in the form
of land (only that which is already shadowing the
Unseelie border) lakes (as before) and the claim of
Starlight (which ever shines brightest.)
I understand no other payments will be required of
me and that further contact with the Unseelie will
be forbidden and consequences for seeking the
attention of the King or Queen shall be high.
I have read this contract in full and fully
understand the implications of attempting any
breach of contract. However in the event of my
death this contract will with immediate effects be
declared null and void.*

There was a space left at the bottom for my signature, and I accepted the quill Niven handed me. "There's no ink."

Niven handed me a knife, her arched brows lifting as she smiled at me. It didn't surprise me that I would have to sign using my blood. Pricking my finger with the blade, I dipped the quill into the blood that swelled up. I glanced at Niven, but her expression gave nothing away. She just sat back and watched.

When I finished, I handed her the papers, unable to shake the feeling I had just handed over my soul.

"Can I go now?"

"Yes," Niven said, the dogs surrounding her feet fading back into simple shadows. "Go play nursemaid."

My hand grasped around the door handle as I made to leave, but I hesitated, turning to meet my sister's glare.

"What?"

"Did you enjoy it?" I asked. "When you slid that knife into Laphaniel's chest, did you enjoy it?"

She lifted her head, a predatory glint in her lovely eyes. "Yes."

My blood chilled at that word, at the way it slid from her lips like a caress. There was something otherworldly about Niven, almost like she was born for the shadows and had finally found her way home.

If Arabelle had foreseen Laphaniel tearing the world to pieces, I couldn't help but wonder what Niven could do to it if given the chance.

I let the door close behind me before I ran, finding my way through the twisting corridors to the winding steps that led back down to Charlotte's lair. My feet skidded on the steps, and I slipped, my arm yanking back as I grabbed at the stone to stop myself from plunging to the bottom. I took a breath and got up, knowing it would help no one if I ended up with a broken neck.

"You said he wouldn't wake up," I snapped, causing Charlotte to lift her head towards me, breaking off whatever she was whispering to Laphaniel.

"I did not say he wouldn't wake, I said he would not miss you," she replied, rising from the bed, taking a wooden bowl away with her. There was a sourness to the room that mingled with the damp. It hadn't been there when I left.

"Is he okay?" I ran closer, avoiding the red stain upon the stone, the only visible remains of Nigit. I took Laphaniel's hand, squeezing his fingers. "Are you okay?"

A neat row of stitches glistened against his pale shoulder, thick bandages snaked around his middle, as if holding him together. I brushed my hand over his face, and his eyes flickered open, glassy and unfocused. He blinked and reached for the drip in his hand, giving it a sharp tug before I caught him.

"No," I said softly. "Leave that. Do you know where you are?"

Laphaniel continued to look through me, but he shook his head slowly, his eyes closing again as I sat by, helpless.

"I managed to cut out the bad flesh," Charlotte began as my head started to swim. "But the infection has got into the blood."

I sat beside him, taking a cloth to wipe over his mouth. "What can I do?"

"Stay by him, talk to him."

I wound my fingers through Laphaniel's and held tight, resting my head gently against his heart, desperately needing to hear it sing to me.

"Am I going to lose him?" Fear coursed through me like poison. I couldn't let him die down in the dark...not so close to everything he feared.

Charlotte reached for me, and I allowed her to fold me against her side. I could smell the cobwebs on her.

"Not yet, little one," she breathed, three of her hands running over my back, while the fourth brushed against my face.

Charlotte withdrew slowly, leaving me to curl back beside Laphaniel. He stirred, pushing away from me. The sheets beneath him were damp.

"You left," he mumbled, beads of sweat trickled down his face.

"Shh, I'm right here." I shifted onto the stool to give him more room. "I'm not going anywhere."

"You left," he repeated. "You were in the water."

"I'm here, sweetheart."

"No...I found you in...in the water." His words came out thick and clumsy. "Face down."

I wrung out the cloth and placed it over his forehead. High spots of colour stained his pale cheeks.

"Laphaniel..."

"You were in the lake." He spoke over me, I didn't even know if he was hearing me. "Your lips were blue...you had...you had pond weed around your... around your neck...and in your mouth."

"I'm right here," I said, my voice hitching. I swallowed, my throat aching. "It's a bad dream, that's all."

He shook his head. "You don't talk when I'm dreaming. You just stay dead."

"You saved me," I breathed. "You weren't too late. You saved me, Laphaniel."

"No." He smacked my hand away. "You're dead...I saw you, I pulled you out. Your eyes were open." He broke on a sob. "I lost you."

I picked the cloth back up, laying it against his neck as a soft moan escaped his mouth, my other hand smoothing back his hair, my lips at his ear in a desperate attempt to drag him back from his nightmares.

"You always talk in your sleep," I began, my head resting against his. "And this is, all this is, a horrible fever dream."

"Do you know where Nefina is?"

I took a deep breath at the sudden change of subject. "She's with Oonagh, Sweetheart."

"Did you know she hates me?"

I had seen the way Nefina looked at her brother, and there was longing behind those sorrowful eyes, also resentment, and yes, hurt. Not hate.

"I tried..." he mumbled slowly. "I did...I just didn't know how to look after her...I tried. I didn't mean for it...for it to end up like it did."

"I know," I replied, placing a finger to his lips. "Shush, try to be quiet now. You're not making much sense."

"I want Teya," he murmured, twisting against the covers. "Please."

"I'm here, close your eyes."

"The Spider came," he whispered, fingers curling around my wrist. "She came out of the dark and cut my legs off."

"No." I brought his hand down to his left leg as he grew more agitated. "Can you feel that?"

He shook his head again, and I had to hold him down as he made to get off the bed. I had no idea where he thought he was going if he believed he had no lower limbs.

"Can you go and get her?"

"Who?"

"Teya...she's in the lake..." His hand tightened on my wrist, not enough to hurt, he wasn't strong enough.

"Charlotte," I called, desperate. "Do something, please?"

She was at my side before I could blink, a hand running over

Laphaniel's face, before settling on his chest. He swiped her hand away.

"Your hands are cold!" he snarled. "And there's too many of them."

"I'm needing them all to deal with you, though, aren't I?"

He looked at her with faraway eyes, all traces of fear ebbed away by whatever she was drip-feeding him. "You smell like rain and blood."

"And you of sweat and vomit. The blood you can smell is your own. Now I'm going to give you something to help you sleep."

"No."

"Yes, because you're upsetting everyone," Charlotte answered, drawing up a greenish liquid from a vial with her clawed hands. "Hush now."

I rested my head against the bed as Laphaniel drifted into an uneasy sleep, tensing slightly when Charlotte curled a hand over my shoulder. The chill of her fingers bit through the fabric of my clothes.

"May I take a look at you?"

I didn't let go of Laphaniel. "I'm fine."

"No, you are not," she said, her hold on me tightening as she coaxed me away. "Just look at what trying to be strong for too long does to someone."

The Spider stood and waited, one hand outstretched to me. I stood reluctantly, laying Laphaniel's hand down upon his chest. For a moment, I just watched him breathing.

"You will be two feet away from his bed, little one," Charlotte began, "I can hear his heartbeat from the far end of this room, likely further if I needed to. Let him sleep."

"I really am fine," I said but didn't argue further.

The spider had me sit beside her desk, she pulled up the sleeves of my hoodie before I could stop her. "Do you want to talk about the bruises on your arms?"

I really didn't.

"There are fingerprints on your skin." She inclined her head to Laphaniel, eyes flashing. "They do not belong to him."

Not a question. I looked away.

"Who gave you these?"

"It doesn't matter," I snapped, moving my hands to cover myself as the memory of filthy paws forced its way back into my head. "It's nothing. They were all killed by the Unseelie knights before they could…they ripped my clothes, that's all."

"Those marks on you say otherwise," Charlotte said, tilting her head. "As do your eyes."

"I don't want to talk about it," I said firmly, struggling with the unwanted memories, the feeling of having no control of what was happening, the look in Laphaniel's eyes while they made him watch. "It's done now, I'll file it away with the other awful things that I've been through."

She gestured to the mark on my arm, where Laphaniel had bitten me, the skin around it already bruised. "Let me at least bind that up; the last thing we need is for it to get infected."

I nodded and outstretched my arm for her quick fingers.

"You have seen more horrors than your young years deserve," Charlotte said, applying a cold salve to the bite before wrapping it.

"And yet here I am."

With a sigh, Charlotte turned to her desk, moving stacks of yellowing pages to make way for a teapot. She stirred in a handful of herbs and placed the pot onto a flame, waiting for it to boil.

"This is a dangerous game you are both playing. Phabian is a twisted little boy who likes to break things. He will try to break you too."

I took the cup she offered me, the honey Charlotte slipped in only just covered the bitterness.

"I'm not stupid enough to trust him, only desperate enough to accept his help. We have nowhere else to go."

Charlotte brought her cup to her lips, her other two hands busy grinding up dried organs for her little jars. "I fear for you, little one."

"Why? You don't even know me. You don't know Laphaniel."

The monster that all other monsters feared smiled at me, baring teeth. "I have always been fond of dreamers. Of those who cling to hope, even in hopeless places."

I warmed my hands against the cup. "Thank you for not eating us."

"It is nice to have company," Charlotte said, dropping tiny mice eyes into a bubbling liquid. "I seldom receive company that I am not to tear apart."

"Do you enjoy it?"

She didn't look up. "Oh, I do. Very much so."

I finished my drink, wishing I hadn't asked.

"Would you label those jars for me?" Charlotte gestured to the vials she was slowly filling. "Keep your hands busy. It will do no good to stand over his bed and worry."

I did as I was told, picking up a quill from a stack on her table. I wrote out the tags while Charlotte worked, only speaking up to question what the vials contained, not wanting to ask what she used them for and if she was giving any to Laphaniel.

As the night passed, Charlotte showed me how to set things over the flame to bubble just right, which herbs to add, and how much, what would heal, and what would poison. I helped her pickle tiny-winged creatures I had no name for, and when I plucked up the courage to ask what she used them for, she just smiled and wouldn't tell. I didn't dare ask again.

Charlotte held up a bottle of silver liquid to the candlelight and frowned. "What does this smell like to you?"

She placed the vial under my nose as I breathed in, my head suddenly spinning as the scent filled my nose. "What is that? It smells sharp and really cold, like snow, but there's something else there, like burning wood and lavender."

"I thought so," Charlotte sighed, tossing the bottle away. "Too much Wintersbreath. In small enough doses, it is a wonderful healing herb, a powerful sedative. Though too much will bring death almost instantly."

"Were you going to give that to Laphaniel?"

"That's why I checked it first. Pass me the other bottle." She took the little vial and lifted it to her nose, nodding. "Yes, much better."

My fingers twitched to knock the vial from her hands, instinct not quite willing to allow the Spider to feed her poisons to Laphaniel. Charlotte noticed, and her eyes narrowed.

"It is hard, is it not?" she began, tipping the vial into the bottle above Laphaniel's bed. "To have him here, with me?"

"Better down here with you," I answered honestly, watching Laphaniel closely as he shuddered, then sighed and went still. "Than anywhere near Niven."

Charlotte continued to fuss over Laphaniel, checking the dressings on his side, the neat row of stitches on his shoulder, her claws lightly following the raised scar over his heart. Her lip curled.

"She did this?"

"She did."

A soft snarl hissed through her teeth. "You are very unlike your sister."

"Thank you."

Charlotte looked up from Laphaniel, her clever fingers changing the bloodied bandages on his shoulder without glancing back down. "I trust you two are being sensible?"

Heat bloomed at my cheeks at the implication. "We've been pretty careful."

She rolled her eyes at me, and I remembered back to the few times we had been careless...stupid. Too lost within a moment to think about anything but each other.

"That is not good enough," Charlotte said, shaking her head. "Female fey ovulate maybe once a year if they are fortunate, for many decades can pass by. To counter that, males are incredibly fertile, to increase the chance of conceiving on the rare occasion a female is ovulating." She paused with a sigh. "It is only due to luck that you are not carrying his child."

"Oh."

"Have you any idea how dangerous it would be to have a child at this point in time?" Charlotte continued, anger chilling her voice. "If gods forbid, you had a daughter. What Luthien would do to another heir to her throne?"

I couldn't bear to think what she would do, knowing how she hunted us, wanted me dead…to put all that pain and fear onto a child was unthinkable. A sick feeling settled deep in my stomach.

Charlotte rummaged high upon her shelves, passing me a vial of a rose-coloured liquid. "Take this every nightfall. Do not forget."

"I won't," I said, tucking the bottle into my pocket, wondering if there was anything at all she did not have a potion for. "What do I do now?"

"Sit and wait for him to come back to you," Charlotte answered gently, tidying away the bottles and jars I had helped her fill, extinguishing the burners with her fingertips.

"And if he doesn't?" The words pushed past my mouth, a question I didn't want to know the answer to. I didn't want to know the probability of losing him, if there was a chance that the time we had together was all there ever would be.

Charlotte said nothing, unable to give me the comfort I was seeking, but she did hand me the bowl of cold water and a fresh cloth, if only to give my hands something to do.

CHAPTER TWENTY

*L*aphaniel woke four days later.

He had barely moved for the days and nights I watched over him, his fever burning so high that even Charlotte's calm demeanour had faltered. I had done little more than sit and wait, only moving from his side to clean myself up. Charlotte had found fresh clothing for me, a shimmering gown of silver spider-silk.

Relief coursed through me when he opened his eyes, new tears trailing down my cheeks. I grasped at his hand, squeezing it tight before bringing it to my lips.

He blinked, squinting against the candlelight. He lifted a heavy hand to rub the sleep from his eyes, missed, and hit himself in the face instead. The pale lilac of his eyes shone bright but very confused. "Where am I?"

His voice was like gravel, rough and pained, but truthfully, I had never heard anything so beautiful in my life. It took me a moment to speak around my tears. "You're safe."

"Where?" he rasped.

I didn't want to frighten him. "Underground in the Unseelie Court," I began, pouring a glass of water. "Are you thirsty?"

He nodded, pushing himself up against the pillows, accepting the glass I passed to him gratefully. He drained it in one swallow.

"What's the last thing you remember?" I asked, filling another glass. "Drink it slowly."

Laphaniel ran a hand through his hair, pushing back the sweat-soaked strands, so it stood on end. He winced.

"I remember the carriage ride here," Laphaniel began, taking a smaller sip of water. He narrowed his eyes while he thought. "Then there were big dogs... I think...I don't know."

"After that?"

He passed me the glass, sinking back into the pillows. "Nothing. I don't know how I got here."

It was a small mercy that he had no recollection of being dragged down to Charlotte's quarters.

"You collapsed upstairs, poisoned by the wound you were hiding from me." I couldn't quite keep the anger from my voice. I wanted to hug him and never let go, and throttle him at the same time. "What the hell were you thinking?"

He stared up at me, and I sighed. He wasn't awake enough for a scolding. With a clumsy hand, he gently touched the faint bruise left upon my skin, the teeth marks, barely visible.

"Did I bite you?"

"You did," I began, "Don't look so guilty, you were delirious and had no idea what you were doing."

"Have you been here all night?"

I swallowed past the lump in my throat, feeling the weight of the long days waiting for him to open his eyes, the exhaustion settling over me like physical presence. "You've been unconscious for four days."

"What?" He sat straighter, glancing around the room, and realising where he was.

"You've been really sick, Laphaniel. Charlotte saved your life..."

"Who?" His eyes widened, gaze dropping to the drip still strapped to his hand. I wasn't quick enough to stop him from wrenching it out.

Laphaniel eyed the long glass needle, watching blood bubble up from the back of his hand. His face turned ashen, eyes suddenly rolling back as he slumped against the pillows.

"Did he just pull that out?" Charlotte appeared at his bedside, glaring at the new bloodstains on her sheets.

I shook him gently, "Laphaniel?"

"He is not the first knight to faint on me, I doubt he will be the last." Charlotte tapped his cheek until he pushed her away. "They do not balk at bloodied wounds, coming to me with their insides hanging out, barely whimpering, then hit the floor when they see my needles."

I stroked the filthy hair back from his face. "How are you feeling?"

Laphaniel flicked his gaze to me for just a moment, recoiling from the Spider leaning over him. Clawed hands lifted the bandages around his ribs before prodding the neat stitches over his skin. The mottled bruising had gone, the angry wound a raised mark that stretched eight inches across his stomach.

"Any pain there?"

Laphaniel tensed, giving her a quick shake of his head. "No."

"Good," Charlotte said, trailing claws up to his shoulder, before pressing the flat of her hand against his forehead. "Your fever has gone too. You will bear scars, a constant reminder that you are not invulnerable, you foolish boy."

"Thank you," I said to her as she slipped past, and she squeezed my shoulder gently.

"You can bathe in a moment," Charlotte began. "The stitches are spider-silk and won't mind the water. Wait until your head clears, or you'll faint again."

He waited until Charlotte had disappeared into the shadows before turning to me. "Teya?"

"Yes?"

"Where the hell are my clothes?"

"They were revolting," I said with a little smile. "I really hope they've been burnt. If it makes you feel better, I was the one undressing you."

He lifted the blankets to look at the mark over his stomach, the stitching so tiny I could barely see them. "I thought it would heal on its own."

"But it didn't." My voice was firm. "You should have told me...I should have noticed. We could have stopped somewhere, anywhere. This didn't need to happen. You need to damn well talk to me."

"I know," he admitted, looking lost. "I'm sorry."

I wrapped my arms around him, pulling him close. "I love you so much, but don't think for a moment I am done telling you off."

"Please don't yell at me just yet," he murmured against my hair. "My head hurts."

I squeezed him tighter, feeling his heart thump against my chest, strong and steady. I took a breath, wrinkling my nose.

"You smell disgusting."

He pulled back, lips twitching into a gentle smile. "I feel disgusting."

"Ready for that bath?"

He took my outstretched hand, accepting my help. "Oh, yes."

Rough stone steps led into the bathing room, a circular space of carved rock with a small sunken pool in the centre. Candles filled the alcoves, the light catching the webbing above us. Fire pits crackled around the edge, smoke curling up and up through vents carved deep into the stone. There was a smell of incense mingling with the fire smoke, pungent and heavy though not unpleasant.

Laphaniel slipped into the greenish water, the steam billowing over the surface in waves of heat. I settled behind him, reaching for the washcloth on the side to run it over his bare shoulders and down his back. My toes curled at the low moan rising from his throat.

"I have missed you so much," I breathed as he ducked his head under the water, washing the blood and filth from his hair. "You were someplace so far from here, and I couldn't get to you."

"I think I dreamt of you," he said softly, closing his eyes when I soaped his hair, scrubbing the clumps of dried blood from the inky strands.

I watched the water take on a reddish tinge, making me want to take him into my arms and never let go. "You kept calling my name, but you wouldn't believe I was there. It was awful, and I didn't think I could feel any more helpless…but then you went quiet."

I swallowed, sucking down a breath before I gently tipped his head back, pouring water over his hair to wash the bubbles out. He ran a hand over his face, slicking his hair back, the violet in his eyes shining brighter than before.

Warm fingers trailed over my face, his mouth brushed against my ear, mumbling words that held a hope so wondrous I feared I had heard them wrong.

"What did you say?"

He shifted in the pool, dark water lapping up over the edge, leaning so close I could almost taste the words. "Marry me."

I blinked. "Charlotte gave you a lot of weird stuff, are you…"

"Marry me, Teya," he repeated, huffing a laugh against my cheek, bringing his warm and soapy hands up to frame my face.

I swallowed. "You're proposing to me, completely naked, in filthy bathwater?"

He grinned, wickedness dancing across his face that sent my heart leaping. I had missed that look. The smile faded, fingers coming up to brush the hair away from my eyes.

"I want you for whatever part of forever is granted to us," he said, touching his forehead to mine. "I want to belong to you in a way that nobody can take away, and I want you to be mine. Marry me tonight, I don't care where or how, I just want you."

Tears of hope and joy slipped down my face and over Laphaniel's fingers as he tried to wipe them away. I nodded against him, my answer barely a breath.

"Yes."

His answering smile was radiant. He said nothing but took a deep breath before relaxing against the side of the pool, laying his head on my legs. I threaded my fingers through his, knowing exactly how good it felt to wash off old sweat and grime.

I was content to just sit by him, listening to the lapping of the water and crackle of flames, enjoying the comforting heat surrounding me. It felt good, and I was beginning to feel sleepy when Laphaniel's head lolled back.

I caught him before he slipped further under the water, my heart a jackhammer in my chest. "Laphaniel!"

He jumped. "What?"

"Get out of the water before you drown yourself," I snapped, keeping an arm around him. "I think we need to find you something to eat, and maybe some caffeine."

"Hmm," he breathed, nipping at my ear. "I can think of something better we could do."

"I'm not getting into that water with you," I said, extending a hand to help him up, watching the droplets slide down the planes of his stomach when he stood. I gestured to a wooden stool close by. "Sit down."

He did as I told him, an eyebrow raised. I found a thick blanket and draped it around him, wrapping it tight. He let me coddle him, his head resting on my shoulder while I breathed him in, gently using the edge of the blanket to catch the cooling water from his face.

I passed him clean clothes Charlotte had left for him, watching him fumble over the buttons of his shirt.

He looked up with a scowl. "You're laughing at me."

With a smile itching at my mouth, I moved to help him. "I have never seen you clumsy before. Do you think you can manage your trousers by yourself?"

"Yes, thank you," he replied, then struggled to get the correct leg in. "No, I can't. Would you stop sniggering and help me?"

"You're putting them on backwards." I laughed, pulling the tangled clothes from his legs. "Hold on to me, that's it, left leg, your other left, my love, and right leg."

"My head feels foggy."

"That's what a coma will do to you," I said, sweeping the wet hair from his face. "Come on, I bet you're hungry."

"Starving," he replied, taking my hand as I led him out of the bathing room. I was relieved to find him already much steadier on his feet.

Charlotte was finishing putting clean sheets on the bed when we returned. She passed me a steaming cup of bitter tea and waited for Laphaniel to sit back down before giving him one.

"How are you feeling now?" Charlotte asked, creeping closer, not seeming to notice Laphaniel's unease as she leant over him.

"Better…thank you."

"He fell asleep in the bath."

Laphaniel glared at me, while Charlotte came closer still, reaching out to tilt his head back, her face barely a breath away from his.

"Charlotte," I began. "He doesn't like that."

"Hmmm," she breathed, ignoring me to press a claw to his throat. "That would be the after-effects of the Wintersbreath. It will pass. Your heart is racing, though."

"Likely because you're looming over him."

"Oh." She patted Laphaniel's cheek gently, an odd look of longing flickering over her otherworldly face. I knew it took everything he had not to flinch away from her—I really hoped she didn't try to hug him. "I'll get you something to eat."

Charlotte moved away, the silks of her gown rustling when she slid off the bed, one pair of hands reaching to fill a bowl with a thick stew that had been left to bubble for hours.

She handed Laphaniel a bowl before passing one to me, along with a large chunk of fresh bread to dip in. I finished two bowlfuls before Laphaniel had finished his, using the bread to finish every last drop I could catch.

"Let that settle, and you can have more later," Charlotte said, plucking Laphaniel's half-eaten food away. He reached for the last piece of bread, and she slapped his hand away. "No more for you."

"I'm hungry."

"Good," Charlotte hissed back. "And you can have some more when I am certain you won't just bring it all back up again."

"Laphaniel asked me to marry him," I said to Charlotte. "Tonight."

"Wait here," the Spider replied, placing a quick, cold kiss to the back of my hands before she darted off, disappearing into the shadows with barely a sound.

"Where is she going?" Laphaniel asked, looking uneasy.

"I have no idea." I shrugged, sensing his fear. "She would have eaten us by now if she was going to."

"If you say so."

Laphaniel hissed a curse as Charlotte emerged from the shadows ahead. She skittered down the wall, her claws scraping the stone. The Spider settled beside him, and he flinched.

"I'll get up," Laphaniel said, but Charlotte's quick hands grasped his arm.

"You will stay where I put you," she said sharply, another set of hands revealing a small box. "These are for you both."

She handed the box to Laphaniel, who glanced at me before taking it. I leant closer, and he flicked the clasp, revealing two rings nestled inside.

Candlelight embraced the near-white rings, catching the tiny fragments of blue and silver held within. My hand hovered over the smaller of the two, not needing to touch it to feel the soft chill it gave.

"We can't take these," Laphaniel began, meeting Charlotte's eyes as she slowly twisted her head to him. "This is dragon stone, it's priceless."

"They're yours."

For the first time, Laphaniel kept the Spider's gaze. "Why?"

"Because I have no use for them anymore," she answered. "Because this world needs more dreamers."

Charlotte closed the lid of the box, her long fingers hovering over the two rings inside for just a moment before the lid clicked shut.

"There is a creature down by the western lake," she said, folding her claws onto her lap. "The one furthest from the castle. For a small token, he may perform the ceremony. He is an ancient thing, older than some of the gods that still like to linger. He likes to play with secrets and forgotten things, with dreamers and those who cling to hope."

Charlotte stood and stretched until her bones clicked, holding out her arms to embrace me. I held her back, closing my eyes against the faint scent of cobwebs and poison that held more comfort and love than the smell of smoke and fabric conditioner ever did.

"Don't let them ruin you, little one," she said against my cheek, her claws scratching the skin on my back. "Stay close to the faerie who holds your heart, and do not give up hoping."

"You could come with us? When this is all over, you could come to the Seelie Court."

Her laugh sang past her fangs. "Oh, little one! I would torment that court for fun; I would revel in its terror and feed on its nightmares." She shook her head, claws coming up to cup my chin. "I belong to the darkness. I am darkness and fear and longing, and this is my home, right here with the shadows."

"I won't ever forget you," I said, a hollow pang echoing in my stomach.

"No, you won't."

"Is that a promise or a threat?"

Her eyes sparkled with wicked delight, her cold lips pressing softly to my cheek. "Both."

Laphaniel rose from the bed, keeping his distance from Charlotte. He looked desperate to escape the damp underground chambers and the monster within it.

"I have something for you," Charlotte said, releasing me to stand before Laphaniel in a flurry of silk, her movements so quick he bumped into her. She wrapped her arms around his neck, and he froze. She pulled away to tuck something down the front of his shirt. "To keep the bad dreams away."

Charlotte released him, and he stumbled back a step, taking my hand before backing up towards the exit. The Spider smiled, fangs glinting.

"The Wintersbreath will wear off in a few hours or so," she said, already turning back to her table. "Seek me out if you start to feel cold and sleepy. I used more than I wanted to save your life, I am a little concerned I may have poisoned you."

I whirled around. "Charlotte!"

She continued with her potions, not looking up at me. "Tiny chance, little one. I am simply being overcautious."

"I'm fine, Teya," Laphaniel said, tugging me away. "Let's go."

I gave one more glance to the Spider, then allowed Laphaniel to lead me up the steps and away.

I could feel all eight of Charlotte's eyes on our backs as we left.

CHAPTER TWENTY-ONE

*T*hick and heavy clouds bled against the night sky, hiding the stars behind a swirl of purple and black. Thunder bellowed over the trees, loud enough to shake the ground beneath us. Lightning ripped holes in the world above.

The night was alight with a cacophony of shrieking birds and the baying of unknown beasts, while the distant crash of water against rock thundered over the unearthly cries. It all added to the wild and feral dance, calling to the darkness, warning those who feared the shadows to stay away.

It was my wedding day, and the world was screaming.

We stood, soaked to the bone in front of a sprawling lake. Laphaniel wore Unseelie black, the darkness of his shirt seeming to swallow up all light. All light, save for my borrowed, shimmering gown of spun spider-silk, glowing beside him with every flash of lightning. It clung to my skin, neckline low and sweeping, the sleeves flowing down to end in points at my fingers.

Mist coiled up from the water, ripples forming where dark heads emerged from the depths. Black eyes peered from the murk, slick heads tilting sideways before vanishing without a whisper.

The imposing shadow of the Unseelie Castle loomed in the

distance, its twisting spires cutting through the storm clouds whirling above it. I could feel its presence from where we stood, a thrum of strange Glamour that set my teeth on edge. I knew Laphaniel felt it too, his Glamour wavered around him constantly, edgy and restless.

I stared down at the newly-skinned corpse of a hare lying at our feet, then to the blood coating Laphaniel's hands. It was our offering to the hooded creature standing in front of us.

Blood ran in trickles from the fresh meat, the skin glistening with the raindrops washing it clean. A gnarled hand reached forwards, the folds of a tattered cloak lifting to reveal white bone with the remnants of torn flesh still hanging from it. The hare was lifted from the ground, the sound of it forcibly torn in two echoing sorrowfully across the lake.

"Kneel."

We obeyed without question, Laphaniel taking my hand as we lowered ourselves onto the sodden earth. A rotting hand cupped my chin, tilting my head up so I could glimpse the face beneath the ruined cloak. I wish I had looked away.

Pit-like eyes met mine, soulless within a face of twisted muscle. A lipless mouth gaped open, a maw of inch long teeth jutting from pale gums that dripped with chunks of our offering.

I closed my eyes, shutting out the nightmare in front of us. How could something as wonderful as marrying Laphaniel be a thing of love and hope when it involved so much blood and darkness and fear?

It seemed to follow us everywhere, tainting everything we held dear with black and red, leaching away any good that was still within us. I had to wonder what would be left of us when it was all over.

Blood swept across my forehead, hot and wet. It trailed down the bridge of my nose to slide against my lips. I turned as Laphaniel was anointed in the same way, red streaking across his face in a primal ritual that had nothing to do with love.

The ceremony was Unseelie incarnate. I couldn't help but think that Laphaniel imagined his wedding day to be something far removed from the blood and sacrifice he was kneeling for.

I could visualise the indulgent ceremony the Seelie would have held if he had wed Luthien and became king...the enormous feasts lasting for days, the music…the utter abandonment of morals and clothing as the wine flowed like water.

A celebration, not a sacrifice.

"The rings?" the cloaked thing rasped, holding out his hand for the box.

He emptied them onto the filthy ground, scattering the remains of bone and sinew over the muddied rings, whispering under his breath. I didn't understand the words he spoke, but I felt Laphaniel tense beside me.

With a quick swoop of bony fingers, the rings were dropped into our waiting palms—the larger one nested within my hand, while Laphaniel held onto mine.

So very gently, he lifted my hand and slid the ring into place. "Wherever our lives lead us, I will always be at your side, to whatever end, Teya. I am yours, and only yours, and we are bound so tight that even death cannot pull us apart. I will love you for all time, and for whatever lies beyond that until there is nothing left."

I nodded, blinking away the tears in my eyes so they streaked through the blood, smeared over my face. I took a breath, clinging to Laphaniel's hand as I slipped his ring onto his finger. It fit so perfectly it was if it had been made for him.

"I could never have guessed," I began and paused, waiting for my voice to steady. "that when I first met you, I would end up loving you in a way I never thought was possible. My life was a thing of darkness and regret and shame…a hopeless place. You gave me hope when I had nothing, love when I believed I deserved no such thing." I smiled through my tears. "You took away my guilt and became a bright light in a very dark sky, and for that, I am yours, for every last moment of forever."

Laphaniel leant in to kiss me, meeting my mouth with a hunger that made me ache for him. I could taste the rain on his skin, cold and crisp mingling with the scent of spice and fresh soap that overpowered the taint of blood, so there was nothing but him.

We broke apart at the rasping words of the hooded creature. "The ceremony will be complete upon consummation, and what was done here upon sacred earth shall never be broken."

We both turned, but the creature had gone, disappearing into the shadows and leaving nothing behind but a pile of bones. Laphaniel scanned the tree line, letting go of my hand to push the soaked hair from his face, his eyes widening as he turned back to me.

"What are you doing?"

I grinned as the wet earth chilled my exposed skin, the raindrops sliding down my neck to my bare breasts and along my stomach. Laphaniel watched them trickle down, his breath catching, fuelling the fire that was raging up within me.

Black swallowed up the violet of his eyes, his gaze turning wholly predatory, his lips parted, a low snarl slipping from his mouth. I knew he could see me...all of me. Not just naked skin, but everything beneath, my beating heart...my soul.

Unfettered, wild Unseelie Glamour swarmed around us, feral and as dark as night. It was alluring in a way I had never experienced before...frightening, but oh so tempting.

"Consummating," I answered, my words almost lost to the wild winds. "Were you not listening?"

He swore, my name an oath against his lips before he joined me. His mouth found mine, biting down while his hands knotted in my hair, tugging my head back so he could kiss my throat. Teeth nipped the soft skin at the hollow of my neck, moving slowly down to the swell of my breast.

I dragged his shirt off, my fingers running over the raised mark on his side, before trailing lower and lower still. He gasped against my mouth. I didn't stop until there was no longer a barrier between us until there was nothing but rain-slicked skin moving together with a passion that outshone the storm that continued to rage around us.

We lay together, entwined and panting for breath, Laphaniel still atop me as he planted little kisses down my nose until he reached my mouth. I kissed him back deeply, arching my hips so I could pull him closer.

"Again?" he said, breathless.

"Unless you feel you're not up to it?" I teased, rolling my hips again, enticing a lovely moan from him.

"Not here," he said, cradling me close, his mouth at my ear, "Not in the cold, in the rain."

I stared up at him, my hands running lazy circles over his back. "Do you want to go back to the castle?"

"I wish it were anywhere but there, but I want you spread out on a bed, surrounded by furs beside a roaring fire. I want to find the wine cellars and drink them dry with you."

The rain did not ease up while we made our way back to the castle, our sodden clothes clinging to our skin. I began to shiver beneath my borrowed gown, the spider-silk stained with blood and dirt and Laphaniel's muddy handprints. Despite the rough treatment, it hadn't ripped.

I clung to Laphaniel while we raced through the gardens. Even the oppressive misery of the Unseelie labyrinth couldn't crush the joy thrumming within me. I clung to the feeling and savoured it.

We found a servant's entrance that led through the vast kitchens. Fire pits roared to life set deep within the floor, and bubbling pots overflowed into the flames, making them hiss. Giant spits roasted entire carcasses, turned by imp-like creatures with bulging eyes.

A great beast with the head of a bull shouted curses at scurrying faeries, spittle flying from blackened lips. It turned to us, hands coated with blood and flour.

"If you are not here to help," it roared, "or to be skinned and served for supper, get out of my kitchens!"

We fled through the wooden doors, ducking as the beast flung a heavy pot our way. It missed and caught something else; instead, it's squeals of pain and outrage following us up the winding stone steps.

I paused for breath, leaning against the wall. Laphaniel rested his head beside me, sniggering.

"That's the first time I've heard you laugh in too long," I said, not wanting him to stop.

"There is something oddly freeing about running with you, Teya Jenkins."

I ran a finger over my wedding band. "Am I still Teya Jenkins, then? I've never asked if you have a surname or not."

"Would you take it if I did?"

"I would, yes."

A lovely smile lifted at his lips. "Faeries don't really have a second name, not in the way you do. Royalty and Nobility usually follow an ancient name to prove legitimacy, but that ceased to be important once Sorcha cursed us. I do not know who fathered me, so I have no family name to give you." He paused for a moment, suddenly looking unsure. "Some fey use the season and place of their birth."

"Which would make yours?" I prompted.

"Winteroak."

"Was it a particular oak tree, or a forest of them?"

He gave me a sidelong glance before pushing himself away from the wall. "An oak tree, somewhere far away, by the docks in the east. I think she was waiting for my father to return."

She. His mother.

I smiled, threading my fingers through his. "Laphaniel Winteroak."

"You can have it, too, if you like it."

Oh, how I loved him.

"Teya Winteroak." The name sounded perfect upon my lips. "I think it will do nicely."

We found our room on the fourth floor with little difficulty, and without incident, which I was thankful for. I pushed open the heavy carved doors, yelping when Laphaniel swung me up into his arms to step into the room.

"I know it's not our home," he began, not letting me go. "but it is considered good luck, and we could always use a little more of that."

He settled me down onto one of the plump sofas, the dark velvet soft and luxurious. Furs dripped over the edge, with large silken floor pillows scattered over the rugs sweeping the floors.

I tilted my head, my eyes following the thick branches that ran through the walls. The stone had cracked around it, scars led down to the floor, and ivy had begun to grow in the crevasses, a glimpse of green amongst the black. The tree was nothing like the beautiful bough curving around Laphaniel's bedroom, with its changing leaves and soft blossom. Rot had set in, the black bark cracking just like the wall. It trailed above us, stagnant, unmoving, nothing but twisting petrified wood.

The enormous bed dwarfed most of the room, made entirely of the deadened ebony wood. Its four posts nearly touched the high ceiling, the points sharpened like arrow tips. Heavy black curtains oozed to the marble floor like shadows, and more furs lay heaped over the mattress, soft and white, and warm.

All the walls gleamed with the same black obsidian that dominated the castle, polished to a high shine and left bare, with no tapestries or paintings to soften it.

Laphaniel joined me upon the velvet sofa, shrugging his soaked shirt off before catching my mouth with his and kissing me deeply.

The flames blazing in the fireplace warmed my storm-chilled skin, though Laphaniel's hands were still cold as they moved over me. My stained dress rumpled further beneath his fingers. I felt the bruises on my skin as his hands wandered.

I swallowed.

He caught the tangles of my hair, forcing my head to the side to nip at my neck.

I closed my eyes, my words the barest of whispers. "Please stop."

He was off me before I could blink, anguish painted across his face. "Did I hurt you?"

I shook my head, swiping the tears from my cheeks. "I'm being stupid...nothing happened...I'm just..."

"No," Laphaniel cut in. "You were attacked, and it was awful, and you have handprints on your body." A low growl rumbled from him. "You have every right to..."

"We literally just had sex by the lake," I said, choking on the memory. "I didn't freeze up then, I didn't even think..."

"Exactly, you didn't stop and think," he said, so softly. "And now you're thinking and remembering."

"I thought..." I began, my hands trembling as I reached for him. "I thought I was okay...I..."

The rest of my words fell into a strangled whimper, bubbling from my throat with a raw sob.

Laphaniel shifted, so I was cradled against him while my body shook in hollow gasps. He said nothing as he held onto me, his hand tight against the back of my head, his body stopping me from fraying completely.

He waited for me to stop dragging air into my lungs to release the frantic hold I had on his arm before he spoke. "Do you want to talk about it?"

I shook my head, not meeting his eyes.

"Do you want to talk to someone else?" he continued gently. "You seemed friendly with the Spider." There was no judgement in his voice; only a deep need to take my pain away. "Is there anything I can do?"

I blew a rasping breath through my lips, feeling oddly cathartic after sobbing in Laphaniel's arms. My head ached, the last few sleepless nights creeping up upon me. "Can we lie together, in bed, to sleep? Just for tonight?"

Laphaniel scooped me up once more and carried me over to the bed. He lay back against the soft pillows and wrapped his arm around me, so I rested against his chest. "For as long as you need."

Outside, the wind threw the rain against the windowpane, the storm continuing to rip apart the night. I fell asleep with surprising ease, dragged under into an exhausted and thankful slumber.

Hazy, strange sunlight woke me. The new dawn spilling violet shadows through the heavy clouds. I had been wrapped in a bundle of furs with my head barely poking out, snug but a little too warm. Wriggling loose, I stretched, causing Laphaniel to shift beside me and roll over, one hand over his face as he slept on.

Reaching over, I gently picked up the wooden disk tied with a leather cord around his neck, running my thumb over the carved marks etched into it. It looked so simple, so ordinary, but watching him sleep undisturbed was a wondrous thing to see.

He was relaxed, snoring softly, his whole body no longer tense to fight off his nightmares. It was the first time since he had been dragged back that I hadn't been woken by his screaming.

"How long have you been watching me?" he said, his eyes still closed.

"Not long enough."

Laphaniel rubbed the sleep from his eyes. "For a moment, I forgot we were here."

"For a moment, I did too," I said, resting my head on his chest. "For just one fleeting moment, it was just us, curled up together a thousand miles away."

The fire burned low, the candlelight soft and still. In the distance, the sounds of shrieks and cackles spilled over into the quiet.

"About last night…"

"Don't you dare apologise, Teya," Laphaniel warned. "Pretending everything is okay, nearly killed me—learn from my mistakes."

"Maybe we should try again?"

"No," he replied, tugging one of the furs up over us both. "I'll still be here whenever you're ready."

"What if I'm never ready again?"

He traced a hand down the side of my face, his eyes fixed on mine. "I'll still be here."

Closing my eyes, I leant into him. The feeling of heavy paws and rancid breath lingered too fresh in my memory, the bruises on my skin still tender.

But memories fade,

as do bruises.

Even scars fade given time, and I had lived around my share of them.

"Laphaniel?"

"Hmm?" His sleepy rumble made me smile, but it faded at what I was going to say next.

"I signed a contract with Niven," I began. "While you were unconscious."

Laphaniel pushed himself up. "What kind of contract?"

"I signed it in blood," I continued, sitting up beside him. "I had to sign, or she threatened to throw us out, and you were too sick, you wouldn't have made it through the night. I have no idea if it was the right thing to do."

"What did it say?" His face was unreadable.

"The Unseelie want land from us, some stars as well. They are going to sever contact with us when everything is over and execute anyone who dares trespass. I think that's everything."

"We can deal with the loss of land when the time comes and will be more than happy never to deal with them again." He took my hand. "I would gladly give up every tree, every rock, and glittering star if it meant keeping you safe."

"You're not mad that I signed something I don't really understand?"

"No, I just wish I could have been there for you."

I sighed. "I think Niven planned it, so you weren't."

"I don't doubt it."

The door to our room clicked open even though we had locked it. Mist and shadow curled around the tall form of a faerie with cloven feet and arms that stretched down to the floor. Long white hair tumbled over her naked body, and her green eyes darted to all the corners of the room before settling upon us.

"I bring food," she began, her words strangely soft and lovely. "And clothing."

A tray appeared from the mist, settling without a sound upon the table. The green-eyed faerie kept her gaze upon us, head twisting like an owl.

"You are to meet with the King at noon rise," she sang. "Do not be late."

She vanished without a trace, the door shutting silently, leaving behind only the echo of her lilting voice.

"Why even bother to have locks if they can just poof inside?" I said while Laphaniel stared at the doorway.

"I hate this place," he muttered under his breath, slipping from the bed to the table of food.

"Is that fresh coffee I can smell?"

Laphaniel rolled his eyes and poured me a cup. I sat opposite him, accepting the steaming coffee gratefully.

Gleaming red apples lay piled in a bowl beside a platter of thinly sliced meat, and fat grapes, full to bursting draped beside wedges of cheese. Steam rose from a chunk of fresh bread.

My mouth watered.

"Anything I shouldn't eat?" I asked, taking a sip of my coffee and feeling it warm my very soul.

Laphaniel popped a grape into his mouth, closing his eyes before plucking a few more from the stems. He swallowed before plucking them from my reach.

"These are overflowing with honey wine," he said, sucking the juice from his fingers. "Everything else is fine."

I could smell the sweetness over the table. "Can I have one?"

"No." A lovely mischief danced in his eyes. "These are to be savoured under a moonlit summer, beneath singing boughs and whispering winds. Not here."

I could almost taste the promise, the warmth of a breeze on naked skin, drunk on love and happiness, and too much wine. "I will hold you to that summer."

"Then I promise you, when we leave this nightmare behind, when everything is as it should be, I will feed you wine-soaked fruit until you can no longer feel the world beneath you."

Oh, the thought of it. "And then what would you do?"

He tore off a chunk of bread, slathering it with jam. "Whatever you wanted me to do."

I spluttered into my coffee, and he sniggered, the sound dark and wicked and wonderful.

We finished breakfast together, the enjoyment of eating good food overshadowed by the knowledge we had to meet with the King. I could not shake the fear that it would all be futile in the end.

I could not envision an outcome where we faced Luthien and won.

CHAPTER TWENTY-TWO

*T*he throne room was quiet. No fey lingered within the shadows that dripped down the walls, no shrieks or hisses crept up from the quiet. Even the flames within the fireplace kept their peace.

The Unseelie King sat upon his throne, dressed in black shadows that roiled and shifted as he moved. A cloak of inky feathers hung from his shoulders, stirring around him, still longing for flight. He peered down at us like we were insects he longed to crush. Niven sat beside him, her midnight gown looking as if it were made of nothing but the night sky. Her haunting beauty eclipsed the ordinary face of the King.

"I do not recall permitting you to elope," the Unseelie King said, voice carrying across the empty room. Shadows scattered; the candle-light cringed within their holders.

Laphaniel tilted his head to meet the cold stare of the king. "I never asked your permission."

The darkness watching from the walls seeped to the floor in black puddles, slithering to the raised stone dais to swarm at the Unseelie King's feet. A wine glass materialised from the black, shining with blood-red wine. He drank deeply, the red staining his lips.

"I wonder what you would give to protect your new bride?" Mist circled the Unseelie King's glass, trailing over his fingers. His smile was chilling.

"Whatever it takes," Laphaniel answered.

The Unseelie King drained his wine and tossed it aside, the cup evaporating into wisps of darkness. He pulled two more from the shadows. "I thought as much."

Niven took the cup offered to her, lips already stained with wine. "Is there anything you would not do?"

Laphaniel turned to my sister. "No."

"You know I was not always like this," the Unseelie King began, gesturing to the shadows tangling around him. "I once was weak, powerless. Human. I am none of these now. I am a true king of Faerie, and my fey and the shadows tremble before me."

"Teya already has the backing of many Seelie fey," Laphaniel said.

"Only a scattering few." The Unseelie King switched his gaze to me, lip curling. "The Seelie will not accept a mortal queen."

Laphaniel took a step forward, voice rising. "They have—"

"But would they, I wonder?" the King interrupted, leaning forwards. "Or better yet, would you accept one if it were different? If it were any other girl but the one at your side, would you happily slaughter her to put Luthien upon your throne?"

"I wou—" The words caught in Laphaniel's throat, and he stopped with a hiss of pain.

A lie.

"As I thought." A strange calm settled over the shadows, they stopped moving as if waiting. "Faeries are all the same, really. Bloodthirsty and restless. I love it all."

I looked between Laphaniel and the King, unsure if I understood what was implied. "You mean for me to become like you?"

He cocked his head, feathers rippling around him. "Could you be someone like me, Teya?"

"Never in a thousand lifetimes."

A slow smile lifted the edges of his mouth. "Wait until you have lived a thousand lifetimes, and we shall see."

"Are you truly suggesting Teya becomes fey?" Laphaniel demanded. "In the same godsdamned experiment that created you?"

"Yes."

I blew out a slow breath. "Didn't turning you fey kill the previous Unseelie Queen? What foolish creature do you intend to sacrifice for me?"

Niven pointed, tendrils of mist dancing over her fingertips. I couldn't stop the quick bark of laughter that escaped my mouth.

"Have you completely lost your mind?"

"To be like me, little Queenling," the Unseelie King began, lifting the darkness from the corners, snuffing out candles as he called more and more shadows to his feet. "You will need someone willing. It is of the utmost importance that they are willing and share a connection with you. A connection of the heart will do, the soul all the better." He cast a glance at Laphaniel, a smirk upon his lips. "Without this, the essence has nothing to adhere to, it has nothing calling it home."

"We are done here." I turned, a hand at Laphaniel's elbow.

Niven's voice sounded behind me in a caress of darkness. "He doesn't have to die if you don't want him to."

"How?" Laphaniel pulled away from me, stepping up to the knotted thrones.

"We leave just enough of what makes you fey behind to keep you alive," the Unseelie King replied with a small shrug.

"No, Laphaniel." My mouth was dry, my stomach a churning mess. I longed for a glass of the too red wine but didn't dare ask. "There has to be another way. Niven is every inch an Unseelie queen, and she is still human."

"Niven is a psychopath."

My sister grinned from her throne, tipping her glass in Laphaniel's direction.

"This may be the only way we can win, Teya," Laphaniel said. "It could put you on equal footing with Luthien."

"And what will it do to you?"

"It's a risk I'm willing to take."

"You would lose your Glamour," I breathed. "Everything that makes you who you are."

"Not everything," he replied. "You are a part of who I am now. I am doing this so I do not lose you."

I closed my eyes, fingers coming up to run over the points of the star at my neck. "Laphaniel—"

"How is it done?" he asked, cutting me off.

The Unseelie King trailed a lazy hand through the shadows, stirring them up into beasts and monsters before shredding them apart. "We go down into the pools deep beneath the castle, the Spider will do the rest."

"Do what?" I dared ask.

Something dark and cruel sparked in the Unseelie King's eyes, transforming them from ordinary brown to something otherworldly.

"You will see."

The doors to the cavernous room swung open, and Charlotte swept in without a sound, the delicate folds of her gown floating around her like fog. She stopped close to the knotted thrones and curtsied low, sweeping across the floor in a graceful move that was as elegant as it was mocking.

"You have kept us waiting, witch," The Unseelie King began, and Charlotte bared her fangs at the insult. "I trust you are ready?"

I stepped in front of the Spider. "Did you know about this?"

"Does it make a difference if I did, little one?"

Betrayal, cold and swift, hit me harder than I thought it would. Charlotte did not owe me loyalty, I knew that, but it was crushing all the same.

"Did you just save Laphaniel's life so he could sacrifice himself?"

Hurt flickered across her face, gone in a flash. "I did not."

Slipping past me, the Spider outstretched one hand to Laphaniel, waiting without a word for him to take it. He hesitated before closing his fingers around hers.

"Come then," Charlotte said.

We followed down narrow corridors of perfect black, the candle-light burning from the gaps in the stone, snuffing out when the

Unseelie King passed them by. Niven ran her nails along the smooth stone, setting my teeth on edge with the noise they made.

Shadows raced after us, curling from the walls, the floor, and the dripping ceiling high above us. Swathes of black laced around my legs like cats, they flowed up over my shoulders, noosed loosely around my neck, teased my hair.

Down and down and down we went. The air grew wet and close. The obsidian walls became rough stone, with thick vines curling down the cracks to tumble to the ground in a tangle of green. Stalactites dripped from above, huge and pointed. As sharp as daggers.

More than once, I lost my footing on the slick ground, grabbing at the equally slick walls to keep from falling. Niven glided over the treacherous stone without so much as a wobble. Charlotte led Laphaniel down, her hand still in his, not letting go.

Carved doors opened to a sprawling antechamber; monstrous serpents had been etched deep into the stone, their eyes fixed with luminous blue gems. Wide smooth steps led down to countless pools of water, the steam rising from the surface to coat the air around us in a strangely scented smog. Orbs of dazzling light skipped overhead, catching the green in the silent waters. The pools were deep and bottomless and utterly still.

Stone columns rose up from the ground, more serpents winding around them, impossible wings stretched out to touch the vaulted ceiling. The skittering orbs lit up the blue gems embedded in their eyes, fracturing the light into streams of colour.

"Remember not to kill him, witch. I would rather not have to fish his corpse from my pools."

The Unseelie King's voice rang out over the cavern, echoing his malice over and over. He leant against one of the misshapen columns, arms crossed while he watched on. Niven stood beside him, her blue eyes bright.

"You will need to get into the water," Charlotte began, addressing Laphaniel. She caught his arm when he made to move. "But not quite yet."

Charlotte held up a vial for us all to see. The thick substance inside glowed faintly, sliding down the glass in gloopy streaks.

"This will turn your Glamour into something corporal," Charlotte continued. "Something I can mould with my hands and pull out."

"What will you leave behind?" I asked, unease settling over me like a cloak.

"Enough so that he lives." Charlotte lifted one of her glass needles from a pocket of silk. Laphaniel took a step back, the colour leeching from his face. "Take off your shirt and boots. You may keep your trousers on. It may be best if you sat down, angel."

Laphaniel did as he was told and sat at the edge of the pool. I sat beside him, keeping his gaze while Charlotte twisted his arm around.

"Deep breath," I whispered so only he could hear. He gave a tight smile before closing his eyes. He flinched as Charlotte slid the needle into his arm, one hand curling around the edge of the pool.

Blue light instantly glowed from his veins, rushing around his body in flashes. It raced towards his heart, spiralling around it before splaying out into countless tendrils.

A gasp slipped from his mouth, but before I could say anything, the Spider shoved him backwards into the water.

Charlotte slipped in after him, the silks of her gown swirling around her. "Stay there!" she hissed at me. "Do not get into the water until I tell you."

She gave me a sharp shove, and I stumbled back from the water's edge. With one set of hands, she gripped Laphaniel's shoulder and dragged him up, and he managed to suck in a quick mouthful of air before she forced him under again.

Bubbles slipped to the surface, the greenish waters lapping frantically over the stone as Laphaniel fought back.

Charlotte didn't allow him up.

I scrambled forwards, jolting when my arm was yanked back. My feet left the ground when I was tossed against the wall.

"Do as you are told," the Unseelie King snapped, towering over me. "You are to watch."

"As he drowns?" My words were desperate.

I lifted my head, fighting the need to crawl back to the water's edge and stop it all. From above me, I could hear Niven snicker. I couldn't look at her. I wouldn't.

Shimmering tendrils began to creep around Charlotte's claws, coiling over her wrists to dance across the deep waters. The green ripples glittered, swirling and swirling in a secluded tempest until the waters moved so frantically, it revealed Laphaniel struggling against its relentless tide.

Laphaniel thrashed, again and again, both hands curled tight over Charlotte's wrists. She held him tight, the ruined pieces of her gown beating around her.

The pool came alive with light, rushing up in a whirl of foam and magic until it reached the vaulted ceiling high above us.

I could no longer see them. Not through the storm of wild waters. My heart crashed at my breast, my lungs burning as I held my breath... I'd take another when he did...

The water dropped like rainfall, slipping back into the pool without a ripple. A sheen of glowing light covered the surface like oil, bubbling in golds and pinks and lilacs.

Laphaniel's Glamour, floating all around him.

"Get into the water, little one." Charlotte outstretched her hand, beckoning me forward. I ran to Laphaniel instead.

He clung to the edge of the pool, panting, head resting on the stone.

"Are you okay?" I demanded. "Laphaniel?"

He nodded, not looking up. With a grunt, he hauled himself from the pool, the glimmering water running off him in streams of colour.

"I am an excellent weaver, little one," Charlotte said, plucking threads of gold from the water. "But even I cannot weave Glamour once it turns back to whispers and wishes—get into the water now."

"Go on," Laphaniel said, his breathing rapid. "I'm fine."

I made to touch him, the remnants of his Glamour sparking against my fingers like static. He shivered under my touch, his clothing in tatters.

With a snarl and a rush of shadows, Niven stepped up beside us and gave me a sharp kick. I tumbled, plunging headfirst into the waiting water.

Darkness, thick and heavy, swallowed everything up. Claws scraped along my arms, my legs, over my chest, everywhere and nowhere. They left behind flashes of heat, followed by a rush of cold. Within the black, my skin glowed with dazzling threads, as the Spider wove the tangled Glamour deep into my skin.

I wanted to scream. To cry… to breathe. Anything.

But I fell instead.

Falling and falling and falling into blackness and silence. There was nothing else but darkness and unending pain that felt like it was tearing me apart.

Then nothing.

CHAPTER TWENTY-THREE

I opened my eyes to screaming. A hollow, agonised cry that charged through the air until there was nothing left but the sound of pain.

Columns of smooth white stone surrounded me, all wound tight with lush vines bursting with pink flowers. Silken panels draped over tall open windows, sweeping across a mosaic floor of swirling golden patterns. The air was crisp and cool, sweet with the scent of pine. Snow covered the mountain tops I could see from the window, standing tall and imposing over an evergreen forest.

The deep underground cavern of the Unseelie was gone. Where I was, I had no idea.

Below the window, just beyond a rolling garden, a lake stretched out as far as I could see. Waterfalls crashed down from the hills surrounding it, the rivers above tumbling over the sides with a constant roar of water.

The beauty of it all seemed so crude against the echo of screams.

A willowy faerie ran by, wings buzzing behind her. I pressed myself against the wall to avoid her colliding with me, but she took no notice. She clutched a bundle of sheets to her chest, and looking closer, I noticed they were covered in red.

The faerie stopped briefly to place a clawed hand upon a small child I had not noticed. He sat with his back to the wall, hands clamped over his ears, eyes shut tight, his mess of dark hair hanging over his face. Not a word passed between them; the passing faerie barely glanced down.

"Are you okay?" I asked the boy gently, walking towards him. I took another step, turning as a man stormed by and passed straight through me like I was a ghost.

Beside me, the boy flinched, curling up to make himself smaller.

"Altha!" A silver-haired man caught the arm of the willowy faerie, dragging her back to him. "Do I have a son?"

"A daughter, my lord…" Altha stammered, pale wings fluttering nervously behind her. "A beautiful sister for your eldest…"

"A sister for the bastard?" The silver-haired man's face burned red with fury as he reached out and dragged the young boy up by his hair. "This was suckling at his mother long before I had her. She spat him out and has left me with a girl? What use have I for a girl?"

"I don't know, my lord."

The grip on the boy's hair tightened, forcing him up onto his tiptoes, a small whimper slipped from his lips. He looked no older than five, with the tips of his ears peeking up through near-black hair. His eyes shone wide and terrified, not yet the deep purple I had come to love.

"What of my wife?" The man added, almost as an afterthought, using his free hand to brush his silver hair from his face, revealing bright blue eyes.

"Dead, my lord."

"A disappointing day," he muttered, releasing his hold with a sneer of disgust. "I will retire to my study. Do not disturb me."

The faerie bobbed a curtsy. "Yes, my lord."

The silver-haired man walked away without another word, the news of his dead wife seeming to settle over him as an inconvenience rather than a tragedy.

"Come, boy," Altha said, outstretching her long fingers. "Come, say your goodbyes."

I didn't want to see anymore. I hated the thought of wallowing through Laphaniel's memories, especially ones he had never talked about. It felt wrong, a deep intrusion that I couldn't walk away from...

I tried.

But it was like there was a thread pulling at me, and there was nothing I could do but follow it.

It led me down a wide hallway, light flooding through from the arches on either side. The room I walked into was equally as bright and airy, and it should have been filled with joy. But instead, it hung heavy with the scent of blood and death.

"Mama?"

I wanted more than anything to take him into my arms and never let go.

"Mama?" Standing on tiptoes, he pulled back the covers, revealing the painstakingly beautiful woman beneath.

She looked so serene; she could have been sleeping. Someone had brushed her hair, so it lay soft over her shoulders, shining jet black against the white of her skin. Her nightgown was clean, as were the bedsheets she lay upon, but there was a stillness to her that forced away any hopes of her waking.

I watched, unable to touch him, as he crawled beside her, his little legs struggling up against the height of the bed. Then he sobbed and sobbed and sobbed, while my heart broke for him.

"Come away now, boy," Altha coaxed, taking his arm to gently pull him away from the bed. "Come meet your new sister."

She led him to a cradle by the window and scooped up a bundle into her arms, bending low so he could peek inside.

He rubbed the tears from his eyes with the back of his hand. "I don't like her."

The servant smiled, passing the wiggling infant to him. "Your mother would have loved her as she did you, but now she has no one to love her, just like you. Perhaps you could learn to love her a little?"

He looked down at the squirming lump in his arms, lip curling. "Maybe."

There was a shift to the air, a sudden blackness that sent a wave of dizziness spiralling through my head. The thread tugging from my middle went taut then loose, slamming me into another memory with such force it took my breath away.

I blinked away the fog, just as another scream sliced through the darkness, a shrill cry filled with terror and panic.

"Laphaniel!" a voice cried out, young and frightened. "Nell, please!"

"What have you done?"

Light filtered through the dark, revealing a vast windowless library, lit only by candle stubs that hung above within dusty chandeliers, the meagre light barely illuminating the maze of bookshelves below.

"I dropped it...I can't catch them." A young girl stood frantic within a flurry of tiny lights, shattered green glass lying scattered around her feet.

"What are you doing down here?" Laphaniel demanded, grabbing her hand and giving her a shake. He looked a little older, though not much. "Why are you touching his things, Fee?"

"It was just a game! I was being careful..."

He shook her again, forcing a startled cry from her lips. "It doesn't look like it!"

Both children jumped at the sound of a door crashing open, wide eyes fixing on each other. Laphaniel dragged his sister over the glass, shoving her under a low table before scrambling in after her. He barely managed to tug the cloth down before a furious roar erupted around the dark, unloved room.

"Keep your mouth shut, understand?" Laphaniel hissed.

Nefina nodded and squeezed her brother's hand. Her lovely blue eyes widened as the cloth lifted, and Laphaniel was dragged away.

"Did you do this?" The silver-haired man snarled, dangling Laphaniel by his wrist so his toes barely scraped the floor. He didn't answer.

A crack echoed across the library, and Laphaniel's head snapped back with the force of the slap.

"Answer me, boy."

"It was an accident." Laphaniel gave a familiar smirk, red gleaming against his teeth. He grunted with the next blow, the grin fading.

"Excuse me?"

"It was an accident," Laphaniel forced out, red slipping over his chin. "Sir."

"I will beat respect into your hide, you miserable bastard," the silver-haired man snarled. "Did you do this?"

Laphaniel nodded, wincing.

"Did you do this, or did your sister?"

"I…did…"

Faeries couldn't lie. To see Laphaniel force the untruth from his lips was awful. Blood bubbled up over his mouth, he twisted against the hold on him, one hand holding his stomach. But yet, I could still see the ghost of a smirk etched upon his face.

"I should have had you drowned, boy."

The smirk bloomed, red and defiant even as he was thrown to the floor. "Run, Nefina!"

She darted, lightning-quick from her hiding place, another shout from her brother forcing her to flee.

The silver-haired man watched her go, then lifted a heavy boot and brought it down upon Laphaniel. Bones crunched.

I turned away, unable to watch, but unable to leave as Laphaniel was dealt blow after blow after blow. He curled into a ball and never uttered a sound.

The memory flickered, then slumped into a heavy blackness.

"Wake up, Nell…"

Everything continued to flicker, shifting between darkness and a too-bright light.

"Get up."

"Did he touch you?"

Darkness again.

"Please, wake up."

Light filtered slowly through the thick black, tilting…moving.

"Your hair is all sticky."

"Fee? Did he hurt you?"

"I got away," she answered, crouching over him, her little hands covered in red. "You need to get up."

"Help me up."

Nefina pulled Laphaniel to his feet; he leant heavily against one of the bookcases and heaved, a dry hacking retch that brought up nothing but spittle and blood. Nefina patted his back, standing on tiptoes to reach.

"It should have been me," Nefina said.

Laphaniel shook his head, wincing at the movement before pulling his sister into him, kissing her tenderly on top of her head.

"No, it shouldn't."

The room shifted and faded, the memory slipping into another.

I stood in a bare room with no furnishings save for a dirty mattress upon the floor and a battered wooden desk and stool. A tiny fire flickered in the grate, its flames not strong enough to push back the creeping chill.

Laphaniel sat on the stool while Nefina hovered nearby, wringing her hands as she watched him wash dry blood from his mouth. Nefina was still just a little girl, her pale hair falling below her shoulders, her eyes shining with an innocence she had still managed to cling to.

"We can't leave...Papa will kill us."

"If we stay, Fee, I will end up dead," Laphaniel said, his voice was a little deeper, a little older. "What do you think will happen to you then? You're growing up, do you know what that means?"

She shook her head, and Laphaniel sighed, raking a hand through filthy hair, revealing old bruising to his face.

"It means you won't be safe anymore. You're a pretty girl with no useful talent..."

"Well, you're just some worthless merchant's bastard!" Nefina snapped, though there was no malice behind her words, only fear.

"Better a bastard than a whore, don't you think?" he snapped back. "As soon as you are of a certain age, you will be sold off to whatever lord wants you. They will come for you, and I won't be able to stop them."

Tears trickled down Nefina's cheeks. "And you will keep me safe?"

"I will always keep you safe, Fee," he said, dousing the candle beside him. "Go get some sleep, we leave before dawn."

Nefina wrung her hands. "I don't want to be on my own."

"Stay here then, but you'll be cold."

"Do you not have another blanket?"

Laphaniel shook his head but gestured to the bed, tucking Nefina beneath a moth-eaten blanket. He waited until she fell asleep, then leant back against the wall and closed his eyes.

Brightness took me away from that cold, damp room. The chill around me warming as I found myself in a magnificent circular tent. Silk panels draped down the sides, all in rich hues of red and gold and green. Candlelight danced over the jewels twinkling from the walls, bouncing from a large, gilded chandelier that hung overhead. It had been shaped like a birdcage, filled with tiny shining birds that hopped in and out of the flames without catching alight.

"I'm hungry," Nefina said, sitting on the edge of an elegantly carved bed, nervously thumbing the tassels on the velvet throws.

"I know," Laphaniel answered, pacing the plush rugs spread over the floor. "I don't have anything, just keep quiet."

"Go ask the pretty lady for something to eat. She seemed really nice."

"No."

"Shall I go ask?"

Laphaniel turned on her, the movement so swift it made her yelp. "No."

"Why?"

"Because I told you no, that's why. Be quiet."

"I'm really hungry," she persisted, a whine entering her voice. "Why won't you go ask?"

"I haven't paid for the room yet, so just get used to being hungry. You are not to leave this tent without me, do you understand?"

"Are you cross with me?"

Laphaniel sighed but didn't stop moving. "No, Fee."

"It smells strange here, doesn't it?" Nefina said, tugging a thick fur around her shoulders. "I don't like it. I don't want to stay long."

The tent faded into darkness, taking the memory with it, lurching sickeningly into the next. Nothing focused, a blur of colour spun around and around and around to a melody of a calliope. Fairground horses spun and spun, up and down, mad grins slashed across their equine faces.

Laughter bubbled up over the music, haunting and lovely. A flash of red drifted by, golden skin dancing upon bare feet. Nothing focused. Nothing stayed still.

"Come with me."

Another tent, perfumed smoke billowing around in coloured clouds. I coughed as the sickly fog filled my lungs. I could taste it on my tongue, heavy with the scent of dreams and despair.

"Over there."

A woman drifted into view, dressed all in red, glistening skin dripping with rubies, black hair adorned with them.

Everything shifted, disappearing into black.

"Stay awake."

I wanted to tear away from the tent, but I couldn't move. I wanted to drag the red woman from him, but I couldn't. I couldn't stop it, couldn't help, couldn't do anything but watch as she climbed on top of him.

She guided his hands, his mouth, the silk of her clothes sliding with ease from her body. She showed him how to move, how to please her until she was writhing, and I was sobbing.

She laughed in his face when she was done.

"I will make my fortune from you," she panted. "Be my best, and perhaps I will not touch that little sweet thing you brought with you."

"If you so much as look at her, I will kill you," Laphaniel snarled, his words thick and heavy.

The red woman grinned, her face alight with a poisonous type of beauty. "Oh, I bet you would."

The light began to fade, everything blinking in and out, flashes of light eaten up by a foggy dark. The music played on, playful and filled with misplaced joy, a crude decoration within a carnival of whores.

"Where have you been?" Nefina crouched low, hovering over Laphaniel while he stared up at her. "You've been gone for so long."

"It's fine." He reached out for her and missed, slumping forwards. "It's all okay…we can stay here…it's fine…"

"What have you done?" She tried to pull him up, failed. "What's wrong with you?"

Laphaniel smiled, a tiny lift of his lips that was utterly humourless. He lifted a finger to his lips and chuckled.

"Where did you go?"

"Nowhere," he slurred, closing his eyes. "Go away and leave me alone."

Everything stayed in a haze, blurring and swaying and never for a moment staying still. Everything remained in darkness, broken now and again with a sudden flash of colour, of bright silks and choking perfume.

There was the sound of laughter.

The sound of singing.

Though it was all forced, all fake. An illusion of happiness. I could hear the music and feel the heat of bodies pressing skin to skin. There was the exchange of gold for a fragment of soul, the stealing of dreams, all beneath an ever-present smog of cloying smoke.

The smothering fumes of Ember; the drug of whores and gutter-rats.

Around and around and around, up and down, up and down, up and down and…

"Where's my sister?"

"She grew beautiful," the red woman smiled, lazing back along a couch draped in furs. She cupped her breast, widening her legs. "Do you want this?"

"Nefina was never part of our bargain. Where is she?"

The red woman ignored him, lifting a vial, so the light danced off the glass. "Or do you want this?"

She rose from the bed, placing the vial into Laphaniel's hand, folding his fingers around it. I couldn't ignore the way his hand shook.

"How much is she worth to you?" Her mouth trailing over his jaw, her hips pressed against his.

"Tell me where she is," he demanded, though he didn't move away from her.

"Give me back my little potion, and perhaps I will." She opened her hand, and he dropped it into her palm, his breath catching in his throat. "But there will be no more."

She crushed the glass with a quick squeeze of her fingers, revealing ash coloured dust mingling with glass shards and blood. Laphaniel stared, fists clenched at his sides, and I could see him struggling to choose between the bloodied fragments and his sister.

"Where have you taken her?"

I gasped at the sudden crack of her hand slapping Laphaniel's face, striking him with enough force to snap his head back. He staggered, spitting blood.

"Go find her yourself," the red woman said, sucking the dust from her fingers.

"I hope one day you choke on the souls you devour." Laphaniel wiped the blood from his lip, smearing it across his face. He pushed himself to his feet, and without another word, he fled, shouting his sister's name.

The tents were a maze of silk. A colourful warren of nightmares that stretched on and on and on, circling around the twisted carousel in the centre of it all. He yelled for her, clawing back throws and silken sheets, pushing against fey with vacant eyes until at last, he found her.

Nefina covered herself when he walked in, lifting the furs to hide her bare skin and the bruises along her arms. She took a breath and held her chin up, reaching on the nightstand for a hairbrush, which she carefully pulled through her soft, lovely hair.

"Sixty blood-red rubies," she said, tossing a bag at her brother, her eyes cold. "What do you think Papa would have got for me?"

"Nefina." Laphaniel took a step closer, his eyes falling onto the discarded clothes littered around the floor.

"Is that a good price for my virginity?" she asked, carefully braiding her hair. "What did you get for yours?"

"Fee...I'm sorry...I..." He moved again, as broken as she was. "This wasn't meant to happen."

"Pass me some clothes, I'm cold."

He handed her a robe, looking away when she stood. The bedcovers fell to the floor in a tangle of rumpled silk and fur. She covered herself, the flash of life in her eyes I had marvelled at...gone.

"You were meant to be safe here."

Something fragile within her snapped, and she launched herself at Laphaniel with her teeth bared, fists colliding with his chest, nails raking across his face.

"I was never safe here!" she screamed at him. "I was never safe with you. You promised you would keep me safe, and instead, you forgot about me. I loved you, and you have destroyed me."

Laphaniel made no move to restrain her, allowing her to beat against him until she let out an agonised howl and sunk to her knees. He dropped with her, and she clung to him like a drowning girl, sobbing against him while he gripped her tight, his knuckles white against her back.

The threads tugging me from memory to memory snapped, sinking me back into an empty darkness that slowly swallowed up the reds and golds surrounding me. The music faded, the laughter and the weeping too. The lingering haze of Ember was the last to disappear, trailing after me into blackness.

I heard raised voices,

My name...

Again...

The sound familiar and panicked and mine.

CHAPTER TWENTY-FOUR

hy isn't she waking up?"

"Do not take that tone with me, boy."

"She's been out for hours." Laphaniel's raised voice pounded against my head. "She's fitted twice. What the hell have you done to her?"

"Your Glamour is coursing through her body, changing her. It is a lot to endure."

"Laphaniel?" I opened my eyes, blinking against the too-bright light. "Why is everyone yelling?"

His hands were on me instantly, helping me sit, running over my cheeks to check I was okay, threading through my hair when I told him over, and over that I was.

I was back in our room, lying against soft pillows, surrounded by furs and throws. The fire crackled in the grate, the logs inside splitting — the flames spitting. The candles were all lit, flooding the room with a light so bright it hurt my eyes. I closed them again, my head filling with the quick thudding of something achingly familiar.

It beat too fast, a panicked drum.

A strange taste coated my tongue, sharp and cold and strangely sweet. It faded with the slowing of Laphaniel's heartbeat, taking on the scent of spice and black liquorice that I would recognise anywhere.

"You were frightened," I said, squinting through half-open lids. "I could...I could taste it."

Darkness bloomed at the corners of the room, candles curling up into grey smoke as Charlotte doused all but a small handful.

Laphaniel gave a tight smile. "You terrified me."

I placed my hand over his chest. "I know, I heard your heartbeat."

"Can you feel it?" Charlotte placed a claw beneath my chin and tilted my head up. "The Glamour?"

The Spider's heart thrummed like a hummingbird's wings, almost silent. There was a flood of new sensations overloading everything, tastes, and scents and sounds...but nothing else.

"I don't know."

"Keep searching for it," Charlotte replied, claws scraping back the tangles of my hair. "It is there, deep inside you."

With a shaking hand, I ran a finger over Laphaniel's delicately pointed ear before touching my rounded one. "I'm still human."

"You are still you," Charlotte said, passing me a hand mirror. "but no, not entirely human. Not anymore."

I lifted the ornate glass, focusing first upon my very human ears, relieved they had remained the same. Freckles still scattered over my nose, though my skin was smoother than it had been before.

The biggest change was my eyes.

Before, they had been an ordinary green, pretty perhaps, but ordinary. Even in the dim light, my eyes seemed to glow, a luminous green speckled with flecks of bright gold. A ring of deep amber circled my pupil, darkening as I stared in shock. Slowly, slowly it deepened to black, swallowing every last bit of emerald.

I dropped the mirror, not wanting to look any longer. I whirled around to face Laphaniel so quickly, I made him jump. "Your eyes are blue."

The lovely purple had faded away, the silver around his pupil dulled to a soft grey.

"A small price to pay," he said, glancing at Charlotte, who continued to hover around us. "Your hair has got longer, look."

He brushed it across my shoulder, fingers running through the deep reds, golds, and blacks that now threaded through it. It was at least six inches longer, thicker and bouncier.

"Oh," I breathed. "I like this."

"But not your eyes?" he smiled gently, our hands continuing to explore the changes in each other. "Because they change colour?"

I nodded. "They are very not human."

"They are beautiful, though."

Heat spread across my cheeks, and I snorted. "Do you feel different?"

Apart from his eye colour, he looked just like he always had. Though he had lost some of the stillness that would settle over him, even sat beside me, I could detect a restlessness that hadn't been there before.

Laphaniel hesitated. "I don't know yet."

"Do you think you can lie now?"

My question piqued the interest of Charlotte, who cocked her head, eyes bright. "Tell us an untruth, angel. Tell me that the sky above burns red."

Laphaniel turned to the window, at the calm Unseelie sky of violet and black. "The sky is red."

The words came out in a quick tumble, and he winced, bracing himself for the pain that would normally follow the lie. His eyes widened, then a grin spread over his lips, bright with wonder and wickedness.

"I think you're going to need a little practice," I said, laughing. "Your poker face needs some work."

Charlotte scurried closer, stopping a breath away from Laphaniel's face. "Do you still fear me?"

"No."

The single word hitched ever so slightly, slipping past his lips with just enough unease to paint it as the lie it was. It wouldn't have mattered if he hadn't faltered. The scent of cloying sweetness lingered at my nose, the taste of that fear chilling upon my tongue.

Charlotte withdrew, smoothing down the faded grey silks of her gown. "I shall be in my quarters if either of you needs me."

"I no longer believe you're going to eat me," Laphaniel said, surprising myself and Charlotte when he reached for her hand. "But, your stories were whispered over my cradle in the darkness, and they are very hard to forget."

Charlotte's answering smile revealed the rows of neat white fangs. "One day, you will tell me these stories."

"If you would like."

Her eyes glittered, black and huge in the dim light. "In the darkness?"

Laphaniel nodded. "It is the best place for them."

"Would you be afraid?"

"Oh, most likely."

The Spider grinned, the smile turning wistful as she ran a claw over the smooth band upon Laphaniel's finger. "Perhaps, one day, I will share a different story over a different cradle."

"Perhaps," he replied after a pause.

"Keep searching for that Glamour, little one," she said to me. "It is there. Find it and work with it."

Charlotte turned in a whisper of silk, her claws clicking upon the marble floor as she left the room.

Laphaniel sat beside me on the bed. "Ready to see what you can do?"

I met the strange blue of his eyes before glancing back down at my hands, wanting to feel the thrum of Glamour in them. "Where do we start?"

"Summon a flame," he answered. "It's the easiest trick to learn."

HOURS PASSED.

We had been trying for hours.

Outside, the strange violet sky darkened to a deep indigo, bringing to life countless stars that glittered in the pitch. Laphaniel re-lit the candles with a match.

My hands shook with the effort of calling up magic that had never been a part of me before. My heart thumped, quick, and jittery. My palms so slick I had to keep wiping them on the bedcovers to get enough friction to click my fingers.

Laphaniel's heartbeat remained steady, his hands cupping around mine while he explained over and over how to call heat to my fingertips.

"Try again," he said, a harshness taking over his voice as his patience finally wavered. His hands hovered above mine. "Again."

I shifted upon the mound of furs I sat upon, my body aching with its newness. My head thumped with the sounds of the crackling fire, the echo of footsteps, the clipped tone of Laphaniel's words.

"Again, Teya."

I moved my fingers like he showed me, trying to feel for the heat that just wasn't there, that spark of magic I had taken from him, trying to get a flame to ignite. Nothing happened. My fingers were sore from nothing happening.

"I'm sorry."

Laphaniel fell back against the pillows, a frustrated grunt slipping from his lips as he blew out a breath. I didn't blame him; it should have been easy enough.

I could feel the Glamour raging within me, deep beneath the surface, a constant thrum of energy that set my nerves alight. I marvelled at how Laphaniel could have ever controlled it and moulded it to his will when I couldn't even reach it.

"Hold your fingers together," Laphaniel said again, shifting beside me. "Can you feel it tingling?"

I shook my head, feeling nothing but the weight of failure.

"Concentrate, don't touch your fingers together yet. Wait until you feel the heat, then click."

I did exactly as I was told, wincing as he raked a quick hand through his hair, muttering beneath his breath.

"I'm really trying," I gritted out, prickling at his impatience. A part of me feared that it was because the Glamour wasn't mine, like it truly didn't belong to me. "This is all new for me."

"You're just assuming you can't do it, so it isn't working."

"Could you give me more time?" I snapped, feeling the tension crackling between us. "I was human this morning."

Laphaniel gritted his teeth. "And I wasn't."

He pushed himself off the bed, running a hand over an unlit candle on the nightstand, flexing his fingers above the wick as if he could still feel the heat in them.

"Do you want to talk about it?"

He started to pace the room. "I can't hear you."

"I said…"

"No." He shut me off, still pacing. Restless. "I can't hear you like I used to. I could pick out the sound of your heartbeat within a hundred beating hearts, and now I can't hear it. You smell different, too. Everything does. I'm afraid that if I can't see you, I won't be able to find you."

"I think we'll always be able to find each other," I said, watching while he rummaged through an ornate liquor cabinet. He pulled out a large bottle and poured two generous glasses of thick, dark amber liquid. I took the glass he offered me, grimacing at the burn it left as I took a sip. Laphaniel swallowed his shot and poured another.

"Do you regret what you did?" A question I was unsure if I wanted the answer to or not.

Laphaniel rubbed his eyes, swirling the whisky in his glass before drinking. "I can't really, can I? Not if it helps in the end, not if it means we can destroy Luthien."

"It's still okay to miss what I've taken from you," I said, reaching for him when he passed me. "Even if it's…"

"Wasted on you?"

I pulled back my hand in surprise, waiting a moment for him to apologise, but he said nothing and poured yet another drink, downing it like the other two.

"I'm doing my best."

"Then, do better."

I glared at him. "I need time. Stop drinking and help me."

His eyes narrowed, looking at something over my shoulder. I turned to see nothing but the dark sky of Unseelie. When I faced Laphaniel again, he had another drink in his hand.

"Can you feel the Glamour inside you at least?"

"Yes."

Laphaniel took a smaller sip before placing the glass down. "Okay, good. Reach for that thread, see what happens."

Nothing happened.

Nothing,

Nothing,

Nothing.

"Why can't you do this?"

I stood, tilting my head to meet his eyes and hissed, "I need more time."

Laphaniel closed the gap between us, towering over me, his face too close to mine. I could smell the tang of liquor on his breath. His hands gripped the tops of my arms, and he gave me a quick, rough shake.

"We don't have time, Teya!" he growled at me. "Don't you understand that? You need to figure this out right now, or you're going to kill us both."

"Get your hands off me!" I shoved him away, startled and furious. "Don't you dare touch me like that."

He stumbled back with a forced laugh, swiping up the bottle of whisky again. "This isn't going to work, is it?" he said, shaking his head while he took a deep drink. "What are you going to do when you face Luthien? Click at her?"

I wanted to snatch the bottle away from him, but I forced a distance between us. "I have seen the dregs of your memories, you know," I breathed, anger surging upwards like a tide. I could taste it upon my tongue.

He faltered. "What?"

"I saw you as a frightened little boy, and I saw you with Nefina." Something prickled up my spine, glorious and hot. "You couldn't save her—are you afraid that you won't save me?"

He backed away, the anger dissolving into something else, but he took a breath, feeding that fury and aimed it back at me without mercy. "I'm afraid I'm going to end up dying for you again."

I felt sick and fought the urge to strike him. "What do you want from me?"

"I want you to stop disappointing me."

"You don't mean that..."

We both jumped at the sudden crash of thunder that sent sheets of rain to beat against the windows.

Laphaniel tipped the bottle in my direction, sloshing amber liquid onto the rugs. More thunder boomed against the sky.

"Oh, but I do," he began, his words beginning to slur together. "I am so tired of having to keep dragging you up. You keep expecting people to drag you up, to help you, to comfort you. Do something for yourself, Teya! Help your damned self."

"I never asked you to die for me," I said, while the wind picked up outside, turning the rain into fine sleet.

"And yet I still did," Laphaniel answered coldly, taking another drink and then another until I snatched the bottle from him and launched it into the fireplace. The bottle shattered, the pieces glittering. He turned away and smirked at the lightning ripping the sky apart.

Furious tears began a slow descent down my face. I felt like my world was breaking. "No wonder everyone you love leaves you."

He closed his eyes briefly, and I knew I had hurt him, but when he opened them again, they were dark and angry. "I left Luthien, and right now it would be just as easy to leave you."

The skies outside crackled, and I could almost taste the storm, feel the way it was trying to split the night in two. I was so angry, so hurt... so in pain that I could taste blood against my lips.

"Then, get out!" I shouted at him. "Get away from here. Get away from me!"

I screamed, and the world screamed with me. The glass in the windows shattered, the candles exploded into flame, and a cacophony of broken things bellowed through the room. It tore Laphaniel from his feet, tossing him against the wall with so much force I heard his head crack before he slumped to the floor.

I followed him, ignoring the sound of broken glass beneath my feet, unable to see past the red haze that covered my eyes, barely hearing anything but the sound of my rage. My fury was a palpable thing, heady and wild and satisfying, flowing through my veins like a drug.

A screech tore through me, a banshee cry that teased winding vines through the broken windows to creep around my feet. They looped around Laphaniel, pinning him up like a puppet, grasping at his throat until he was forced to suck in a pained breath. I tightened my hold and squeezed.

The storm was mine, and I was not letting go.

"I...I...can't...breathe."

More lightning flashed, thunder rolling across the skies while hail pounded the castle walls, spraying the floor with ice. I saw only red— beautiful, beautiful red.

"If you can still talk, you can breathe," I hissed, power coursing over me in dizzying waves.

"You...lit...the...candles."

I turned, the mist fading instantly when I saw that every single candle in the room was ablaze, the light dancing over the destruction I had caused. My gaze snapped back to Laphaniel, and I choked on my scream when I realised what I had done.

The vines uncurled and dropped him, and the winds died down. I caught him when he fell to his knees, gasping. He sucked in rasping breaths against my shoulder, the noises catching in his throat as he struggled to get them in. His hands tightened on my arms, panic taking hold.

"I could have killed you," I said, drawing back, my hands trembling against him. "I nearly killed you."

Laphaniel leant forward, resting his head against his knees as he calmed his breathing. He sat there for a few minutes before he looked up, his neck bright with livid red marks. "Then, just imagine what you'll do to Luthien."

Thunder erupted at the sound of her name, and Laphaniel grinned while I fought against the surge of emotions raging within me. "You didn't mean anything you said."

"No," he replied, touching his forehead against mine. "But you believed me."

I held onto him, my hands snaking through his hair. There was blood on my hands when I pulled them back, trickling slowly from a cut near his temple.

"I would have loved to…to have the time to show you properly," he began. "We just didn't have the time. I didn't want…I didn't want to hurt you."

I took an uneasy breath, tears threatening at my eyes as the anger ebbed away, leaving me exhausted. "You've never been able to lie to me before. I believed you because I wouldn't blame you for having enough. I've dragged you through hell, and I guess everyone must have their limits, I thought you had finally reached yours. You gave up so much for me, and I was still useless."

Laphaniel looked around the room, at the destruction and chaos I had caused, a lovely, wicked smile spreading over his face. "You have just destroyed an entire room in a temper tantrum. I wouldn't call that useless."

I returned his smile. "I can't believe you drank a bottle of whisky just to piss me off."

"And I would gladly do it again," he said, pushing himself to his feet, clutching the broken bedpost as he stumbled.

"That drink has hit you harder than it used to, hasn't it?"

"A little bit," he admitted, lowering himself onto the bed. He looked around at the blazing candles, shedding erratic light onto the shattered pieces of furniture, then back at me.

He looked at me with such pride in his eyes that I felt heat rise to my cheeks. The pain of his words melted away beneath that look, and I found myself longing to be closer to him, to undo the doubt and the hurt and the anger that had caused me to completely lose control. Words that niggled at the back of my mind, knowing that perhaps there was a little truth to them.

I slipped into his arms, the broken bed creaking under our weight as I kissed him hard. I could taste the raindrops on his mouth, the subtle tang of blood and sweat and alcohol, but beneath that...him. He tasted like the woods, like spice and warmth. Of home.

I moved my lips to his neck, and he arched up against me, a wonderful moan slipping from his mouth, his whole body turning to press against mine. I could feel the Glamour swirl around us, teasing the flames, touching Laphaniel in light, feather-like touches.

"You don't have to do this..." he murmured.

"Do you want me to stop?" My lips grazed over his cheek. "How drunk are you?"

Laphaniel sniggered. "Worried you're taking advantage of me?"

Glamour eddied around us, the anger, the fury, the hurt all gone. It lifted around my hair, curling around Laphaniel with barely a thought, as if some part of it still wanted to be close to him.

He closed his eyes while threads of glimmering light teased at him; his heartbeat quickened, an erratic song. I remembered how it felt to have the press of Glamour around me, to have it coax feelings I had no words for from my body, to have my head swim with the delights of it, to be held within someone's arms as they made the world implode for you.

"Does it feel weird to you?" I began. "For me to use your Glamour on you?"

"Yes," he breathed. "But I don't want you to stop."

His kiss swallowed up the gasp he enticed from my mouth, his laugh rumbling against me as I made the candles snuff out.

"Should I try to control it?"

Laphaniel shook his head. "No."

We made love upon the remains of the broken bed deep into the night, my Glamour around us like a tangible thing, winding around us to set every bared nerve alight. We kissed goodnight, one last kiss, one last embrace that moved us together again as if our very souls couldn't bear to be parted.

It was near dawn before an exhausted sleep dragged us both down, still entwined, into a dreamless black.

CHAPTER TWENTY-FIVE

I woke to the delicious smell of fresh coffee, the bed empty beside me. Laphaniel sat at the cracked table, his head in his hands while he rubbed his temples. A mug of half-finished coffee rested beside his arm, steam curling upwards.

"Be careful of the glass on the floor," he murmured, not looking up as I joined him.

"Sore head?" I enquired, surveying the damage I had wreaked upon the room with no small amount of satisfaction.

"It feels like something crawled into my mouth and died." Laphaniel poured more black coffee into his mug, then heaped sugar into it.

"Is this your first hangover?"

He nodded and winced, hands curling around the mug as he brought it to his lips. "And my last."

"Everyone says that," I said with a smile. "You'll feel better if you eat something, trust me."

I passed him a piece of toast while he looked like he was fighting just to keep his coffee down. "A greasy bacon sandwich works wonders, but this will have to do."

Laphaniel groaned.

"Or a big cooked breakfast."

"Please stop."

"With the egg all runny, and jiggly…"

He darted to the bathing room, knees slamming on the marble as he retched into the toilet. I rubbed his back, sitting down beside him.

"I promise you'll feel better once it's all up," I began. "There's no point waiting around feeling rotten."

"So, this isn't payback for the things I said?" He rested his head against the bowl.

"I said some awful things too."

"I didn't mean them," Laphaniel said, taking the damp washcloth I passed him. He ran it over his face and sat back. "None of it."

"The words maybe, but the frustration was real. I think some of the anger too."

"I'm not angry at you."

He got up from the floor, and I followed him back to the table, where he poured a large cup of fresh orange juice and gulped it down. I helped myself to the glistening pastries that were still warm from the oven, waiting for him to continue.

He sighed, picking at a cold piece of toast. "I still think that perhaps it could have been different."

"If you had kept me Glamoured?"

"No. No, I will always regret that, Teya. Always. I will never forgive myself for doing that to you."

"I forgave you."

He gave me a tight smile, but it didn't reach his eyes. "I sometimes think what would have happened if I had just been honest with you, right at the beginning. If I hadn't tried to force you to stay."

I reached for his hand across the table. "We would end up here. I would still have gone looking for Niven, and you would still go with me. She would still shove that knife…that knife through your heart." I faltered, swallowing quickly. "You would still end up dying in my arms, and the curse would break. We would end up here. It's okay to feel angry and bitter about it, because I do too. It's okay to wish for something other than this, it's okay to vent to me because you're my best friend and I love you."

His eyes met mine, still wary. "I want the life I promised you all those months ago, but no matter how this all ends, I can no longer give that to you. It's a dream that no longer exists, but I can't just let it go."

I ran a finger over his wedding band and smiled. "It was my dream, too, in the end. More than I ever realised."

Laphaniel continued to pick apart his breakfast, looking tired, but the tension that plagued him seemed to have lifted slightly. It made me wonder if his outburst hadn't only awakened my Glamour but been a much-needed release for him too.

The sound of the door slamming open, startled both of us. Laphaniel was instantly in front of me, still inhumanly quick. I was on my feet before I knew I was moving, Glamour sparking unsteadily at my fingertips.

"What the fuck happened in here?" Niven demanded, storming in, her eyes darting around the room before settling upon me.

Laphaniel met her furious look with his own. "Teya is learning how to control her newly acquired gifts."

Niven swept a hand through the air, gesturing at the destruction I had created. "Does this look like control?"

"It looks as if she is going to tear Luthien down," Laphaniel answered. "With more time…"

"Oh, it looks like you found time for other things." She nodded over to the rumpled bed before sneering at my barely covered body. That look…she made me feel ashamed. And dirty.

"Did we disturb you?" Laphaniel said, voice cold. I knew he noticed me shrink beneath Niven's gaze.

"I was hunting in the Broken Wylds," the Unseelie King began, pushing past Niven to look upon the chaos surrounding us.

He was soaking wet, copper hair plastered against his face; trails of blood seeped from a deep wound on his cheek. From the look on his face, I couldn't tell if he was impressed or livid.

The shadows began their slow dance for him, inching away from the walls, the nooks, to gather at his feet.

"Six of my horses bolted in the storm you created," he continued, stirring the shadows into two giant wolves. "I was riding one of them."

"Oh." I reached for my clothes, slipping a black silken dress over my head, so I was no longer the only one in the room half-naked. "I'm sorry. Were you hunting deer or pheasant?"

The Unseelie King clenched his fists, and the wolves at his side snarled, hackles rising, lips curled up, revealing very real looking teeth. He took another step towards me, muddied boots crunching upon the shards of glass. "Would you really like to know, Teya?"

My heartbeat quickened, the flames around me flaring. The shadows flickered, withdrawing back to their master. The King of Nightmares smiled, and it was terrifying.

"Is it tied to your emotions?" he asked, head tilting while he ran a hand over the beasts beside him. "How much control do you have?"

"Not much," I answered, holding onto the Glamour buzzing at my fingertips, afraid to let it go. "I'm not ready yet, I need more time."

The Unseelie King's smile widened on his bloody face as he snapped his fingers. The wolves tore forwards, lunging for Laphaniel with cruel teeth and mad eyes. They sprang up at him, made from more than shadows and darkness. They were things of hatred and nightmares, made real by a desire to hurt…to draw blood and create misery.

I leapt forward, dragging Laphaniel back as I spun in front of him, my hands coming up in defence as a surge of energy and power burst from me, turning the wolves back into nothing but mist.

"You leave at sunrise," the King said, swirling his hand around the candlelight, calling more wolves from the shadows.

I still had my arms shielding Laphaniel while I stared up at the Unseelie king, my chest heaving. I had no doubts that he would not have called off the wolves if I had failed.

"I'm not ready."

"I don't care," he replied, and for one stupid moment, I looked to Niven for help. Her cool eyes remained impassive.

Laphaniel gripped my shoulder. "She needs to practise; what if she faces Luthien and freezes? We will lose, you will lose…"

"I am not waiting any longer," the Unseelie King hissed with deathly calm. The shadows stilled, the darkness waited, even Niven flinched. "I know how long it can take to control this." He raised his hands, sending the skies into chaos again. "I will not wait while Luthien gains strength. You go tomorrow, and you take my knights and destroy her."

Laphaniel untangled himself from me and faced the Unseelie King without an ounce of fear. "What will you do if Teya fails?"

"I'll go to war and butcher her myself."

With a movement too quick for me to stop, Laphaniel launched forward and cracked his fist across the king's face. "You're sending her to test Luthien's hold on the Seelie court? To see if you can dispatch her without dirtying your own hands?"

The Unseelie King struck back, the blow rocking Laphaniel on his feet, but he kept his balance, spitting blood at the King's feet.

"I have turned your whore into a weapon. She has but one task, kill Luthien and take the throne, else I will bring war upon this land and bathe in the blood of those you love."

"You are a coward," Laphaniel hissed, red staining his teeth, straining against my hand as I pulled him back.

"And you are nothing," the Unseelie King said, a breath away from Laphaniel's face. "Not fey, not human, not quite alive but not yet dead. A filthy mongrel. One day, I will have you pay for striking me."

I held Laphaniel firm, my fingers digging into his arm while Phabian goaded him. I tried and failed to use my Glamour to calm him like he used to do to me. I didn't achieve anything except to gutter out the candle beside me.

The Unseelie King turned his back on us, outstretching his hand for Niven, who curled her fingers around his without a word.

"Sunrise, Teya," he called over his shoulder. "Live or die. I have no other choices for you."

I stared after him, open-mouthed as they left. I still held onto Laphaniel. I could hear the furious sound of his heartbeat, scent the anger whirling around him, a strange bitterness against the familiar spice.

"He threw those words at you to get you to react. It's all a game to him."

"They're true, though. I don't even know what I am anymore."

"You're mine."

I pressed my forehead to his, allowing him to be angry, to feel helpless and lost because he needed to, because even if I could...I shouldn't control what he felt.

"I shouldn't have hit him."

"No, probably not."

Laphaniel sighed, taking a steadying breath. "You need to practise calling your Glamour."

"I know."

I did need to be better, much better if I was going to defeat Luthien and save our court...our friends. My thoughts shifted to Oonagh and then to Nefina, wondering if they were still safe, if they still lived at all. I thought of Nefina, of everything she and Laphaniel had endured as children, my heart twisting for the cold and vindictive faerie.

"I saw what happened with you and your sister," I said quickly. Laphaniel instantly began to shut down, closing me off before I could even begin. "I know you don't want to talk about it..."

"I don't."

"But I don't think Nefina hates you, I've seen her look at you and..."

His eyes darkened, not with black, but with a sharper blue that flashed cold. "Not now, Teya."

"I saw what happened," I continued, knowing too well how guilt and shame ate away at everything good. "You were so young and alone. What happened was not your fault."

"My sister was raped, Teya, because I was out of my mind elsewhere."

"You came for her," I said, needing to lift some of the lingering darkness in his eyes. "You still came for her."

His face hardened. "What did you see after that?"

"Nothing, I woke up."

"Do you think we escaped out the back? Ran off into the night to beg for shelter elsewhere? That we fell into Luthien's lap and were welcomed with open arms in the castle?"

I shook my head, but a part of me, a foolish part of me, hoped the story had a happier ending.

"I didn't leave," he continued. "I couldn't."

"You went back to the red woman?"

Laphaniel nodded. "And so did Nefina."

"Did you give her Ember?" I asked, remembering the cloying smell of the drug, the thickness of the smoke. I could still taste it from the dark blur of Laphaniel's memories.

"She took it from me," he said, the deep blue of his eyes chilling. "And I nearly killed her for it."

"Laphaniel…"

He snatched his arm back as I reached to comfort him. "I don't want to do this now, Teya. Stop digging through my head, you won't like what you find."

"I just want to be there for you, to understand." I held my hands up, not wanting another fight. "Talk to me."

"You can't absolve this for me. I couldn't look after Nefina, and I can't look after you. I even tried to find her a safe place within Luthien's court, I failed at that, and I am failing at this."

"Laphaniel…"

"Just leave it. I am asking you because I can't deal with this right now. You need to practise using your Glamour, not picking apart my memories."

"I'm not judging you on your past," I said softly as he continued to back away from me, physically and mentally distancing himself. "You have centuries on me, Laphaniel; that's a huge amount of history you have that I am not a part of."

"Right now," he gritted out. "Your Glamour is swarming around the room, and you haven't even noticed. It's wrapping around everything I am not ready or willing to talk about and is dragging it all up. My head is aching from it all. Stop it."

"I didn't even know I was using it." I held out a hand, searching for the threads I had unwittingly sent out. They were scattered around me, knotted and taut, searching and poking. I pulled them back, and they snapped away from Laphaniel with more reluctance than I would have liked.

Laphaniel closed his eyes, drawing in a deep breath. "Thank you."

"Do you have any Glamour left?" I asked gently.

He looked down at his fingers and splayed them out, turning them over as if searching for any glimmer of magic. "There's an echo. Nothing I can reach or use."

"You never created storms with it, or shattered rooms."

Laphaniel perched at the edge of the rumpled bed. "I was not a king. Our Glamour is tied to Faerie itself. It gives only what is needed. What it wants."

"Is that why Luthien is so powerful?"

"As a true princess of Faerie, her gifts always were stronger."

"And if you had married her?"

"I guess we'll never know."

"But you are a king of Faerie now," I said, confused. "You married me."

"In name only, Teya," Laphaniel said, lifting his hand, so his wedding band caught the candlelight. "I no longer have the Glamour needed to conjure storms."

"Then why can Niven?"

He said nothing for a moment, looking troubled. "I don't know."

"I never wanted to take this from you."

"You took nothing from me," he replied, firm. "I gave it to you. I knew what I was getting into."

"Neither of us knew what we were getting into," I replied, sitting beside him.

His lips twitched into a barely-there smile as he rested his head against my shoulder. "See if you can make me jump out of the window."

I snorted a laugh. "You once told me a faerie couldn't make you do something that deep down you didn't want to do. Unless you really do want to throw yourself out?"

"You're my queen," he began, a teasing smile erasing the haunted look from his face. "You should be able to make me whether I want to or not. You command me, and I'll try to resist."

"No."

A wickedness danced across his face. "No? Afraid you won't be able to do it?"

"I'm not going to ask you to jump, Laphaniel."

"You may not even be capable of doing it."

I heard the challenge in his voice, and I bristled with the need to prove him wrong. "Jump, then."

He grinned at me but didn't move.

"You're able to resist because you married me," I accused, and he laughed.

"You wouldn't have been able to throw me across the room or mess with my head if that were true. I'm your consort, Teya. You do what you want with me."

"I don't want to hurt you."

He shrugged. "Because you can't."

I laughed, the warmth of Glamour slipping across my hands. "That's not going to work this time. Go on, then, get up."

He tensed slightly, barely a movement, but I heard the breath he took and the sudden quick dip of his heartbeat.

"Get up," I whispered, and this time he jerked. Glamour swirled around us, dancing close like tiny fireflies. It wrapped around us in a fog, changing my voice into something softer and lilting and tempting. Oh, I remembered that tone. How it felt to listen and give in. More threads reached out to dispel fear and reason, to replace caution with a sense of misplaced trust.

Laphaniel still didn't move, but his fists curled at his side as he fought against me. I was worried I could break his mind if I pushed too hard, but that fear quickly fled when I couldn't even get him to stand up.

With a new resolve, I pushed harder, focusing on the glittering strands of Glamour, winding them around Laphaniel. His smile faltered as he fought me, his legs twitching, beads of sweat breaking out against his skin.

I took a breath and concentrated, feeling out for the tug against my will, and gently pulled it apart. The brightness in his lovely eyes went out, glazing over as he blinked and stood. He took one step and then another, not seeming to care about the shards of glass that littered the floor.

My delight quickly turned to revulsion at the thought of controlling him, of having that amount of power over someone. I knew the moment I took over his thoughts, breaking down a barrier he was trying hard to keep up, and it felt wrong, a grotesque invasion that I vowed I would never enjoy.

"Laphaniel, stop."

He moved closer to the shattered window, hands curling over the frame while the wind started to batter at his face. I hadn't asked him to go to the window...just to stand up, the Glamour was listening to his command...his dare, not my simple request.

"Stop!"

He didn't turn, didn't slow. The threads holding onto him had snapped away in my panic, and I couldn't get them back up again.

"Laphaniel!" I grabbed at his arm as he continued forward, precariously close to the window's edge. I gathered up the spluttering remains of Glamour, sensing it struggle against my fingertips. "Get down."

Forcing a silken layer into my voice, I remembered how he used to sweet talk the darkness away for me. He pulled away, one foot hanging from the gaping window. I grabbed at him, but he yanked his arm back and nearly toppled over.

"Stop." I found my control again, barely recognising my voice, "Stop this, and sleep instead."

Laphaniel crumpled like someone had cut strings from him, and I only just managed to grab him as he fell, hauling him away from the ledge and onto the floor.

My breath caught in my throat, my heart pounding, so angry with myself that I shook. Laphaniel lay entirely still against me, breathing soundly, completely oblivious.

I shook him hard, fighting the urge to smack him. He stirred and blinked at me, meeting my furious glare with confusion.

"What?"

"Don't you what me!" I hissed. "Don't ever ask me to do that again!"

He sat up, rubbing a hand over his eyes. "You did it. I could feel you in my head, nudging against me until all I could hear was you. Nothing else mattered."

"It felt wrong."

"It won't always," Laphaniel said, reaching up to wipe at the blood that had begun to trickle from his nose.

"Are you okay?"

He nodded. "It takes a lot to override someone's will to live. You did amazingly."

"That is the singular most awful thing you have ever said to me." I swept the hair from his eyes. "And you've said some pretty appalling things."

He stood a little shakily and moved to sit by the cracked table. The breakfast things had all disappeared. "You are going to have to do some awful things as Queen."

I didn't sit but moved my hand over the stumps of candle wax dotted over the table, coaxing flames up from the ruined wicks. With a quick clench of my fist, the flames raged upwards before I snuffed them out.

"I have been like this for less than a day," I said, unable to stay still. "And already what I can do frightens me. I can feel this power, this Glamour inside me, and it's getting stronger. A few hours ago, I couldn't light a candle, and now I feel as if I could burn this castle to the ground with a whisper. I hurt you because I lost my temper—what if I lose my temper again? I don't want to become a monster, Laphaniel."

"You're the rightful Queen of the Seelie Court," Laphaniel said. "You need to be feared."

I swallowed. "I don't want you to be afraid of me."

He pulled me to him, stopping my pacing. "I'm not afraid of you. I never will be. I fear for you because I don't think you understand that defeating Luthien is only the beginning of everything."

I rested my head on his shoulder. "I don't want to die."

Laphaniel brushed a kiss to my lips, saying nothing as he looped his fingers through mine. The strange chill of his wedding band pressed against my skin as I clung to him. With his free hand, he reached for my star pendant, his fingers running over its crooked points. It was a symbol of everything he meant to me, of a constant light within an eternity of darkness.

A beacon of hope in a hopeless place.

CHAPTER TWENTY-SIX

*M*orning came slow and black and cold. Sunlight barely broke over the horizon, oozing feeble violet light through the low storm clouds spitting drizzle over the damp and misty ground.

Neither of us had slept, we hadn't talked much either but just stayed quiet in each other's company and waited for dawn.

"I'm terrified," I admitted, my back to Laphaniel while he tightened the stays on my borrowed dress, a flowing thing of sheer black. "More than I have been in a long time."

He kissed the nape of my neck, hands running over my hips. "So am I. I love you, Teya. More than anything, more than I thought was ever possible."

"I feel like you're saying goodbye," I said, stretching out my hands, rooting for the Glamour beneath my skin. "How long until we reach Luthien?"

"It's a good week's ride, longer perhaps. We can't risk cutting through Seelie lands until we absolutely must. We need to be able to surprise her."

I nodded, turning to face him, smoothing the fabric of his dark shirt. "Then tell me goodbye another day."

I laced my boots, the soft leather reaching high up my legs, the deep black the same shade as my dress; Unseelie clothes, all made from darkness and shadows that settled over my skin like mist.

The neckline was lower than I would have liked, fitting snugly against my breasts before flowing in sheer drapes down my legs. The weightless silk caught the slightest breeze and moved in ribbons of darkness around my body, the sheer sleeves stopping at my wrists to keep my hands free.

It was the first time I had felt like a queen, standing in front of the mirror shrouded in shadow with my hair bright and wild around my shoulders.

"Will you fight differently?" I asked, worried that I had compromised his ability to make me stronger. "Now, you're not quite fey?"

Laphaniel pulled his boots on before shrugging into a leather jacket as black as ink. "It will be an adjustment—it's being unable to see in the dark that bothers me most…"

"You could see in the dark?"

"Not in total darkness, no." He smiled at me, passing me a hooded cloak lined with midnight fur. "I never realised you couldn't. It didn't occur to me that your sight may be different to mine. Your hearing is pretty appalling too, I always thought you were ignoring me half the time."

I shook my head in disbelief. "Do you not understand how humans work? My ears are little and rounded, my eyes never changed colour. Technically we are different species…which is pretty weird if you think too long about it."

"The only thing I knew about humans was that they screamed when you locked them away."

I cradled his face in my hands, feeling the way guilt rose up within him.

"Niven didn't."

He took a breath. "I should never have chosen her."

"Then you wouldn't have found me."

"I think I would have found you eventually," he said, sweeping a soft kiss against my lips. "And you wouldn't have had a reason not to stay with me."

His words sent a pang of regret through me, though it was wonderful to believe that fate would have pushed us together one way or another.

I had no appetite to eat but knew that riding out on an empty stomach was a bad idea, so I forced down a few mouthfuls of porridge. Laphaniel picked at his own breakfast, mainly consisting of the thick and bitter coffee favoured at the dark court.

The knights were waiting for us in the throne room, standing still and ominous in their dark armour and raven feather cloaks. They watched us as we entered, eyes narrowing in distaste at me, before darkening to hatred as they set eyes upon Laphaniel. They began whispering between themselves when we walked forwards towards the two knotted thrones, only silencing when the Unseelie King lifted a lazy hand.

"Quiet." The single word barely echoed but brought with it a sudden silence. Not a soul uttered a sound. The King turned to me, beside him, my sister watched on. A Queen, surveying her court. "I have six knights for you, Teya. Do you think that will be enough?"

I gritted my teeth against his tone, forcing a grateful smile onto my face. "I hope so."

The Unseelie King smiled back, showing teeth. "Ever hopeful, aren't you?"

"It's all I have left."

"Then I wish you luck, Queen of Seelie. Try not to die."

I bowed my head, sensing the curt dismissal and turned my attention to my sister. She leant back into her throne, cigarette at her mouth, her hair an untamed cascade over her bare shoulders.

"Would you mourn me if I failed?" I asked as she blew a plume of smoke from her lips.

"Maybe we will find out."

I turned away from her, following the Raven knights as they led us out of the throne room and away from the cold, cruel presence of my sister and the mad king beside her.

We rode out upon black horses, monstrous beasts that towered over us. Gleaming twin horns curved back from their heads, two shorter ones pointed forward, ebony black and razor-sharp. They all stomped at the ground, cleaving the half-frozen earth, desperate to run. Steam rose in angry puffs as they snorted their impatience, heads whipping around to knock at anyone standing too close.

Laphaniel helped me up onto my mount, adjusting the stirrups so my feet could reach them. The frigid wind caught my cloak, snapping it behind me, but the layers of shadow I wore kept off the morning's chill. Laphaniel leapt up beside me, holding the reins of his horse in one hand while he checked my own.

The Raven knights flanked us, each sitting cold and proud upon his own beast, their feathered cloaks whipping back in the wind. Every now and then, I would catch their eye, and they would glower back, dripping wet and miserable beneath the relentless rain.

Laphaniel rode beside me, his black leather jacket slick with rain. A sword hung at his side, a knife too, and upon his back was a large bow and a quiver filled with arrows.

"How well can you shoot?" I asked, wanting to fill the silence with anything but the sound of rain and wind.

"I can hit a target," Laphaniel replied, causing one of the nearby knights to snigger.

With one swift move, he notched an arrow and let it fly over the horses, sending it straight through the flesh of an apple held in the hands of a knight at the front of our group. The yelp of surprise caused his horse to rear up and toss him from the saddle, dumping him with a thump into the dirt to the sound of cheers and laughter.

"Not bad," the sniggering knight said. Curling black hair hung over his face, almost obscuring the vivid green eyes that stared back at us with a grudging respect. He held out a hand to Laphaniel. "I'm Cole. The idiot you just landed in the dirt is Liam."

Laphaniel shook the outstretched hand, shoulders relaxing slightly as some of the tension lifted from the group.

"Show off," I muttered to him, earning myself a smirk.

"I was aiming for his hand."

We travelled down the twisting paths of Unseelie lands for hours, the strange twilight overhead barely reaching down through the ancient trees surrounding us. The twisted and black forests thinned, the giant oaks turning spindly as the landscape slowly changed. We passed sprawling lakes, the ground growing soggy underfoot, so the horses struggled and resisted. Mist rose from the murky waters, ripples appearing on the surface as things from the depths drifted upwards.

I was soaked from the waist down, my dress heavy with mud while my frozen fingers clung to the reins. I urged my horse onwards, the creature bucking and snorting its displeasure.

"Would it be better to dismount? We're weighing the horses down."

"Jump off at your own risk, girl," shouted one of the knights, unsheathing his sword in one fluid motion. The others followed, the sound of metal cutting through the eerie softness of the swamps. Laphaniel drew his weapon, his eyes following the ripples in the water.

"Mermaids," he whispered to me. "Bring your legs up, make sure you're not touching the water."

"But it's so shallow…"

Laphaniel pressed a finger to his lips, taking the reins from me and dragging my terrified mare onwards.

I watched the water, noted how the horses twitched and shuddered. The knights ahead were silent, swords poised and ready.

The tension was stifling, unnerving. Glamour awoke with the growing fear, pouring down my arms to my fingertips. I outstretched my fingers, waiting for the surge of power to ripple through me.

"No," Laphaniel whispered, reaching out to still my hand. "Don't."

I lowered my hand, noting how the Raven knights' eyes were all trained on me. I glanced at Cole, who shook his head with the barest of movements before nodding to the sword he held.

With a sharp signal, we began to move again, and I tried to calm the swirling Glamour inside me. It pulsed through my body, humming in panic…stirring the waters beneath us.

Something surfaced, ducking back under the shallows before I could take a good look. A tail flicked out, long and black, as slick as an eel.

I caught the subtle movement beside me, barely a ripple, and I couldn't tear my eyes away as a head emerged. Milky white eyes stared back, unblinking within a bleached face. Tendrils of greasy black strands curled over its bony shoulders, spilling like oil around it. A smile, bloodless and stretched, widened over its lips, revealing rows of cracked and jagged teeth.

Others emerged from the swamp, pushing up from the shallows to rest upon outstretched arms. They watched us pass with a mild curiosity, eyes trained upon the weapons the knights held in their hands.

For a moment, I thought they would let us pass, but then they opened their mouths and sang.

It filled that eerie twilight with a song so haunting...so soul destroying, I felt as if my heart would break. It consumed me...everyone, even the horses, stilled.

I willed myself to look away, digging my fingernails deep into my palms to force my attention elsewhere, the pain grounding me. I kicked my horse forward, grabbing my slack reins from Laphaniel's hand and snapping them harder than I wanted to. The sharp sting caused her to jerk and jolt forward, horned head slashing through the mist.

I grabbed Laphaniel as I passed, pinching him hard on the underside of his arm. He barely flinched, didn't look at me as he stared out at the swamp, his fingers loosening around the blade in his hand, so it slipped uselessly into the waters.

The song lilted and drifted around us, lulling and tempting and soft and wonderful...deadly. My nails bit into my skin.

One by one, the knights dropped their weapons, their faces blank and slack while the mermaids closed in.

Without much thought and driven by sudden blinding panic, I threw my hands out, sending a wave of Glamour over the horses. I sent white-hot pain into nerve endings, causing them to scream out and bolt forwards, taking the dazed knights with them.

I struck Laphaniel's horse, but it reared up instead and startled a petrified mare beside it that had yet to move. It threw the dark-haired rider off, plunging him into the waters beside Laphaniel. The heavy hooves missed their heads by sheer luck. My shout echoed across the lake as Laphaniel stood and staggered, hauling the fallen knight to his feet beside him. His hand fumbled for a knife still sheathed in his belt.

With a screeching halt, the song stopped, and every slick body snapped its head toward the two faeries in the water.

"Stay there!" Laphaniel shouted. "Don't you dare get off! Go!"

Laphaniel launched a rock at my horse, hitting it hard on the rump, so it reared in pain and began to bolt, taking no heed to me screaming at it to stop.

I leapt off beside the Raven knights and spun around, fighting against the strong arms that locked around my waist.

"Let me go!" I demanded, but the hands just held tighter, pulling me up the embankment where I could do nothing but watch as the creatures swamped over Laphaniel and the struggling Raven knight.

Laphaniel slashed with his knife, swinging at anything that got too close, the roar at his lips drowning out the poisonous song of the mermaids. They rose up over the Raven knight, hauling him down into the black water until I could see nothing of him.

One of the knights darted past me, the mirror image to the faerie lost in the waters. He barely made it to the water's edge before Cole snatched his arm and dragged him back. "Move again, and I'll knock you out, Fell."

"Ferdia!" bellowed the Raven knight, his voice merging with mine as I screamed for Laphaniel.

The oily creatures screeched, clawed hands raking to drag them both down, but Laphaniel kept slashing with his blade until the waters ran red, and they began to slip away, teeth bared…but silent.

"Laphaniel!" I cried out, shoving away from the hold on me, slipping down the bank with the knight called Fell close behind, followed swiftly by the others.

Laphaniel dragged the limp body of Ferdia through the thick water, blood running in trickles down his face.

"Move!" Cole shoved me aside as Laphaniel dropped to his knees with his arm still around Ferdia. "Is he breathing?"

Laphaniel shook his head, fighting with too slick hands to remove Ferdia's breastplate. Cole tossed it aside before slamming his hands against his chest.

Again,

and again.

"Wait," Laphaniel hissed, shoving Cole to the side before forcing Ferdia's head back. He reached into his mouth and hooked out a coil of thick green weed. Ferdia drew in a guttering breath, dark eyes flying open before he spewed up a stomach-full of brackish lake water into Laphaniel's lap.

"Wonderful," Laphaniel muttered, rising to his feet.

"I could have gone in after him," Fell, Ferdia's twin, snapped, whirling on Cole. "I could have got him out!"

"I am not losing good men on this ridiculous quest," Cole answered, giving me a pointed look. "Both of them got out by the skin of their teeth."

I ran my hands over Laphaniel. "Are you okay? Look at me, are you okay?"

He nodded slowly, his eyes not meeting mine.

Cole stood, giving Laphaniel a sharp slap on the back. "You have our thanks. We'll camp beyond the lake here tonight. All of you, clear the area, get the fires lit. Ferdia, get up and walk it off. Faolan and Liam, retrieve the fucking swords, and be wary of any remaining slippery bastards. Oliver and Angus go and get food. Fell, see to the horses."

Cole was met with a chorus of shouts, an echo of his orders as the Raven knights began to move. Faolan and Liam eyed the shallows with caution, shoving each other closer to the bloodied water, bickering who would be going in first.

With a broad hand, Cole swept the dark curls from his face, turning to Laphaniel.

"You didn't let him go," he said, eyes narrowing.

"No."

"Get yourself something to eat, and a stiff drink, though don't accept anything Liam offers you, he brews it himself, and it tastes like satyr piss."

"Would you have left him?" I asked before he walked away. "Would you have let my husband drown?"

Cole held my stare, unflinching and unapologetic, then he simply nodded and turned his back on us.

I took Laphaniel's freezing hand to lead him down to the camp that was slowly forming not too far away, feeling it tremble against mine.

"I just need a minute." His voice hitched, breathing ragged. He wrenched his hand from mine, shoving the sodden hair from his eyes. "One minute."

"What's wrong?" I asked, pulling him close. He swallowed down breaths, fingers digging into my back. "Laphaniel?"

"I pulled pond weed from your mouth too." He forced the words out, struggling against me.

The water, the mermaids. I had no idea how deeply it had affected him because he didn't speak of it...only once beneath the Unseelie Castle while in the grips of a fever dream.

He sucked in another breath, a gasping sound I had heard countless times before, the noise he made before he woke screaming. The noise I had heard him make upon a bloodstained floor in a ruined castle.

A shuddering, awful breath after what had nearly been his last.

He had gone under the water and couldn't breathe.

"You're fine," I whispered to him. "You're fine."

He shook his head, eyes wide. I placed my hand over his heart, feeling it jackhammer back at me.

"It's okay." I could taste his panic, sharp and unending. "Close your eyes, I'm not going anywhere, close your eyes."

He did as I instructed, squeezing his eyes shut, growing agitated while I held onto him.

"Hold your breath."

He shook his head again, pulling away from me

"Hold your breath," I repeated, digging my fingers into his shoulders, until he obeyed. "Now let it go."

It hissed through his teeth, angry and scared.

"Again."

He opened his eyes, and he blew out a breath, steadier as the panic started to ebb from his eyes.

"Again."

"Teya…" Laphaniel began, his voice catching.

"Shh, it's okay," I said, but he just shook his head, his fingers fumbling for mine.

"No…I saw it." He stumbled over the words. "I slipped under the water…I must have blacked out for just a second…but it's waiting. It's waiting for me and it's so angry."

Dread prickled at my spine, at the memory of shadowy fingers hovering over my husband. I had felt its wrath in that cursed tower, its reluctance at giving up what rightfully belonged to it.

"Perhaps it was only a flashback?" I began, desperate to comfort him. "Like your nightmares?"

"No, it was different…"

"You felt it try to drag you back? Wherever you went before?"

Laphaniel met my eyes, the strange blue clouded. "I don't think I get to go back there."

"I won't let that happen," I said to him, running my hands up and down his arms until he at last stopped trembling. "I will journey through the pits of hell to find you and drag you out if that is what I have to do. It'll be another adventure. I'll bring Charlotte and Oonagh, Nefina too, and we'll wreak so much havoc that death itself will throw you out to get some peace."

A thin smile spread over his lips. "I don't doubt you."

"Make sure you don't," I said, reaching out to brush the hair from his face. "We'll figure this out together, you and me. You're not alone."

"I know."

"Come on, let's find a place by the fire, have something to eat, and do all of this again tomorrow."

We made our way through the thin and crooked trees, their limbs covered in thick moss that dripped from the branches. The blackened wood looked dead, rotten; pieces ripped open to reveal an abundance of fungus thriving within. Life still clung to the branches, blooms of vivid orange flowers stretched up towards the strange Unseelie light, tiny buds of purple flourished along the cracks and crevices. Some of the trees even held onto their leaves, blackened things with pointed edges that caught against my clothes when I brushed past.

The others barely looked up as we joined the camp, but Cole caught my eye and gave me a slight nod before gesturing to the spit hanging above the roaring fire.

We settled a little way away from the group but close enough to feel the benefit of the generous fire. We ate readily, the wild pig filling my stomach while the sound of the Raven knights' chatter filled my ears. Drinks were passed around, strong spirits that burned my throat and tasted like the earth, both muddy and gritty.

I sat between Laphaniel's legs, his head resting against my shoulder, arms loose around me. Together we listened to the stories the Raven knights shared, of the battles they had seen, the things they had fought against, the friends they had lost. I listened as their tales slipped into laments, and with the drinks flowing they soon turned into bawdy songs that I couldn't help grinning along to.

CHAPTER TWENTY-SEVEN

We rested beneath the stars, the warmth from the fire keeping some of the night's chill at bay, but not enough that I couldn't feel the damp settle deep into my bones. I huddled beneath a thick blanket, the sound of Laphaniel's steady breathing in my ear. His hand rested in my lap, head tilted back against the tree trunk he leant on. I couldn't sleep.

Restless, I carefully untangled myself and tucked the blanket back around Laphaniel. I made my way to the centre of the camp, mindful not to step on the fingers of the sleeping knights. Snores and grunts lifted from the mounds of blankets, drifting into the star-flecked skies to join the distant howls and cries that filled the Unseelie night.

Picking up a log from the stacked pile, I tossed it into the fire and watched the sparks dance. The flames eased the numbness from my fingers, bringing warmth back to my aching joints.

"Do you want some company?" I asked the faerie taking watch, and his deep brown eyes met mine, almost black despite the firelight.

"Is your lover boring you?" he answered, flashing teeth.

"My husband is sleeping." I threw another stick into the flames. "I needed to stretch my legs."

"Can't sleep?" His eyes flashed, head tilting. "Does a group of hostile men worry you?"

I tensed, instantly returning my gaze to Laphaniel's sleeping form, not far from us. "Should it?"

He scrubbed a hand down his face, scratching against the reddish stubble on his chin. "No, you're safe enough with us."

He shifted to make room for me on the thick log, and I sat beside him, accepting the flask he passed to me.

"You look very young to be meddling in things you don't truly understand."

"Don't I know it," I replied, taking a hearty sip from the flask before passing it back. The Raven knight took a long sip, eyes still on me, waiting. "I would rather not be here; I'd rather not be meddling in all...this."

"Where would you rather be?" He turned slightly, so he faced me, the inky feathers on his cloak rippling with the movement, the firelight catching the deeper hues of blue within them.

"In a house made of stone," I answered, closing my eyes so I could see it. "Where it rained blossom inside, and the walls breathed. I would rather be on a bed made from fallen trees, piled with threadbare throws and soft furs. A place where I was loved beyond anything else."

"You wouldn't go home?"

"That was home," I said, rubbing at the sudden ache within my chest, a longing that had rooted deep within me.

"Would you not want your sister back?"

"No, you can keep her."

He snorted into the flask, choking on the mouthful he had just taken, and I found myself grinning.

"What's your name?"

"Faolan," he said, a lopsided smile still on his face. "Cole is an ungrateful shit, but the rest of us won't forget what your husband did for Ferdia, least of all Fell."

I glanced back at Laphaniel, smiling. "He has a weird thing for damsels in distress."

Another laugh, rich and genuine. "Careful, Queen of Seelie, else I may end up liking you."

"Would that be so awful?"

"It wouldn't be wise, seeing as our courts are longstanding enemies."

And always would be if all went well. The contract I signed made that abundantly clear.

"What kind of queen is Niven?"

All traces of humour vanished from Faolan's face. "It is treason to speak ill of one's sovereign."

"I wasn't going to tell her, obviously."

Faolan leant closer, the liquor on his breath strong and unpleasant. "You may hold your tongue, but the trees are listening. I am rather fond of my beautiful head remaining attached to my body."

"Do you fear her more than the Unseelie King?"

His breath tickled against my ear, and I fought the urge to flinch. "Phabian is the King of the Unseelie. Your sister is human."

"You didn't answer my question."

"Any sane creature would be wary of Niven."

I smiled, pulling away. "That still isn't an answer."

"It's all you're getting, Queen of Seelie."

I stayed a little longer and warmed myself by the fire, watching over the sleeping bodies of the Raven knights, a sea of shimmering black feathers beneath the even blacker night sky.

From where I sat, I could just make out the hands clasped around sword hilts, fingers curling around the handles of daggers, of knives. I was not mistaken to believe they were deeply asleep...that they wouldn't leap up at the first sound of trouble. It led me to wonder if they ever slept peacefully if they knew how it felt to sleep long and deep without fear.

Because I didn't.

"There's a few hours before dawn," Faolan said, his dark eyes scanning the campsite. "It's going to be a long day tomorrow. You'd better try and get some rest, otherwise, you'll slow us all down if you fall from your horse."

"Goodnight, then." I stood and dusted myself off. Faolan nodded, kicking a few more logs into the hungry fire.

"You're nothing like your sister," he said to my back, leaving me to wonder if he meant it as a compliment or not.

Laphaniel stirred when I crept back beneath the blankets, flinching at the touch of my cold fingers.

"Sorry," I whispered, huddling closer. "I didn't mean to wake you."

"What is it with you and wandering off?" he said, shifting on the damp ground, trying to get comfortable again. "Your hands are freezing, Teya."

But he was warm, so wonderfully warm. He hissed at my hands, sneaking beneath the layers he wore, but he didn't fight me off. The blankets tightened around me, my head tucked beneath his chin as he pulled me closer.

"I couldn't sleep," I said, closing my eyes to the sound of his heartbeat. "I don't think I'll be able to rest until this is all over. If it'll ever be over."

"Your Glamour will only be more unpredictable if you're exhausted."

I sighed, and he ran his hand down my back in long, soothing strokes. "It's already pretty damned unpredictable."

"You can ride in front of me tomorrow if you need to, it might be easier to sleep if you're moving."

I tilted my head up, meeting his eyes. "That won't look very queen-like, though, will it? What will the Unseelie think of me, dribbling on your shoulder?"

"I don't care what they think," Laphaniel answered, hands still moving across my back, fingers needing into the knots twisted beneath my skin. "I care about you."

I lifted the pendant hanging from his neck, my fingers stroking over the smooth wood, following the strange etches carved into one side. "Were you dreaming?"

"Before your frozen fingers woke me up? Yes, I was."

"About what?" I asked, grinning.

"Usually, it's you, for you are a cause of constant worry," he said, huffing a laugh when I elbowed him. "Tonight, I dreamt of Nefina."

"Do you think she's safe?"

"She's with Oonagh, so I want to believe so," he answered, unable to hide the flash of regret upon his face. "But I can't shake the feeling that I've left it too late."

"It's not too late," I said, entwining my fingers through his. "We'll find her again, and you can spend the next hundred years making it right for her."

He took a breath. "What if she's already dead?"

I had no answer for him, at least nothing that could offer him any sense of comfort, because I simply did not know. I only had the hope that our friends were still alive, but that was not enough. Hope was a fickle, cruel thing, and we both knew that.

Dawn came slowly and too soon, the dark skies lightening to a mercifully clear day, the morning light glowing violet down through the spindly trees. Dew glistened over the coarse grass, the barest hint of frost lingering upon the ground.

I stirred after a restless night, damp and cold from sleeping on the floor, my bones aching as I stretched some life back into them. Quiet chatter drifted around; most of the raven knights were already awake and up, gathering around the fire where something was cooking for breakfast. I nudged Laphaniel, and he opened bleary eyes, scrubbing a hand over them before I pulled him to his feet.

Cole glanced up at us from his seat on a weathered log, gesturing to a pot bubbling over the flames. "Get some food while it's still hot, because it's foul when left to cool, it starts to congeal."

"What is it?"

A smirk crept over his lips. "The remains of what was left from last night, some hot water, a handful of herbs and oats. You won't find fine dining here."

I ladled some into a bowl with a shrug. "I've eaten worse."

We ate the salty, grey stew with little complaint, scraping what was left of the meat off the bones floating within it. It was warming and filling, just enough to keep the chill off for a little while.

I helped douse the fire while Laphaniel packed up the horses, the entire camp busy and organised. There was little chatter, just shouted orders for everything to be stripped away, leaving no sign that we were ever there.

We rode, and we camped, and we rode again. For six long days, we continued through the Unseelie lands. Slowly, the damp, swampy landscape hardened into clearer plains, to crashing rivers and jagged rocks. Colossal trees intertwined together to create natural bridges high overhead; the boughs so thick they made walkways that hung over the furious waterfalls that flowed beneath. The land dipped and fell into deep gorges that scarred the miles of open ground as far as the eye could see.

The nights crept in colder, the days gave little relief from the biting chill. The eerie permanent twilight sky remained clear and cloudless and bitingly cold. Within the span of a few days, autumn had given up its lingering fight and allowed winter to creep in. In the mornings, the frost had stopped melting.

Tempers frayed, and Cole had his hands full, splitting up scuffles between his men.

"This is fucking bullshit," Oliver, a towering knight with cropped blond hair, snapped. "Remind me again why we're freezing our bollocks off for this brat?"

"Would you rather be all tucked up someplace nice and warm?" Laphaniel answered tightly.

Oliver spun his horse around, and Laphaniel's hand instantly went to the knife at his belt. "Yes! Wouldn't you?"

Laphaniel paused while the others exchanged wary glances. Cole tensed his shoulders, readying himself to pull the two fey apart if they started. Slowly, Laphaniel's fingers relaxed, and his knife remained sheathed.

"Anywhere but here," he answered finally, earning a curt nod from Oliver.

"Surrounded by a swarm of whores and endless ale," the broad knight said. "Ever been to a brothel, boy?"

"I've seen my share of them," Laphaniel replied through gritted teeth, jerking forwards as Oliver clapped him hard on the back.

"Happiest places on earth." Oliver snapped the reins of his horse. "Hook yourself up with an Unseelie whore while you're here, I swear you'll never look back."

"He's married!" I yelled to him, earning myself a cackle of laughter from the knights. I turned my attention to Cole, who eyed me with an exasperated look on his face. "I thought you said it would take a week to get to Luthien? We've been travelling for six days, and we're still on Unseelie soil."

Black flooded his eyes. "Really? Do you think I had not noticed?"

Laphaniel slowed his horse, remaining close, one hand still lingering on the hilt of his knife.

"I was just—"

Cole cut me off with a snarl, his horse nickering. "Perhaps you think I'm lost, Queen of Seelie? Or that I am leading us around these forsaken rocks for the sheer fun of it?"

"I didn't mean…"

"Would you like to lead us? Have you not noted how winter is creeping in earlier than it should? Which leaves the Mourning river impassable, too cold to swim across, and the ice will be too thin to walk upon. Do you even know where the Mourning River is? We could go up through the Northern Caves, but the Cleavers dwell up there and would likely take all our heads. Oh, not yours though, they'll use you for breeding. Or, what we could do is stay on this fucking path, which is passable and should only delay us by a few days."

"Point taken," I said, shrinking beneath Cole's furious gaze.

"I don't take the safety of my men lightly, Seelie Queen," he said. "Or yours, for what it's worth. I choose the path we take." He held a hand up, cutting off Laphaniel before he could speak. "Do not question me. The safest path is the one we are on."

A screech tore through the air, cleaving the world apart, shaking the ground even before a great shadow soared over us.

My mare rose, an awful sound escaping her mouth. She bucked, striking my face with the back of her head, and pain exploded behind my eyes, then up my back as I struck the unyielding ground.

I whipped my head up, just in time to see curving talons pluck up my terrified horse like she was a grape. Around me, the earth lifted with the force of gigantic leathery wings beating against the sky. Pieces of rock slammed into me, the world suddenly filled with nothing but the sounds of chaos.

My mouth opened, not a sound slipping through as I remained frozen, head tipped back to stare dumbly at the skies. They ripped through it with a hideous grace, bodies long as jet planes, the rippling midnight scales drinking in the violet light. Teeth flashed, so did the talons. Red dripped from the claws.

Dragons.

They were dragons.

I found my voice, raw and desperate. "Laphaniel!"

A plea and a question.

I couldn't see anything. Dust whipped around me in a choking smog. Glamour pulsed at my fingertips panicked. The threads wouldn't still, wouldn't allow me to work them into anything but a frenzied tangle.

"Laphaniel!" I screamed his name.

"Get up!"

Cole grabbed my arm, hauling me onto the back of his horse. It bucked, and claws scraped inches from us. So close...too close. I felt the heat from the scales, could smell the fire beneath the armour.

Cole kicked sharply, tugging on the reins to turn the petrified beast around. I clung to his waist, cringing into his back. A head snapped down, serpentine and massive. A maw opened, teeth longer than my arm glinting against a mouth of never-ending black. Foul breath hit us, hot and stagnant.

Terror bubbled in my stomach, erasing everything else out. Everything. I could taste Cole's fear. Sharp and real, hitting me in waves until there was nothing left. Nothing at all.

Warmth trickled down my legs, I didn't know if it was sweat or...I didn't care.

Cole slammed the reins, again and again. Teeth clashed beside us, talons gouging chunks of earth up, missing us by a breath. Cole forced the horse to zigzag, his head bowed over its neck, my own body pressed tight to his.

Blackness lashed out, razor-tipped and swift. A guttural rasp followed the spray of blood, and the horse buckled forward, collapsing over itself, drawing both of us beneath it.

Something cracked. For a merciful moment, the world stopped.

Cole landed on top of me, his body heavy and limp. I could feel the warm, sticky mess of his head pressed against mine. Agony shot down my shoulder, my neck. Everywhere.

"Get up," I breathed, tasting blood on my lips. "Please."

I tried not to look at the remains of the horse or the way the massive teeth had ripped through it with such ease. One bite, and it was gone.

"Cole." The word shuddered from my mouth. The knight groaned, gaze vacant as he lifted his head. Bone gleamed through the knotted curls. His eyes rolled back, body tensing before convulsing beside me, every movement sent blinding pain over my broken bones.

"Look at me," I hissed through the darkness slipping over me. I choked on a sob. "You need to get up."

My bones ground together. I clung to consciousness by a thread.

"Can you move?" The voice didn't belong to Laphaniel, but Faolan. He crawled closer to me, body pressed close to the ground. "I can't carry you and Cole...my orders are to keep you safe."

"I can't run..."

"Don't run." Faolan dragged himself closer, face caked in blood and mud. "If you're still, they can't see you, if you move slowly..."

"Please don't leave Cole," I said, and he glanced between us, face tormented and terrified, wanting to choose him over me. "Please."

Faolan gritted his teeth. "Walk straight ahead, keep to the trees and the rocks. There's a dip...there's a slope, and it leads to a cave. Don't run."

Tears slid down my cheeks, a gasp ripping from my lips as I forced myself up. With a hand tight around my middle, I took a step forward and braced myself. I took another, then another and another. I dared a glance, I needed to.

It rested too close to me; its head tilted back to scent the air. Great horns protruded from its plated head, smaller ones lined at its neck and throat. Yellow eyes shone bright and alert from hooded lids, while steam rose in waves from its slitted nostrils, hissing when it struck the frigid air.

It rose, stretching its enormous wings, so it blotted out the sunlight. Red glowed from its throat, scales becoming like molten ore as it spun its head around. Heat smacked against me, slamming me with the stench of decay upon ancient breath, a promise of death.

Faolan swore, grabbing my arm, so I barked in pain. "Use your Glamour, quick!"

"I don't know how…"

"Imagine a protective bubble around us, glittering and real…now… do it now!"

Faolan yanked me close as if he could shield me if I failed. I pulled upon the skittering pieces of my Glamour, weaving them tight, feeling them fray the more I pulled.

Seconds. I had seconds to drag the flickering bubble around the three of us before flame erupted from the gaping jaws and flooded towards me.

The heat was unimaginable. Sweat pooled and steamed from our skin, the flames licking up high, burning blue, charring the ground to nothing. It burned up the air, crackling along the fragile knots of my bubble, splitting it.

I held onto it, aching. Everything aching.

"Move!"

The bubble shattered around us, and I sucked in a lungful of air at the same time Faolan did. I choked on the oily smoke, unable to see anything in front of me. Faolan's hand clamped around mine, hauling me forward. His other hand stayed tight around Cole's legs, the unconscious knight hanging limply over his shoulder.

I heard a screech but saw nothing through the curling black smoke.

We ran, and the sounds of raking claws followed us. The earth boomed with each footfall, the wind crying out at each flap of mighty wings.

The ground finally dipped, the entrance to the cave appearing behind a scattering of scorched trees.

"Laphaniel." The word rasped past my lips, nothing more than a guttural whisper as I saw him race forwards. He crashed against me in an embrace that reeked of smoke and sweat, lifting me into his arms without a word.

Others passed us to grab Cole, hauling him into the cave. Someone caught Faolan and dragged him forward and away from the crashing jaws that missed him by a breath.

CHAPTER TWENTY-EIGHT

ocks crashed around the cave entrance, teeth and claws tearing down at them, the edges glowing red as scorching breath growled around it.

"Get back into the tunnels!" Faolan bellowed. "Make up a bed for Cole, hurry."

The others rushed by, all dirtied, bloodied, limping.

"Is he alive?" Oliver's cropped silvery hair was coated in ash.

"I don't know," Faolan answered, glancing at me in Laphaniel's arms, and his hands tightened around me, fingers gripping into my shoulders. My husband had yet to say a word to me.

"Is anyone else hurt?" I asked, cringing away from the furious shrieks thundering from behind the cave mouth.

"Liam," Ferdia began, leaning heavily against his twin. We followed him down and down into an antechamber deep within the cave. Skittering light danced from above, shards of sunlight peeking down from crevices high up to scatter over the crystals embedded in the stone. "The beast lifted him from the ground, the talons went straight through him and his horse."

The smell of blood hit me before anything else, the low moans exaggerated by the cavernous room, so they echoed misery and pain around us. Candles had been hastily stuffed into alcoves, giving off jittery light that barely touched the corners of the cave. The walls glittered with the unsteady glow, dancing off the sharp-edged jewels embedded in the rock.

Laphaniel carefully set me down on my feet, and I took a step forward, regretting it instantly. He kept a hand at my back, staying close. Beneath the sweat and the stench of smoke, I could smell the fear swarming him, the panic mingling with dizzying relief that left him speechless. Because it wasn't me lying on the cold floor.

Liam lay sprawled on the ground, black hair sticking to his face, the feathers threaded through it, limp and broken. His mouth hung open, pale lips murmuring words that no one could make out; dribbles of red slipped from one corner.

His armour had been shredded like it were made from tin foil, exposing a mess of ragged fabric and torn flesh, and most of what was supposed to be on his insides...no longer was.

"A scratch," he rasped, blood splattering his lip. He made to move his hand over his stomach, but I just couldn't bear the thought of him feeling his guts, so I reached for him instead. His hand curled tight around mine, the skin cold.

"Can you save him?" I tilted my head to look at Oliver, who crouched nearby, his hand squeezing Liam's shoulder.

"What do you expect me to do?" he growled, blood shining against his teeth. "Shove his stomach back in and sew him up?"

I glared back. "Yes."

Oliver's face softened, but he shook his head, reaching up to wipe at the blood spilling from a wound on his forehead. "War has casualties, your Majesty."

I clutched at Liam's hand, refusing to look at the pool of blood seeping from beneath him. The knight drew in a long, shuddering breath, the sound hissing through his teeth before his lovely blue eyes clouded over and he stilled. There would be no ancient magic to bring him back.

Someone, I didn't know who, gently untangled Liam's hand from mine and set it upon his ruined chest. Above me, they murmured a few words beneath their breath, a fragment of song I had no place knowing. As one, they each drew a sole black feather from their cloaks and placed it upon him.

Looking closer, I could see gaps between the feathers, some of them were bent slightly as if many fingers had reached in and plucked them out, a feather for each fallen.

"You need to lie down," Laphaniel said, breaking his silence. "You won't heal unless you sleep."

I took in the bloodied knights around me. "I can't. I need to do something useful."

"Teya." My name was a warning on his lips. I stared him down.

"I'll rest when everyone is settled."

"There is nothing for you to do. We can't move Cole, and you can barely walk, let alone ride. Get some sleep and heal." His hand came up to cup my face, eyes bright. "I thought I'd lost you."

The crack in his voice ensured I wouldn't argue. We had come too close...so close to losing each other. With a small nod, I allowed him to help me down upon a hastily made bed. Blankets were piled up upon the cold floor, a bag used for my pillow.

Cole lay on a similar heap of blankets at my side, unmoving.

"What do you want us to do?" Fell asked, stripping cloth into clean bandages while Ferdia inspected the gore around Cole's head.

"What?" Laphaniel looked up. The Unseelie knights were looking to him, their faces expectant.

"Cole is unresponsive, your Queen can barely keep her head up—as king, you are next in line of command. What would you have us do?" Oliver said, taking a breath before he added a forced, "Your Majesty."

"Find clean water," Laphaniel said after a pause, not moving from me. "Food, if you can get it, obviously don't go outside. Do you two know what you're doing?" Fell and Ferdia nodded, barely glancing at him while they carried on working on Cole. "Treat any other wounded. Treat the remaining horses before they die of shock. Someone needs to get rid of the body."

There was a silence, tense, and short-lived.

"The body?"

Laphaniel stood. "Yes, will that be a problem?"

"The Unseelie burn their dead," Oliver growled, "Liam deserves a funeral fit for a knight of the Unseelie, he died for your Queen."

"He died for your King," Laphaniel replied, staying calm. "Are you really going to burn him in this cave? With nowhere for the smoke to go, we'll all suffocate. If you are suggesting we leave him over there, until we are ready to move out, then it's going to get messy. We won't be going anywhere for a few days, and it's humid in here."

"He deserves better."

Laphaniel stepped closer to him. "Life doesn't care what we deserve. Dispose of the body before it draws the rats in."

"And if that body was your wife?"

Laphaniel closed the gap between them, and I swore I could feel the barest echo of his Glamour flare up. "Then, I would no longer need any of you."

"You would allow Luthien to take the crown?" A nasty smirk lifted the side of Oliver's mouth.

"Yes, and I wouldn't lift a finger while she tore your world apart."

"All this because you love her?" Oliver pointed a finger at me, shaking his head as if he found the very idea unfathomable. "You're a fool."

"I've been called worse." Laphaniel shrugged. "Dispose of the body. Mourn another time."

Oliver didn't reply; a snarl slipped from his lips before he stormed off. I didn't fail to notice how he was the only one who spoke up, the only one fighting for his friend's dignity. The others understood that Laphaniel was right. We couldn't afford to honour the dead, not when it was so hard to take care of the living.

A strange sense of order quickly descended over the cave, and water was fetched from a trickling stream that ran through the tunnels, small silver fish were caught within the waters, and beds were made with the last of the supplies that had survived the attack.

A hush settled over us, whispered voices echoing around the dim cavern. Injuries were cleaned and dressed; burns wrapped. A tribute was made for Liam. Then quiet.

Laphaniel remained close to me, eyes darting around the cave at the knights as they settled to get some rest, to Cole at my side. Assessing, organising, leading. I squeezed his hand, and he looked down at me, a tired smile on his lips.

"You have no idea how thankful I am that you're no longer quite human," he said, bringing my hand to his mouth. "That your bones will heal tonight."

"Your bones won't do that anymore." Fear gripped around my heart. "If you break, I won't be able to put you back together."

"I didn't break, Teya." His voice was soft, sounding a little too far away. "Stop talking and go to sleep."

My eyes closed as blackness set in, a heavy force just too compelling to ignore. It brought with it the promise of a painless sleep, and I could fight it no longer. The last thing I saw before I gave in completely was the broken form of Cole as he foamed at the mouth, shaking violently against the folded blankets that made up his bed.

CHAPTER TWENTY-NINE

I stirred to darkness and hushed whispers, the shadowed edges of the cave lit up by candle stubs that did little to expel the smothering pitch. One flickered beside me, illuminating a cup of cool water.

The pain lingering in my body was nothing but a distant throb, a stiffness in my neck and ribs, nothing more.

Turning my head on the bundle of a lumpy bag that was my pillow, I turned to face Cole. The left side of his face was unrecognisable, even in the dim light. One eye remained swollen shut, a mess of livid bruises raged against his skin, and where once there had been a finely pointed ear, nothing but raw and bloodied flesh remained.

His eye flickered open, a moan slipping past his split lip as he moved his head, his gaze locking onto mine.

"Hey," I whispered, reaching a hand across to his bed. "Don't try to sit up yet."

He stared at me for a moment, then down at my fingers holding his.

"Can you squeeze my hand?" I asked, but he slumped back and didn't move again.

"We found nightstar flowers growing in one of the tunnels," Laphaniel said, appearing beside me, placing a few more candle stubs in the alcoves above my head. "It's the same herb found in Goodnight Kisses. We've given Cole a fair amount of it, so I doubt he will be making any sense for a while."

I sat up slowly, stretching out my limbs. "Will he be okay?"

"He stopped fitting a few hours ago, and his wounds are clean. We'll be able to tell more when the nightstar wears off." Laphaniel settled beside me, then traced the lingering bruises on my skin with a gentle finger. "How are you feeling?"

I shifted so I could lie against him, breathing him in, hating the way he smelled like dragon fire and blood, of stale sweat and fear.

"Still a little sore," I replied. "Is everyone else okay?"

"Nothing that won't heal quickly." Laphaniel glanced behind him, listening for something I wasn't aware of. I tilted my head but heard nothing. "Would you like something to eat? The fish aren't too bad, but you have to eat them raw."

As lovely as food sounded, my head still had a strange heaviness to it. "Can I sleep a little longer?"

"As long as you need."

He helped me lie back down, tucking me under his cloak until I was almost unbearably warm. The fabric smelled like him, comforting despite the filth coating it.

"I can stay with you if you want me to."

"Are you needed elsewhere?"

Laphaniel looked out into the darkness, to the sound of voices down the tunnels. "I am…"

"Go, I'll be fine here."

"I won't be far away."

"Laphaniel?"

He turned, waiting.

"I love you."

"You first told me that in another damp cave," he said, candlelight dancing over his eyes, making the blue glow.

"I remember." I closed my eyes. "Beats saying it for the first time drugged up on troll poison."

I heard his laugh, felt the warmth of his mouth on mine as he brushed the ghost of a kiss onto my lips. "I meant it, though."

Sleep settled over me like a safety blanket. Quick and warm and heavy. Dreams floated through the darkness, of soft sunshine and blossom-heavy branches within a house of stone.

"QUEENLING?"

I winced at the jabbing to my arm, groggily swatting it away.

"Queenling?

Another jab, harder this time. Then a pinch.

"Teya?

I opened my eyes, my wonderful dream disappearing as quickly as it had come. "What?"

"Oh, good, you're awake," Cole whispered, his face so close to mine that I startled. "Where the hell are we?"

Dark bruises still mottled his face, the left eye still swollen shut. "We're in some cave, having narrowly missed being eaten by dragons. You took a nasty blow to the head." I took a breath. "I'm glad you're awake."

"Did everyone else make it?" He moved back at the look on my face. "Who?"

"Liam," I answered, and he brought his head down into his hands. "I'm so sorry, Cole—there was nothing you could have done."

"I chose the wrong path."

"You weren't to know," I said, sitting up. "This isn't on you."

He shook his head. "I made the choices; the blame lies with me."

I touched his hand again, and he let me take it. "How are you feeling? You were in a pretty bad way when they carried you in."

"Everything is spinning, and I feel like I'm going to hurl my guts up." He pressed a hand over his good eye, wavering. "I need to go see what's going on."

He tugged his hand from mine and made to get up, but I grabbed his arm and forced him down again. "Laphaniel is handling it, lie down."

"I need to get up." His voice rose, and somewhere in the darkness, someone stirred.

"Shh, everyone is asleep. Calm down."

"I don't know where I am."

"Sit down."

A snarl rumbled up from his throat, black swallowing up the green in his eye. I sensed his growing panic; gone was the imposing captain of the Raven knights, gone was the sureness of an immortal who had lived within the shadows and nightmares of the Unseelie Court. Fear coiled around him like smoke, and I was wary of frightened and vulnerable fey, especially those in pain. It brought out the barely concealed feral nature of faeries.

"Shh, Cole," I whispered, wincing at the sudden hold he had on my arm. "You're safe here."

"I don't know where I am," he repeated.

"You're…"

His fist cracked against my face, and I swallowed my cry of pain, catching his hand when he made to strike again.

"Don't," I said, shoving him back. "Lie still, listen to me."

I wove the temptation into my voice, tasting it against my tongue like a lullaby. I remembered the feel of it, the warmth at my lips, the buzz against my skin. I remembered how it felt to listen to it, to allow that softness in. I remembered how I had made Laphaniel's feet move against his will, while I inched him closer to an open window. I had almost forgotten how good it felt.

"Listen to me." My voice was a song on my lips. "Are you listening?"

Cole nodded slowly, the fear and panic ebbing from his face.

"Let go of me." He dropped my arm, swaying slightly. "Lie down, that's it. Slowly, don't hurt yourself. Close your eyes, and keep listening to me. We are safe here. I am the Queen of Seelie, and I will not let anything happen to you or your knights. Go to sleep. Sleep until the bones in your skull heal until everything stops spinning. We can wait."

I brushed his hair from his face while I spoke, listening to his heartbeat slowing within his chest. Glamour continued to weave its way into my words, threading them through with the desire to rest, my entire body tingling with the power it wielded.

He snored a little, mouth open, fast asleep. I covered him with the cloak and hoped that the next time he woke, he would be functioning better, because as good a job as Laphaniel was doing, we needed Cole. We needed him to navigate us across the bleak Unseelie lands, to stand with his knights to face Luthien.

I stood up to the eerie silence of the cave, the lingering aches, and pains in my body, all gone. My stomach grumbled loud enough to echo, and hunger gnawed at my belly like a beast. Searching the shadows for Laphaniel, I carefully stepped over sleeping knights stretched out upon the cavern floor. I wondered who was on watch…and where they had gone.

The three remaining horses lay unmoving upon the cold ground, candlelight glinting off their curved black horns.

It shouldn't have been so quiet.

I called his name, my voice too loud within the heavy silence, finding him close to a curving tunnel with his head propped against Fell.

"Laphaniel?" I shook him gently. "Something's wrong."

I shook him again when he didn't stir, pressing my hand against his chest to feel the slow thud, thud, thud of his heartbeat.

"Wake up."

I nudged Fell, my fingers digging into his shoulder as I shook him too. He didn't move but slumped forwards against me.

"Fuck." The curse echoed in the silence, lonely and pointless. "Laphaniel? Wake up…please."

I tried to pull the Glamour back into my words, but it wouldn't come. Swallowing the panic, I tried again and again until sweat broke against my skin, and my throat felt raw.

"Open your eyes, for me, please." My breath hissed through my teeth when his eyes flickered open, and I slapped his cheek before they rolled back again. "Stay with me, okay?"

He nodded very slowly, his eyes closing.

"No, no, no, I need you." I propped his head up, tapping his cheek. "I think I've put everyone to sleep."

"Yeah?" he murmured, the single word thick and heavy.

"I don't know how to fix it." My voice caught. "What do I do? No! Stay awake, I need you!"

He forced his eyes open, leaning a clumsy hand against me. "What?"

"What did I do?"

"Hmmm."

"I Glamoured Cole to get some sleep, and I think it spread to everyone." I shook him when his head lolled against my shoulder, and he groaned as he pushed himself back up. "Keep your damned eyes open."

"When?" The word slurred over his lips.

"Just now, about five minutes ago."

"Until…until when?" Laphaniel forced out, blood seeped from his nose as he fought the compulsion to close his eyes. Perhaps the lingering whisper of Glamour he held onto recognised the power now within me, making it possible to resist.

"Until he's healed," I said, "How long will that be? Laphaniel? When will he get better?"

Fear suddenly brightened his sleep-addled eyes, breaking through his haze for a split second. "Don't…"

"Don't what?"

He took a breath, leaning his head against my shoulder. "Tunnels."

"What's in the tunnels?"

It was then that I noticed the two swords lying beside Fell and Laphaniel, the sharp blades red with blood.

"What's in the tunnels? Laphaniel?"

But he didn't answer, his body slumping awkwardly against mine. Easing his head to the floor, I stood and looked around the cave, noting all the shadowy corners where things could hide.

Backing away, I didn't dare linger too close for fear of disturbing whatever Laphaniel and Fell discovered within the tunnel. The rest of the knights slumbered on, and nudging them, shaking them, pinching them, did nothing to stir them. They stayed asleep, unmoving and uncaring, and, although I knew it was all my fault, I felt abandoned.

Making my way back to Cole, I knelt beside him and checked his wounds, peeling away the old bandages to wash the bloodied mess of his head. Pink flesh was beginning to show, the wound slowly knitting itself back together.

"Hurry up," I whispered to him, stroking back his matted hair. "I need you to wake up quickly, Cole."

"Teya."

My head shot up at the sound of my name, the disembodied voice echoing with malice around the too-quiet cave.

"Teya."

I rose, tensing my shoulders, flexing my hands to feel for the spark of Glamour I knew was there.

"Come down here, Teya. We can see you. We can see you are all alone. Come down here with us, Teya."

"What are you?" I shouted back, fighting to feel the familiar surge of power at my fingertips. Nothing came. I grabbed for one of the discarded swords beside Fell and Laphaniel.

"We are hungry."

With the sword clutched in my hand, I swallowed the rising fear and gripped the hilt tight. Wrongness seeped from the tunnel. A wrongness that hadn't been there before.

"What do you want?"

"We are hungry."

I stood in front of Laphaniel and Fell as if I would have any success in defending them against whatever lingered within the darkness.

"Feed us."

Something screeched past me, a whip of stale air and rotted cloth. It flew around the cavern with a shriek at its lips, a sound brimming with fury and hunger.

"Feed us."

It shot towards my face, barely a breath against me. Hollow eyes, buried within grey skin that hung from its skull like the rags from its body bored into me. With my own scream joining the cacophony of echoes, I slashed down upon it, my sword jolting as it struck bone.

It hissed, mouth unhinging to let a howl of rage escape. Blood dripped from the slash I created, dripping from my sword and the mouldering cloth covering its body.

Staggering back, I swung again, aiming higher. The head sliced from its body as if made from butter, bouncing once on the harsh ground before rolling to a stop at the centre of the cave.

Before I could draw breath, before my triumphant shout had finished echoing, the headless wraith floated towards its severed head, picked it up from the ground, and forced it back into the ruined tendrils of its neck.

"So hungry."

It turned, sweeping back over the sleeping forms of Fell and Laphaniel. A clawed hand hovered over them, nails black and long and so very sharp.

"Don't!"

It retracted its fingers, a snarl forming over its maw as it twisted its head back to me, dark blood seeping from the edges of its neck.

"Empty."

"What?"

"Empty." It repeated the word, hissing it through thin, needle-like teeth. "There is nothing within."

Those long fingers moved away from Laphaniel to run across Fells' face. It trailed them down his neck before splaying them across his chest.

"I can almost taste this one."

"Taste what?" I knew the answer before the word slipped like a caress from its hideous mouth.

"Soul."

My world stopped. "Laphaniel has a soul, I feel it."

"Empty," it rasped. "Even hell will not take those without a soul."

I wouldn't believe it, even when some distant thought rose up unbidden. He had come back different, distant…lost. He had come back to me saying something was missing.

And I hadn't noticed.

Warmth spread to my fingertips, a surge of strength and magic flooding down through my veins, as the Glamour lying dormant within my body, began to stir at last.

I snarled the next few words. "I'll get it back."

"You can try."

"What will happen to him?" The words escaped my mouth before I could stop them.

A smile stretched over cracked lips, a horrible glee dancing within the hollows of its eyes. It stretched its arms out, beckoning more and more wraiths from the shadows.

"Hungry."

My desperate cry rebounded from the walls, echoing back my fury, my pain, my desperation to prove it was wrong. Glamour spilled from me, a wave of magic I had no control over. It fled from my fingertips, feeding off my horror, off the fury that had clenched around my heart so tight I could scarcely breathe.

I held the wraith within that power, hatred pouring from it like spilled ink, oily, and black. Without a second thought, I tore it to pieces until there was nothing left but a dark stain on the cavern floor.

There was a collective hiss around me, hungry mouths widening over the still forms of the sleeping knights, clawed hands outstretched to cleave away the souls encased within.

Red mist settled over my eyes, Glamour threatening to consume me as it had done back at the Unseelie castle. I sucked in a trembling breath. Another, straining against the flames coiling at my fingers, forcing them forwards. Every burning thread of Glamour struck out. A rope. A noose.

The storm within me soared until I lost the battle with myself, the rush of Glamour pouring over me so euphoric, I let it consume me.

I drowned in it.

There was nothing but the heat of magic, my tempest crashing around me. It stole away my breath, my reason.

Everything but the need to set the world on fire.

With fingers outstretched, the threads curled tight around my wrists. I pulled. Tighter and tighter, looping the glittering strands around my hands. The sounds they made were exquisite, low moans joined by the snapping of brittle bones.

With my screech following theirs, I thrust out my hands until nothing was left of the wraiths but black dust and a dying echo.

CHAPTER THIRTY

or three days, I sat alone in the cave, drawing water from the shallow river that trickled through, gnawing on the tough jerky I found in one of the camping bags. I had managed to drip water into the mouths of the sleeping knights, into Laphaniel's. Most of it had dribbled over them, but they had swallowed some. Just enough.

The blast of Glamour had left me aching and exhausted. A weariness settled into my bones, along with a creeping unease at how much I had enjoyed it all.

The revelation about Laphaniel had left me hollow. I wanted to believe that his soul still sang within him.

I needed to.

Cole began to stir late in the afternoon, just as the sun hit the glittering stone on the far cave wall, the only slice of light save for the candle stubs. I only lit them when I could bear the darkness no longer, when it felt like the shadows would reach up and smother me if I did nothing to banish them.

During those long hours in the pitch, I had clung to Laphaniel, not daring to close my eyes in fear of what nightmares would come to torment me. It made me powerless, and I hated it.

"Cole?" I knelt beside the knight, having spent the morning

unwrapping the new bandages on his head, relieved to see the skin beneath white and shiny. "Cole, wake up."

He opened his eyes and glared back at me, swatting my hand away. "I am awake."

Slowly, he ran his fingers over the left side of his face, touching the coils of scar tissue running from what was left of his ear, to his cheek, and finally to the scars that pulled up his lip into a permanent snarl.

The swelling was gone, the bruises fading, but his left eye had clouded over to a milky haze.

"Girls love scars," I said, reaching to pull his hand away from his face.

"Even if they're half blind?" Anger lingered in his voice, and shame.

"You can wear an eyepatch, like a pirate. Everyone will swoon over you."

His gaze flicked to his knights sprawled over the floor, some just beginning to stir now my Glamour was slowly wearing off.

"What did you do?" A sharp accusation.

"I was trying to help."

He groaned as he stood, placing a hand on the rough wall to steady himself. "How long have they been like this?"

"Three days."

He whirled on me. "Three days?"

I flinched. "I Glamoured you to get some rest. I didn't know it would put everyone to sleep."

"You couldn't undo it?"

"No."

"Why?" he demanded.

"I couldn't reach it...my Glamour. I panicked and I couldn't reach it."

"You could have killed everyone."

Tired, pitying tears pricked at my eyes. "I know."

"You are a foolish girl," Cole hissed. "Playing foolish games. Get them all up, now."

"I didn't ask for any of this." I forced myself to meet his livid stare. "None of it."

"You are incredibly lucky you don't have my knights' deaths on your hands," Cole began, voice soft and lethal. "Or your husband's."

With equal simmering calm, I replied, "You are incredibly lucky, Cole, that a foolish girl took pity and refused to leave you as a buffet for the dragons."

Shock flashed across his face. "My knights were under strict orders from the king to keep you safe until we reached Luthien. You were the priority."

I shrugged. "Well, it looked like a really shitty way to die."

"You need to work on controlling your Glamour," he said, barely backing down, but the edge to his voice had softened. "Start gathering water; everyone is going to be thirsty."

He turned his back on me, striding over the stone floor to his knights. I swore at him under my breath before I made my way over to Laphaniel.

Fell shifted on the ground, his head lifting from Laphaniel's shoulder. He blinked up at me, eyes narrowing.

"Are you okay?"

Fell didn't answer, but turned his gaze upon his sword, not knowing the tunnels stood empty.

"What the hell happened?"

"I made a mistake," I said, passing him one of the cups of water I had filled. He gulped it down, eyeing the second one. "I managed to kill the wraiths."

Fell fought to get up, nudging Laphaniel to free the arm that was trapped behind him. Laphaniel groaned and stirred.

"Get off," he mumbled, giving Fell a sharp kick.

Fell shoved himself to his feet, keeping a firm grip on his empty cup. He wove on unsteady feet to the clear waters running through the rock, pushing aside the thirsty horses to swallow down more water.

"Teya?" The sleepiness was gone from Laphaniel's eyes instantly as he sat up, his hands firmly on my shoulders while he looked me over. "Are you okay?"

"I'm okay," I said, passing him the water. He drank deeply before he trailed one hand over my face, then the other, eyes searching for any signs of hurt. "I'm okay."

"How long were we out?"

"Three days." The words caught in my throat. "I could have killed you all. I'm sorry, I'm so, so sorry."

He pulled me to him, hugging me close, his lips were at my cheek, his face against mine while he breathed me in.

"You were alone down here."

"Not quite."

He drew back. "Where are they?"

"All gone."

"Did they hurt you?"

I shook my head. "I obliterated them."

"You controlled your Glamour?"

"It controlled me," I said, closing my eyes, remembering the way I had freely lost myself to it. "And the most awful part was, I loved it. I snuffed out the lives of those things like they were nothing, I didn't think twice. I could have easily destroyed you all, and I don't think I could have stopped myself."

"You did stop." Laphaniel didn't move away from me.

"This time," I answered, unable to shake the worry of how easy it took over everything. How quickly.

"I vote we get out of these forsaken caves!" Oliver bellowed from the other side of the cavern. "And find some food, I'm starving. Then we can march straight to Luthien and stick the bitch's head on a pike!"

A roar erupted from the Raven knights, a battle cry that revealed their own thirst for blood and mayhem. It had almost been too easy to forget they were Unseelie, that their lives were filled with shadows and lust for chaos in a way that the Seelie were not.

They never hid those desires behind a pretence at civility, they were proud to bare their teeth and unsheathe their claws.

"Pack up, boys," Cole called over the still rebounding echo. "Tonight, we'll feast on meat and toast Liam's legacy until the gods themselves hear us!"

Another roar, a shout filled with the promises of violence. Loss and pain lingered within the echo, an undercurrent of grief no one would voice.

"To honour our dead," Ferdia began, his black hair a dishevelled mess around his head, "the Unseelie drink until they pass out. The wake can last for days and days, usually at least a few more die in the aftermath, and we then must honour them too. The longest funeral spanned eight moons, and we lost count of how many souls departed."

"So, it's an excuse to get utterly wasted?"

The answering grin upon Ferdia's face was nothing short of depraved. "And to bathe the paths in red."

He gave a cutting glance at Laphaniel, before winking at me, saying nothing else as he re-joined the rest of the knights already filtering out of the chamber.

We followed the empty tunnel, walking beside the clear stream that flowed through its bowels. Silver fish swam in little shoals against the gentle current, gliding between the rocks that had been worn smooth with the passing of water. Overhead, giant stalagmites hung from the tunnel roof, creeping down so low that we had to duck around them. They dripped water, crystal droplets leaking down from above to pool in mirror-like puddles upon the floor.

Nothing crept within the dim light but us, our only source of light what was left of the candles and the flames the fey could conjure from their hands. My own burned painlessly against my fingers, and I caught Laphaniel look at his own hands with longing.

"You miss it, don't you?"

Laphaniel dropped his hands to his sides. For a moment, I thought he wouldn't answer. "I keep reaching for it—because it is…was, as natural as breathing, but it's not there anymore."

Something else he had lost. I had no idea how I was going to tell him that, along with his Glamour…the very essence that had made him who he was, he also no longer had his soul.

He saw the look on my face and misread it. "I guess it will get easier when Luthien is gone, when I can feel like it meant something."

"It does mean something," I replied, taking his hand in the darkness. "More than I can ever say."

He squeezed back, touch strong and sure. "I want to wake up six months from now, a year maybe. I want a glimpse of how this feels when it's all over."

"And spoil the surprise?"

"I think I've had enough to last a hundred lifetimes."

"Can you picture it then?" I asked, ducking low to avoid the rocks overhead as the cave narrowed and finally revealed an exit. "A life after all this?"

"I try to." He let go of my hand and clambered out behind me, blinking in the sudden light.

Moonlight, fat and bright, glowed overhead in a cloudless dark sky. The stars blazed back within the inky hues, racing across the night in blurs of silver. Thick, sprawling evergreens towered up and up, the rich scent of pine mixing with the sharpness of the frost upon the ground. The night was cold and brisk; the frost wouldn't be melting anymore.

"What do you imagine?" I asked, following the Raven knights down into a shallow clearing.

"I imagine simply being able to love you without the fear that something is going to snatch you away," Laphaniel began, bending down to scoop logs from the hard ground. "That one day, I'll be able to lie down beside you and wake up in the morning without wondering where the hell I am. I just want to be able to fall asleep again without help. Without the nightmares. I imagine staying in one place, to have a home again, with you."

"Do you ever see children in that future?" I asked, regretting the question instantly at the look on his face. "Not now, obviously. Not for a long, long while, but someday?"

"No."

He didn't hesitate as he spoke that little word, instantly shutting down the conversation, one I knew we would have to bring up again at some point, somewhere quiet and private and away from everything else.

My fantasy was so close to his, all except for one little detail, and I couldn't shake it. Ever since the River of Tears, a little raven-haired girl had snuck into my hopes for our future and taken root. I wasn't sure if I could let that go, if I could let her go.

"This isn't the place to talk about this," I said, and Laphaniel's eyes flashed as he looked up from where he was gathering wood. The others glanced up and quickly busied themselves with tasks that took them away from us.

"No, it's not."

The memory of that little bed wouldn't leave me, the scent of the wildflowers hanging from the painted door lingered too. I could still hear laughter, the call to watch. And it didn't matter that it wasn't real, that it wasn't even a memory, not really. The part of me that so desperately wanted to belong to something pure and unbroken longed for it.

Even little Alice had awoken something in me. My heart ached at the thought of her clinging to Laphaniel, at her terrified screams. How his arms had tightened on her as the Scara made to snatch her away.

I didn't know if a life with just Laphaniel would ever be quite enough.

"Are you coming with us, Seelie boy?" Fell called out over the clearing, spinning a knife in the air before catching it by the tip. "See if you can hit anything, not two feet in front of you."

Laphaniel caught the bow that was flung to him and swiped the quiver of arrows from beside the few remaining packs we had.

"I won't be long," he said.

"Bring back a stag," I called after him, but he had already disappeared into the shadows.

I ignited the campfire and helped Oliver tie a spit over it while the others hunted for food. We were all hoping for meat for dinner; after three days of sleeping, my companions were starving, and it would have been utterly foolish to even think about storming Luthien on empty bellies.

Oliver said little, his knife lying across his lap while he ran a sharpening stone across the blade in long, slow strokes. I caught him shooting glances my way while I poked the fire, looking like he wanted nothing more than to pull the edge of the knife along my throat.

"I never wanted anyone to die because of me," I began, not taking my eyes off Oliver's knife. "I didn't get to know Liam…"

"You don't get to speak his name," Oliver hissed. "You do not know any of us, Queen of Seelie. You never will. Just pray we can take down your enemy before my King wipes the entire Seelie Court from these lands."

"I almost forgot you were Unseelie," I said, forcing calm into my voice even though my heart hammered at the pure rage in his voice. "Thank you for reminding me."

The stone glided down the blade one more time before the knife sang through the air and landed a breath away from my feet. "I doubt you'll forget again."

I would not.

"Slim pickings," Cole said, striding back to the campfire, tossing a skinny doe onto the ground with a wet thump. "Everything else has moved deeper into the woods or underground. The snow is coming, and the wolves are out. We rest up here, gather strength, tomorrow we end this." He paused, noting the blade I held in my hands. "What's going on?"

"Just admiring Oliver's knife," I said, fingers tracing the intricately carved marking on the hilt. "He was demonstrating how swiftly it flies through the air. It's remarkable, really, isn't it, Oliver?"

The fair-haired faerie said nothing, hand shooting up to snatch the handle from in front of his face as I whirled it back at him.

"You should be careful nobody slits your throat for it."

Laphaniel looked between us, hand reaching for his blade. "Did you throw that at her?"

A sneer began to lift the edge of Oliver's lip. "And if I did?"

Cole grabbed Laphaniel by the shoulder, pulling him back before he could strike. "If you did, you ignorant fuck, I'd beat you until you wept for whatever whore birthed you. You would draw blood on what we are charged to protect? The sister to your Queen? A Queen in her own gods-damned right? I don't give a shit if you're happy with our task, none of us are, but we get it done, understand?"

Oliver said nothing, glaring, his sneer nowhere to be seen.

"I said, do you understand?"

We all startled at Cole's tone, at the sheer command within his words.

"Yes, sir," Oliver said, baring teeth. He refused to look at me.

"Why is everyone standing around?" Cole continued, causing me to jump to my feet. "Get the deer gutted so we can eat it."

The others scattered, busying themselves away from Cole's temper. Oliver stormed into the shadows, flicking his knife over in his hand, so it glinted in the moonlight.

"He blames me for Liam's death," I whispered to Laphaniel, kneeling beside him while his skilled hands freed the deer from its hide. "He's not really wrong."

Laphaniel worked the knife cleanly up the middle, slicing it to remove the insides, passing them to Ferdia, who added them to a bubbling pot.

"It's easier to blame someone," Ferdia began, wiping blood from his hands. "Because it's easier to deal with anger than anything else. We all volunteered for this; Cole gave us the choice. We all thought it better to come along than stay behind and risk the wrath..."

He stopped, barely able to conceal his flinch. With a quick tilt of his head, he scanned the treetops, no doubt wondering if they were whispering back to his king.

"Can I help?" I gestured to the deer, earning a grateful nod from Ferdia.

Laphaniel handed me the knife and showed me where to cut, which bits were worth saving, and what to throw away. I helped tie it over the fire, watching as fat trickled down the meat to spit in the flames below.

"Back home, meat was all cut up ready for you," I said to no one in particular. "With plastic wrapping and labels. My mum hated touching it, she would always prise the plastic off and toss into a tray. It would be cooked for about six hours, too, until it was utterly ruined."

"What a waste," Ferdia said, towering over me to dip his fingers in the discarded pieces of deer before sucking on them.

"I suppose it was."

"What do you prefer?" he asked, his lips red.

I glanced down at my hands, tinged with blood, at the carcass charring on the spit, the wild scent making my mouth water.

"This."

Ferdia tore a strip of meat from the spit, ignoring Fell as he smacked him away. "When did you realise that Faerie was your true home?"

"Far too late," I said, brushing my hand over the flames, so they danced over my fingers, coaxing the embers up until they tangled over my hands, dangling over the firepit like puppet strings. "But I know it now, and that's all that matters."

I stirred up the wood smoke, swirling it into lazy spirals before conjuring up the shapes of animals. Wolves and bears came to life at my hand, miniature beasts that danced and twisted in the flames, burning blue within the ashen smoke.

The others watched, all settling down around the fire before they made their own monsters appear from the smoke. Imps and goblins and creatures with wide, open mouths all writhed over the fire, spinning, and flailing until the flames spat with the excitement of it all.

The Raven knights took turns in destroying each other's creations, revelling in the violence of it while I sat content with making my animals twirl and spin for me. Laphaniel sat nearby, and for a moment, I mistook the look on his face for yearning, but then he leant forwards, his arms resting against his knees.

He watched my bears dance with a look of wonder, so entranced that he didn't notice me staring at him. His head tilted to the side, strange blue eyes following the wolves as they leapt over the logs. I had them dance for him, changing them, so they stood upright, forms melting into two dancers that swayed to music made only for them.

Over the flames, over the spirited smoke, he met my eye, and he smiled, a real smile, one I had missed and longed for and feared I wouldn't see again. It brightened everything, lighting a hope deep inside me, reminding me of what we fought for...a chance of happiness. Our happiness. Our forever.

CHAPTER THIRTY-ONE

*W*e made it to Luthien's mansion before the twin suns reached their summit in the sky, walking without rest while the snow began to fall heavily around us. We had walked until the odd light of the Unseelie lands lightened, revealing the brighter, but no less treacherous, land of the Seelie. Above us, the clouds gleamed, showering us with unblemished snow.

Nothing came for us; no one came.

Within the snow drenched gardens, there was not a sound. The trees themselves remained still, as if watching. Our footprints marked the only paths through the snow, so I could almost believe the place was deserted.

Almost.

Luthien's mansion stood perfect, winter roses bloomed fat and proud around the white stonework, trailing up around the towers, heedless of the cold. There was bated quietness to it that unsettled me, like it waited.

"Where is everyone?" I whispered the words, tugging my cloak tighter, not trusting the leering trees.

The Raven knights surrounded me, swords ready, bodies as tense as mine. Glamour flickered in the air, crackling and on edge. Laphaniel stood at my side, his blade in his hand, looking every inch my knight.

"She knows we're coming," he said, eyes focused upon my hands as I worked my Glamour into them. The threads fumbled, panicked, and weak.

"Then why not come out to meet us?" Oliver's voice rumbled over the gardens, his echo joined by the indignant cries of a few restless crows.

I stared up at the cold beauty of the mansion, dread coiling tight in my stomach at the memory of the last time I set foot inside its halls. How it had changed everything. "Because she's waiting for me."

We moved on silent feet through the eerie gardens, the unnatural stillness raising the hairs on my neck. My hands trembled at my side, fear creeping up my spine to send waves of Glamour pulsing from me. I caught the sparks and held tight. I didn't dare let them go again.

Beneath my feet, the garden began to awaken. Grass shot up to wind around my legs, the branches from the quiet trees stretched closer, blooms of pink bursting from slumbering limbs.

"Careful," Cole said, placing a hand on my shoulder. "Control it."

I took a breath, coiling the glittering threads tight around my hands. Snow buried the new shoots of green, the blossom I had awoken, withered to dust, and was carried away by the wind. Glamour ached beneath my skin, thrumming with wild energy I could barely contain. It wanted out. I wanted to let it out.

Laphaniel curled his hand around mine, steady and grounded. We had both faced the towering mansion together once before, hand in hand, and had walked away from it. My free hand went to the star at my neck, a symbol of the light in the darkness, of hope in hopeless places.

"Luthien has no idea you have Glamour now, Teya. Take her by surprise." Laphaniel squeezed my hand, drawing me close in a quick embrace. "You might only have the one chance."

I swallowed, my throat suddenly dry and parched. Held tight against Laphaniel, I breathed in his scent, memorised the spice and liquorice and the woodsmoke that now clung to him. I memorised his heartbeat, the song it played, the chorus to my own.

I memorised it all.

The grand doors made no sound as we passed through them, no faeries lounged upon the steps or lingered in the halls. The Raven knights walked ahead, braced and alert, casting quick glances at one another.

Our footsteps echoed on the pristine floor of the long hallway, the tall windows allowing the winter light to flood through, banishing the shadows. Vases stood upon ornate tables, overflowing with winter blooms and curling ivy that trailed down to coil at the floor. An illusion of softness, of comfort. Nothing more.

I stepped inside the great hall, where once I had bowed and scraped and begged. The armchairs had all gone, the overstuffed velvet cushions too. Heavy brocade curtains covered the back wall, the mirrors upon the other walls all remained untouched, so no matter where I looked, I could see everything, all of it.

Luthien rose from the single chair in the room, the sheer fabric of her pale gown rippling around her feet. The smile on her lovely face was abhorrent. She raised an arm, fingers splayed as she gestured to the horror before her.

"Behold your followers."

They hung from the vaulted ceiling like grotesque marionettes, swaying with the breeze Luthien made as she swept her hand at them. Dull eyes watched back, the life that had once danced behind them leeched out, snuffed away for the unforgivable crime of choosing me.

Amongst the swinging corpses, gilded cages dangled from the ceiling, glittering in the bright winter light. The fey held inside were thin and filthy, haunted eyes not daring to meet mine as they cowered against the polished bars. I saw no sign of Oonagh or Nefina.

"What have you done?" I uttered, my breath catching, noting the scent of death in the air, almost masked by the overpowering incense that burned around the hall. Laphaniel stepped close, Raven knights circling the both of us.

I grappled for the Glamour that just moments before had been flaring beneath my skin, to find nothing. Not even a spark. There was only a deep well of darkness that went on and on as if it had sensed Luthien and fled.

Laphaniel felt the emptiness too. I knew he did because he stepped in front of me.

"I am eliminating a threat," Luthien replied. She took a step closer, the gossamer of her dress sighing around her. It clung to her like winter mist, pale and cold.

If the arrival of the Raven knights concerned her, she hid it well.

"I thought I wasn't a threat to you."

I reached and reached. Knowing it was there. I knew it was there.

Luthien smiled, beautiful and dark. "Oh, Teya, my sweet, I will not underestimate you again."

Luthien angled her head, stretching out her hands, so she disturbed the bodies while she stalked closer. A small whimper bled from one of the cages, muffled and terrified. Luthien turned her head, her lips stretching out in a delighted smile.

"Don't!" I cried.

With a lazy stretch of her hand, she severed the chain holding the cage up, turning to face me as it smashed upon the marble below. A soft sigh blew past her lips when the cries within silenced.

"You're mad." The words tumbled from my lips, unable to tear my eyes away from the carnage she had created, at the fey that bobbed and swayed above me. "This is madness, Luthien."

"Do you think?" She smoothed the folds of her dress, frowning at the speckles of blood that mottled the skirts. "Some would say the same about allying with that filth."

Beside me, the knights tensed, hands tight on their weapons, ready to strike. They had taken in the horror with blank faces, utterly unmoved by the amount of death within Luthien's home.

It was a bitter reminder that we were not on the same team, not truly.

"I did what I had to do."

"Indeed," Luthien drawled, unfathomable eyes trailing over each of the knights. "Like a cockroach."

"You are alone, Lady," Cole began. "Surrender now, before the full force of the Unseelie crashes down upon you..."

Luthien struck, quick as an asp, and plunged her hand deep within Cole's chest. His eyes went wide, words dying at his lips as she dragged her hand back, fingers curled tight around his heart.

She dropped it beside his body like it were nothing, streaking the blood from her hands down her already ruined gown.

"The Unseelie are a plague," Luthien snarled. "One, I plan on erasing from this earth."

With a snarl rumbling up his throat, Oliver lunged forwards with his sword high, face twisted with rage and hate and loss as he made to strike Luthien down.

My shout went unheard, my warning unheeded, my voice a lost echo sounding around the elegant hall.

Oliver was dead before he hit the floor, his face forever a mask of horror. From where I stood, I couldn't see a mark upon him. I heard the sound his neck had made, though, like a dry twig.

The Raven knights backed up, their Glamour swirling around them, ruffling the feathers on their inky cloaks. Candles guttered, the cages above swayed.

Luthien didn't move, didn't blink. The hall went black, the skies outside darkening until no light filtered through. Chains snapped and fell. The sound of broken bones filled the silence.

"You were sent as cannon fodder," Luthien sang from the shadows. "The trees whisper to me of a new king, a mad king. Perhaps one day, I would like to meet him upon some distant screaming battlefield and tear this world to shreds."

"Do something," Fell hissed beside me, his fingers straining at the hilt of his sword. "Do something, you useless girl."

I stared at the two bodies lying in front of me, searching deep inside for the sparks of Glamour I knew...I knew were there. Warmth bristled at my fingertips, a suggestion of something bigger, but nothing more.

I had killed us all.

One by one, the candles flared to life, catching the twisted gold bars of the cages Luthien had sent crashing down. Nothing moved within. At my side, Laphaniel stared at the carnage before glancing up at the cages still swaying. I noted his gaze didn't linger upon the bodies strung beside them.

"Looking for something?" Luthien swept up to Laphaniel and placed her hand upon his cheek, streaking it with Cole's blood. "Or, perhaps, someone?"

"What have you done with her?" he demanded, pulling away in an act of defiance that curled the edges of Luthien's mouth.

With a small gesture, the curtain at the far end of the room dropped to the floor, the heavy red fabric pooling to the floor like old blood.

"Take her down!" Laphaniel hissed, grabbing at Luthien's hand when she made to walk away. My heart lurched, fearing Luthien would tear it off.

Luthien didn't react, but only slid her almost black eyes to Laphaniel's hand before turning them to his sister.

Nefina was alive, I could see that. See the breaths she took, her bare chest heaving as she strained on her tiptoes, hands bound tight above her head. Bruises snaked over her skin like a tattoo.

"Take her down!" Laphaniel demanded again, the words echoing around the bated quiet of the room.

Luthien stared down at the hand still upon her wrist, twisting it slowly, so her fingers entwined with his. "I don't think I will."

"You cannot win this, Luthien," Laphaniel began, shooting me a quick desperate look. "If you kill us, more will come."

"Then let them."

My heart froze within my chest as she pulled him to her, stealing a lingering kiss that made me want to rip her in two. Glamour pulsed through me, finally awakening.

At last.

With a hiss, Luthien pulled away from Laphaniel, her teeth bloodied where she had bitten through his lip. She grabbed him again, hands either side of his head, forcing him to his knees with a hard thud.

For a moment, disbelief flashed across her face, quickly replaced with disgust. "What have you done to yourself?"

"What I had to."

"You're an abomination," Luthien whispered, and Laphaniel flinched. "A mongrel, you have no place here."

"I don't belong at your side, Luthien. I never did."

The resounding crack rattled my teeth. I heard bones break in Laphaniel's cheek as Luthien backhanded him so hard her fingers snapped back.

"Stop!" The single word erupted from me, my Glamour fuelled with weeks and weeks of rage, hunger, and fear. It shrouded me like mist, pouring from me in waves as, at last, at long last, it finally surfaced.

The edge of my vision darkened, shadowing everything but Luthien. Lightning forked outside, thunder rumbling in answer to the storm I was creating. It all beat to the booming rhythm of my heart.

Another Raven knight fell by Luthien's hand, neck twisting to the side, eyes wide and mouth gaping. Ferdia. A hollow cry echoed behind me, raw and broken.

The windows exploded in a burst of feral power. Luthien threw her head back and laughed.

"This is different," she began, treading carefully through the shards of glass. "Are you controlling it, or is it controlling you?"

I knelt on the floor beside Laphaniel, his hand cradling the side of his face. More lightning crackled as I stared Luthien down. "Come closer and see."

She did, not because I compelled her but because she chose to. I was pushing hard, but she didn't even flinch.

"I think I should have killed you a long time ago, Teya Jenkins."

With glass breaking beneath my feet, I stood. My hands splayed at my side, and the marble floor began to crack. Creepers rose from the fractures, snaking up the walls, around the beams high above us.

"We only ever wanted to be left alone."

"No," Luthien uttered with a tilt of her head. "No, Teya. That is not what you wanted. Not what you asked for. If you had kept your word, then this would not have happened. Those that lie dead are because of you. Their blood stains your hands, taints your soul." Luthien paused before waving a hand to make the bodies above us dance again. "Perhaps they would all still live if not for your deception?"

She waited, daring me to contradict her. "I..."

"A hundred years alone in that castle, in return for your sister. Was that not our bargain?"

"Yes...but..."

"I gave you back that wretched girl, and in return, you stole him and ruined him!" Luthien thrust her hand towards Laphaniel, and in her fury sent him slamming against the wall, the mirrors shattered. "You broke our bargain; everything you have suffered since is your own doing."

"That's not..." I spluttered, feeling a painful burn creep up my throat. I choked, tasting blood.

"Lies hurt, don't they?"

Laphaniel forced himself up, blood trickling down his face. He made to storm towards Luthien, fury in his eyes. Fell and Faolan stalked closer, teeth gritted, eyes as black as the cloaks they wore.

I pushed them down, wrapping Glamour around each of them to force them to the ground. They snarled in outrage; Laphaniel's wide eyes met mine, and he shook his head.

I didn't let him go. Too many had already died because of me.

Glamour trembled at my hands, stirring up the storm outside. The ground rumbled, shaking the cages so the chains holding them up creaked, threatening to send those trapped inside plummeting to the ground. Some cried out, weak moans filling the room with the sound of desperation and fear.

"Do you think you can save them now?" Luthien said, lifting a hand to tempt my storm to her.

I moved quicker, fear fuelling the magic inside me. I sent her to the floor in a reel of shattered glass and screeching wind, flinging her across the marble. Fury, hot and wild, surged through me, taking over the fear that had almost overwhelmed me. Without thought, I picked her back up again, only to send her crashing back down with all the force I could summon. If she had been human, I would have killed her.

With blood at her mouth, Luthien rose, her dark hair a wild mass around her shoulders, her eyes black. She pushed back with surprising force, a scream leaving her lips to sway my storm.

Lightning struck a breath away from me, scorching the floor, so it cracked further. Great forks of power ploughed down from above, hitting the ground with frantic booms that tore the great hall in two.

I flung my Glamour out to snatch at Faolan before he slipped through the divide, not caring that I heard his shoulder snap when I hauled him back.

Above me, three of the chains gave way, sending the fey trapped behind bars crashing to the floor. The noise broke through everything else, the screams and the crack of bodies silenced the sound of our war, until it was all I could hear.

"Give me your life, Teya," Luthien called over the chaos. "Your life, for everyone in this room."

"I am not here to bargain with you," I replied, standing on the very edge of the scar she had created.

"You are not fit to be queen," Luthien snarled, the storm teasing the wild strands of her hair. "You are not made for difficult choices."

"You have no idea what choices I've had to make."

A laugh rang out over the ruins, a musical sound that was grotesque, given the circumstances. "Would you choose love over duty, Teya?"

She moved before I could answer, spinning around like a deranged ballet dancer until all the cages above us swayed and rocked, their chains creaking with the motion. The ceiling began to crack, allowing the chains to slip down just a little, teasing and testing.

I started forwards, reaching out to steady the cages, while Luthien's Glamour looped around Laphaniel, forcing him upright until he stood on his tiptoes. He gasped, clutching at his throat as Luthien choked him from the other side of the room.

"Stop!"

Luthien heard my panic and grinned, madness twisting her beauty into something monstrous.

"Stop what?" she asked, "Do I cease trying to crush these traitorous creatures, or cease strangling your mongrel?"

With a wave of her hand, she sent the cages rocking, flinging the terrified fey against the bars. The chains creaked further, dust from the ceiling raining down to the floor. Inside they reached out for each other, hands grasping through bars to touch those just out of reach.

My fey.

Not Luthien's.

Mine.

"Keep dawdling, and you'll lose them all," Luthien sang, lifting her other hand to jerk Laphaniel's head back. "Choose wisely."

Laphaniel twitched, one foot scraping along the marble. He had resisted me, fought against me when I had tried to Glamour him, and almost won. If he could break away from Luthien…

With a breath and a silent prayer, I sent a wave of Glamour up towards the swinging cages, severing each chain with a screech of wind and rain. They plummeted to the ground in a cacophony of screams and grating metal before thick vines shot through the ruined floor and knotted through each one, stopping them all mere inches away from the marble.

Out of the corner of my eye, I saw Laphaniel lurch forwards, blood streaming from his nose. Luthien's hold on him was undone.

From the other side of the divide, Fell launched himself at Luthien, sword raised to slam through her chest, a scream at his lips. She howled in pain and surprise, tossing him aside with a furious sweep of Glamour. Her fingers wrapped around the hilt, and she tugged the blade, so it slid out with a squelch.

The blade sang through the air, sailing through the empty space where the Raven knight had stood a heartbeat before. Laphaniel collided with Fell, sending them both slamming to the ground, the blade missing by a breath. It hit the wall behind with enough force it shattered.

Luthien's hand lingered at the wound to her chest, lifting the tattered fragments of her gown to watch the blood seep through.

"You gave up everything for a human girl," she said to Laphaniel, a softness creeping into her voice, "And now you risk your life for that filth?"

"Jealous?"

The storm around us stilled, the world hushed as Luthien strode through the ruins to Laphaniel.

"You once offered up your soul for her," she said, crouching low, while I fought to regain control over the storm. "Would you still?"

"In a heartbeat," Laphaniel said, wincing as she cupped his face in her hand and squeezed. She began to laugh, her body shaking with it.

"But you no longer have one."

Laphaniel jerked his head away, eyes wide while she continued to laugh at him. "What?"

"There is nothing there," she grinned, blood on her teeth. "You know what awaits faeries without souls, what you'll become when death at last claims you." A nasty pause, that grin widening. "Again. There is nothing for you but endless dark and eternal hunger."

"You're wrong," Laphaniel said, but I could feel the fight seep away from him.

"And you will always be my greatest disappointment."

Her hands tightened against his neck, and I felt him tense, heard the sudden intake of breath when she began to twist.

My hand shot out, bile rising in my throat as I forced her fingers away and poured all I had into dragging her away from him. Something popped in my eye, turning my vision red.

Anger, wild and frantic, coursed through me and set every nerve in my body on fire. It was something I couldn't stop, didn't want to stop. There was nothing left of me but a desperate need to sever her head from her body and watch her die.

I dragged her kicking and screaming across the broken marble and forced her to her knees. I held her there and turned to Laphaniel, sensing his fury—I could taste it, but stayed silent, quietly pushing Luthien to the filthy ground. She could wait. I made her wait.

There was an eerie quiet while everyone watched Laphaniel, his footsteps mingling with the hushed sound of sobs coming from the cages.

He pulled a knife from his belt, and, without a word, severed the binds holding Nefina, catching her as she fell into his arms. So very gently, he wrapped her in his cloak, and for a moment, she was lifeless. He sunk to the floor with her in his arms, murmuring words with his head buried in her hair. Then she was clinging to him, her sobs drowning out anything else as she fell apart in his embrace.

I blinked my tears away and turned back to Luthien. "Where is Oonagh?"

She said nothing.

"Where is…"

"She was taken to the cellars," someone called from the cages.

I looked to Fell, who stood back, face pale beneath the blood caked across it. "Please, go find my friend."

He hesitated, and for a moment I thought he would refuse me.

"Please."

He gave a quick nod, eyes utterly black, and walked away.

"You lose," I breathed to Luthien. "These fey are mine."

I dragged her back up, baring her throat as I forced her to stand, forcing her to look at each one of the captive fey. Within the cages, the faeries hissed and clawed at their bars, desperate to get out so they could tear her to pieces. Teeth glistened, and blood lust seeped heavy in the air.

"Will you follow me?" I called out, closing my eyes at the unified answer. I could sense every one of them as they accepted me, feel each heartbeat, taste the uniqueness of their Glamour.

"All mine," I hissed, tossing Luthien to the ground while the storm around me, newly awoken, growled. I felt her heartbeat too. It was quick, frightened, defeated. I pressed against it, and she gasped. I smiled.

Pressing harder, I watched her squirm. I wanted to break her heart, I wanted to crush it, so I wrapped my Glamour around it and stopped it beating. I could have killed her with barely a thought.

"Teya," she gasped, her eyes wide, the beautiful chocolate dulling as I squeezed harder. "Don't…"

"Don't what?" I snarled, seeing nothing but a yawning black. It would be easy to tumble into, wonderful. "You are misery, Luthien."

Luthien would not have granted me mercy. She would have pulled out my heart just as she pulled out Cole's. She would have crushed Laphaniel's windpipe without blinking and sent the trapped fey to their deaths. Luthien was cold and cruel, and I truly believed she deserved to die.

But I wasn't cruel.

With the storm calming around me, I hesitated. The feel of her heart sickened me. I had never taken a life, I didn't want to feel someone's heart slow and stop in my hands, no matter how they deserved it. I would never be able to wash that away.

"Exile," I snarled the word, and it echoed around the room as if I had shouted. As did the cries of outrage. "I grant you exile, Luthien, not death."

"Where do you expect me to go?"

"I don't care," I said each word slowly, and they hissed past my teeth. I barely recognised my voice. "Go rot somewhere."

Drawing upon the memory of the Unseelie King's shadow dogs, I made my own out of mist and rain. They were barely corporal, just the faint idea of hounds, but I was sure their teeth would still be sharp. With a click of my fingers, they snarled, lunging forwards for Luthien.

She scrambled to her feet, ripped gown billowing behind her as she tore from the room, and my hounds gave chase.

The fey waiting within the gilded cages watched in silence, unmoved, unimpressed. Leaving me to wonder if I had just made my first mistake.

CHAPTER THIRTY-TWO

We buried the dead under frigid earth, as far away from Luthien's mansion as we could carry them. Flowers bloomed over the mounds, forcing their way up past the snow to flock over the gravesites, covering the ground with a bloom of colour and hope.

The Unseelie took their own further away. Cole, Oliver, and Ferdia were each placed upon pyres, two black feathers upon their breasts, and set alight. The flames reached so high they seemed to lick the heavy clouds above us.

There would be no drinking, no funerals lasting for days for the knights who had fallen. Faolan had given me a solemn nod from my place away from the rising smoke. Fell wouldn't turn, his head bowed low beside his twin's pyre. Out of the six knights who had chosen to help me, only two would be returning home.

A knot twisted in my stomach, grief, and guilt taking root deep inside. I wanted to say something, anything. But there were no words to give, nothing I could do to give any sort of comfort, not when so many of their friends had perished on Seelie soil, for a Seelie Queen.

They left before the embers had died down, silent and cold as shadows. Any bond that had begun to build between us vanished with the ashes eddying into the wind.

The surviving fey, my fey, stood uncertain and lost, something deep within them broken. They gathered around me, too thin and dirty, all malice stripped from their lovely faces as they waited for me to do something. They looked to Laphaniel standing beside me, expectant. I was not a fool to believe they would ever follow me without him by my side.

I was exhausted.

Every part of me ached and burned, but I could still feel my Glamour at my hands, sparking in response to the faeries around me. I could taste their fear, their hunger, and beneath all that...a spark of hope. Just an ember at that moment, but a spark at least.

Laphaniel stared out at the Court of Seelie, the streaks of crimson on his face, barely hiding the livid bruises on his cheek, around his neck. He leant forwards and pressed his lips softly to mine before dropping to his knees at my feet.

"Long live the Queen."

Laphaniel's words echoed through the fey, repeated with a fervour that betrayed their worn and weary faces. All knelt before me.

Oonagh bowed her head, tears streaming through the filth on her face. She had been carried from the cellars by Fell, the fingers in each hand broken. The silver-haired faerie had barely whimpered while Laphaniel reset them, refusing outright to be coddled.

Nefina knelt beside her, not meeting my gaze and still wearing her brother's cloak. Others I recognised too, ones that had once sneered and mocked and threatened me. Others peered through matted hair, tentative smiles upon their faces.

I caught the bronze eyes of Gabriel, the golden-haired fey who had danced with me at the New Moon ball so many months ago. The smirk was gone, the glint in his gaze less wicked, but he winked at me, and I couldn't help the smile that bloomed at my mouth.

Laphaniel took my outstretched hand and stood, and I wrapped my arms around him, resting my head on his chest.

My words were only for him. "We made it."

I felt him swallow, his hand tightening. "We did."

THE DAYS FLOWED after that with surprising swiftness, with so much to rebuild and organise and attempt to set right. The abandoned Seelie Castle was the first on the list.

Thousands of tiny elves descended upon the sprawling stone, transforming it into something of beauty and light. They worked endlessly, forest green skin slicked with sweat despite the winter's chill. They spoke little, each baring jagged little teeth if anyone so much as stepped into the shadow of the castle.

We camped nearby in splendid tents of gold and red, all of us together watching the home that had been denied to the Seelie for so very long, be brought back to life.

Their excitement buzzed through me, their longing for home so strong that I found myself weeping with them. They reached for my hands when they passed by, lithe and graceful beings, holding onto me as their strength began to renew, and I embraced them back, slowly feeling like I was where I belonged. Not a word was spoken about Luthien's exile. I heard no discontent at the decision I had made, but I knew it lingered there, beneath the relief.

"Do you think I should have killed her?" I asked Laphaniel, finally voicing the question that had kept me awake at night. We stood at the threshold of the castle, the moon high above us, the elves waiting with strange little smiles to show us what they had created.

Laphaniel tilted his head, looking up and up and up at the towers twisting into the skies, at the flags that beat proudly in the wind. "Only you can decide that, Teya."

Not an answer.

"Would you have?" I pressed.

"I don't think I would have shown her the mercy you did," he answered after a pause. "But you did show mercy, and I love you all the more for it. But I can't tell you if it was the right thing to do or not. Time will tell, and we'll deal with it together."

"The Seelie wanted blood."

He shrugged, "Faeries always want blood."

The elves insisted they show the two of us in first, chittering and snarling at anyone else who wanted to come and see. They took my hand, sharp claws wrapping around my finger to lead me through the maze of glittering white corridors. They had banished the shadows and the darkness completely, bathing everything in a wondrous light, covering every surface with plush rugs or pillowing drapes, in furs and cushions. It no longer felt like a nightmare.

We both halted at a patch of polished wall, the seams blended so perfectly, it was almost impossible to tell anything ever lingered behind. It had been our only request.

I would never unsee the blood spreading out from Laphaniel, or the sound of his last heartbeat, the knife dripping red in my sister's hand. Laphaniel still re-lived it, bore the scars both seen and unseen. We had asked for the tower where the curse had been broken to be destroyed.

The elves led us up wide and open staircases, greenery already snaking up the banisters, blooming with little silver buds that caught the moonlight.

The hallway we walked down had been beautifully restored. Jewelled lanterns hung from the ceiling, holding a dozen candles in each, and the white marble floors were adorned with thick red and gold rugs that were the softest things my feet had ever touched. Full-length windows looked out onto the grounds, dressed only in white gossamer so the light always shone through.

It held none of the darkness it once did.

Stepping past one of the elves, I squeezed Laphaniel's hand before I walked into our rooms. Underfoot was polished marble, adorned with more sumptuous rugs so I could scarcely see the gleaming stone beneath. There were sofas and armchairs and plump floor cushions, all in velvets and silks. An enormous fire crackled over by one wall, filling the spacious room with warmth and light.

I wandered through the double doors to the side, pushing them open to reveal our bedchamber, my heart thudding. Laphaniel held my hand tighter, and it shook within his.

Home. We had finally found our way home.

The four-poster bed dominated the space, and as I climbed on top of it and sat back, I could look out of the window and see six waterfalls cascade into a vast lake. Laphaniel climbed in next to me, waiting for me to say something.

Tears ran down my cheeks instead, and he reached across to brush them away with his thumb, at a loss for words himself.

The room was beautiful, simplistic and elegant. As well as the giant bed, there was a pretty dressing table, a writing desk with a gilded key, two more fat armchairs, and an overflowing bookcase. I had no idea where the elves had found so many books.

Sliding off the bed, I knelt before one of the elves, taking its long green hands in my own. "Thank you."

The green of its face darkened, the others chittered beside it, teeth showing as they grinned.

"For all of this," I said. "Thank you."

They left in a bubble of excited noises, clapping each other on the back as they vanished into puffs of greenish smoke. I wanted to offer them payment but refrained after Laphaniel explained it would insult them greatly.

"What next?" I said, re-joining Laphaniel on the bed. He had his eyes closed, one hand tucked behind his head.

"Everything," he replied, not moving. "But everything else can wait for a moment."

I pressed a soft kiss to the dip of his neck. "Even this?"

He made a wonderful sound at the back of his throat, and pulled me closer, his mouth finding mine in a kiss that stole all other thoughts away.

His quick fingers untied the stays of my dress, a flowing gown of heavy gold velvet, complete with fur tipped sleeves and collar. It wasn't an easy dress to get into. The fabric tore beneath his hands, but he stopped when they brushed over the thick leggings I wore underneath.

"It's freezing outside," I began, snorting at the look on his face. "Do you expect me to wear gauzy silk in this weather?"

Laphaniel lifted the hem of one leg, shaking his head at the thick grey socks I wore. "Those are mine."

I grinned. "Ours."

His teeth nipped my lower lip. "I liked it when you wore my shirts, and they would graze just here." His hand trailed over the top of my knee, moving higher. "And you would sleep in them, so they smelled like you. Everything did."

"Do you think I could wear just your shirts as Queen?" My breath caught as Laphaniel moved his mouth across to my ear, then down and down, to the soft skin just below my collar. "And nothing else, or do you think that would cause a scandal?"

"I think," Laphaniel began, a huskiness to his voice, "that you have far too many damned layers on right now."

"And she'd better keep them on," a new voice said from our doorway. "I am sorry to disturb you…"

Laphaniel dropped his hand with a soft groan. "What do you want, Oonagh?"

Musical laughter rang around the room, and the bed dipped further as another body joined us. "You two have a Court of eager fey at your command. You have much more to do before you…" Oonagh paused with a wicked grin. "Retire for the night."

I sat up, adjusting my gown, calling back the glittering Glamour that had begun to snake its way around Laphaniel, who made no attempt to reorder the buttons on his clothing.

"Is there a rule forbidding anyone entering the royal bedchamber unannounced," I asked, "let alone their actual bed?"

"Perhaps you should make one?" the willowy faerie sang.

"Oh, I think I will."

Oonagh opened her arms to me, and I fell into her embrace. She still felt too thin in my arms, but the bruises had gone, the cuts healed, and the light in her strange eyes was finally back. She pulled away, eyes glistening, and without warning, threw herself onto Laphaniel and squeezed him tight. He embraced her for a moment before dumping her onto the bed beside him.

"I know you are both exhausted," Oonagh said. "But the Seelie have been without proper rule for so long, no one knows what they're supposed to do. Laphaniel, you need to organise your knights, name a captain, figure out the Queen's guards." She turned to me. "You, my beautiful girl, need to organise your council, start discussing new laws, a new order of things. I have a few girls for you to interview for your maid..."

"I don't need a maid."

Oonagh scoffed. "And who will tie your corsets, Teya, when your husband is otherwise engaged?"

"Perhaps I won't wear a corset. I am the Queen, so I can damn well wear what I want."

Oonagh stood, lifting a slender pale eyebrow, her glare icy. I knew, without doubt, she would be standing as my chief council, just as I knew I would likely be wearing a corset for the rest of my life.

"I'll interview them later."

Oonagh curtsied, the fluid movement sweeping her silvery gown across the floor like water. There was a smile to her lips, warmth against her mouth, and I returned it in kind, forever grateful to her.

"Your Majesties." Oonagh curtsied again, her parting words sounding strange and utterly unbelievable. We were the Queen and King of the Seelie Court, our castle rebuilt, our fey waiting for us.

"Will it always be so busy?" I asked, swinging my legs off the bed, the reality of everything not quite sinking in.

"You'll always have more to do than you have time for, Teya, but it will get easier." He slipped from the bed, outstretching a hand to me. "and I will always be right beside you."

I placed my hand to his chest, right over his heart, my fingers splayed to catch every thump, every song beat. "We'll get it back." He knew what I meant. "Even if I have to travel the ends of the world, I will get it back for you, I'll bargain..."

"No." The word was quick, final. "No more bargaining, promise me."

"I will pay any price, Laphaniel."

"But I don't want you to," he said firmly. "I don't want to get something back only to lose something worse."

"The wraiths…" The word caught in my throat, the memory of them raw. The hunger, the emptiness, the utter void of anything good or whole. "I can't make that promise to you. I'm sorry but I won't."

"Teya…"

"Don't argue with me."

He bristled, eyes flashing. "Is that a command?"

I didn't want to fight, not on our first night, but it was not something I was willing to back down over. "Yes, it is."

Hurt flickered over his face, and he opened his mouth to bite back, but just shook his head instead. With a mocking bow, he turned on his heel and walked out.

FEY FILLED THE THRONE ROOM, and they all wanted something from me.

Laphaniel was absent, his throne beside mine empty while he sparred with knights in some courtyard away from me. He had chosen Gabriel as his captain, the golden-haired faerie I had once danced with so long ago in Luthien's ballroom. Gabriel had healed slowly from the wounds Luthien had dealt him, his bones splintered in places. He still had little memory of his time spent in the dangling gold cages.

Laphaniel had not hesitated in choosing him.

The two thrones stood high upon a dais of glittering stone, both made from smooth wood that wound around each other, before splaying across the floor. Winter had stripped it bare, save the ivy snaking around it, but in spring, I had been promised, it would come alive with blossom.

The throne room ceiling towered high above, the beams all green with winter foliage. Balls of curved wood hung low, each holding a bright blue flame that filled the entire room with wondrous light. Pillars rose from the floor, carved with deer and hares and towering oaks.

Music filled the space, as did the soft sound of chatter, and laughter. I could sense the unease of the gathered fey, but also their excitement, their curiosity, their hope.

Gazing out at the seemingly endless line of faeries that Oonagh had directed at me, I noticed Nefina standing a little way from the crowd, out of place and alone. I beckoned her forward, and she curtsied graciously, ebony gown bathing her like a night's sky. There was no light, however, no warmth behind her eyes. I very much doubted we would ever be close.

"This is for you, Nefina," I said, handing her a small silver key, which she took with little enthusiasm. "It opens the door to the North Wing. There are four rooms in total with a balcony overlooking the forest and the White Rivers. Your ladies in waiting are Lara, Summer, and Rose." I gestured to three young fey hovering nearby, still nervous at their new occupations. "You are a Princess of the Seelie Court, and you shall be treated as such."

Nefina stared at me, her face softening as her eyes glistened, and then widened as the entire Court dropped to their knees in acknowledgment. She tightened her hand around the key, hands shaking while she fought to compose herself. Her parting curtsy was still elegant, and no one but me would have seen the slight tremor in it.

"What are you three standing there for?" Nefina snapped at her waiting ladies, causing the girls to jump, iridescent wings quivering at her tone. "We have much to do, are you meant to be serving me, or gawping?"

I gave a quick apologetic smile to Rose, the smallest girl as they flittered after Nefina, feeling a little sorry for inflicting Laphaniel's sister upon them.

"You may have created a monster," Oonagh whispered from her spot beside me. "Albeit a loyal one."

"I hope so."

"You have just given that faerie her dream, everything she has fought for since she was a little girl. She may not ever show it, Teya, but you've made a friend there."

I took her hand, her smooth skin cold against mine, and gave it a gentle squeeze. "I reward my friends, Oonagh."

"Hmm," she smiled, eyes twinkling. "With everlasting work, it would seem. Now please continue to deal with your subjects, my Queen, if you ever want to get back to that ridiculously large bed of yours."

Light began to dwindle through the enormous stained-glass windows, the sun sinking below the hills to bring dusk, and finally nightfall, to the castle. With a sweep of my hand, I ignited every unlit candle in the room. After hours and hours of talking and planning, I was nearly finished, and just a few patient fey still had to receive my attention.

I glanced up from the list Oonagh was creating when the doors swung open and smiled despite my weariness when Laphaniel walked in. He took up the throne beside mine, and the few lingering fey dropped to their knees. He was clean and had changed out of his sparring armour into a loose shirt, but a sword still hung from his belt. I wondered if it always would.

Laphaniel lowered his head to me, speaking so that no other could hear. "I'm sorry I stormed off."

I turned, my forehead touching his. "I'm sorry, too, for the way I spoke to you. You are not mine to command."

"But I am yours," he said. "Always."

He looked as exhausted as I felt, his hair still damp from the bath I envied him for. "You don't have to stay; I'll be finished soon."

"I'm not leaving without you, Teya. Our first night here will be together, however long that may take."

I turned back to the waiting faeries, all wanting a place within my court. Cooks and hunters and stable hands. Maids, and valets, blacksmiths, and so much more, all needed to keep the castle and the Court thriving. There was a place for all.

My voice was hoarse by the time the hall emptied, and I longed for nothing else but to curl up beside Laphaniel and close my eyes. To spend the first night together, the first night of the rest of forever.

We did not expect anyone else, no one else was announced, I was so, so close to being finished. Yet more came, two knights, I did not recognise strode up to the dais where we sat, followed swiftly by my knights, swords drawn, faces fearful.

Oonagh was instantly alert, the papers she was scanning forgotten as she stepped up close.

The two Raven knights remained calm, their black feather cloaks shimmering like oil around their shoulders. I did not know their faces.

"You are not welcome here," I called out. Laphaniel rose beside me, his hand upon the hilt of his sword. "Your King knows the rules, he was the one to make them. What is it you want?"

The knight on the left bowed slightly, his eyes like flint. "We have come to collect payment."

"Our castle is newly standing, and you demand payment now?" Laphaniel began, his voice hard and cold.

"What does your King demand?" I placed a hand on Laphaniel's forearm, stopping him from drawing his blade.

The other knight stared back with black eyes, and I felt a shiver run through me. "Starshine, Queen of Seelie, as agreed by yourself."

"Take the stars you want then, there are many more."

"The King has no use for ordinary stars, your Majesty. Only yours."

My hand went to my pendant, the cool silver a reassuring weight in my hand. "What does Phabian want with trinkets?"

"Oh, nothing at all, your Majesty," he replied, a slow smile creeping across his face. "We are here for your own star, your starshine, that bright light within the darkness you desperately cling to."

"I don't understand..."

He cocked his head. "Don't you?"

Everything went cold, as slowly, exactly, what I had signed crept over me like a ghost.

Who I had signed over.

I met those black eyes, unflinching. "No."

The Unseelie knight handed a roll of parchment, and I didn't have to read what it said to understand what it was. I recognised my signature.

"You signed the contract, your Majesty."

"I said, no."

Laphaniel looked at me, not understanding yet. The other fey in the room whispered to one another, hushed voices quick and worried. Oonagh stepped forward, taking the paper from my hands, eyes scanning it while all colour leached from her face.

"The contract is binding, Queen of Seelie," the Raven knight said, baring teeth. "With your life as forfeit. Without its Queen, your court will crumble, and the Unseelie will destroy all that remains. All will die. He no longer belongs to you."

I felt the realisation hit Laphaniel, heard the sudden thud of his heart, the quick intake of breath, the fear, as he finally understood.

I stepped down from the dais, snuffing out all the candles, calling up a wild wind that began to whirl around the throne room. "He is not yours to take!"

"But he was yours to give away," the Raven knight replied, ignoring the whirlwind spiralling around him. "It is bound in blood."

I glanced frantically at Oonagh, who stood dumb, her face a shocking shade of white.

"Did you sign?" she asked, her eyes pleading. "Is this your signature, Teya?"

"Yes...but I didn't know." I whirled back to Laphaniel, Glamour snatching at the heavy fabric of my gown, at my hair, at Laphaniel's. "I didn't know, I swear I didn't know... Oonagh, do something."

"It's a legal document, Teya." Oonagh stared back at me, her hands trembling. "There is nothing I can do."

I grabbed Laphaniel's hand, but he pulled away, staring dumbly at the two knights in front of him.

"Chains, Seelie whelp?"

"What does your King want with me?" Laphaniel asked, his voice surprisingly steady. The answering grin on the Raven knight's lips was a terrible thing, a nightmare.

"Oh, you'll see."

They took a step toward him, binding his hands as they made to snatch him away from me. Laphaniel stood frozen, still not looking at me until I clutched his arm and wrenched him back.

"Tell your king he can have anything else," I implored, ready to get down on my knees and beg. "Name his price."

"He already has."

They began to tug him away but turned as one, feathers whipping around them in the flurry of Glamour that would not calm.

"We are expected back to the Unseelie Castle unharmed. The King will lay waste to your shining new home and all who dwell within if we dally."

"Please..."

"Such manners, Queen of Seelie. Say your goodbyes."

They thrust Laphaniel back to me, and he finally met my eyes. The chains around his wrists clanked against me.

"I will bring you home."

He brushed a tiny kiss against my lips, touching his forehead to mine as he whispered to me, his voice lost. Defeated. "Do you ever stop to wonder why it is so hard for us to be together, to be happy? Why fate is so devoted to destroying us?"

Tears swam down my face, unchecked. "You once said fate doesn't care about us."

"I think I was wrong."

They wrenched him back, the chains rattling as he gripped my fingers tight before he was ripped away. Terror flashed across his face, and I fought to hold on to him. Tendrils of Glamour surged forward, reaching for him, calling out to the echo lingering deep within him.

"I will bring you home."

They dragged him away.

And I watched him go.

I watched him go.

My knees thudded upon the marble, my gown spilling around me. My too heavy gown with too many layers.

Our bed was waiting for us. Huge and warm and inviting. Because it was our first night, and we would go up together.

But I watched him go.

My star.

Mine.

Someone sank beside me. Oonagh. Cool arms held me close, so close, I could smell the salt from her own tears. She murmured something, barked orders at someone. I didn't know what or to whom.

I was drowning, and there was nothing I could do.

I didn't know how to save him.

"My Queen?" A whisper, soft and gentle. I lifted my head to meet the bronze eyes of Gabriel, all wicked humour had gone from his face, leaving it stark. "They left this at the gates."

I took the letter from his hand, reading it with blurred eyes, scarcely daring to believe the whisper of hope behind the ink. A bleak hope.

Queen of Seelie,

As agreed by yourself, your husband now belongs to me as payment for the aid I gifted to you and your Court. Be warned that any attempt at reclaiming him will bring instant and merciless death. I will not hesitate, there will be no warning. You have no claim over him now, he is mine to use as I see fit. As a grand gesture of goodwill, I will grant you the three days over midwinter to visit. That is three days each year for the rest of forever. More than any mortal would have in a lifetime. There is nothing more to be said.

Until midwinter,

Phabian, King of the Unseelie.

ACKNOWLEDGMENTS

I have so many people to thank, so buckle up my lovelies.

My first thank you goes to my readers. To those of you who picked up my first book and then this one, wanting to continue Teya and Laphaniel's journey with me. There's more to come.

Thank you to my wonderful Beta readers. Your comments, your wisdom and your guidance has been invaluable. You are superstars. You are all welcome in Faerie anytime.

To my critique partner and Unseelie fiend, Chesney Infalt, thank you for everything. For the guidance, the pointers, the notes. All of it. I would send you an entire herd of Garys' if I could!

My best friend, Love Solman. You know what you did. Every step of the way…from the beginning, you've been there. You are awesome in every way and I love you more than words can say.

A massive thank you again to Jorge Wiles for the outstanding cover! I knew you were excited to start this…and you outdid yourself! It's beautiful. Thank you for having the patience to work with me again. Can't wait for book three…

I would like to thank my wonderful and oh, so patient editor Lynne Raddall, I have enjoyed our long faerie chats over a good cup of tea.

Thanks again to Leila, for not only taking the time to beta read for me again but for helping in some early formatting. You are wonderful.

Louise Elms, thank you for your keen proofreading eyes and for tracking down any wayward typos (Yes…I added extra kissing just for you.) Thank you!

The absolute gorgeous interior is all thanks to Nicole Scarano, you are pure magic. Thank you so much!

Thank you to Mum and Dad for all the support, for feeding me on constant fairy-tales and allowing me to run wild in the dark woods beyond our cottage. For all the haunted corners, the night-time trips to lock up the old church…the walks through the forgotten parts of Dorset.

Thanks again to my Matters, my Husband for supporting my writing journey, for not questioning why I need yet another notebook when I have six blank ones…Thank you for giving me the time to write, for more coffee…more snacks. Thank you for feeding me in books.

To my girls, my Imps…

This one is for you. They're all for you.

ABOUT THE AUTHOR

Lydia Russell grew up on a farm deep in the Dorset countryside along-side her three elder brothers, using the fields and woodland as their playground.

As an adult with two young children, she has used the memories of the wild woods of her youth to write The Wicked Woods Chronicles.

Stories of lost sisters, whispering oaks and dark romance.

Oh, the woods are dark and wicked.

intothewickedwoods.wordpress.com

 twitter.com/fey_girl63
 instagram.com/intothewickedwoods